Born and raised in Sydney, Charles Purcell is a journalist with more than 20 years of experience in newspapers, magazines and television, including as an entertainment writer for the Sydney Morning Herald. He has a deep interest in military history - particularly that of ancient Greece - and is a lover of pop culture, DVD box sets, quality literature, good food, fine friends and anything featuring that peculiar breed of warriors known as the Spartans.

He currently works as a freelance journalist, writer and social media blogger.

Game Of Killers is his second novel.

The Spartan: Game Of Killers

By Charles Purcell

First published in 2017
This edition published by Charles Purcell

https://charlespurcell.com/

Game Of Killers: The Spartan

EPUB format: 9781925579307
Print on Demand format: 9781925579314

Cover design by Red Tally Studios

Publishing services provided by Critical Mass
www.critmassconsulting.com

It was one word.
Spartan.
A name.
Spartan.
A call sign.
Spartan.
A blood oath.
Spartan.
A way of life.
Spartan.
And America's only hope.
Spartan.

Chapter 1

Fighting Dog awoke to find out his whole world had been set on fire.

His alarm clock had been the huge explosion outside the front of his heavily fortified compound. The blast had blown out all his expensive imported windows, covering his bedroom with glass. His ears were ringing, his nose assailed with the smell of smoke and harsh chemicals.

The head of Juarez's Scorpion cartel quickly got out of bed, put on his white robe and slippers and, careful to avoid the glass all over the floor, stared out of the shattered windows.

It was as if the fist of God had descended upon his front yard. A tower of dust and smoke stretched up to the sky. His men were dead everywhere. Luxury vehicles were ablaze. Guard towers and small buildings were destroyed. The dying wailed for first (or even second) aid.

The Juarez cartel boss wasn't sure what pained him more – the sight of his wounded men or the destruction of his garage full of million-dollar cars.

Probably the cars. They were harder to replace.

"What was that?" asked the pretty nude brunette in his bed, afraid.

"Shut up, Ximena," said Fighting Dog, then kicked the bed. "Get the fuck out of here."

As Ximena fled the room, covering herself with a sheet for modesty's sake, Fighting Dog struggled to decipher what had just happened. It seemed unbelievable that someone would bomb his HQ. Was this an old enemy striking at him? Or a new, undeclared one?

An ill wind had been blowing in the valley recently, a miasma known to the superstitious locals as "The Devil's Caress". Now something even more malign had blown onto his doorstep. Without thinking, Fighting Dog performed the Sign of the Cross. Then he ran out into his hallway, roughly colliding with a hulking bodyguard toting an assault rifle.

"What has caused this destruction?" demanded Fighting Dog, all attempts at politeness now gone.

"We have no idea, patron," came the nervous reply. "There was no warning. One second – nothing. The next – boom!"

Fighting Dog grabbed him by the head and pushed him down the hallway.

"So what are you doing here? Go find out what it was!"

As the bodyguard bolted off, Fighting Dog's No.2, Angel, ran into the room, armed with a C14 Timberwolf sniper rifle. Known for being tougher than Chuck Norris's toilet paper, the muscular, lazy-eyed sniper had saved Fighting Dog's life many times.

Perhaps today would be another.

"You need to get to safety, sir," insisted Angel.

"Who is doing this, Angel? Who would *dare*?"

"We don't know yet," said Angel, shuffling edgily in his snakeskin boots, as gunfire rang out outside. "But what I do know is that we need to get you to the panic room."

As Angel went to grab Fighting Dog's arm, the cartel boss shook him off. If word got out he had cowered in a panic room while his compound was being attacked, his reputation would be ruined. Already mockingly known as the *jefe* who couldn't put a troublesome policewoman in the ground, he would no longer command respect. The *narcocorridos* singers would probably pen a mocking song about the cartel boss who hid like a coward while his men fought and died.

So he would face this threat. He had to.

Fighting Dog suddenly remembered his mentor, shot in the shower by unbribed Mexican special forces. Killed while squeezing zits on your *culo* was no way to go.

"I won't retreat," Fighting Dog insisted. "I'll fight with the men. But tell the domestic staff to leave."

"As you wish, patron. I'm going to higher ground, see if I can find any targets."

"Do it. *Rapido*!" As Angel disappeared, Fighting Dog heard the snap and crack of gunfire. He was about to stick his head out of the window to look but bullets smashed through the little glass remaining.

A cold sweat instantly broke out on his back.

Startled by the near-miss, he retreated and went to his closet. He retrieved some black body armor and quickly put it over his chest, tying the straps in place. Next Fighting Dog changed into pants and boots.

He grabbed his cell phone and called the local police chief. Fighting Dog knew he wasn't being attacked by the *policia*. For one thing, they phoned ahead when they were about to launch a raid. And they liked to be greeted at the front door with money, not guns. Mexican cops were entrepreneurial rather than homicidal.

"Cesar," he barked, "I need your help."

"Ahh, Fighting Dog … how are you, senor?" The cartel boss then knew something was seriously wrong. For one thing, Cesar's tone was a far cry from its usual servile nature. The police chief sounded almost smug. Insolent, even.

"There's trouble at the hacienda. I need you to send your men right away."

There was a suspicious pause over the sound of battle. "I'm afraid I can't do that."

Fighting Dog was surprised. He'd never heard the word "no" from Cesar before. He'd heard "please" and "don't" and "mercy", but never "no".

"This isn't a negotiation. Get your fat *culo* over here now, Cesar."

The police chief snickered, which only infuriated Fighting Dog more. "So rude, *senor*. Then again, I understand. I used to be an asshole, too. But it doesn't matter. Your days are numbered. Well, everyone's days are numbered … just yours are in the single digits."

"What are you blathering about, you fool?" said the cartel boss, irritated that the police chief wasn't addressing him as if he was El Diablo himself.

"You've made the Yankees very angry. Angry enough to launch a Reaper drone strike against your house."

"A … Reaper strike?"

Cesar chuckled again, clearly enjoying the other man's discomfort. "I know. Trust the Norteamericanos and their love of overkill. But they want you gone. The missiles are just to soften you up for their foot soldiers. And no one on this side of the Rio Grande is going to stick his neck out to save you."

Fighting Dog couldn't believe what he was hearing. A high-tech drone attack? The Americans on the war path? The cartels … this *pinche* cop … refusing to have his back?

"Here's the rub, senor," continued the police chief happily, "No one likes you. *I* don't like you."

"Is that because I put my cigar out on your face that one time? Because that can happen again, you know."

"You were too greedy, too quick to kill, too slow to negotiate, too … difficult to do business with. You never shared the bounty from your table during the good times. The other cartels are tired of you. So they have already agreed to abandon you to the Yankees."

"I don't believe you. The Jaguar would never …"

The police chief found that last statement particularly hilarious. "*Who* do you think gave you up?"

Now Fighting Dog was forced to pause.

The thought that the Jaguar – the unofficial kingpin of Fighting Dog's part of Mexico and one of Fighting Dog's staunchest allies – had abandoned the cartel boss silenced him. The Jaguar was a strategic ally, but also a potential rival. Now, it seemed, he had become an actual rival. *Beware of the old man in a hurry.* Unfortunately, Fighting Dog's warning had come too late.

"It's good to give the Yankees someone occasionally," said Cesar, his tone light and philosophical. "It keeps them happy and off our backs, lets them think they're winning their futile War on Drugs."

Fighting Dog's head swam. He was temporarily lost for words, baffled by all the new and shocking information.

"Your plaza has already been divided," explained the police chief as gunfire continued to ring out. "And the new management has agreed to pay me a higher percentage."

"You're talking about me as if I don't have any say in the matter," snarled Fighting Dog, pacing down the hallway as his soldiers rushed downstairs. "Like I'm a powerless *cabron*. Don't you know who I am?"

"I know who you *were*, senor."

The use of the past tense troubled Fighting Dog. He was forced to do something very much against his nature ... beg. "Quit messing around, Cesar. I'll double what I pay you! Triple!"

The police chief laughed. "Ah, yes, it is the old saying, no? For the money, the monkey dances. But I shall dance for you no longer, senor. Today, you will be the monkey." The police chief ignored Fighting Dog's furious swearing in response. "Adios, dead man. Go get buried." Cesar hung up, his insolence ringing in Fighting Dog's ears.

This was not good at all, thought Fighting Dog. If the cops and the cartels had sold him out, he was now in mortal danger. It was a truism in the gangster world that your enemies never came at you when you were strong, but rather when all your allies had abandoned you. Fighting Dog paced around the top floor, furiously thinking, searching for a way out of his predicament.

He rang the local army chief. Yes. That was the right move. He'd prove loyal, surely. He'd been paid enough money for his children to go to college in Houston.

Yet when he heard Fighting Dog's voice, he started laughing hysterically. And hung up.

The word had spread. Fighting Dog was alone ... all alone. Just him and his remaining soldiers against whoever was assaulting his compound. But who would they send to attack him? Fighting Dog, feared across Mexico? His men, figures of terror from Cancun to Juarez?

As gunfire continued to ring out, Fighting Dog had a flash of insight. Surely this couldn't have anything to do with *her*?

Chapter 2

Vasquez, silenced MP-5 up, took cover behind the ruined front gate of the Scorpion cartel's HQ.

"Remember, lover," she told the giant soldier beside her. "This is my revenge. Fighting Dog is mine."

"Affirmative," said the Spartan, Squad Automatic Weapon in his hands, on the other side of the gate.

Vasquez readied her weapon as a flaming tyre rolled past. "Let's do this, then. Though we walk through the valley of the shadow of death we shall fear no evil, because we are heavily armed, and are the baddest motherfuckers in the valley."

"Oh yeah."

"Going dark now," whispered a voice over their comms as their eye-in-the-sky surveillance logged off.

The Target: Fighting Dog. Occupation: head of the Scorpion cartel. Identifying features: vertical scar over left eye, missing right pinkie finger, scorpion tattoo on left arm. Wanted dead or alive (preferably dead) for the murder of Vasquez's family.

Mission operatives: the Spartan, Tier 1 soldier, mid-thirties, 250 pounds of tight muscle, cobalt blue eyes, steely brown hair shaped in a buzz cut; and Teresa Vasquez, ex-Juarez cop, special forces trained operative, possessor of the world's only set of invisibility combat armor, late twenties, brunette, beautiful, smart.

They sprinted towards the front of the house through the thick dust and smoke in the air. Vasquez went left, leaving the Spartan to take the right. They ran past demolished vehicles, burning rubble and men blown to bits like a scene from the Somme. The Hellfire missiles had done their work well. Real Shock and Awe. The target's forward defenses had been "softened". Now for the final kill.

The Spartan spotted movement at one of the top windows. He raised his SAW, sending rounds through the shattered glass. Whoever it was ducked away in time. The Spartan refocused his attention directly ahead.

"Target 12 o'clock," he shouted, firing at a Scorpion near the doorway setting up a .50 caliber machinegun. The Spartan's target dropped his weapon and dived through the doorway, screaming in Spanish.

"He said you shot him in the *culo*," shouted Vasquez as she fired.

The Spartan went down on one armored knee, lined up the fleeing Scorpion in the iron sights of his SAW and fired. There was another howl, followed by more fractured Spanish.

"What about now?"

"I think that translates into something like, 'ahh, you got me, Slim'," said Vasquez. The screaming abruptly stopped. "No translation required there," she said dryly.

A heavy-set Scorpion in jeans and a checked shirt jumped out from behind a marble column and fired at them with his Heckler & Koch G36C. The pair took cover, before Vasquez leant from cover and shot him in the head and chest. He slowly fell backwards, the gun clattering to the ground.

Vasquez attempted to move forward. Yet a tango with a combat shotgun appeared almost right next to his slain muchacho. When he saw what Vasquez had done, he went from resting bitchface to raging bull in the blink of an eye. The loud, promiscuous firing from his SPAS-12 forced Vasquez to dive behind a flaming Hummer. Vasquez fired blind from behind cover, strafing left to right.

The Spartan held up a closed fist, gesturing for Vasquez to stay put. Vasquez fired another burst, then one more, deliberately exhausting her clip. Click, click. The shotgunner sensed victory. A Pyrrhic victory of the worst sort. The Spartan had outflanked him.

"No!" the shotgunner screamed. He spun and fell as the Spartan sent him low.

Vasquez slammed in a new mag.

"Clear," shouted the Spartan. He swung his head back to look at Vasquez.

"Look out!" she screamed.

The Spartan turned back as a grenade flew straight at his head. On pure reflex, he swung his SAW like a baseball bat, hitting the fragmentation device back to where it came from. Return to sender. Two Scorpions were blown to smithereens. Blood began to flow down the white tiles.

Vasquez joined the Spartan outside the smashed front door.

"Don't try that at home, folks," she said. "Plan?"

"Blind and disorientate the enemy. Then kill them all."

"Roger … popping smoke," said Vasquez as she hurled a smoke grenade down the hall.

"Flashbang," said the Spartan as he lobbed his own device. The flashbang exploded. The smoke enveloped the area.

The Spartan and Vasquez ran down the hall, firing all the way.

Together they charged into the entertainment area – decorated in typically garish drug lord style, gold leaf on white furniture, portraits of Fighting Dog on the walls – and jumped over the two dead men killed by their own grenade.

Scorpions were choking and staggering about, blinded by the flashbang light of thousands of candles. The grenades had done their work. But the tangos were still trying to shoot, spraying and praying across the room, seizing their chance to do that most prized things among international gangs and insurgents ... kill an American.

The Spartan hit the floor beside a couch just as the wall behind him was peppered with fire. A blinded, choking cartel member was ratholing at the couch. The buff Scorpion grabbed the Spartan, farm-strong hands choking him. The Spartan seized his lapels and head-butted him. Those farm-strong hands released their grip. The Spartan used the breathing space to draw his *xiphos* short sword and stab the choker with the sharp steel, puncturing his lung. O happy sword, here is thy sheath. The gangbanger gurgled and slumped face down.

The Spartan gingerly pushed him away with his boot, wiped his *xiphos* clean on the couch, and sheathed it.

Meanwhile, Vasquez was taking care of business topside. MP-5 writhing in her hands, she exhausted her clip, strafing from left to right ... taking out a pistolero by the TV as well as the TV itself, a rifleman with an AK-47 by a pot plant (ditto the pot plant), a shotgunner futilely trying to unjam his weapon (always check and clean your weapon before combat), and a stocky hombre with a Kriss Super V submachine gun (cool weapon: Vasquez wanted one for Christmas).

Vasquez emptied the remainder of her clip into a garish painting of Fighting Dog. It fell to the floor. Death by art criticism.

"If you're finished screwing around you can get up now," said Vasquez as the Spartan got to his feet. "Thanks for the assist."

The Spartan swung his SAW around and nailed a Scorpion creeping down the stairs, Vasquez in his sights. The gunman screamed before tumbling down head first, quite dead by the time he landed near Vasquez's feet.

"Don't mention it," said the Spartan, deadpan.

Vasquez poked out her tongue as she reloaded.

The Spartan examined the slain and mortally wounded Scorpions, noting Vasquez's superior gun work. "Annie Oakley here."

"Fuck your Annie Oakley. I'm Mexican."

The pair stared at the faces and hands of the Scorpions, searching for their high-value target. The Spartan used his heavy boot to roll over a face-down body. "Is it just me or do all of these guys look like Danny Trejo?"

"It's just you."

"On the plus side, I've never shot anyone wearing a cowboy hat until today."

"Fewer jokes, more checking for Fighting Dog, *mi amor*."

One body bearing two upper-torso bullet wounds drew Vasquez's attention. She suspected the gangster was faking it. Vasquez "eye-thumped" him with the hot barrel of her MP-5, the idea being that no one still alive could fail to react to such a blow.

The concept was sound. The faking foe cried out and sprang back to live.

Vasquez finished him off with three rounds to the chest.

The Spartan frowned. "I thought you said these guys were bad-ass. So far they've been about as dangerous as a mariachi band."

Vasquez made her own face. "I wish I knew how to quit you."

"I don't see Fighting Dog here. You?"

"No such luck," she said. They could hear more movement on both levels. People who wouldn't get with the program. And beyond that ... the killer of Vasquez's family. Vasquez grabbed the hood of her invisibility suit, her Ghost Armor, and powered it up. She looked *fierce*.

"I'll go stealth and head topside," she said. "You take the ground floor. We'll cover more ground that way." As she began to go invisible, then fully disappeared, she said over her shoulder, "And don't forget – Fighting Dog belongs to me."

Chapter 3

Vasquez felt the old familiar sensations of excitement, fear and adrenalin as she faded from view. Slowly and silently, she padded up the stairs, moving one foot a second. The intel on the house wasn't very precise – Fighting Dog hadn't filed floor plans with his local council – but they knew that it held a panic room and living quarters for a few dozen trigger pullers.

Plus Fighting Dog, the murderer of her family.

You can do this, she told herself as she advanced cautiously, quiet as a ninja, her noise discipline impeccable.

Vasquez admired the décor as she glided through the hacienda. Fighting Dog had lived well in the years since he had killed Vasquez's parents and young brother. Too well. He had dined on riches while she ate the ashes of future revenge. Revenge she would now claim.

She eyeballed a scared young guard in front of one partially open door. Armed with a new-looking AK-47, the teen rookie nervously glanced back and forth. He practised combat breathing with quick intakes and outtakes of breath, set to the count of four.

Then he stopped combat breathing and stared straight at Vasquez. She froze, waiting to find out if he was one of the tiny percentage of people who could detect the presence of someone in the Ghost Armor. But then his eyes moved on.

Only God could see her now.

Still, Vasquez needed to know who or what he was guarding. She kicked the back of his knees, making him kneel. In the same rapid movement, Vasquez drew her slender, sharp knife and plunged it down into his neck. He gasped, hands immediately going to his throat. Vasquez caught his body before it could thud on the ground, then gently lowered it, the teen's head lolling to the side.

He was barely a man, thought Vasquez. Yet Vasquez didn't feel too sorry for the youth. He'd chosen to join the cartels and embark on a career of kidnapping, extortion, drug dealing and murder – and now it had cost him.

Blood in, blood out.

Now visible, she sheathed her knife, equipped her MP-5 and snuck into the room through the door, checking the corners. At the window, lying on the ground with his back to her, was a tall, muscular killer, staring through the scope of a sniper rifle. Was he there to shoot anyone else that was part of Vasquez's team? Or Vasquez and the Spartan themselves when they left, guard down after successfully completing the mission?

Either way, his presence required the same response.

"Hola," she said softly.

To his credit, the sniper reacted quickly. With uncanny speed, he swung around on his belly, pulled up the rifle and attempted to re-aim it at Vasquez. It was an impressive performance, but it was too late. Vasquez stitched him up from crotch to collar.

Then she shot him again, because in real life sometimes people kept shooting at you after you'd shot them for the first time.

Staring down, Vasquez felt like she had just killed someone senior in the cartel. Someone dangerous, too, judging by how quickly he had reacted to her presence. Not for the first time, she was grateful of the combat edge her Ghost Armor gave her.

She kicked the sniper rifle aside and positioned herself behind the doorway. She stealthed up again. Magic time. High-tech Eye of Newt.

Yet some sound must have carried out of the room. Two neckless thugs with AK-47s charged down the hall towards her, moving swiftly like the ex-Mexican special forces they probably were. They fired into the room, ricochets pinging around the walls. One round thudded wetly into the dead sniper. Two came dangerously close to Vasquez, striking the wall near her ear.

She held her MP-5 up to her chin, took a deep breath, exited cover and fired. Phht phht. Phht phht. Two perfect double taps for each man. Shots right in the center ring. Textbook. They collapsed where they were, clutching their weapons like prayer books.

There were loud roars of gunfire coming from below. Vasquez could tell by the familiar sounds that the Spartan was busy with his SAW. She hoped he was OK. She waited until she was invisible again before moving on down the hall.

A large room gave her pause … and not just because of the smell of Mexican cuisine inside, which made her instantly nostalgic. There was loud, rapid talking in Spanish audible through the wooden door. The Scorpions were debating what to do. Stay put, just in case another explosion went off? Or throw themselves, gun blazing, into a possible meat grinder? The tangos seemed torn 50–50.

Vasquez decided to be the tie-breaker. She fired a three-round burst through the door, then took cover on the left-hand side.

"You're all scum and deserve to die," she yelled in Spanish. "But we're not here for you. We're here for your boss. Drop your weapons and leave. Or stay and die. Your call."

"Shut your bitch mouth!" shouted a voice. Small-caliber bullets sailed through the door, sending splinters flying. So much for negotiation.

"Fire at will!" came another loud, angry voice, along with more rounds. *What's Will ever done to deserve that*, thought Vasquez. Boom boom. After a few seconds the fusillade stopped. Maybe Will was finally dead.

Vasquez slapped a proximity mine to the door, stepped back out of range, then waited. And waited. And waited for curiosity to do its business. Then … kaboom. The mine went off as a Scorpion reached for the door handle. Curiosity killed the cats.

Vasquez didn't dally. She raced into the room, ignored the two dead bodies before her and the gore on the walls, and lined up the first of four shocked goons in her gunsights. She pressed the trigger, scoring three headshots before they could react, red mist flying. The fourth dived down, the falling bodies preventing Vasquez from getting a clear shot.

But Vasquez was on him before he could aim. Her foot was on his wrist as he fired, his burst going wide.

"Not the face!" he screamed, holding up his hand.

"Yes, the face," she said as she shot him through his palm and into his temple.

Vasquez slammed in a new mag. *Things were getting bloodier than expected*, she thought. They say that if you're after revenge you should dig two graves ... but by her reckoning, Vasquez had already exceeded her grave quota by at least 10.

So much for a quick, surgical op.

In the background one of the soldiers whispered the Spanish word for mother before he expired.

She scanned around what were clearly living quarters for Fighting Dog's soldiers, checking to see if anyone was hiding underneath the bunk beds (nada – Mexican gangsters were too macho for that).

Vasquez examined the room's armory. There were enough guns and ammunition to invade Southern California. Well, Grenada anyway. Lots of Russian-made grenades. Hopefully the Spartan wouldn't be facing too many of these party favors downstairs.

The security panels in a corner interested her. Maybe they would reveal Fighting Dog's location, save them the trouble of more fighting. Yet the screens were all white static. Perhaps the Hellfire missiles had taken out the cameras or damaged the mainframe.

Just as Vasquez was tapping on the keyboard a Scorpion cautiously entered the room. He dropped his jaw and raised his AK-47. Yet Vasquez was quicker. Without turning her body, she aimed her MP-5 with one arm and let fly with a lethal volley. The Scorpion emitted a high-pitched scream before collapsing onto his AK-47.

Vasquez felt a sudden pain in her side, winding her. The now-twitching Scorpion had shot her. Catching her breath, she nervously checked her back for an exit wound. Nothing. Her armor had taken the blow. She was bruised but not bloodied. She could still move. And movement was life. She left through the door, which was hanging off its hinges.

Vasquez continued her search, inching invisibly along the hall like an astronaut slowly walking along the moon. Some rooms showed signs of people leaving in a hurry. Others were used for storage.

One simply – and ominously – contained a chainsaw, a lone chair, some rope and walls covered in red. Vasquez swallowed hard. She'd seen torture chambers like that in her previous incarnation as a cop in Juarez. It was a sight one never fully got used to … and a reminder of the sort of scumbags she was up against.

She continued on.

After many slow, deliberate steps she came to a room with a luxury white door. Its frilly brass nameplate – "Ximena" – suggested the occupant was female. But Vasquez wouldn't take any chances. The female of the species could be as deadly as the male. She herself was proof of that.

She opened the door, tossed in a flashbang and backed away as it went off. Flash. Bang. She entered the space, weapon at the ready.

Nothing.

Vasquez heard something from the walk-in closet. She grabbed the handle and hurled the door open, thrusting the muzzle of her MP-5 into the space. Lying on the ground underneath a fur coat was a young, expensively dressed brunette. Ximena herself, perhaps. The would-be Ximena was immaculately made up. And beautiful. And scared, brown eyes wide with fear.

"Get up, *chica*," Vasquez ordered roughly. "We're here for your boyfriend, not you."

The shivering beauty nodded and got to her feet. Vasquez was about to say something more when the beauty turned dragon, screaming and lashing out with her red-nailed fingers, trying to rake Vasquez's face. Vasquez stepped aside and slapped her, hard. The beauty went down, face red, long hair covering her bare knees. Vasquez shook her head, unhappy that she had had to strike a woman and a civilian.

She regarded Ximena, not unkindly despite the attempted assault. She knew how the cartels treated women. Beautiful women were considered possessions, prisoners in luxury cages. Even Ximena's obvious, over-the-top breast implants probably weren't her idea, but rather Fighting Dog's fetish.

"Fighting Dog isn't going to survive the day ... Ximena," she said to the cowering woman, whose eyes flickered at the use of her name. "Take what you can and go. If anyone asks, I'll say you defended him like Satan incarnate." The last bit was to assuage Ximena's fears that the Scorpion cartel would hear that she let an invader into the house without resistance.

Ximena nodded slowly: this strange woman understood her dilemma. Ximena gathered some clothes and jewellery before fleeing like she was performing a Walk of Shame.

"Gracias," Ximena said softly to Vasquez. Vasquez watched her go, shook her head ... then continued her search.

Eventually Vasquez came to the panic room. There was a keypad next to the solid steel door, but unfortunately she had no idea what the code was. Was Fighting Dog inside?

Time to find out.

She slapped two demolition charges on the door, set the timer and stepped back into the hallway. Fire in the hole. Boom.

Rather than being blown off its hinges, the door was slumped at a 45-degree angle. She tossed in a flashbang, waited for its detonation, then charged forward, gun up, going visible.

Yet there was no sign of Fighting Dog or anyone else. The panic room was empty. Empty of humans, that is. Gold coins lay strewn on the floor. Cocaine danced in the air, covering everything in a fine white powder. Paper money was on fire. There was a pair of pistols with fetching golden grips. Rolexes worth more than the average Mexican family made in a year. But no cowering cartel boss.

One coin looked familiar. It was Carthaginian, a symbol from a dead empire. She pocketed it. *The Spartan will find this one interesting*, she thought.

As she exited the doorway, still lightly covered in cocaine dust, a heavyset Scorpion stuck a shotgun against her stomach ... then fired. It was only pure reflex and years of intensive training that saved Vasquez's life. She immediately tilted sideways as the blast went off. A lightning bolt of energy flew through her, as if her body had just been pierced by an adrenalin syringe.

She seized the warm shotgun barrel and used her foe's thrusting momentum to hurl him against the wall. As he wrestled for possession of the gun, Vasquez booted him in the groin. New balls, please, umpire. He grunted and released his grip. Vasquez struck him in the throat with the butt of his own shotgun. She heard a satisfying crunch.

"Stop," he gasped. The killer held up a hand, his eyes wet and pleading like a rescue puppy's.

Sometimes defeated foes begged Vasquez for mercy, hoping for clemency because she was a woman.

They never received it.

Instead, Vasquez leapt up and, while still in the air, slammed the butt against his temple. He cried out and fell to the wooden floor, poleaxed. She kept bashing him in the head with the butt. Again. Then again. Then again, until she saw white bone and beyond. It was done. Her suit was splattered with blood, her heart pounding.

Stupid, she told herself. *Stupid! Get it together! You've come too far to die now.* She took a deep, calming breath, then another, and another, until she focused and became invisible again.

Vasquez continued her mission. Her movements became automatic. Clear the next room and move on. Clear the next room and move on. All the while looking for Fighting Dog.

At last Vasquez accounted for all the rooms on the level, having exhausted her supply of flashbangs in the process. Checkpoint completed. Either she'd missed something – doubtful – or Fighting Dog was on the ground floor.

As she made her way to a staircase back down again she stared through a large cathedral-style window. It was then that she saw the face burned into her mind. Fighting Dog. Outside. Retreating to the stables with a large case in his hand. She quickened her pace.

Chapter 4

Fun fact: the gunfight at the OK Corral lasted a mere 30 seconds.

The Spartan's current gunfight was lasting considerably longer.

Despite his previous wisecracks, the Tier 1 soldier was finding his first op on Mexican soil hard-going. The defiant gangbangers were brave and determined, making him fight for every inch of the house. They reminded him of the Taliban, fanatics willing to keep fighting to the end … on crutches and with multiple gunshot wounds if need be. Unable to retreat, they had one choice: win or die.

Like the Spartan.

The Spartan's previous rapid advance had slowed to a crawl as he battled it out with foes that ducked and dived in and out of doorways and corners and took cover behind walls and furniture.

Every 10 seconds he was capping another foe. More bodies for the Boatmen. But they needed to wrap this up before Fighting Dog was reinforced.

Bullets and taunts came his way. He knew every taunt an enemy could throw at him by now: they tended to be variations of "Come and face me you son of a goat", "We're going to mail you home in pieces" or, just simply, "die, Great Satan". None worked. However, the choice of insult could determine where he shot someone and whether he started with the crotch or the knee first.

He heard someone say "soldado" … soldier. At least, that's what he assumed it meant: he didn't speak Spanish, preferring to communicate with the Scorpions in the international language of Violence, which he spoke extremely well.

But no, his foes weren't true soldiers, thought the Spartan as he slew a Scorpion leaping through the air between two walls like he was in a video game. They weren't Taliban or Persians or even Chinese special forces. They were just armed criminals. Pushers of poison who had gorged on the wealth from their feckless customers to the north.

A round flew past his ear, whispering an intimate, private threat. Time to move. The Spartan performed a combat roll just as bullets raked his position. He now flanked a veteran gangbanger who was aiming at the space he had just vacated. The portly foe was holding his Glock in a modified Weaver stance. Maybe he was a cop once. Now he was just a dead man. The Spartan's SAW hummed its deadly song.

Two Russian-made grenades hurtled towards him, forcing him to dive out of the way again. He rolled as they went off. Fortunately, he wasn't hit by any shrapnel or debris from the Cossack daisy cutters. His ears rang but he could tell his eardrums weren't perforated.

Then, just as he rose to his feet again, moving low, six screaming Scorpions raced into the room. Five waved evilly sharp machetes. The sixth, the smallest, yet the real danger, brandished an expensive Austrian-made pistol and was using the cover of his comrades to shoot at the Spartan.

Here it comes, he thought. The moment of close-quarters combat. The way combat was meant to be fought. That old familiar moment when it was time to win or lose. Do or die. Fuck or walk.

The Tier 1 soldier let his SAW go slack on its strap and drew his Spartan short sword, his *xiphos*. A part of him welcomed the encounter. There was nobility in fighting with a blade, of fighting at arm's length rather than at a cowardly distance.

Tapping into an ancient, primal fighting spirit, the Spartan evaded the first wild machete swing, then slashed a Scorpion in the stomach as the gang of bladesmen reached close-quarter distance. As he tore away his *xiphos* and the Scorpion folded like a red accordion he knew he had delivered a fatal wound.

The Spartan immediately sidestepped as the pistolero aimed for his head. The gunman shouted for his colleagues to get out of the way. The Spartan blocked one, two, three, no, four, savage blade attacks, one eye on the edged weapons, the other on the gunman lurking at the back. The bladesmen were so close he could see their teeth bared in anger, stained yellow from tobacco.

The Spartan moved aside again, batting away the machetes with great effort. The impatient gunman shot one of his own men in the back and pelvic girdle. The Spartan watched the macheteman's face contort in agony. As the Scorpion's front exploded outwards, the Spartan realized the pistolero was using dum-dum bullets, which caused a small entry wound and a large, explosive exit wound. He wasn't sure if his armor would stop a such a vile bullet. Best not to find out.

The Spartan bashed the pommel of his *xiphos* into the nose of the Scorpion next to him. He stepped aside as the stunned

Scorpion swung his machete at the Spartan's shoulder, caught the blade with his free hand and, continuing the swing, guided the blade up into the man's genitals. The Juarez bladesman screamed to high heaven. Now *that* felt like a critical wound.

"Next," he announced boldly.

The Spartan immediately had to raise his *xiphos* in self-defense as the others swarmed him. A massed blade attack was difficult to defend against: just ask all those convicts stabbed with shivs in prison. Few survived the old prison gang rush.

The remaining three fought well together. They had clearly done this before, battling as a co-ordinated pack, timing their attacks in sync with each other. The Spartan blocked, parried and counter-thrust as the gunman moved around looking for a clear shot, again shouting at his comrades to get out of the way so he could shoot the intruder. But they were fighting for their lives, too.

The Spartan dodged as two bullets came worryingly close to his head. Lining himself up with the gunman, he kicked a macheteman hard in the groin, sending him tumbling backwards over furniture towards the shooter. The Spartan watched with satisfaction as their legs became entangled. He had bought himself precious seconds to deal with the other two machetemen.

One Juarez bladesman was a major threat, wielding his machete with skill and authority. The scars across his face and body suggested he had been in many knife fights. The Spartan needed time to give him the attention he deserved.

The Tier 1 soldier rolled to the side – receiving a machete blow absorbed by his back armor plate – and came up next to the veteran's compatriot. The cartel member had a dotted line tattooed across his neck. *Cut here.*

The Spartan raised his *xiphos*, blocked the two-handed attack on the edge of his blade, pushed the machete aside and slashed straight across his opponent's throat. *Cut here? Wish granted.* Another Scorpion removed from the field.

He grabbed his fallen foe's machete and hurled it straight at the gunman, who had escaped from the limbs of the other Scorpion. The Spartan aimed for his head, but had to settle for hitting the shoulder instead. The gunman screamed but didn't drop his weapon. Still, he wasted precious seconds trying to pluck the blade from his flesh.

Taking a risk, the Spartan charged at the pistolero, ducking a vicious slash aimed at his throat from the remaining macheteman. As the gunman raised his pistol to fire, the Spartan severed his hand at the wrist. The gunman howled and grabbed his bloody stump, unable to believe that his hand was now gone.

"No one uses dum-dums, scumbag," growled the Spartan.

He had no time to rejoice, though. The expert macheteman was back, screaming and hacking at him with speed and ferocity. The Spartan barely parried the blows. As their blades pushed against each other, metal screaming, the macheteman planted a hard foot into the Spartan's sternum.

The Spartan struck back, only for his opponent to simultaneously parry and punch, striking him in the face with his machete-filled hand. The Scorpion's further kata of kicks and punches – culminating in a wicked hack that came close to carving up the Spartan's shoulder – made the Spartan realise he faced a master in jeet kune do, the late Bruce Lee's martial art.

The macheteman succeeded in hitting the Spartan with a leading straight punch. The Spartan reeled. Believing victory in sight, the macheteman went "off label" and performed a high spinning kick, aiming for the Spartan's head.

But the Spartan was ahead of him. He ducked and slashed through the macheteman's leg, through flesh and tendon and into bone. His assailant howled in the manner of savagely wounded men everywhere as he fell.

The Spartan straddled his chest, then, two-handed, thrust his *xiphos* into his heart.

"You fought well," said the Spartan. "But you're no Bruce Lee." The veteran macheteman coughed up blood, as if he was about to offer a last retort, a last complaint about the intimacy of dying by the sword. Then he died.

The Spartan was filled with the thrill of victory that came from slaying a man hand-to-hand, a joy hardwired in the human brain ever since caveman first killed caveman with a big-cat bone. Yes, this was where he made sense ... in the midst of war. He didn't belong anywhere else. He didn't fit in into the world of civilians.

Crying caught his notice. The last remaining Scorpion was still clutching his ghastly red stump. The Spartan slowly sheathed his *xiphos* and raised his SAW.

"You don't deserve the honor of dying by the sword," he uttered. Then he finished him with a rapid burst.

The Spartan checked that everyone was dead – or were about to be. He was a man who took pride in his work. And in this case, his work was thorough.

The carnage prompted a rare moment of introspection. Sometimes folk asked him why he did what he did, fought for his country, hell, fought at all. A quote from George Orwell came to mind: "We sleep soundly in our beds because rough men stand ready in the night to visit violence on those who would do us harm."

Well, there was part of the answer. The Spartan was one of those legions of rough men watching vigil over his country, ready to do what others wouldn't – or couldn't – do. He was a rough man. A necessary man.

A Spartan.

Introspection over, the Spartan advanced forward to the entry of what was clearly a kitchen/dining area. Then he saw him again. Fighting Dog. Vertical scar on left eye. Missing pinkie finger. General sense of entitlement. More than passable accuracy. He was a wily opponent, running and gunning through the house with his Desert Eagle, coming close to striking the Spartan several times. And the last thing the Spartan wanted was to be hit by one of those .50 caliber rounds.

Judging by the rate of fire, the Spartan calculated there were at least four foes in the kitchen, including Fighting Dog. A technical challenge.

Then he heard an odd noise to his left-hand side that raised the hairs on the back of his neck. It sounded like something metallic had hit a nearby wall. Actually, it seemed as if it had come from *inside* the wall. Perfidy. Villains unworthy of death by forged steel.

The Spartan had honed his instincts to a fine edge serving as point man in special forces. Those instincts were serving him now.

Hefting his SAW, he adjusted for the height of the average Mexican man – shorter than the typical, well-fed North American male – then let fly a burst of 30 rounds into the seemingly solid obstacle. Screams were the response. Blood trickled out of the bullet holes, followed by moans and the sound of guns clattering to the floor.

Yes ... there had been men hiding in those flimsy, tricked-up walls, waiting to jump out and surprise him. He'd seen that trick in Afghanistan before. Seen experienced special forces soldiers fall to such "Athenian" trickery.

The Tier 1 soldier heard cursing and yelling coming from the kitchen. Someone didn't appreciate their trap being prematurely sprung.

"Why, it's the American superhero!" cursed a loud, angry voice. "Where's your spandex suit, *cabron*?"

"That you, Fighting Dog?" shouted the Spartan back, taking the opportunity to load a fresh 200-round mag into his SAW. "Vasquez has come for you."

"*Bueno*! I'll kill her, too! Then I'll shove that big gun up your ass!"

"*Molon labe*," uttered the Spartan. *Come and take it.* The classic Spartan taunt.

Fighting Dog spoke loud, unknown words to his associates. The Spartan triangulated the source of the sound, leaned around the corner, and fired, blowing most of Fighting Dog's right ear off. The meat flopped wetly to the floor. Friends, Spartans, countrymen, lend me your ears. Or just take one of mine.

"Arrgh!" cried the cartel boss-slash-Mexican Van Gogh.

Fighting Dog was enraged … and an enraged enemy is a careless enemy. The Spartan listened as Fighting Dog barked rapid instructions to his underlings, incentivising his workforce at gunpoint. Two of Fighting Dog's soldiers charged towards the doorway, firing and yelling.

It was a futile, suicidal move, but just what the Spartan was hoping for. He raised his SAW. The Spartan watched their expressions change from anger to agony as he first fired a burst across their legs, causing them to collapse to the floor, before delivering the coup de grace.

However, the pawn sacrifice had bought enough time for the king to escape, for Fighting Dog to crash through the glass doors leading out of the kitchen. The Spartan tried to track him with his SAW, rounds following the fleeing gang boss like tracers, but to no avail. Fighting Dog was gone.

"Vasquez, I've located Fighting Dog, over," he said into his throat mic. But all he heard over the coms was a giant explosion. Tremors ran through the ceiling. He hoped Vasquez wasn't caught up in whatever that was.

As the Spartan headed through the kitchen, boots crackling on glass and spent shell casings, a giant in a white singlet popped up from behind a counter. The Spartan raised his SAW to fire. But this new foe was unarmed, holding his huge hands up like a boxer.

The Spartan realized that, rather than this being an act of surrender, he was being challenged to hand-to-hand combat. *Mano e mano*. Welcome to Fight Club, Juarez branch. And if the Spartan had a weakness, it was his inability to resist a duel, a one-on-one battle, a call to honor.

The boxer gestured towards himself with his hands.

The Spartan slowly nodded in approval. This wasn't the smart thing to do, but it was something he wanted to do – and who went through life always doing the smart thing to do?

Besides, he sensed he had broken the tempo and rhythm of the enemy's attack for now.

He slowly put his SAW on the counter, all the while carefully watching the other man for sudden movements. Huge biceps, cauliflower ears, broken nose, teardrop tattoos next to his eyes to signify murder ... yes, this brute was a killer, perhaps claiming those lives with his bare hands.

A worthy challenge.

"Accepted," the Spartan intoned. He would settle this with honor.

The giant smiled, showing off a diamond-encrusted tooth. "Bueno, bueno," he said.

Then he snarled, raised his thick hands and came at the Spartan, throwing a haymaker at the Spartan's head. The Spartan dodged the blow and the right hook that came after it. The bruiser followed up with a left jab that the Spartan blocked with his own muscular forearms.

The giant dropped his hands and pummelled the Spartan in the stomach three times, then once in the ribcage. The Spartan grunted, the blows painful despite his body armor.

The Spartan jabbed, ducked a counterpunch, and slammed a left hook into the giant's face. The giant tottered, but recovered quickly. The Spartan landed another punch to the head. Then another. The Spartan felt the impact of his punches all the way up his arms. The giant lost his diamond tooth to a brutal left jab worthy of Tyson. Yet it was if the brute wasn't bothering to defend himself, just soaking up the Spartan's energy until …

Wham. The giant slugged the Spartan with a mighty uppercut. The Tier 1 soldier felt like half his head had been taken off.

The Spartan tasted blood in his mouth.

His foe took advantage of his dazed state and slugged the Spartan hard in the temple, again twisting the Spartan's head around. With his next blow, he struck the side of the Spartan's skull, where human bone was weaker. The Spartan saw stars in his eyes, like he was looking through a kaleidoscope. This colossus knew how to throw down. Evidently the bigger they are, the harder they hit.

The ham-like hands kept coming. They slammed the Spartan's kidneys once, twice, no, three times for good measure, making the Tier 1 soldier grimace. Just because he was Spartan didn't mean he didn't feel pain.

But then the Mexican Muhammad Ali made a grievous mistake. He grabbed the fridge door and swung it into the

Spartan's stomach, then shoved the winded Spartan against the kitchen cabinets and pressed his forearm into the Spartan's throat. To the Spartan's mind, his assailant was now cheating. He was using more than just his fists. By employing other moves he had strayed into *pankration* territory, the form of hand-to hand combat favored by the ancient Greeks.

It meant more than just fists was on the menu. It meant anything goes.

The Spartan began by boxing the giant's ears with his flat open hands. The hulk moaned, ears ringing, his equilibrium disturbed. He staggered but keep his crushing forearm on the Spartan's throat.

The Spartan hit the Scorpion in the chin, inflicting further damage. He grabbed the giant's windpipe with his thumb and fingers and squeezed. The giant was stricken … but still the forearm pushed down on the Spartan's neck. Both men were in agony, the Spartan's throat full of fire-like pain.

The Spartan blacked out for a second. Images of his special forces training flashed in his brain. "Ring the bell," said the instructor. "You know you want to quit."

But he would not quit. Not now. Not ever.

The Spartan fought through the agony, maintained the pressure on his opponent's windpipe and booted the giant hard in the stomach. And again, tenderising the meat. Then, as the giant slumped, finally releasing his forearm of the Spartan's neck, the Spartan kung fu kicked him hard in the forehead.

The giant half-slipped, hand grabbing the table corner for balance. But it was too late. The Spartan grabbed the hand and bent the wrist back in a horrible, unnatural direction, breaking it. Not waiting for the giant's pained reaction, the Spartan expertly snaked one arm around his neck and another hand on his head. The hulk fought back as strong as any man the Spartan had ever faced, trying to resist what was coming next, thrashing back and forth, slamming the Spartan's back against cabinet and tables. The battle went on for a few more seconds. But it was futile. The Spartan's grip was inexorable. And he was angry, offended by his opponent's breaking of his unspoken word.

"Oathbreaker," he spat. Then he snapped the pugilist's neck.

He allowed his inert opponent to slither down to the ground.

The Spartan stared at the giant as he rubbed his own sore neck. A good fight, if short. Too bad his foe had spoiled it by "cheating". Then the Spartan grabbed his SAW and double-timed it in the direction of Fighting Dog.

Chapter 5

"Say hello to my big friend," whispered Fighting Dog as he took cover behind the stable door, watching the Spartan approach.

The harried cartel boss hefted an XM-25 grenade launcher in his hands. Nicknamed "The Punisher", the rare US Army weapon fired 25mm high-explosive programmable rounds that could detonate in the air precisely above opponents. Pretty much all you needed to do was stare down the electronic scope, aim the range-finding laser and fire. The XM-25 would do the rest, programming each round's range as it left the chamber.

The "anti-defilade" weapon could thus eliminate soldiers who were even dug in or in cover ... as the Spartan was now, taking cover behind a tractor. Even the Taliban had come to fear it as they hid behind walls, praying that they were safe even as the XM-25's laser locked onto their position.

How Fighting Dog managed to procure one was a story in itself, but in short, weapons often disappeared from the battlefield, the gun trade between America and Mexico was *insanely* lucrative, and cartel money could buy just about anything. Including an XM-25.

And if things were going to go last-scene Scarface, *thought Fighting Dog, this was just the weapon for it.*

Fighting Dog savored the prospect of blowing this blue-eyed soldier to bits. He'd killed men for far, far less than invading his home. This gringo soldier deserved a violent, bloody death.

Adding insult to injury was the fact that he was being assaulted by a North American. He felt such an attack was almost patronising, as if his older big brother from the north had come to discipline his unruly southern sibling. Fighting Dog expected to be shot at from time to time.

What he didn't like or expect was to be *judged.*

In normal circumstances the cartel leader would have loved to have captured the northerner alive and tortured him for information ... but this particular gringo was simply too dangerous to live. The trail of dead he had left in the hacienda was testament to that fact.

Fighting Dog felt the thrill of fear as well as anticipation. It had been a long time since the cartel boss faced an operator like this grim-faced killer with the downturned mouth. It was disturbing about how he had methodically worked his way through Fighting Dog's men, gunning and gutting them down one by one.

But if anything could stop this indomitable intruder, it would be the XM-25.

Ignoring the pain of raising the weapon up to the place where his earlobe used to be, Fighting Dog aimed the range-finding laser at his foe's rough position, then fired. He sensed that the gringo had jumped away at the last moment, perhaps even recognising the weapon. The almighty explosion set the tractor on fire, but on the other side, as if he had suddenly been expelled out of a black hole, lay the foreign soldier, shaken and wounded.

Quick on his feet, the intruder began running again, firing an accurate burst of machine-gun fire that forced Fighting Dog to duck behind cover, splinters flying as bullets hit the wood.

By the time the cartel boss judged it safe to peer out of cover again, the strange soldier was nowhere to be seen.

But there were only three other possible places the gringo killer could have taken cover: a cart, a jeep and a generator. Fighting Dog had five high-ex rounds left. He would shoot all three targets. He ranged in the cart, then fired. Boom. Behind him the horses whinnied in terror. Yet there was no movement behind the cart. Either Fighting Dog had succeeded or his opponent wasn't ratholing there. He had to assume the latter.

He blew away the generator next. He detected no movement behind the ruined, smoking mass. The horses whinnied again, million-dollar horseflesh quivering in fear. Again, he sensed that the foreigner was still alive. But there was only one place left for him to hide.

A smoke grenade landed in front of Fighting Dog as he aimed, clouding the area in white gas. Door number two it was, then. The cartel boss smiled. He had already had the jeep ranged in with the laser, even if he could no longer see it with his own eyes. Time to die by your army's own weapon, gringo. Adios.

Then he felt a cold gun barrel pressed against his head.

"Drop it," a voice said.

* * *

"On your knees," insisted Vasquez as she tore off her hood, letting her hated enemy see her face. "Do it." As he knelt, Vasquez kicked the XM-25 out of Fighting Dog's hands.

"You've ruined me, you stupid sow!" yelled Fighting Dog. "The cartels have abandoned me!"

"It pleases me to hear that."

"You think this is about you! You're just a gun someone else is aiming at me!"

"As long as the end result is you dying, that's fine by me."

Vasquez regarded her mortal enemy. He was older than she remembered. Older, but still strong. Still dangerous, even on his knees. They glowered at each other, years of mutual hatred pouring out of their eyes.

Eventually Fighting Dog said: "Don't pretend you're still a cop. You can't arrest me."

"I'm not here to put you in cuffs," declared Vasquez, keeping her MP-5 trained on him. "We both know you'd just bribe your way out of any jail." Vasquez stared at Fighting Dog's torso. "The body armor. Lose it, too."

Fighting Dog tore off his protection and tossed it at Vasquez's feet in disgust. "Do you expect me to beg, orphan? Scream?"

"There would be no point in begging. But you will scream by the time we're through."

"Never, *puta*."

Vasquez flinched. She could face knives and bullets with relative equanimity, but being called a whore made her red-faced and angry.

The Spartan made his way into the barn and observed the scene.

"Saved your ass back there," said Vasquez.

"I had it under control," came the cool reply.

"Who is this gringo bastard?" asked Fighting Dog, staring at Vasquez. "Why have you *involved* him?"

"That's classified," replied the gringo in question. He stared at Fighting Dog, then picked up the XM-25. "Where did you get this, asshole?" he said, gripping Fighting Dog by the collar. "This is a US Army weapon. And a rare one at that." The Spartan loomed over him like a cocked rifle.

"Let him go, Spartan," ordered Vasquez.

The Spartan reluctantly released his prisoner. Fighting Dog stood again. He was short for a man and Vasquez was tall for a woman, which made them about equal.

Vasquez stared at Fighting Dog's missing ear. "Your work?"

"You said alive. He's alive."

"And your bruised eye?"

"Boxing match." I came, I boxed, I broke his neck. Vasquez nodded. The two of them stood over Fighting Dog. "So ... what now?"

"I finish it my way. Cover him."

Vasquez stepped aside, dropped her MP-5, then slowly removed her Ghost Armor. The cartel boss and the Tier 1 soldier watched as she tossed aside her bullet-proof vest and other equipment until she was wearing only shorts, boots and a singlet. She slowly unsheathed her knife.

"My family has been waiting a long time for justice," said Vasquez venomously. She turned to the Spartan. "Whatever happens, don't stop the fight."

The Spartan nodded.

Vasquez gestured towards the knife Fighting Dog had strapped to his side, which resembled a US Marine Ka-Bar. "Fill your hand, *pendejo*."

The cartel boss gleefully drew his weapon. Fighting Dog's knife was longer and heavier than Vasquez's slender stealth blade ... yet her blade was incredibly sharp, like a samurai sword that would cut a butterfly in half if the butterfly dared rest on it.

Vasquez breathed in and out, shook her head from side to side and flexed her limbs, warming up. Fighting Dog watched her closely, trying to get her measure, the Spartan's SAW still pointed at him. Finally, she pointed her knife towards Fighting Dog in open challenge.

It was on.

"You indulge yourself, Teresa," said Fighting Dog as he circled around Vasquez. "I grew up fighting with knives. I've never lost a fight."

"Today you will."

As if angered by her words, Fighting Dog suddenly lunged at her stomach. Like a matador allowing a bull to pass, she dodged his lunge, then flicked her blade across Fighting Dog's face, drawing blood. He immediately spun around and returned the favor with a backhanded slash that ran across her cheekbone.

Fighting Dog feinted, pretending to stab Vasquez in the chest. But with his other hand he roughly seized her long hair and used his strength to force her body down, his knife poised above her throat.

Yet before the cartel boss could deliver the killing stroke Vasquez ran her knife across his other wrist, the sharp, stinging pain forcing him to release her hair. She darted away and resumed an upright fighting stance.

"Don't get tired yet ... we've just begun," yelled Fighting Dog, spittle flying from his mouth.

They went at each other some more, slices, stabs and parries that came close. Both combatants were filled with rage: Vasquez, over the death of her family, and Fighting

Dog, over the destruction of his position with the cartels and his humiliation at the hands of a woman. Fighting Dog was an agile, experienced opponent. And Vasquez, normally so controlled in combat, was furious, her anger potentially overwhelming all her training.

To an outsider, the fight appeared evenly balanced.

The cartel boss swiped at Vasquez's face. She ducked and, in the same movement, slashed Fighting Dog on the side. He made a growling noise, seemingly angrier at getting tagged than the actual pain.

Fighting Dog let fly with an arabesque of bladework, all of which missed, but brought him close enough to Vasquez to punch her in the left breast. Vasquez's free hand flew to the spot, all the while her left foot found his groin. The pair staggered back to absorb the pain of their respective wounds.

"I always meant to tell you, Teresa," taunted Fighting Dog as he circled around. "It's your fault your family is dead."

The taunt had its intended effect. Enraged, Vasquez screamed and raised her knife high for a savage downward attack. Before it could land Fighting Dog responded with a horizontal swipe that almost disembowelled Vasquez. Almost. Vasquez had twitched aside at the last moment, so the blade ripped open her singlet at the waist and left a red ribbon of pain underneath.

The Spartan saw movement out of the corner of his eye. Scorpions at the back of the house, trying to muster up the sack to attack. The Spartan seized the XM-25, stared down the scope and fired. The high-ex round whistled through the air, scoring a direct hit. The enemy was schwacked.

By the time the Spartan turned back to the knife fight, both combatants had fresh wounds. Fighting Dog kicked at Vasquez's left knee, hoping to bring her low. She danced out of the way, then delivered a front kick to Fighting Dog's stomach. He grunted, but managed to slash Vasquez's leg as she quickly withdrew it, leaving a shallow wound.

Fighting Dog attacked Vasquez's head. The lunge masked his true purpose, which was a follow-up strike with his elbow, which landed home. Vasquez tottered.

Flushed with triumph, Fighting Dog raised his knife to strike downwards. Vasquez grabbed his arm just in time. But Fighting Dog was stronger. He pushed the blade down with all his considerable strength. All Vasquez could do was to divert the blade until Fighting Dog plunged it into her shoulder. Vasquez screamed.

"Time to join your family!" he hissed in her face.

His mistake.

Vasquez yelled and savaged his lip with her teeth.

Woman bites Dog.

Fighting Dog bled profusely down his chin. Vasquez spat out flesh.

She struck Fighting Dog's elbow so he released his grip on his knife. With the blade still in her, Vasquez allowed her body to go limp, seemingly falling down. The Spartan could see Fighting Dog was puzzled by the move.

Once down near the grass Vasquez seized Fighting Dog's left ankle and, with a firm, savage slice, severed the tendons there with her knife.

As Vasquez had promised he would do, Fighting Dog screamed.

She did the same with the other ankle, cutting through tendons and gristle. Fighting Dog howled again. Vasquez's attack was reminiscent of an old Triad punishment where all the tendons of the victim were cut, leaving the target quivering but alive, unable to move. If it had been anyone else but this evil man, it would have been a pitiable site.

The stricken cartel boss reached for the knife still embedded in Vasquez, but found he couldn't stand.

Vasquez rushed him, her face terrible. Fighting Dog slurred something only Vasquez could hear. He smiled, lips torn and red.

As Vasquez attempted to deliver the coup de grace with her knife, Fighting Dog seized her wrist with his hand. She leant down and delivered the type of forearm smash that would've made Ronda Rousey proud. The cartel boss moaned and released her wrist.

Knees upon his chest, Vasquez plunged her knife deep into Fighting Dog, who screamed in agony.

But her old enemy wasn't finished. He reached up with bloody hands and seized her throat. Vasquez gurgled. Fighting Dog kept choking her, eyes alive with a revenant's anger. For her part, Vasquez kept stabbing. It was a race against time to see who would be killed first.

Control his body, Vasquez, thought the Spartan. He made a step forward, as if to intervene. He was concerned Vasquez could die right here, with victory in hand, while he just stood there and watched.

Yet he backed away. Vasquez had asked him not to intervene … and had done the same while watching him fight others to the death. So he owed her that.

After several more agonising seconds, his faith was rewarded. Fighting Dog's hands loosened and fell by his side. He had bled out.

Vasquez took a deep breath, air canal now free, and kept stabbing, unaware he was done.

Now was the time to intervene.

The Spartan said, "Enough, Vasquez. He's dead. You've won."

As if hearing the words from afar, Vasquez halted her actions. She left the knife in the cartel boss's corpse. Her hair fell on her face, matted with sweat. Vasquez suddenly looked exhausted, every last ounce of rage spent.

But she had closed the eyes of her family's killer forever.

The Spartan knew better than to offer her a hand up. Instead, he gestured at the knife in her shoulder: "You want me to get that?"

Vasquez stared at the weapon, as if suddenly reminded that she was wounded, adrenalin shielding her from the pain. "Oh. Yes."

"Brace yourself." The Spartan held Vasquez's shoulder and swiftly removed the blade, tossing it onto the ground.

"Ouch." Blood flowed swiftly from the wound. Vasquez tore off part of her singlet and bandaged herself, tying the material tight until she was satisfied.

The Spartan performed his own ocular triage on Vasquez. She was bleeding from many wounds, but none were fatal. Most were mere surface wounds, testament to her speed and skill. Thus, further medical attention could wait. He was glad.

"Good fight, Vasquez."

"*Gracias*. He was better than I imagined."

"The worst ones often are." The Spartan went and collected the XM-25. "I'd like to know how he got his hands on this."

"I'm just glad the *pendejo* is dead."

He glanced at Vasquez, who was now staring at Fighting Dog, thinking unknown thoughts. He gave her another moment. The Spartan knew the effect mortal combat had on the mind and body, the need to reckon with oneself after the kill. But they still had to leave, and quickly. This was a foreign country and they weren't welcome here.

"Ready to go?" he said after a suitable pause.

"Roger. We're done here."

The Spartan gestured towards Vasquez's blade, still stuck in Fighting Dog's chest. "You going to take your knife?"

"No, leave it. It has found its true home."

As Vasquez grabbed her MP-5 and her Ghost Armor, the Spartan suddenly stared at the hillside, as if he could detect something was there, then reached for his radio to call for an extraction.

* * *

One hour later the *policia*, politely waiting on the hill for the Americans to leave, came to check that Fighting Dog was indeed dead ... and to ransack his hacienda. The police chief Cesar laughed as he saw Fighting Dog's bloody body. He struck a match against the corpse to light his cigar, then took a celebratory puff. Fighting Dog continued to stare vacantly at the sky with his dead eyes, a halo of blood around his head.

Here lies the mighty Fighting Dog, Cesar thought ... stabbed to death, according to his men watching from above with binoculars, by a woman. A fittingly ignoble end for his former "employer", one who had terrorised both police and cartel enemies alike. One who had, in a moment of pure, power-drunk arrogance, forced Cesar to kiss his boots at gunpoint. The police chief could still remember the taste of that expensive Italian leather on his tongue.

Just one of the many reasons it was good to see Fighting Dog dead.

Even better was the news that Fighting Dog's treasury was intact. The drone strike had been confined to the front of the hacienda. It would be a nice payday for Cesar and his men. He deserved it for having to endure Fighting Dog's brutal reign.

The scene inside the hacienda was bloody carnage. It was hard to believe that the duo his men had seen had caused so much damage. Truly they were a pair to be feared.

Yet sadly for those who believed that the War on Drugs was winnable, Fighting Dog's death was merely a blip on the radar. As Cesar had told the late, inconvenient cartel boss, Fighting Dog's terrain had already been divvied up among his fellow cartel leaders. Trucks were busy transferring drugs from various warehouses, factories, storage units and strongholds. There would be no interruption in supply for the hungry nostrils and lungs of America, no end to the War on Drugs as long as the gringos kept buying them. The only dividend to be gained was by those who personally wanted to see Fighting Dog dead … and on a personal level, that list was many.

Including Cesar and his men.

Cesar suddenly felt sorry for his beloved Mexico. Like many long-suffering Mexicans, who had watched the drug violence spread across the country, he wished the cartels gone. But he wasn't a young man any more. Rebellion against the established order was for young men, men without families to feed and with nothing to lose. And the cartels were the established order. They were simply too rich and powerful for most to defy. Even for police chiefs, who were given the same choice as everyone else: silver (bribes to look the other way) or lead (in the form of a bullet to the back of the head).

Perhaps one day the cartels would all destroy each other and Mexico could breathe again. Until then, there was only the business of compromise and survival. Cesar would allow himself to succumb to the gravity of submission and mediocrity.

Cesar turned back and looked at the hacienda and its riches.

"Take everything valuable," he told his men, even as he was stripping the Rolex off Fighting Dog's wrist. "Fill the cars. We'll divide the cash and gold later. But I want his plasma TV."

His men obeyed his orders ... mostly.

Except when it came to Fighting Dog's gold-plated Desert Eagle.

A trophy hunter pocketed the cartel bosses' gun and sold it on the internet to another cartel boss for $US10,000.

* * *

One month later the *narcocorridos* single, *The Shameful Death of Fighting Dog At The Hands Of A Woman*, reached No.2 on the Mexican Top 100 charts.

* * *

Two months later Vasquez received an anonymous letter in the mail. The plain white piece of paper had only two things on it. The words "thank you". And a symbol of a jaguar.

Chapter 6

One of the greatest mysteries of the post-World War II era is what happened to the Honjo Masamune – perhaps the greatest Japanese sword ever made.

Forged by the legendary swordsmith Masamune in the 13th century, the Honjo Masamune is regarded as a National Treasure in Japan. This singular samurai sword was considered so special it was the official weapon passed between the shoguns, the military rulers of Japan. The Japanese Excalibur, if you will. A blade for conquerors.

A far cry from the samurai sword imitations crass Westerners kept on their mantelpieces, bought from gift chain outlets to let a faux air of Japanese culture to their garish living rooms.

The Honjo Masamune belonged to the ruling Tokugawa shoguns. Handed down through the generations, it was still in the possession of the Tokugawa family when Japan surrendered in 1945 at the end of World War II.

Determined to rid the newly surrendered nation of all weapons – including edged ones – General MacArthur demanded that all samurai swords be handed in to the new occupying power to be melted down and destroyed. Many of these were ordinary swords that had no special purpose or history, merely mass produced for Japanese soldiers to wear into battle. Blades without names.

Yet others had survived for centuries, baptised on the battlefields of ancient Japan. They were more than mere weapons: they were sacred heirlooms. As much works of art as weapons of war, they represented a precious, vanished world of honor. And the mighty Honjo Masamune was the best of them.

Many Japanese objected to surrendering these special swords to their barbarian conquerors. But the Emperor had ordered the nation to surrender and Japan's citizens were honor-bound to hand in these priceless treasures. And so, the Tokugawa clan, determined to endure the unendurable at the command of the Emperor, handed in more than a dozen of the family's swords – including the Honjo Masamune – to a Tokyo police station.

The Americans later repealed their edict, recognising the genuine cultural significance of certain legendary blades, but by then it was too late.

According to the available information, the Honjo Masamune and other swords were collected by a US cavalry sergeant called Coldy Bimore from the Tokyo police station and then promptly vanished. No record has ever been found of the GI, which led some to believe that the Japanese police recorded the soldier's name wrong.

The official history is that the sword was never seen again: that Bimore, whoever he was, kept the sword as a war souvenir, and that it languishes in some dusty attic or basement somewhere in America.

But the official history is wrong. The Honjo Masamune has been found ... and it lies in the hands of Japan's enemies.

Many decades after World War II, an agent of that foreign power was stunned to discover that the blade was being sold in a garage sale in the American south-west. An aficionado of Japanese swords, he recognised the blade from drawings and etchings made centuries ago. Scarcely believing his luck – and the astonishing ignorance of the sellers – he purchased the weapon for a middling price rather than the untold millions it warranted, shook his head again at the ignorance of Westerners, and took the blade home to his house.

He permitted himself a precious day with the blade, marvelling at its beauty and sharpness, wielding it in his dojo: even holding it up by the light of the moon to see if, according to legend, it shone in moonlight. He swung it again and again until he collapsed to the ground, exhausted.

Reluctantly, for he had already fallen in love with the sword by now, he arranged for the Honjo Masamune to be delivered to his homeland. Then the agent left America forever, lest the Japanese discover his purchase and his identity.

The Japanese continued their frantic efforts to find the blade, unaware that it was being passed around by the military elite of one of its enemies. Even today they search for it still. But to no avail.

Now the blade has a new owner. And he has brought the Honjo Masamune back to American soil ... to christen it in American blood.

Chapter 7

I shouldn't be doing this, thought Colonel Garin, as he walked the grim streets of New York.

As Homeland Security's top troubleshooter, with extensive connections to the army and its special forces programs, there were a thousand other pressing things that demanded his highly-paid attention.

After all, America was still reeling from the aftermath of the plague delivered by China's canister conspiracists. The worst of it was now over, the noxious spread of the plague on US soil halted, but the American death toll was in the unknown millions. Just about everyone knew of someone who had died. The country was one race, color and creed united under fear.

And violence.

America's cities and suburbs had become war zones, its suspicious, scared residents becoming paranoid and hostile after rumours that those taken to "quarantine zones" were never making it out alive. Thus once-compliant keyboard warriors and soccer moms were fighting the police tooth and nail in the streets. Molotov cocktails crashed against plastic shields. Riots that made Watts and LA look like bonfire parties were breaking out in all the major cities. Many areas had become or remained W.R.O.L – Without Rule Of Law.

If truth was the first casualty of conflict, then innocent civilians were the second, with law enforcement officials coming a close third.

Many police officers died.

Looters roamed the streets. Snipers were exercising their Second Amendment rights by shooting down news helicopters.

Up was down. Black was white. One and one made three.

The only disaster missing was a Sharknado.

"It's chaos out there," Garin said aloud, causing nervous citizens on the streets of once-fair Gotham to avoid him.

The authorities were doing the best that they could, but the United States hadn't experienced this level of disruption and paranoia since the Spanish Flu epidemic of 1918, which killed more than 3 per cent of the world.

The main difference now in the current age of entitlement was that, half the country was heavily armed and had access to the still-functioning internet, listening to every crank and tin-foil hatter claiming that the government had released the plague on purpose. Some citizens had even refused to take the cure, holding up siege-style in their houses, thoughtfully infecting all their loved ones in the process.

Many called for war against China for its part in the plague – someone just *had* to take a major hit after the death toll in America. The only reason that the stealth bombers weren't already fuelled and dropping the Mother Of All Bombs on Beijing was because China had suffered just like America, and the canister conspiracists had been rogue agents rather than state-sanctioned operatives.

So, in fact, the only folks happy with the situation – apart from the one per cent of the population who were psychopaths, who thought all their Christmases had come at once and were busy bringing their darkest fantasies to life – were the doomsday preppers eating tinned meat and hoarding toilet paper in their bunkers. They could finally point one Nomex-gloved finger at the liberal media and say "I told you so", their paranoid choice of lifestyle vindicated at last.

The country had had, to use the Chinese phrase, to *chi ku*: to eat bitterness. And after pampered years as the world's lone superpower, the United States neither had the taste or the stomach for much bitterness.

Then there was the rest of the world. The world had changed. And not for the better.

The global economy was in the crapper: to quote Garin's son Robbie, the craven investment banker and economic hit man, fruit of his loins if not his soul, "Wall Street can't make any money in this environment!"

"Damn punk kid," Garin muttered.

China was holding Japan's ships hostage for "reparation for World War II crimes", while ramming Vietnamese vessels in the South China Sea. It was also taking advantage of the world's distracted state to build what was being called "The Great Wall Of Sand" in the South China Sea, claiming as much territory as it could despite the objections of its neighbors. If the world had had any lingering doubts about how China posed an existential threat to the current global order, such doubts had now vanished.

Meanwhile, Japan was making ominous noises about rewriting its post-World War II constitution so it could re-arm itself. It had rushed through bills allowing its soldiers to fight overseas for the first time since 1945. Japanese and Chinese fighter jets were flying so close to each other in the South China Sea they were colliding mid-air.

North Korea sensed weakness and was launching probing attacks on its border with South Korea.

Africa was divided along tribal, religious and economic lines.

The Germans ran Europe again.

The Middle East was its usual mess.

Taiwan remained occupied by the People's Liberation Army. Hong Kong? Well, everyone knew what had happened there.

Meanwhile, the UN was left holding its various multinational dicks in its hands.

Among its allies, America's impotence in allowing the tragedy to happen was noted, its status as the world's sheriff in question.

More and more people were saying the world had gone from a unipolar world dominated by Uncle Sam to an unstable bipolar world where it had to share power with China: a development viewed with suspicion and fear by many.

In the face of all this, Washington was paralysed with indecision, partisanship and horror. Barbed wire was everywhere in the homeland, like some Martian weed, as if to suggest that the country was undergoing some horrible transformation.

In short, it was a darker world. A darker America.

Garin watched as a homeless man screamed incoherently to himself on a street corner, trying to ward off some invisible evil.

"I know how you feel, pal," Garin thought.

He was reminded of a quote from his more religious days: "Outside the church there is no salvation." But Garin was not about to get down on his knees and start reciting the 23rd Psalm. He wouldn't cry or scream or pray to the Lord, the Sky Father or even Oprah. That was not his way. That was the not the special forces way.

And as they liked to say in special forces: the only easy day was yesterday.

Besides, life went on, not matter how wretchedly, thought Garin as he walked down the street, pulling his sailor hat down lower as an unmarked black ops helicopter armed with a Vulcan cannon flew overhead. The poor and the homeless were disproportionately hammered, but the rich, like cockroaches, always seemed to survive. That was what occupied Garin's mind as he stood across the road from an upmarket retirement home in upstate New York.

Garin crossed the street towards the home, chiding himself about how indulgent it was of him to focus on the fate of one individual right now. It was the sort of off-mission bullshit he always berated the Spartan over. If he didn't know any better he would have accused himself of survivor's guilt, of attempting a token gesture in the faces of all those millions of graves.

Maybe there was something to that last thought. It was always a soldier's worst fears that he would fail in the job and others would die. As Homeland Security's ace troubleshooter, he had failed to prevent the plague from reaching America's shores via Taiwan, even if he had helped stop the six plague canisters they'd found in the American homeland.

You think you're a savior, whispered a voice. *You're more like Shiva the Destroyer.*

Garin ignored it.

Back to the mission.

There were multiple stubbed-out cigarettes in front of the twin security guards at the door, suggesting that their watch had been long. The pair threw Garin a cursory look as he slowly climbed the steps. Garin was unrecognisable from his former guise as a US Tier 1 special forces killer. The guards could not tell that he was once a fully operational member of that famous warrior elite, also known as the finest soldiers that had ever walked the earth.

The finest warriors who had ever walked the earth, except, perhaps, for one other tribe. The Spartans.

Moving slowly, almost limping, Garin seemed like just another crusty old duffer. Not a trained soldier who could kill either man with a single, swift blow.

As Garin came closer, the larger guard stared into Garin's eyes, looking for signs of bad-assery. Yet Garin had removed the steel from his eyes. Perhaps if the guard had thought to pat Garin down he might have noted something amiss: that under those loose-fitting clothes lay a military-fit body. But he didn't. He bought Garin's cover story of Old Spice meets Old Money. Besides, Garin knew the guard's brief was to keep out street rats and angry mobs targeting One Percenters, not the One Percenters themselves.

"Have a good day, sir," the guard said.

Garin was through the front door.

As he entered, he heard one guard say to the other: "That dude looked just like Lee Marvin."

Which was not the first time he'd heard those words.

The other guard replied: "Ask him to sing something from *Paint Your Wagon*, then."

Which was definitely the first time Garin had heard those words.

The inside of the elite retirement home boasted the sort of wood-meets-marble-meets-money look that rich retirees and Bohemian Grovers drooled over. Judging by the level of comfort and the contented demeanor of its occupants, the casual observer would never think that the mighty USA was suffering outside. This was a port from the storm, an oasis of calm in the surrounding scorched earth.

Garin shuffled along the blond wood floor past patients, nurses and doctors, keeping his face hidden under his sailor hat, until he came close to the door he wanted. Checking to make sure no one was watching, he silently let himself in.

Inside, the room's single, white male occupant – a man in his mid-80s – was sleeping lightly, snoring under the blankets, his nose making a whistling noise.

Looking at him, he seemed like just another old coot … hardly the man behind one of the 20th century's most terrible crimes.

Garin recalled images he'd seen of his suspect: first as a vital young Turk, then as a middle-aged powerbroker with his face blacked out in secret photos, and finally as he was today, thinned out, face like sandpaper. Yes, it was him. Eyeball confirmation. *Target is green.*

The colonel pulled a chair from the corner and brought it near the bed, the chair complaining with a squeaking noise. As he moved closer, Garin looked at the cross above the patient's bed. He smiled a wry smile, briefly remembering his own holier-than-thou youth. It had been a long time since he had heard His voice. And he probably never would again … regularly coveting his neighbor's ass was the least of his trespasses against the 10 Commandments.

Meanwhile, the asshole in the bed kept snoring.

Garin grabbed the vase, threw out the flowers and tossed its water into the man's face. A second or two later he spluttered. Joe Patient's eyes came to life.

"What? What?"

"It's time for your sponge bath, sir," said Garin merrily.

"Who are you?" said the other man, eyes blinking rapidly. "What are you doing in here?"

"What, you're not buying the sponge bath story?" said Garin conversationally, removing his hat, folding his legs and taking a seat. "Anyway, who am I is classified. I could tell you who I am, but then I'd have to kill you."

The patient stared at Garin warily. "I don't know you. Get the fuck out of here."

"And here I thought all men were brothers."

"To hell with this," said the patient, reaching out for the control with the "nurse" button on it. Garin gently removed it from his liver-spotted grasp.

"Ah, ah. Don't be naughty. Leave nursey and her giant, unpaid student loan out of it."

"If you want money there's some in the drawer," said the man, now afraid.

"It's not about money."

"Then what do you want? Get to the point, then get out," said the man in the bed, pointing his eyes at the door.

"No foreplay? Fine. Why am I here? JFK." Three letters that hung in the air like an accusation. An accusation that travelled through the decades of history, begging for an answer that never came.

The man opposite looked like he'd just seen a ghost.

"JFK?" he croaked.

"Yes, John F. Kennedy, former President of the United States of America. Someone you know only too well."

There was another long, fraught pause, interrupted only by the sound of the humming air-conditioner.

"Everybody knew JFK," came the weak reply.

"Some better than others. Like you. Even if your name never came up during the Warren Commission. Even if your finger wasn't on the trigger that day in Dallas." Garin leaned in. "Only the rest are now horse glue. You're the last. And I'm not about to let you get away clean."

Garin then said the man's real name. The patient made a strange, choked-off noise, as if he hadn't heard those unfamiliar words in a long time. His hands shook. If it were another man, Garin might have placed a gentle hand on his to calm him. Yet he didn't. Instead, he said: "You're at the end of the road. So why not bare your soul?"

The man's eyes lit up in panic again. Then, a certain acceptance came over them. Then calculation.

"You open the kimono first," he said slowly. "Who are you?"

"My name is Colonel Garin. Lover, fighter, retweeter."

"I've heard of you. What was it, special forces? SOCOM?" SOCOM being short for United States Special Operations Command.

"And Homeland Security, among other things."

The patient fixed Garin with a malevolent look. "Are you like one of those assholes who never got over Vietnam?"

"Wrong war."

"Correct me if I'm wrong, *colonel*, but don't you have better things to be doing right now? Have you looked outside the window? The country is godforsaken. FUBAR, even."

Garin's eyes were drawn to the window in the room, then back towards the patient. "I *do* have better things to do. But I thought you didn't deserve to die peacefully in your sleep. You and your friends robbed the US of a great President."

The patient shifted under the sheets. "Didn't you hear? Oswald did it."

"Very funny. But I do the jokes here."

"Who sent you? I can't imagine anyone giving you clearance for this."

Garin laughed. "You're the first person I ever met who hoped that red tape would save them. No, I sent myself. One of the benefits of giving orders. Occasionally you can give one to yourself."

"You still can't do this. This is America."

"This *was* America."

Garin's target exhaled as the weight of a great secret left him. "I always wondered if someone like you was going to turn up on my door one day. For years, I used to check underneath my car for bombs. I watched for strange cars in the driver mirror. I woke up in the middle of the night, covered in sweat, expecting to find a hitman in the bedroom."

Garin nodded. "Guilty conscience, eh?"

"But after so many decades, I realized no one was coming. So, I got on with living my life. A rich, full life I may add, asshole." Garin didn't react to the barb. "Now I suppose you want to know *why*. Like every other dime-store detective out there."

Garin nodded.

The patient sneered. "*Why* is a child's question. You already know why. Because it had to be done. JFK was soft on Communism. Hell, he let the Beard install nuclear weapons in Cuba. On our very doorstep!"

"Permit me to 'Greedo' you here …"

"What?"

"'Greedo'. It's *Star Wars* speak for violently cutting someone off. Which is what I'm doing over your claim that the Commies unilaterally installed nukes in our backyard. Because we had our *own* Jupiter missiles in Turkey. Right on the USSR's doorstep. So it was natural for the Russkies to respond by putting theirs in Cuba."

The patient was unimpressed. "So what? That doesn't mean Kennedy shouldn't have backed our boys during the

Bay of Pigs. JFK was losing the Cold War. The arrogant bastard was threatening our interests all over the world. He was going to splinter the CIA into a thousand pieces. If we'd left it to him he would have cut off our balls and handed them to the Russians.

"So ... we did what needed to be done. We acted. With the help of our friends."

"Your friends ... I know all about those 'goodfellas' of yours," Garin said with disdain.

"You hypocrite," spat the patient. "Are your hands clean? What have you done for God and country?"

Garin nodded his head slowly, finally agreeing with the cur on something. "You're right. I've done a lot of things I'm not proud of. But I've never had a President assassinated."

"The world is full of sin," came the reply. "Is this what you've been reduced to ... avenging one sin at a time?"

Garin carefully considered this surprising riposte. Eventually he said: "In the end, every man draws a circle around himself and says, 'Everything inside this circle, I accept. Everything outside this circle, I cannot accept.'" Garin pointed his finger at the other man. "And you, I cannot accept." Garin then stood up, reached over and removed the man's pillow from under his head. "Anyway, you seem uncomfortable. Let me fluff up your pillow."

The JFK conspirator knew what was coming. In Garin's experience, men could be divided into two categories at this point: those that attempted to beg, plead or rationalise at the end; and those that said "fuck you" in the face of oblivion.

The JFK conspirator was the latter.

"Damn you to hell!" he shouted. "It was 50 years ago! No one cares any more!"

"I care," said Garin sadly.

"Who do you think you are, some kind of hero? Who will ever know what you've done here?"

"*I'll* know. And in some strange way, history will know."

The prone figure laughed bitterly. "History won't know dick." He laughed again, then shook his head. "Whacking a senior citizen in a retirement village ... they'll give you the Medal of Honor for sure!"

"Hush now." Garin loomed over him, holding the pillow above the man's head. "Incidentally, the pillow's not for your benefit. It's for the maid's."

"I regret nothing!" yelled the conspirator with his last ounce of strength. "I'm a patriot! I did my duty!"

"I'm doing my duty, too." Garin bunched up the pillow, feeling feathers in his fingers and the rush that always came before the kill. "JFK sends his regards."

The pillow descended.

Chapter 8

Private Duane Halen couldn't shake the feeling that he was being watched.

For weeks the 19-year-old US soldier had felt eyes on him as he stood on guard duty at Prometheus Labs. He imagined unseen presences scrutinising him as he served on the midnight shift outside the classified buildings in California, guarding the next generation of military technology. It was a feeling that harkened back to the days when man was genuine prey to the creatures that lurked out there in the dark, the days long before man became top of the food chain.

The feeling refused to go away even when he'd taken the guard dogs and scanned the perimeter ... or did the rounds with his buddy and fellow guard Aaron, always finding nothing.

Then again, he was taking *a lot* of speed.

Speed was just the thing to get you through those late shifts staring out into the night. Guard duty had been deathly boring ever since the days of Roman legionaries staring over

Hadrian's Wall, searching for hairy barbarians on the horizon. Only those tired ancients didn't have modern pharmaceuticals to keep them sharp and stay awake. They probably let the odd barbarian past the watchtower by mistake.

And, as Duane's superiors took every instance to remind him, he couldn't afford to make mistakes.

Apparently, the projects going on inside those sterile white buildings behind him were vital to national security. It was secret squirrel stuff. Omega-level clearance only. Which was why the labs were also home to their own rapid-reaction strike force, ex-special forces bad-asses ready to rock and roll at a moment's notice.

During the past year the lab was host to many important delegations and visits by civilian scientists. There was one dude in particular that Duane had seen several times: a tough-looking colonel who resembled Lee Marvin. (Aaron didn't know who Lee Marvin was, refusing to watch any movie that was made before the first *Star Wars* came out.)

One day Duane summoned up the nerve to ask this full-bird colonel what it was the scientists were working on.

"Are we building a flying saucer in there?" he said, despite Aaron kicking him in the shin to shut up. The colonel laughed at the "flying saucer" reference. The old man looked like he enjoyed a good joke. He put his arm around the private's shoulder in a friendly manner.

"Don't ask, lad," he said. "The 'Greys' would be angry if I said anything." The colonel caught Duane's frown and laughed again. "Anyway, you wouldn't believe me if I told you."

That had only piqued Duane's curiosity more, but Lee Marvin wasn't dropping any more crumbs of information. Nor were the geeks in white lab coats who travelled back and forth each day dropping any nuggets of information, no doubt sworn to some insane level of non-disclosure, forbidden to talk about what they were doing to friends, family and lowly grunts on the gate.

Yet after the plague had swept across the US and the world, security had become lax. Most of the rapid-reaction force had been deployed elsewhere. The previous 50-strong guard had been whittled down to a mere dozen as soldiers were removed to fill gaps elsewhere. Other levels of high-tech security remained in place – iris checks, passwords, voice recognition software – but the number of actual boots on the ground was at the lowest level ever. Duane wondered if "Lee Marvin" knew just had critically vulnerable his pet project had become.

Hence the speed. Just the thing to keep you sharp and get you through shifts that were growing longer and longer. Duane felt his paranoia was due to some unseen external threat rather than the speed. Then again, if you regularly took speed, were you in any good mental state to assess what was *really* making you paranoid?

One night he'd taken that paranoia to extremes. Scenting prey, the guard dogs had gone beyond the fence to chase a white rabbit. For some reason the incident pushed all of Duane's paranoia buttons. He'd never seen any rabbit around here before. So why a rabbit now?

And why a *white* rabbit?

He seized the radio and summoned what remained of the rapid-reaction force to sweep the area.

"I've got a bad feeling about this," he told them.

The depleted force found nothing, except the dogs fighting over Bugs. The angry soldiers glared at him as if he was some spaced-out white trash tweaker who claimed he'd just spotted Sasquatch ... before, grumbling, they returned to base.

Aaron was similarly unimpressed. He told him to switch to coffee or that soldier's favorite, Ripped Fuel, before the next surprise round of mandatory drug testing.

"You sound just like my old lady, nagging me about the speed," complained Duane. "What's *your* problem?"

"Besides peaking in high school? I don't want to break in a new guard duty partner. You need to knock it off with the blue meth before the sarge makes you pee into a cup."

Duane wasn't particularly worried. The military needed every able body it could muster right now. Regulations were being overlooked on all sorts of things post-plague.

He cut down on the speed like Aaron suggested. Yet the feeling that he was being watched persisted.

And was only confirmed one night when a tall figure crept up behind Duane as he was playing Fruit Ninja on his smartphone and stuck a 13th-century samurai sword through his chest.

"Aww, man," complained Duane.

* * *

The slain, drug-affected private had been right. Intruders *had* been watching the base.

Each night 12 highly trained men had observed Prometheus Labs through night-vision goggles. The men in black had spent many hours crouching in the shadows in their ghillie suits at the periphery, staring through the NVGs, looking for a weakness, an opening.

Yes, they knew they could be discovered at any time. But by all reports, the prize inside was worth the risk ... a prize only winkled out when American cyber security had been at its weakest following the plague pandemic. (Incidentally, the group had penetrated America's black ops data bases by hacking their heating and cooling systems: proving that a spy in the right place, even on a keyboard, was worth 20,000 troops on the battlefield.)

It had been too risky to attack while the lab was heavily guarded. Hence their patience. All they could do was wait in position. And probe. And test for vulnerabilities.

The other fly in the proverbial ointment was the raging paranoia of that one young guard. He had foiled their probes one too many times. Some ancient sense had been triggered in him, alerting him to the malevolent presence hiding in the dark.

The incident with the white rabbit only served to increase the guard's paranoia. Their leader had almost been caught when the guard had spotted their white rabbit, sent out as a decoy for the K9 units. He barely escaped when the heavily armed rapid reaction force arrived in jeeps, summoned by the jittery guard who had found the rabbit a bad omen.

Still, they waited.

One day they saw the sign that they had been waiting for. The rapid-reaction force was called away. Soon more soldiers disappeared, no doubt redeployed to handle the chaos raging across America. Only a mere handful of guards remained. A skeleton staff. Soon to become actual skeletons. Not enough to protect the precious treasure within.

And so, on the night that they sensed the private's powers of observation were at their weakest, they struck, starting with the guard. (The leader made sure to twist the blade, irritated at the guard's interference.)

The masked, armed men made their bloody way past the guard posts, past the K9 units (no time for sentimentality now), past the electronic defenses for which they were already prepared for (one guard's severed head, a victim of the Honjo Masamune, was used to pass the retina scans), and past the desultory remaining opposition.

They lost two men to gunfire – well within their accepted casualty figures – before they killed the last of the brave defenders. Before long the intruders made it into the main labs.

"Five minutes," said the leader, setting his watch, as the men in black efficiently went from room to room. The silent intruders inserted USB-style sticks into computers, the sticks armed with programs that both sucked all the information from the computers and then deleted the computer's data and that of any backups off-site. The intruders collected files, equipment, rare materials, even mechanical components. Information from security cameras was deleted. Explosives were placed on machines and walls.

Finally, they seized the most important item of all: the lead scientist behind the project, the brains trust without whom all the rest would be worthless. A luminary described in the mission notes as being as important to his own field as Wernher Von Braun was to rocketry and the Space Race.

The remainder of the white-coated scientists were forced into a corner. The intruders' leader coldly observed the scientists. Also watching by his side was a fierce-looking woman, armed with a submachine gun, with whom he exchanged frequent glances.

The leader separated the lead scientist and held the tall, scrawny man hard by the neck.

"Who are you?" he gasped.

"A consequence," said the leader. "Now watch. And remember."

Then the leader nodded. His men opened fire. The rest of the scientists were slain. The surviving scientist howled with grief.

"Time to leave," ordered the leader.

The intruders escaped into the night in vehicles with their dead, their hostage and their stolen cargo. The leader personally detonated the explosives from a safe distance, watching flames lick up into the night sky. He and his men shared a moment of giddy excitement, smiles all round, scarcely believing what they had achieved, the fruits of so many years of training.

Yes, a good night, he thought to himself. *And so it begins.*

* * *

With a heavy heart, Colonel Garin heard the bad news several hours later. When the lab had failed its latest comms check, a rapid-reaction unit had raced over to find chaos. The fresh corpses of men and scientists lay strewn in corridors, bloody red handprints on white antiseptic walls like something out of a zombie movie. Lab equipment and computers were destroyed. And, worst of all, there was no sign of the equipment used to manufacture the Ghost Armor invisibility suit.

Nor was the body of its creator among the dead. That had been the first thing Garin had asked.

That lone act of mercy also felt very deliberate and planned. Professor Eisenstein was the one visionary who knew how all the pieces fell together. Without him, building the Ghost Armor suit would have been impossible.

Now, even though the US had built the first suit, it would face an uphill battle to replicate the painstaking manufacturing process with much of the information missing and the professor gone.

Garin felt like the ancient library of Alexandria ... they'd both been burned.

When Garin, furious, had demanded to know how this had all happened, considering the amount of security he had arranged for the lab, he was told that most of his rapid-reaction unit and almost all his other guards had been requisitioned by another officer. Unfortunately, this officer didn't know just how important the lab and its contents were because he wasn't in the information loop. In fact, very few people knew what had been going on in the labs – a decision that had now come back to bite Garin.

Compartmentalisation. Most of the time it worked. Sometimes it got people killed.

Garin grasped his head as if in agony. They had no firm leads as to who was behind the daring raid. There was no footage to examine – the cameras and their back-up data banks had been deliberately destroyed. Nor was there any satellite, surveillance or electronic intel yet. The United States was the world's leader in signal intelligence, but the NSA, with its vast reams of data, had nothing to offer him. Nor did the CIA or any other agency.

Like the canister conspiracy, it was yet another example of America's over-reliance on electronic intercepts. As his Russian friend Marchenko said, America's weakness was always to rely on signal intelligence rather than human intelligence: the latter helped the Russians outfox America many times during the Cold War. There was no substitute for people on the ground infiltrating groups and gathering intelligence the old-fashioned, human way, rather than simply rely on Big Data to do all the heavy lifting.

It was a military maxim that every weapon ever invented had been used at least once. The colonel couldn't imagine the new owners not wanting to try out their new toy.

But however the thieves used it, he could bet it wouldn't be used for "good".

Garin's didn't look forward to sharing this information with the President. Already under tremendous strain, POTUS had begun quoting Winston Churchill circa WWII. Never a good sign.

His protégé and favorite Luddite, the Spartan, had been right all along – the disruptive technology had been destined to escape from the labs and fall into the wrong, presumably non-American hands.

Garin could almost hear the Spartan's gravelly voice telling him "I told you so".

Chapter 9

They kept the scientist alone and in darkness for the first day, only turning on the lights in his cell whenever he tried to sleep.

On the second day, the men in black refused to feed him.

On the third day, they silently beat him in a manner as painful as it was confusing. "Not the face or hands," said the tall, slender man the scientist knew to be the leader.

On the fourth day, they tortured Professor Eisenstein by using martial arts on his nerve endings. The pain was unendurable. Yet no mark was left. Nor were any questions asked.

On the fifth day, they asked, "Will you build the suits for us?" He said no. The torture continued. The lights stayed on so he couldn't sleep. He received almost no food. He was forced to drink water on the hour every hour until he was sick.

On the sixth day, they showed Professor Eisenstein a photo of his wife and two children. The photo was recent. "We have your family. Will you build the suits for us?" they repeated. He said no.

On the seventh day, they tortured him even more intensely than before, applying chillies to his eyes, even waterboarding him. They showed him the picture of his family again. The leader said: "I have one question. Do you want them to live?"

"How do I know you have them?" he gasped.

"How difficult do you think it was to snatch four unguarded civilians when we destroyed an entire military facility to get at you?" said the leader.

Professor Eisenstein thought about that. "Let me talk to my family."

"No."

"How can I trust you?"

"You have my word we won't harm them if you co-operate. We're not interested in your wife and children. We're only interested in your work. Which is brilliant, if I may say so." The leader paused, standing above the scientist. The tall man still had the samurai sword strapped to his back. "The death of your loved ones is inevitable without your help. I won't lie: you can't save yourself. But you can save them. Make your decision." Then the leader left.

On the eighth day, Professor Eisenstein agreed to build the suits.

Chapter 10

Four months later

Colonel Garin had an 8am visitor to his apartment: the Spartan.

Both soldiers had already completed their 10-mile runs for the morning. Neither men exercised to look aesthetically pleasing: they exercised to enhance their ability to fight and, ultimately, kill.

But now was not the time to think of fighting. Now it was time to break bread, drink coffee and swap war stories in New York's Little Belgium.

Garin eyed the man mountain in a black tracksuit sitting on his couch as the morning sun peeked through the bullet-resistant blinds. He smiled at his protégé with the ease of a friendship long established over many strange and awesome circumstances.

"It's great to see you, son," he said. "Thanks for making it over this early. I know you had to catch the red-eye from Fort Bragg."

"No problem, sir."

"I guessed you might be up for breakfast coffee. Because I wasn't about to suggest brunch. No soldier should ever do brunch."

"I don't believe in 'brunch' either, sir."

"They never served it in special forces," breezed Garin. "Why start now?"

Ever the gracious host, Garin reached over to serve his guest a strong coffee from the plunger. Next, he took a sip from his cup, which was emblazoned with the words "World's No.1 boss".

"Ahh, sweet coffee," said Garin as he sipped his drink, "what miracles have been achieved under your power. Do you know the President drinks the same blend?" Replenished, he said: "So what have you been up to lately, my son of Sparta?"

"The usual … shooting tangos, sir."

"I hope they had it coming, then."

"They all did, sir," said the Spartan, his huge knuckles wrapping around his mug. Some scientists believed the human hand evolved the way it did so humans could punch better … and one look at the Spartan's hands and you'd believe it, too.

"At ease, son. You don't have to keep calling me sir."

"I'll try to remember that, sir."

Garin smiled, perhaps realising that his star recruit would never drop the "sir". He teasingly placed a spoon into the sugar bowl. "Sugar?"

"You know I don't take sugar, sir."

"Because you think sugar is leading to the downfall of America."

"Sugar IS leading to the downfall of the United States, sir."

"Maybe you're right." Garin topped up his own coffee, his robe coming close to the brim of the cup. "Don't see too many people taking sugar in their coffee at Fort Bragg, either. All those special forces heroes watching their waistline. Like me back in the day.

"Two sugars for me now, though. Hope you don't think that's too Athenian, soldier." For Athenian, read soft and decadent. Read "non-Spartan".

"You get a special dispensation, colonel, for your years of service," said the Spartan, sipping his dark coffee.

The colonel raised his coffee cup. "To fallen comrades."

The Spartan mirrored the colonel's gesture. "To fallen comrades."

They drank silently, remembering friends fallen in action in dusty battlefields, al-Qaeda nests, deniable operations in Third World slums, Second World drug compounds and First World terrorist lairs.

"Right, then," said the colonel as he took a seat opposite the couch. "Let's get down to business. I haven't see you in person for a few months – not after all our work on the canister conspiracy – so I just wanted to talk in person, see that everything was all right."

"It's fine, sir. Thanks for asking."

"The uniform still fits?"

"The uniform still fits, colonel."

"Still happy to 'sing of arms and the man'?" asked Garin, quoting Homer.

"Always, sir. There's no better song."

"I agree. Once you've tasted war, nothing else really touches the sides, does it?" Garin gave his favorite soldier the ocular once-over. Every soldier's body told the owner's tale: and judging by the number of scars and healed wounds on the Spartan's, his tale was rich indeed. "So ... how are the ribs?" asked Garin.

The Spartan looked down, glancing at the space where flying debris had struck his body armor and cracked said rib with its dispersed energy on a recent mission. "Already healed, sir."

"Suicide car bomber in Iraq, wasn't it?"

"Affirmative. We got him as he came down the highway."

"Well done, son."

There was a moment of silence between them. In general, as a man of action, the Spartan didn't talk much – like his namesakes, he was quite laconic, and special forces soldiers tended not to talk too much about their missions anyway – so when the Spartan did get the chance to talk with Garin, he tended to binge. The Tier 1 soldier treasured the moments he spent with the colonel, who was perhaps the only person alive who truly understood him.

The Chinese special forces soldier known as the Monk may have fit that category as well, but no one knew if he was alive.

As Garin sipped his coffee, the Spartan took it as his cue to speak.

"And how are you, sir?"

"I thrive, soldier."

The Spartan examined his commander and old friend.

Garin did indeed look as if he was in fine fettle for a man approaching his sixth decade on this earth. Physically, the Spartan and Garin were almost polar opposites – the Spartan built like a Mack truck, Garin lean and wiry – but Garin possessed an uncanny strength in his frame that many had underestimated to their misfortune.

Indeed, Garin had been one of special forces' star hunter/killers in his time. He was also one of the only men ever to beat the Spartan in hand-to-hand combat, a feat he had accomplished close to 20 years ago when he first met the raw recruit, cementing a bond that lasted to this day.

The Spartan sipped his coffee, then said: "And your family?"

"They're fine. My ex-wife is OK. Took my advice and got out of the plague's way while the getting was good."

"And your son?"

Garin made a "tssking" noise. "Still an insufferable, greedy little shit. That's civilians for you. But he's family, so what are you going to do, right?"

The Spartan noted Garin's continued irritated expression at the mention of his son. A sore topic best dropped. Instead, he looked away and scanned the apartment.

The Spartan's trained eyes took in the rest of Garin's funky pad, filled with both mod cons and military souvenirs. He had been in Garin's apartment many times, one of rare individuals so honored. The Spartan had had seen the apartment change and morph over more than a decade, changing along with the tastes of its owner as well as with the fashions of the day.

Garin noticed the Spartan's scrutiny.

"Looking for something in particular, son?" he asked with a touch of amusement.

"Just looking for the arrow on the ceiling pointing towards Fort Bragg, colonel."

The colonel laughed. "Been meaning to get one."

The Spartan's eyed stopped at two weapons in cases on a nearby wall.

"Those pistols, colonel … I don't think I've seen them before." He gestured with his head.

"Good eyes, son. I wondered if you'd notice them. Remind me never to underestimate your powers of observation." The colonel rose and slowly took one of the pistols out of the case, turning it in his hands to admire the weapon.

He continued: "They're a pair of Carl von Clausewitz's duelling pistols. Not sure if he ever used them. A gift from the Germans. The Krauts came out of the plague pretty well after our tip-off and our actions. Seems they don't do as much trade with Taiwan as we do. They got their borders down before the worst of it hit. Which is good, because Europe needs their help." Garin held the pistol close so the Spartan could examine it. "Look at the engraving and metalwork. Magnificent, isn't it?"

The Spartan peered closer. The weapon looked both beautiful and old. Unlike most members of his generation, he appreciated old things. "Are they functional or merely decorative, sir?"

"Straight to the nub of it as always, soldier. Why don't we find out right now?" Garin adopted a duelling stance.

"They're a hell of a thing to load, though. Watch this." Garin sat on the couch. "First, you half-cock the pistol. Then, check the barrel is empty." Garin emptied some of the contents of a small pouch into the barrel. "Add some gunpowder, place a patch with a ball at the top, ram in the ball in with the ram rod, open the frizzen pan, pour in more powder ... Christ, how they ever even got around to the duel with all this nonsense I'll never know ... full cock and then ... let's just hope it doesn't blow up in my hand ... blam!"

Garin discharged the pistol into a nearby pillow. The noise was loud in the confined space, yet neither man flinched, having been under fire too many times to count.

Garin examined his hand first to make sure it was OK – it was – then peered down at the hole left by the ball. The hole was small but presumably fatal to a real person.

"Still works. That's good to know ... just in case I get challenged to a duel any time soon. Ha." Garin waved the pistol at the walls. "Don't worry about the neighbors. They won't complain. They've heard worse things going on in this apartment."

Garin finally returned the pistol and all its bits and pieces to the glass case, then slowly closed it. Then he resumed his position opposite the Spartan. "Anyway, let's return to the 21st century. I've seen the reports from your last 10 special forces missions, son. Sterling work as always."

The Spartan glowed at the praise. The soldier did not fear knives or bullets or his fellow man – only a look of disappointment in his commander's eyes. And today he saw no such disappointment. "Thank you, sir. We got the job done and brought our boys home."

"That latest job was hairy, though. I heard you saw more action than that suicide bomber."

"Took bullets in my front and back. AK rounds."

Garin looked at the Spartan's back, as if expecting to see a bullet there. "I think the Russians must have left the world's supply of AK-47s in Afghanistan when they left. Now they're everywhere. And those rusty old pieces of shit still work fine. Special forces are as busy as ever, then?"

"Yes, sir."

"And new spheres of operation are springing up all over the globe. Africa, Asia, South America, the Middle East," said Garin, counting them off on his fingers. He sipped his coffee, then said: "Is it just me or is the world becoming a more hostile place?"

"It was always a hostile place, sir. Humans have been at war for nine-tenths of recorded history ... and from my personal experience, I don't see that stopping any time soon."

"I mean, since the plague and all. It might be my imagination, but there seems to be a lot more people angry at us. And not just our enemies. Our friends as well."

The Spartan was untroubled by the observation. "Nothing we can't deal with, sir."

"I *want* to believe that. Yet I sometimes wonder if we've bitten off more than we can chew. As a country, I mean. As an unofficial empire. I fear imperial overreach. I feel blowback blowing our way."

"Did you have something particular in mind, sir?" asked the Spartan. By the expression of Garin's face it seemed as if for a moment Garin was about to tell him something, to reveal some pressing secret. Then the colonel seemed to change his mind.

"Hopefully it's nothing. Or it's a nothing that will get straightened out in the end. But you know how I like to worry, son. I'm a professional worrier. "

The Spartan studied his mentor. He thought he detected a certain level of doubt. Was that due to old age or a generally more threatening global environment, he wondered? Or a specific, unnamed threat that was keeping him up at night?

He was concerned for Garin. It was rare of him to project any doubt. There were few people the Spartan held precious, but Garin was one of them. And Garin himself had always told him that doubt could kill a man quicker than any bullet.

The Spartan leant back and sipped his coffee, trying to mask his concern. Personally, the Spartan had no doubts. He knew what he was. He knew what he was capable of. He loved his job and his mission. And he wasn't about to stop doing that job for anyone.

Not even for the General.

As if Garin had read the Spartan's mind, he said: "Are you working on … any other projects, son?"

The Spartan smirked at Garin's attempts to bring up a perennial topic. "Do you mean that excuse of a man, the General?"

"Yes, I do." The General, aka the man the Spartan had slashed in the face and later gut-stabbed with his *xiphos*. The General, the powerful military leader locked in a fight to the death with the Spartan.

"I haven't heard from him since after our mission to China to kill Commander Lee."

"Good," said Garin emphatically. "Let's keep it that way. He's unworthy of your attention. He's a distraction you don't need."

"You mean an enemy I don't need, sir?"

"That, too. This isn't a game. There are far better uses for your skill set."

The Spartan stroked the sheath on his side that held his *xiphos*. "I'd be lying if it didn't feel like it was unfinished business, sir."

"Well, don't go provoking anything," warned Garin, peering at him over the brim of his coffee cup. "You both had your chance to kill each other already and we saw how that turned out. There's better things you can be doing than pursuing an old grudge."

"I think it's gone well beyond a grudge. It's now a vendetta."

Garin sighed. "I was afraid of that." Garin waved his hand. "You know my views on the subject. I'd prefer if you dealt with your rivalry permanently. This mission needs to be over already. And you barely survived the last time the two of you went toe to toe."

"So did the General," said the Spartan.

"Point. Enough said." Garin munched on a croissant.

The two men sat without speaking for a while. They knew each other well enough to share a comfortable silence. Any soldier who had spent time in the field knew that there were extended periods of waiting in silence for orders or for combat. One had to learn to get used to quiet times: to savor them, even. Often the Spartan and Garin just sat together silently. They shared a special bond beyond words, forged over adversity.

Eventually, Garin said: "How is Vasquez?"

"Good, sir. Fighting fit."

Garin gave the Spartan a shrewd look. "Do I hear wedding bells?"

"Only if you've been standing too close to too many artillery blasts, sir."

Garin laughed, his mirth sending ripples through the surface of his coffee. "You don't have to get married, son, but you don't have to be afraid of caring for her, either. It won't make you any less of a soldier. We're not priests. We've taken a holy vow of violence, but not a vow of celibacy."

"Understood, sir."

"Take it from me: I've been married and it didn't make me any less of a killer." Garin paused. "Then again, I *did* get divorced."

"Maybe that made you even *more* of a killer sir."

"For the first few months, it probably did. I was pretty angry." Garin tilted his head as if recalling the memory. "But back to Vasquez. She's good for you, I can tell."

"She is ... a valuable teammate, sir." The Spartan didn't know what more information Garin wanted. The Spartan wasn't a sharer by nature.

Garin nodded, as if he knew that the Spartan was more comfortable facing the Taliban than talking about his feelings.

"Is she happier now that she's killed Fighting Dog?"

The Spartan paused, considering the question. "I would say so, sir."

The colonel's voice lowered conspiratorially. "Has she figured out the truth about revenge?"

The Spartan's already-gravelly voice also dropped an octave. "That it doesn't completely fill the hole left behind after tragedy?"

Garin gave the Spartan a meaningful look. "Yes."

"No, sir."

"It will come to her. Comfort her when it does." Garin looked away. "I may have to think about her future. I'm not sure she wants to be doing this sort of thing forever. She chose being a cop in Juarez, but she didn't choose the special forces life."

"She's a born warrior sir. I've seldom worked with better."

"A born warrior? Rare praise indeed, coming from you. I always imagined that if they'd taken a sonogram of you in the womb you'd be pictured holding your SAW." Garin smiled. "And to think you could barely stand to be in the same room together when you first met."

"She *was* invisible at the time, sir."

"She may be a natural warrior, son, but that doesn't mean she wants to fight forever. She doesn't have a war-shaped hole in the middle of her like us that she needs to fill with … well, war. She should consider returning to a normal life while she still has a normal life to go back to."

"Yes, sir," said the Spartan, curious to see where Garin was going with this.

"Our way of life can be punishing," Garin continued. "And she's already told me she's had trouble sleeping. It's a frequent problem with special forces soldiers fighting in intense terrains. War wears men out like clothes." Garin touched the edge of his robe, feeling its fabric between his fingers. "And in times of peace, the warlike man goes to war with himself."

That sounded familiar to the Spartan, who had a taste for pithy military sayings. "Who said that?"

"I just did. Just remember, son … Vasquez is too precious to let slip away. No man needs nothing. Even a Spartan. And you're not a man who forms connections with people very easily or very often." Garin flashed him a look. "No offence, soldier."

"None taken, sir."

"The connections we forge with people can make all the difference in life. Treasure them. Remember what we fight for."

The Spartan felt a sudden pang at the notion of Vasquez not being in his life. As Garin had intimated, he wasn't a man who became easily attached. And it was rare to find a partner with Vasquez's qualities, her fighting spirit, her skill at arms, her intelligence, her beauty.

The Spartan wanted her. Did he now also *need* her?

Colonel Garin got up, leaving the Spartan to ponder his enigmatic last remark. "Anyway, son. I won't keep you. I'm late as it is. I have my own mission to take care of today and it's already half past a monkey's ass."

The Spartan looked at his bare wrist. "That's what my watch says as well, sir."

"Maybe you, me and Vasquez can do lunch sometime. I'll cook for you. I do a wicked baklava. Make you lamb Greek style."

"I look forward to it, sir." The Spartan got up and saluted. "Goodbye, colonel."

Garin saluted back. "Goodbye, soldier. Give my best wishes to Vasquez."

Then the Spartan left.

Chapter 11

As the General stared at his scarred face in the mirror, he realized he was long overdue to try to kill the Spartan.

The Spartan, aka the monster that refused to salute his superior officer; aka the beast that told him he was a coward to his face; aka the horror that used his body as a whetstone for his sword; aka the maniac who had not only slashed his face but had later gut-stabbed and left him for dead.

Stab me once, shame on you.

Stab me twice, shame on me.

The General stared at the scar that ran from his eyebrow to his chin, following its path lightly with his thin fingers. The Mark of Cain, he thought. The Mark of the Spartan.

He knew the Spartan seldom laughed. Yet the General still imagined the special forces soldier laughing at him somewhere.

He turned away from the mirror, a sudden regret at the mutilation of his handsome face flickering through his mind. He hadn't encountered the Spartan for a long time now, but he was reminded of his deadly handiwork in that hospital room in Kandahar every day.

It had been months since the Spartan and Colonel Garin had narrowly escaped the General's wrath. The loathed duo had stolen the Zarathustra, the high-tech stealth plane under the General's command, then taken for a global joyride to slay the villain behind the Chinese canister conspiracy. The pair had succeeded ... only to fall into the General's trap upon return to the States, where he intended to throw them in military prison for heisting the plane.

Goodie, goodie. Cue the rubbing of hands in glee, the twirling of the non-existent villainous moustache.

The genius plan was, once the Spartan was arrested by the military police, it would have been much easier to have him killed in a holding cell, unarmed and with no possible avenue of escape.

Certainly, the General's other attempts to kill the Spartan – even having rogue special forces troops do the job – had failed. So had his earlier, less imaginative attempts, such as tipping off the Mafia when the Spartan was about to attack one of their strongholds. And the attempts even before that, when the General had first summoned up the nerve to get rid of this turbulent Tier 1 soldier.

Unfortunately that idiot, the Vice President, had appeared just as the General had ordered the pair to be arrested on the runway. The VP insisted that, despite their illegal requisitioning of said stealth plane – to launch a mission on Chinese soil, for Christ's sake! – that Garin and the Spartan be freed. The release of the plague in Taiwan meant that Garin had become too important and useful to punish.

God, the VP was an asshole, thought the General. *More of a haircut than a man. Someone should put him out of his misery.*

So, yes, after he had failed to end the Spartan, the potent monster was loose on the world once more. And one day, like a bad penny, the General knew he would arrive on his doorstep, accursed sword in hand, refusing to stop until one of them was dead.

Yes … the Spartan and the General had a *history*.

The Spartan, another asshole in his list of assholes, thought the General. *But a different kind of asshole to the VP, who sold his soul daily for fame and profit. No, the Spartan was an asshole with a "code". Didn't every asshole with a "code" realise that they could only live by that "code" because another dozen people were performing the humiliating tasks that allowed the code-following hero to hold themselves above the fray?*

In fact, behind every hero was the lackey who fed their horses, repaired their tanks, fixed their weapons, worked in the factories producing the bullets and ammunition … those little things our putative savior wouldn't design to perform himself because it violated his "code".

But enough rumination, thought the General. Seeing how the Spartan almost killed him at their last encounter, the General was determined to strike first. Every time he looked in the mirror after his morning shave he was reminded of the Spartan's deadly handiwork. He still had nightmares about that cold blade of this, his precious *xiphos*.

His stomach growled, as if remembering being struck by the *xiphos*. Thanks to that near-fatal wound, there were days he just didn't shit right.

So the Spartan had to be stopped: for both the General's own sense of honor – the Spartan's hatred he could live with, but the lack of respect never – and for his peace of mind. Neither was ready to back down until the other was dead.

Nor would the General have his scar surgically removed until the Spartan was six foot in the ground. Consider it a

Post-It Note he wore on his face so he wouldn't forget what he had to do.

But how to do it? How to kill the inconvenient soldier who refused to be killed, who had the uncanny ability to survive even the most dangerous battle or assassination scenario?

There was the rub.

Of course, he had to know where the Spartan was first.

The Tier 1 jabberwocky had proven to be a hard man to find, being constantly on the move. The General had heard rumours of an off-the-books op in Mexico, where the Spartan and his woman had killed a drug boss.

But then … nothing.

The General had no doubt the Spartan was being kept busy: there was so much to do since the plague had spread around the world. The General kept his ear to the ground as he recuperated from the gut-stabbing, but there was little to be heard.

There were some more juicy nuggets about Colonel Garin, however. Rumour was the President was furious because an unknown force had stolen some high-tech equipment Garin was responsible for. No one knew exactly what that tech was – a fancy new killbot? some amazing new gun? – but its disappearance was considered very bad for national security. And considering that having a plague loose on the world was also considered "very bad" for national security, the General was dying to know what this item was that could also potentially wreak such mayhem.

What evil genie had Garin let out of its bottle? The General had sent his minions out to find out what, but so far they had drawn a blank.

The General wondered whether it might be fruitful to target Colonel Garin as part of his strategy against the

Spartan. The colonel had been the Spartan's political shield, protecting him from censure, wielding enough power to let the Spartan get away with just about anything.

Garin's protection had been one of the main reasons the General had had to be careful about striking back at the Spartan. While the Spartan could damage him physically, Garin could wound him politically. Garin had the ear of the President, after all.

Yet this new development surrounding Garin piqued his interest. If played right, it sounded like just the sort of screw-up that could snowball into a career wrecker. So he now had a two-pronged attack: locate the Spartan, and discover more about Garin's missing doodad.

In the meantime, he waited patiently, like a crocodile in a river. Because if you wait by the river long enough, the body of your enemy – or at least his location – is bound to come floating by.

Chapter 12

Jackson was enjoying a few cold brews in an Irish bar in Brooklyn, wondering which of his girlfriends to call bedwards, when it happened.

A wiry young punk in a denim jacket knocked Jackson's elbow, making Jackson spill his Guinness. The bar was packed cheek-to-cheek and these things happened, but Jackson still didn't like it. He took it personally.

Jackson took a lot of things personally.

As his beer dripped on the counter, Jackson turned from his bar stool to stare coldly at the offender.

"Sorry, bro," said the fair-haired punk. Taking a second look at Jackson, he muttered the "n" word.

The veteran special forces soldier shook his head. So much for "post-racial America". So much for all his supposedly color-blind service to his country.

But the main point was … no one was allowed to speak to him like that. Ever.

He slowly set his imported beer aside. It was a bad time to mess with the Tier 1 soldier. He'd been listening to hard rock all day, AC/DC in particular. He was charged up and angry. He was more than ready to fight.

"Say again, asshole?" he said, turning.

As if by magic, the crowd around the bar parted. People stopped pounding back beers and watching the game on TV to watch the real-life drama.

By now the racist punk, who looked like he had some hillbilly blood in him, was backed up by four of his friends. They were all young, white, fit-looking, athletic, glamour muscles stretching out the fabric of their T-shirts.

They wore their sense of entitlement even tighter.

"You heard," said the punk, belly full of liquid courage. "Did I stutter?"

Jackson stared at them coldly.

Surrounded on all sides by hostile, angry crackers – this was Memphis all over again, he thought.

He considered his next move. Jackson knew there were harsh penalties for getting into bar fights with civilians, up to and including what many special forces soldiers feared above all – being kicked out of the "teams "and sent back to join the ordinary ranks of the army, navy and Marines. But right now, he didn't give a damn about any of that.

Jackson stared at them again. To his trained eye, they were all unarmed. It would come down to trading hands, then.

Jackson's lips turned up in a wry smile. Like all young men, these five thought they were invulnerable. They believed they could "handle" themselves because they'd busted up a few wooden boards with bullshit karate moves.

As Bruce Lee once said, boards don't hit back.

But Jackson did.

Jackson put his hands in his jacket pocket, then stood. The five punks now looked doubtful as they took in Jackson's full size.

"Please don't fight in here, sir," begged a scared, middle-aged white waitress.

The young men looked at the waitress as if she was their sudden savior, as if Jackson might take her advice.

But for Jackson, things were past the point of no return.

He stuffed a twenty into her apron. She was going to have a bad night. But not as bad as the gentlemen in front of him.

"Don't punk out now, bitches," said Jackson as he held his hands up, the brass knuckles he had surreptitiously slipped into place falling down around his knuckles. "Come get the white privilege beaten out of you."

The posse saw this, realized that there was no backing down … and immediately raised their fists. The Charge of the White Brigade.

Jackson struck first. His first punch landed straight in the middle of the face of the "hillbilly" who had insulted him. The maimed man dropped to his knees in shock, holding his bleeding mouth, feeling the fresh new gap on his gums. Judging by his sudden coughing, he'd probably just swallowed some teeth as well. No doubt he'd never been punched that hard in his life.

That was real-life violence for you: brutal, shocking and fast.

His bros stared on, aghast. Jackson waited, feet planted firmly in place.

Two of his friends jumped up in the maimed man's place. Jackson planted a hand into the face of one, pushing him back and onto his ass. He would take these fortunate sons one at a time.

A fresh assailant stepped forward and threw a wild haymaker that Jackson easily ducked, the breeze of its passing ruffling his hair. Two more punches whistled through empty air before Jackson tenderised the punk's stomach with a quick left and a right. The youth had strong abs, but they were not strong enough to protect him from Jackson's brutal, combat-honed strength.

Next, Jackson seized his winded opponent and slammed his head into the side of the bar. Glass and screams filled the air.

As another punk came for him, Jackson used the head of the man he held and slammed it into the other man's face. Bone collided with bone in the most horribly audible way.

"Oooo," cried the crowd.

The attacker was dazed, but still standing. Jackson dropped his human battering ram and slammed lefts and rights into his foe's face instead.

Two punches left a detectable impression of the letters on Jackson's brass knuckles: "FUCK YALL." One word for each cheek.

The fifth punch found the punk's glass jaw and shattered it. Another foe combat ineffective.

The second-last punk, the one Jackson had put on his ass with a firm hand, had a brighter idea. He charged Jackson as if they were on the gridiron field. The wide-shouldered boy-man knew his stuff: Jackson was almost forced to his knees. Almost. But gridiron wasn't a martial art. And they weren't playing for touchdowns. This wasn't a minute before full-time at the Super Bowl.

Jackson slammed elbow after elbow into his assailant's back and neck. He heard a pained grunt after the sixth such strike. His tenderised foe went slack. Jackson kneed him in the head, feeling bone impact with bone. His target went limp like a rag doll. Finished.

Jackson grabbed the fifth punk, who looked like he was about to piss his pants.

"Tell me I'm the Duke of New York."

"What?"

"Say, 'You're the Duke of New York. A-Number-One!' "

"Fuck you!"

Jackson applied pressure to the man's throat.

"OK, OK, you're the Duke of New York," stammered the terrified, confused punk, "A-Number-One!"

"Attaboy."

He felt like punching on, to beat these boys into bloody paste. But he could tell that they'd already learned a lesson that would last them for a lifetime.

Instead, he released his captive and gestured to the bleeding and moaning pile of flesh. "Now get your homies out of here. And tell them to watch their mouths in future."

Jackson watched as the punk helped his friends out of the bar. Only two of them – the first and the last – could walk. They dragged their buddies away, keeping a fearful eye on Jackson all the while.

"Thanks for the workout, assholes," he shouted after them. Then he laughed loudly.

They thought they were predators. Now they understood they were just prey.

He put his brass knucks in his jacket and brushed blood off his expensive Brioni suit. There was more blood on the floor, but Jackson had seen worse. He'd beaten people far worse, too, their limbs splayed at crazy, unnatural angles.

Fury and honor satisfied, Jackson turned back to his drink at the bar. The bartender, a grizzled old type who looked like he'd lived a thousand lifetimes and seen a thousand more vicious assaults in his bar, was on the phone.

"Calling Five-Oh?" asked Jackson, an edge in his voice. "Because I wouldn't like that."

Surprised at the interruption, the bartender shook his head. "Not this time, son," he said over his shoulder.

With a flash of insight, Jackson realized who the booze jockey might be reporting to.

"*Him?*"

"Him."

It figured. Jackson was always being watched by "The Old Man", even when he was officially off-duty. The thought displeased him. He didn't need another "Old Man" watching over him. He'd already had one … and pops had run out on him and moms when he was eight. It taught Jackson a very early lesson – that he could only rely on himself and his own strength in this world.

The "Old Man's" knowledge of his favorite watering hole meant Jackson would need to find a new bar. And he liked this place, even with its sudden violence and random racism.

"He's on his way," replied the bartender, not without a tinge of pity, as he hung up the phone. "Sorry, son."

"Tell 'him' I'll be at a booth in the back," said Jackson, picking up his drink and walking off. "He can pay my tab. Get me another round of Guinness and keep them coming. And bring over a bottle of Jack, a shot glass and a napkin. That's how he takes it."

* * *

Precisely 91 minutes later, "Old Man" Garin joined Jackson at the gloomy back of the bar. No one had said boo to Jackson in that time. Hell, no one even dared *look* at him. It wasn't a proper night in an Irish pub unless there was at least one fight – but Jackson's cold professionalism had creeped out the patrons, who were more comfortable with amateur drunken brawling than sober, expert takedowns. Some *craic* tonight had turned out to be.

"Colonel," said Jackson neutrally, looking up from the book he was reading. "Who's out saving the world if you're in here?"

Garin took a seat without replying. Jackson observed that Garin was dressed as a full-bird colonel, which told him plenty about the tone the following conversation was going to take. "Is this the part where you tell me to get a haircut and shine my shoes?" The older man shook his head. He looked mad. He was probably armed, too.

"This is Memphis all over again," stated Garin.

"Funny. I thought the same thing."

"I'm getting tired of cleaning up your messes," said Garin sternly.

"I could say the same thing about you."

Garin offered a sour smile that didn't reach his eyes. "Would you have preferred that I'd left this to the police to handle?"

Jackson sneered. "Anyone tries to Rodney King me, they'll end up the same way."

"They probably would. You know how to fight, I'll give you that." Garin poured himself a shot of Jack, noticing for the first time there was a napkin underneath. He held the napkin up.

"I wasn't sure if it was your 'time of the month', colonel," said Jackson, grinning.

"Blow me." Garin tossed the napkin away. "Did you really have to use brass knucks on a bunch of civilians?"

"Yeah – I did," said Jackson without hesitation. His hands curled around his beer. His knuckles were still bleeding. "Holmes calls me a nigger, he better be ready for what comes next, you feel me?"

"Your civilian targets sure felt you. And by the medical reports, they won't be feeling much except pain for a while. Particularly the one eating through a straw." Garin and Jackson stared at each other over the table. Both soldiers had the habit of rubbing each other the wrong way: Jackson, because he didn't want Garin hanging over his neck giving him orders, and Garin, because the huge warrior had once kidnapped and almost killed the Spartan. They had somehow forged a working relationship, but that didn't mean they particularly liked each other.

All details that informed any dealings between Jackson and Garin, sitting between them at the table like an untouched bottle.

Garin downed his shot and then said: "What if you got killed? What if they put you six feet under?"

"Seven feet under, you mean. You need an extra foot for my dick."

Jackson's levity failed to console Garin. "Special forces are supposed to be shadows in the night. You could have followed the racist into the bathroom and taken care of it there. Nice and quiet. No witnesses. And only one victim."

Jackson drank his Guinness before replying, wiping foam off his mouth with his left hand.

"So that's why you came all the way across town to rap my brass knuckles. Because I didn't take care of things in a 'special forces' manner. That I used 'unnecessary aggression'. That I went freelance with my violence instead of using it on officially approved targets like insurgents and hajjis." Jackson grinned. "So tell me … what's your boy's excuse then?"

"Pardon me, sergeant?" said Garin, surprised.

"I met the General, remember? The fool that hired me to take out the Spartan? He had a sword cut on his face.

That looked like 'freelance' violence to me. And there's only one homie crazy enough to stab a fool who could order the bombing of a city. A certain soldier you'd burn down half the world to protect. Your prodigal son."

Jackson noticed that Garin flinched. The colonel hadn't blinked when they were under gunfire together in China – but he did flinch when his boy the Spartan was put on the spot. Interesting. And maybe exploitable.

"I didn't realise that cutting up a superior officer's face was covered under the Patriot Act," he continued. "I guess your boy deserves special treatment. I guess some animals are more equal than others."

"Don't change the subject – we're talking about you here. What meaning of 'covert ops' don't you understand?"

Jackson laughed. "I've learnt my lesson. I'll never do it again." Then he barked in laughter once more.

The laughter peeved Garin, who replied: "What's so damn funny?"

Jackson tossed over the book he had been reading. "You, thinking we're Dudley Do-rights. That 'democracy' doesn't rhyme with 'hypocrisy'. What we are are motherfucking gangsters."

Garin took in the book's title. "*War is A Racket*," he read.

"It was written by a Marine corps major general called Smedley Butler. Won the Medal of Honor." Jackson had always been a keen reader in special forces, demonstrating the kind of love of literature absent from the Spartan.

"I've heard of him," said Garin, nodding. "He was allegedly asked to stage a military coup to overthrow FDR but said no. Fortunately for the US. We don't have coups in this country. We just help stage them in other countries."

Jackson clicked his fingers. "That's him. He claimed war was a racket. He should know. When he wasn't being asked to shut down FDR's New Deal, he was kicking ass in the name of capitalism on three continents. Smedley said Capone was a pussy compared to the Marines because Capone only operated in one market, whereas the Marines were operating as gangsters for capitalism all over the world." Jackson hesitated, then added: "So yeah, colonel, that's what I think we are: gangsters for capitalism. Which I guess makes you 'OG'."

"OG?"

"Original Gangster."

Garin regarded Jackson with the type of cold, dismissive stare drill sergeants used on raw recruits. Whether he agreed with anything Jackson had just said – even the "OG" quip – he wasn't saying. Instead, he said: "That's some pretty deep thinking there."

Jackson didn't miss the intended sarcasm. "Permission to speak freely, sir?"

"So you finally remembered to call me sir? Granted."

"Then screw you, sir. You think that just because I'm a brother that I don't have a brain?"

"Don't lump me in with the morons you just pummelled, soldier," said Garin, eyes flashing. "That's not why I'm angry. It's the idea of reducing what we do to being a gangster. OG, indeed."

"After all the *Apocalypse Now*-type shit you've had me do, I would have thought you of all people would understand." Jackson thought briefly about some of the missions Garin had sent Jackson on – some of which he knew the Spartan would refuse to even consider because of their dubious character.

Jackson continued: "Hell, just look at the world ... everyone out for themselves after the plague. You need to be some kind of gangster just to survive."

"I'd prefer it if you were some kind of elite warrior," said Garin, before downing his drink and pouring another. He wiped his mouth with his sleeve, then added: "Those fat Mafia fucks wouldn't even make it through day one of special forces training."

"Maybe I like the idea of being a gangster," teased Jackson.

"Maybe, as your commanding officer, I don't."

"If you've come looking for an 'oo-rah', colonel, you've come to the wrong place." Jackson paused, as if thinking. "All right … I'm Tier Motherfucking 1, that's what I am," he finally said, unable to hide the pride in his voice. "An apex predator. Satisfied?"

Garin nodded, relief crossing his face. "That's more like it. We fight for honor and our country, not money. You answered the call, just like the Spartan."

"The call of what?"

"Destiny." There was a moment of silence as the two drank deeply, unexpectedly moved by the mention of destiny, as most men of destiny usually were. Scared eyes darted over to their booth, both at Jackson and to the man who would dare drink with him.

"So … I wonder how much longer I have to work for you to pay off my 'debt'," said Jackson eventually.

"You tried to kill the Spartan. Keep wondering." Jackson kept looking at Garin. Eventually the colonel was moved to elaborate. "You're past the halfway mark," he said, before finishing his shot. "There's still more to do … "

"There always is. The world is a gaping asshole."

"… and your abilities will be useful. Can I count on you, Sergeant?"

Jackson stared at his "commanding officer". He hated owing Garin anything: in this case, his life after his failed attempt to kill the Spartan. But – and this was a big but – he thought Garin understood him in some way. As much as Jackson loathed the idea of anyone being his "boss", there were worse employers to have.

Just as long as Garin didn't give him a Mission Impossible. Or worse yet, set him up to be killed.

Jackson took a good long swig as all this swirled around in his mind.

"I'm in," said Jackson, punctuating his statement by slamming his glass down on the table.

"Good. Because there's plenty of trigger time on the horizon."

"The North Korean thing still on?"

"Could be. Stay tuned."

"Shee-ittt. Guess you'll be calling up the Spartan, too."

Garin nodded.

"You're getting the gang back together again, then? Is this your version of yelling 'Avengers Assemble'?"

"The Avengers don't kill anyone," said Garin. "Well, maybe the Hulk, seeing how strong he is. How could he not accidentally kill some bystanders with all the things he throws?"

"Do you think special forces could kill the Avengers?" asked Jackson with a grin.

"Special forces would find a way," said Garin firmly. "We always do."

"Thus ending a profitable motherfucking movie franchise."

Garin rose. "Thanks for the drink. Please try not to beat the crap out of any more candy-ass civilians. Save your expertise for the paying customers." Garin tossed the book back at Jackson. "And for God's sake, stop reading shit like that."

Then he exited, stage right.

Chapter 13

The leader watched as his men practised with their new garb, moving silently around the obstacle maze in the remote warehouse. His operatives were completely invisible to the naked eye as they reconnoitred the area.

Their intel had been right. This so-called Ghost Armor really worked. It was incredible: an actual, functioning suit of invisibility, almost more a work of magic than man. Lightweight, flexible and comfortable to wear, the Ghost Armor was the perfect tool for infiltration.

Or assassination.

With the threat to his family's safety hanging over his head, the American scientist, Professor Eisenstein, had reluctantly assisted in the creation of the sleek, snake-like garments. Despite their access to their own brilliant minds and high-tech equipment, the leader and his men would never have been able to build the suits without Eisenstein. The American's mind truly was unique: one wondered what other works of genius it could create. But for now, the leader was only interested in the Ghost Armor.

With Eisenstein's aid, they had not only constructed his own custom-made suit, but more than 30. Dozens to send out in the world, worn by highly trained professionals with specific targets to strike.

Perhaps it was good that their enemies never saw them coming. When the prey saw the blade, it spoiled the flavor of the meat.

The leader felt his pulse race at the violence to come. Adrenalin running, he drew the Honjo Masamune, hearing the crisp ring as it escaped the scabbard, admiring the sword's pure form. He swung the sword through the air two-handed. If only all our enemies had but one neck, he thought.

Soon the blade would taste American blood again. And so it should. This was a hungry blade, one that demanded to be used. It didn't deserve to be rusting away in some museum or private collection.

His No.2 – his lover and the only woman ninja on the team, a *kunoichi* – had accused him of loving the Honjo Masamune more than her. He had assured her that there was room in his heart for both of them. Just like the suits, it was a special tool he would use to continue his commander's work.

May he rest in peace. May he soon be avenged.

Meanwhile, the leader savored the opportunity of testing his own suit in the field. *Yes, we shall be lions in the dark,* he thought. *Ghosts moving through men's minds. Shades travelling across the landscape, delivering death.*

True, the suits had their drawbacks. Movement in them was limited to about a foot a second. The user became visible when they moved too fast, fired a weapon or swung a fist or a knife. Dogs and infrared could detect the wearers. There was only room for light weapons under the back pouch such as machine guns, pistols or short swords (the leader's own suit had been custom made to accommodate the samurai sword he wore on his back). The batteries were exhausted after a few minutes of continual use before new ones were required or the suit needed recharging. The body armor that could be squeezed into the suit was light: good enough to stop some rounds, but not anything high caliber or coated with Teflon.

And, very occasionally, the suit could fail for no reason. The leader would have suspected sabotage on the part of Professor Eisenstein, but he had already read in the literature stolen from the Americans that the suits were prone to unexpected failure, just like American cars.

Even more interestingly, some humans – admittedly, a very rare minority – could sense the presence of someone in the suit, even managing to point to their exact position when they were near. Perhaps some primitive sense long suppressed in modern man was still active in a few select individuals.

Their new version of the suit came in silver, rather than white like the American version. It had something to do with the materials and fabric they used – the strike team hadn't been able to seize everything the Americans had in their own labs, and their own rare earth materials and conflict minerals were slightly different. The leader would have preferred the suits in black or blue like his traditional garb, but ultimately the color didn't matter. Only that the suits worked.

The leader watched as one of his brethren moved too clumsily around the obstacle maze and became visible. A colleague swiftly struck him on the shoulder with a wooden sword and ordered him to go back to the beginning of the maze.

The leader had already divided his team into half. Fifteen of his men were already or just about in position, ready to strike. The others remained with him here at the base. They, too, would be shortly sent out on missions.

He was proud to lead these soldiers into battle.

As well as the suits, each operative was highly trained in sabotage, gun fighting and ninjutsu (that last martial art seemingly somewhat culturally insensitive, but in hindsight, the best art for the job). And like ninjas, his men and women feared only the failure of a mission. These suits were a perfect complement to their skill sets.

He thought bitterly about a racist term he had learned in America: a "Chinaman's chance". Or, in other words, no chance at all. The leader suspected that with his abilities, intel, motivation and invisibility suit, this "Chinaman's" chances of success were very high indeed.

He thought of the mythical blinded cyclops, whose mighty strength was powerless against an enemy he couldn't see. He smiled to himself, liking the imagery.

Yes ... with their motivation, elite abilities and Ghost Armor, there seemed little that could stop them. But something still nagged at the leader. One individual remained at large with her own suit. Not only did this soldier know how the suits worked, but she could conceivably dream up ways to neutralise their advantages.

The American operative was an unknown variable, a danger, a loose end. And the leader hated loose ends.

He couldn't afford to leave anything to fate or randomness. Not when they were this close to going operational. Perhaps a practice run of their new armor was required.

And so he summoned his best soldier into his office.

"Will you kill for me?" he asked.

"Now and forever" was the answer.

Pleased, he gave her the mission details.

Chapter 14

The two large soldiers, shirtless and daunting, circled each other in the competition-sized boxing ring.

"I was surprised you asked me to spar, Spartan," announced Jackson as he knocked his red gloves together. "But you came to the right man. Golden Gloves, baby. Golden Gloves. Plus special forces champion."

"They said you were good." The Spartan held his gloves up in defense, body glistening with sweat. "So show me." He lobbed a left hook at Jackson that missed. The Spartan received a hard, almost teacherly left jab in the face in return. The Spartan tasted copperish blood in his mouth.

"Just be grateful I only hit you with my left," said Jackson. "With the left I send you to the hospital."

"And the right?"

"With my right I send you to the morgue." Jackson feinted as he circled the Spartan. "So … you didn't say in your call why you wanted this throwdown."

"I fought a tango a few months ago who got in some hard punches. Thought my pure boxing could use improvement."

"The more you sweat, the less you bleed? Well, don't expect to be walking out of here on two legs, Spartan. I'm going to beat you like a red-headed stepchild."

As Garin's urging, the pair had assembled at a special forces safe house in upstate New York, its location designated only as a set of co-ordinates in a classified file. Vasquez was there, too.

Jackson and the Spartan shared a chequered history – set the wayback machine, Sherman, to last year, where Jackson had kidnapped and tortured the Spartan, the Spartan beating him almost to death in retaliation.

Yet despite this bloody past, the Spartan enjoyed sparring with Jackson. He had trouble finding sparring partners that could keep up with him, and Jackson, Tier 1 himself and a natural warrior, could take the pace and punishment.

And in a perverse way, he respected Jackson for almost killing him. The Spartan was old-fashioned that way.

But back to the fighting.

The Spartan hit Jackson in the breadbasket. And again. Jackson replied with a spirited right hook that turned the Spartan's head.

Jackson pursued his advantage to deliver a wicked set of body blows, followed by a flurry of jabs, some of which made it past the Spartan's defenses.

"Move your feet more, Spartan. You move like old people fuck."

The Spartan danced forward, dodged a right hook and landed his own left jab, which rocked Jackson's skull.

Jackson recovered, then landed some hammer blows into the Spartan's side. The Spartan didn't wince. Instead he attacked Jackson furiously with an eight-punch combo. Two landed, but the effort left the Spartan exposed. Jackson slugged the Spartan so hard his mouthguard flew out.

There was that right hand Jackson was talking about.

The Spartan glared, then picked up his mouthguard and re-inserted it.

"I've been thinking a lot about the last time we fought," said Jackson. "We've had the same training, been to the same places … shit, we've even got the same kind of builds. But I've finally figured out why you beat me."

"Because I'm bad-ass?"

Jackson paused, then answered: "Because you're *crazy*."

The Spartan said nothing. Instead, he rammed his right fist into Jackson's jaw so hard the other man was visibly dazed. The Spartan moved back and gave Jackson a standing eight-count.

That was his response to Jackson's observation.

The Spartan watched as Jackson composed himself. He had the feeling Jackson would never make that observation again.

Eventually, Jackson said: "So … why do you think Garin's got us all together?"

"No idea," said the Spartan, pummelling Jackson as they clinched. Then they separated.

"Garin said the North Korean thing could be still on."

"Yeah? That would be … epic." Sending a special forces team to take out the North Korean leadership before they could launch nukes on the West and the world for its part in the spread of the plague? Yes, that qualified as epic in any language.

"Changing the subject," said Jackson between swings, "how's your woman?"

"We're not going to talk about her."

"Aren't we?" said Jackson, who grabbed the Spartan in a clinch, landed some more body blows, and then separated. "See? All that quality pussy is making you slow." For a second Jackson saw doubt in the Spartan's eyes, as if he believed it, too.

"Shut up."

"And here I thought we were friends."

"If you want a friend, go buy a Jack Russell." Yet even as the words left his lips, he knew they were wrong. That Jackson, if not a friend, was more than just a casual acquaintance.

As if he sensed the same thing, Jackson replied: "That's cold. I know you've got mad love for me."

The Spartan tried, unsuccessfully, to land a right cross on Jackson's jaw. "Tell me, how are you getting on with Garin?" he said, changing the subject.

"He's an expert at busting my balls."

"That's what commanding officers do."

"And I'm getting tired of taking orders from old men," said Jackson sourly. He paused, as if remembering some recent slight.

"Just don't try anything."

"Like kill him while he's sleeping?" smiled Jackson wolfishly.

"Because you know I'd come after you."

"Oooo … now I'm really scared," said Jackson. He smashed the Spartan in the side of the face, pushing him against the ropes. "How about us, though, dog? Are we good?"

"You mean after you kidnapped and tortured me on instructions from the General?" said the Spartan, ducking a haymaker. "And held a gun to Vasquez's head?"

"I figured that was water under the bridge."

"More like blood under the bridge." He dodged a one-two combination from Jackson before landing a devastating right hook to the other man's surprised face. Now it was Jackson's turn to kiss the ropes. "But yeah ... we're good."

Jackson grinned despite the pain in his mouth. "Because you know I'm not going to apologize for any of it."

"I don't expect – or want – any apology."

"All right, then," said Jackson, bashing his gloves together. "Enough yakking. I've gone easy on you, but this shit's about to get real. You ready?"

The Spartan raised his gloves. "I was born ready."

Jackson grinned toothily. "Of course you were." Jackson headed towards him. "Then bring it."

Chapter 15

Vasquez couldn't sleep.

She was lying on her bed in Garin's safe house, wearing only a shirt and underwear. Her eyes were closed, but behind them she was still awake. Thinking. Going over things in her mind. Far from the Land of Nod.

Colonel Garin had kept the promise he had made to Vasquez when he had rescued her from a cartel hit in Mexico all those years ago. He had OK'd a Hellfire strike on Fighting Dog's compound, equipped her with the Ghost Armor invisibility suit, given her the Spartan as an ally and helped her take revenge against her family's killer.

Having secured her revenge, you'd think her body would issue a great sigh of relief and let her relax. That she could rest soundly in bed and get on with the rest of her life, a life long put on hold in the quest for revenge.

But that hadn't happened.

Vasquez had had trouble sleeping for many moons now. The former Mexican police officer was lucky if she snatched a few hours a night. Her youth and incredible level of fitness compensated for the missing zees, but she couldn't remember the last time she'd slept straight through. All the meditations and tea in China weren't helping. And she refused to take sleeping pills because they dulled her edge.

It wasn't bad dreams that were keeping her awake – she had the odd vision of the people she'd killed, yet by and large they'd deserved their fate. However, without realising it, Vasquez had entered what was known as "the red zone", the zone where soldiers were constantly primed for combat, every sense heightened and alert. And she'd stayed there.

Just when Vasquez thought she was out, the world of blood and iron and battle pulled her back in.

Vasquez most likely first entered the red zone when she met the Spartan. Their intense battles against gangsters and rival special forces soldiers had pushed her further and further into a continual state of combat readiness. And when she'd killed Fighting Dog in hand-to-hand combat, the event had been so primal, so emotional, she'd never fully come down back to normality.

Not even after the hot week she'd spent with the Spartan in Cancun afterwards had she returned to earth. (Although she did go to heaven and back in bed daily.)

Maybe after all she'd been through there was no going to back to normality ... to step back into "the green", as it were.

It wasn't a problem for the Spartan to live "in the red". It was his preferred mode of being. He tended to get antsy when he wasn't trying to shoot, stab, punch or kill something. He was addicted to the rush of peak combat experiences, hooked on the adrenal rush of war.

Yet for Vasquez, who'd planned to put aside war once she'd slain Fighting Dog, such a life was disquieting. After years of giving 110 per cent for Colonel Garin she was now a race car stuck in fifth gear, her body and her mind refusing to switch off.

Hence her insomnia.

"The human body is built for survival, not happiness," claimed the Spartan on one restless night. "You're still stuck in survival mode."

"And how long will that last?" she had asked.

"No idea," he said.

Great.

Colonel Garin had been more diplomatic: fatherly, even. He told her that her condition was common. Every grunt or special forces operative who returned from war had to go through the same process, had to re-acclimatise to public life after the massive adrenalin rush and mind fuck of the frontline.

The mind and body had to get used to a daily environment where every sound didn't signify some new threat, where the stranger around the corner was merely going to the local store to get milk rather than trying to stalk and kill them ... that the bag left abandoned at the bus stop didn't contain an IED.

Exiting the red zone, he said, varied from soldier to soldier. Sometimes the process lasted weeks. Sometimes it lasted months.

And, in some extreme cases, it seemed to last a lifetime.

But Garin assured her she wasn't one of the latter. He didn't think she needed to talk to a professional therapist. She just had to ... well, wait.

"I can recognise the lifers," he said. "Like the Spartan. And hell, maybe even myself. But you'll come out of the other side, I can tell. When you do, then we can talk about your future. If you still want to work as an operative, I can still use you – hell, you're irreplaceable."

"Thanks, colonel," said Vasquez, touched.

"Well, you *are* irreplaceable. You and the Spartan make a hell of a team. You would be sorely missed if you left."

"I don't think I'd entirely leave, colonel. 'Leave the saving of the world to the men? I don't think so.'"

The colonel laughed. "Ha! Elastigirl from *The Incredibles*, right?"

"Right."

"Nice one. And the world will need saving. It always does. It's rather delinquent that way. What say for now we keep you on light duties? Grab a copy of *Lonely Planet* and enjoy some R&R with the Spartan. He could use a break, too."

Vasquez liked the sound of that – she was keen to catch up on all her missing vacation time. Unfortunately, the Spartan was a reluctant tourist. He preferred to stay near home just like his ancient namesake … even if he didn't have to keep one eye on a restive helot population threatening rebellion if he strayed too far from the city walls.

"He's not big on R&R," observed Vasquez dryly. "It was tough enough persuading him to go to Cancun."

"Take him to Greece," suggested Garin. "He always likes it there. Hell, it's the only place he ever seems to go on holiday."

"YOLO," laughed Vasquez.

"What?"

"Nothing, sir. Anyway, he'll probably just want to explore the ruins of Sparta. Make a pilgrimage to the statue of Leonidas or something."

"You are doubtless right. I never really ask him what he gets up to over there. Probably some kind of warrior worship." The colonel paused. "It's strange the worlds we create to live in. The Spartan's is perhaps a little different from most."

"He's an unusual man, sir. But well worth the effort."

"I concur, Vasquez. So indulge him in his pilgrimage. Meanwhile, you can kick back in the Greek isles until he's finished." Garin's eyes assumed a faraway look. "Check out Santorini. I've spent a few weeks there, just sunbathing, seeing the sights, drinking Ouzo and eating goat meat."

"Nice. Although I might pass on the goat meat." Vasquez imagined the Spartan sitting uncomfortably on the beach in his Speedos, applying suntan lotion to Vasquez's back. Funny. But also pleasant.

Speaking of her and the Spartan, things were ... complicated. Sometimes she went whole weeks without seeing her strange lover. The Tier 1 soldier was often on missions that took him around the world at a moment's notice, usually at Garin's behest (although Garin occasionally had the decency to apologize to Vasquez for ruining their social plans).

Nor could the Spartan discuss those classified missions in Asia, the Middle East and Africa. So they couldn't talk about his "job". Nor could she talk about the occasional mission she went on at Garin's suggestion, which she now did out of choice rather than obligation.

In fact, the Spartan didn't talk much at all, whether to share choice mission details or to wax lyrical about his feelings. Not only was he adept at the Spartans' laconic turn of phrase, he had perfected the art of the laconic conversation.

Still, he was a listener. He valued her opinion and intelligence. And when he did say something, it was always something worth listening to. So there was that.

In short, she was yet to crack the Enigma Code that was the Spartan.

She fingered the necklace around her neck. The Spartan had taken the Carthaginian coin she had seized from Fighting Dog's house and had it made into a necklace for her.

"So you'll always remember the day you avenged your family," he said.

It was perhaps the closest he had come to being a romantic. The one time they'd watched *The English Patient* on TV, the Spartan had ignored the sweeping romance and instead provided a running commentary on how the desert landscape could be used to its best military advantage.

Sigh.

Still, Vasquez knew he cared, in his own idiosyncratic way. His opponents were wrong to believe that the Spartan didn't feel any emotions. He did. And they ran deep. And she had an undeniable affection for the man she had risked her life with many times. They worked well together ... for now.

And for later? That would depend on when and how she left "the red zone".

Currently Vasquez and the Spartan were the only occupants of the safe house. Jackson had visited, sparred with the Spartan, then left, somewhat bruised (how the Spartan could box with a creep who tried to kill the pair of them, she didn't know ... maybe it was a weird male bonding thing).

The Spartan was now working out in the gym following their epic lovemaking.

She smiled. At least being in the red hadn't harmed her enjoyment of sex. Perhaps enhanced it, actually.

It was nice to get laid regularly – and well – after years of a nun-like existence, moving from base to base and country to country. The Spartan had reawakened an appetite in her.

And special forces sex was just like sex between Olympic athletes i.e. it was awesome.

She bit her lip in the way that men always liked.

Vasquez should tease the Spartan about how much good sex he was getting – such a surfeit of carnality was, for ancient soldiers who barely saw their wives, un-Spartan-like. It was almost "Athenian", the Spartan's catchphrase for anything that smacked of pleasure-seeking and hedonism. Maybe they'd go at it again when he returned to the gym, all pumped up and sweaty.

Mmmm.

As Vasquez considered future pleasures, a long piece of grey thread unfurled itself from the ceiling and rested just above her mouth. Vasquez failed to notice, her chest rising and falling as she continued to breathe just on the cusp of sleep, oblivious to the soundless danger.

A second or two later a black liquid began its slow journey from the top of the string down towards her mouth. The thick drops inched ever closer to her lips. At any moment, the drops would pass through her lips and into her throat to do whatever dark harm they intended.

Then the "red zone" called Vasquez to attention.

Someone's in the room, an inner voice told her. She opened her eyes – to see the thread hovering above her face. She turned away just as black noxious liquid splashed her check.

Vasquez was now fully awake.

With shock, she noticed that the thread appeared to dangle in mid-air. The owner of the original Ghost Armor wasn't fooled. She knew what that meant. She knew that just because you couldn't see your enemy it didn't mean they weren't there. Vasquez reached under her pillow for her MP-5 and raised it towards the point of origin of the thread.

Soundlessly a slender figure in a silver suit became visible as it released itself from the ceiling. The apparition thrust its leg out and down at Vasquez's hand, knocking the MP-5 aside and forcing her burst to go wide.

"Jesus!" cried Vasquez. She gaped at the appearance of the ninja.

Ninja. Also known as shinobi. Japanese special forces of the ancient world. Feared shadow warriors. Skilled assassins. The deadliest of enemies.

The ninja made a grunting noise of disappointment before it attacked again. It raked at Vasquez with the cat's claws attached to its hands. The first swipe missed. The second tore Vasquez's shirt, tearing the "S" from her Navy SEALs logo. The ninja tried a third time, attempting to swipe at her with both claws simultaneously. Seizing the nearest thing – a pink stiletto shoe – Vasquez blocked both claws with the sole.

"Enough with this 'wax on, wax off' shit," she said, thrusting the shadow warrior's claws aside with great effort.

Vasquez grabbed both ninja's wrists before it could strike again. The ninja had a wiry strength. But so did Vasquez. And she was fighting for her life.

"I know what you are," hissed Vasquez. She struck the ninja in the face with her bare foot. It was an almighty kick, borne on the wings of adrenalin. The ninja's head spun heavily. If it had spun any more the ninja would have been Linda Blair in *The Exorcist*.

Vasquez seized the initiative and kneed the ninja in the groin, confirming that she did indeed face a *kunoichi* – a female ninja. A woman of similar size who had her own set of Ghost Armor. The blow had the same effect it would have had on a man, sending rivers of pain through its victim.

Vasquez placed her right foot behind the ninja's ankle, hoping to throw her to the floor. Recovering from the groin strike, the *kunoichi* instead performed a spinning kick in return. She hit Vasquez in the face, freed her wrists and flipped back on her feet in a precise and elegant battlefield ballet.

"Clever," spat Vasquez.

The ninja reached for her side for a weapon. Vasquez didn't want to face whatever it was. She kicked down on the *kunoichi's* hand, forcing her to resheathe the tanto she was attempting to draw. Thwarted again, the ninja cried in rage. She summoned her *chi* energy and took to the air.

"Hai!" she screamed as her leg flicked out like forked lightning. The *kunoichi* kicked Vasquez square in the shoulder, knocking her down and over the bed. Unfortunately for the shadow warrior, she had propelled Vasquez right within arm's reach of her MP-5.

The *kunoichi* dived out of room just as Vasquez grasped her gun and raked the wall with rounds. In hot pursuit, Vasquez took a bead on the ninja's back as the silver-suited figure darted for the stairwell. Without halting her movement, the *kunoichi* plucked some throwing stars and flicked them over her shoulder. Vasquez hurled herself out of the way, but one of the wicked stars tore open her shirt. The stars were covered in the same substance as the thread, but fortunately the shurikens didn't break Vasquez's skin.

Vasquez raced onwards. She combat rolled into the stairwell, just as more shurikens struck the spot on the stairwell wall where her head might have been. She got up and leapt down below, expertly judging the spot where the shadow warrior would be. Vasquez landed heavily on the *kunoichi's* shoulders with the balls of her feet. The ninja cried out in shock as they both went down.

"Who said you could raid my wardrobe, bitch?" said Vasquez as she slammed the butt of her MP-5 into a back section of the Ghost Armor. She knew precisely where to strike to damage its circuitry. This ninja wouldn't be fading away any time soon.

The *kunoichi* yelped from the pain of the blow, strong enough to break wiring. Vasquez pulled her up with one hand and slammed the ninja's face against the wall, just like she had done with perps in Mexico. The ninja pressed herself off the wall and delivered a side kick into Vasquez's stomach. The blow made Vasquez grunt and pause. The *kunoichi* climbed the wall, flipped over to land behind Vasquez and booted her in the face. Vasquez responded with a savage elbow to the chest. The wounds made them separate for a second.

The ninja pulled something small and spherical from her waist and hurled it to the ground. Vasquez's world exploded in a flash. Blinded, she strafed from left to right with her MP-5. She heard a stifled cry as a bullet struck home. As if witnessing a single cell from a projectionist's movie reel, she caught a fleeting glimpse of the ninja clutching her shoulder. Then white light again.

When she could fully see, she followed the blood trail out towards the exit. The Spartan met her there, shirtless and holding his SAW.

"What happened?"

"A fucking ninja attacked me."

As he was about to run out into the street, Vasquez held up her arm to block the Spartan. She nodded downwards. There were small, metallic, pointed objects on the ground.

"Caltrops," she said. "Probably poisoned." And they were both bare-footed.

They leapt out over the caltrops and ran out into the darkened street, following the trail of blood. But the trail abruptly stopped at the kerb.

The *kunoichi* was gone.

* * *

"You have failed." It was a statement, not an accusation.

"Yes."

"Was it your fault or the armor's?"

"Mine."

"Are you wounded?"

"Yes."

"Will you live?"

"Yes."

"Will you fail again?"

"No."

"Then return to base. The Humbling has begun."

Chapter 16

"That was cone snail poison the *kunoichi* tried to poison you with," said Colonel Garin as he, Vasquez and the Spartan sat in a late-night diner drinking coffee, surrounded by tired shift workers, java lovers and insomniacs, a song about pina coladas playing the background.

"It's pretty rare, particularly in that weaponized form," he continued. "And there's no known cure. Thank God you didn't swallow any."

"Ninjas," cursed the Spartan. "I *hate* ninjas."

Vasquez held her throat as if the thought of swallowing the poison made her particularly squeamish. "Fuck those pyjama-wearing assholes for trying to kill me." She turned to Garin. "I thought the only ones running around these days were in Teenage Mutant Ninja Turtles."

"I'll put an APB out for all pizza delivery in the tristate area," replied Garin, chuckling.

It was mutually agreed by soldiers everywhere that gallows humour was the correct response when a total stranger tried to kill you.

The colonel had arrived in a New York minute when he had heard about the assassination attempt. He had ordered Vasquez to put on her Ghost Armor under her street clothes and bring the Spartan to one of the colonel's favorite java haunts in Manhattan. There was *beaucoup* security outside ... and half the customers inside were Garin's men and women.

"Ninjas," exhaled Garin loudly. "This is going to be fun to explain to everyone." He refocused on Vasquez. "But I'm glad you're safe, Vasquez."

Vasquez raised her left hand. "Hmm ... I broke a nail."

Garin stared at her hands, then back at her eyes. "Sounds like your opponent broke more than that."

Garin exchanged a look with the Spartan. The latter could hear Garin's words in his head: "There is no such thing as an uninjured soldier."

The café's other patrons began to stare at the trio, taking in both the fresh bruises on Vasquez's face and the military demeanor of her male companions. To the civilian eye, they were an unusual group, out of place, radiating danger. In particular, they focused the Spartan, the man whose eyes constantly darted towards the exits as if expecting an attack.

The Spartan stared back. The curious civilians quickly lost their curiosity.

The Spartan had that effect on strangers. And for the Tier 1 soldier, anyone who wasn't in the armed forces was a stranger. Sometimes even then.

He sighed. He loved his country, but he wasn't sure how much its people loved him back. He was a warrior in a world where being a warrior was considered an antique profession – a world where a professional soldier was regarded as something to be kept in a glass cage to be broken open only in case of war.

There was a considerable amount of psychic pain to be in that position. Even a Spartan wasn't immune to the thought that few appreciated or understood him. He thought of Kipling's poem *Tommy*, about brutes that were only appreciated when the guns began to shoot.

Those were words he understood in his bones.

"Spartan, you with us?" said the colonel. "Focus, son."

"Sorry, sir. Please continue."

"So, Vasquez, you said the ninja was a Daughter of Eve?" asked Garin.

"I kneed her in the questionables. Definitely a *kunoichi*."

"Ouch," said Garin, crossing his own legs slightly. "No other clues?"

"None. She was masked the whole time. But she was good. Special forces good. She had her own set of Ghost Armor, just like mine, but it was silver." Vasquez paused, recalling the battle. "It was like I was fighting myself ... only I rock the suit better."

"How did the ninja know where Vasquez was, colonel?" asked the Spartan.

"Unknown ... just like a lot of other things, son," replied Garin wearily. "Our security has been piss-poor since the plague. We've had to throw so many resources into dealing with that that we've let other things slide, particularly our security. Who knows what secrets have been stolen? Who knows what has been exposed?

"Plus, it's not like the old days where no one wrote anything important down in case some Deep Throat was around. Now everything's on some database that our enemies can hack into." Garin paused. "I think the Mafia was onto something when they only communicated by whispering into someone's ear. Good luck trying to hack someone's ear."

"Obviously, the secrets of the Ghost Armor were among the information stolen," said Vasquez.

Garin nodded. "Correct. And we don't know who our enemies are. And who knows who many Ghost Armor copies are out there?"

"I told you it was a mistake building that armor, sir," growled the Spartan. "An act of hubris."

"I know, I know, you were right, Spartan," admitted Garin. "But hubris or not, if we didn't build it, someone else would have."

"Someone else *has*, colonel," said the Spartan with heat. "The thing doesn't belong on the battlefield. It's dishonorable."

"What about me?" said Vasquez, flashing him a look. "Does that mean I'm 'dishonorable'?"

The Spartan turned to her. "I'll never like the suit, but I like the person in it." Vasquez smiled and seemed to melt a little.

"Let's ask the other obvious question," said Garin, "why did they target you, Vasquez? You have the only other suit apart from theirs. Maybe that means they wanted to get rid of anyone who knows how they work."

"Which also means they want to bring their own Ghost Armor into play," said Vasquez. She grabbed a cronut and a bear's claw. She was famished after her brush with near-death.

Garin rubbed his chin again, which he did whenever he was thinking hard. "I'll have to put the word out, warn all the VIPs that we have some rogue Ghost Armor out there. So much for keeping this tech a secret. This news will make a lot of powerful people afraid. A skilled assassin in one of these suits could get to just about anyone."

"Including the President," said Vasquez.

"Affirmative." Garin held his head, as if in pain. "I'm going to see him next. He's not going to be happy."

"I'll bet," said the Spartan. "What other technology do you have under your sleeve, sir? Stargates? Rail guns? Robots?"

Garin laughed. "We don't call them robots – we call them 'autonomous weapons systems'."

"The more we rely on technology, the less human we become," said the Spartan with a shake of his head. He paused, then said: "The less we are pure warriors."

Garin nodded towards the Spartan. "Our friend here is just like the Spartan general Archidamus."

"Who?" asked Vasquez.

"The dude who saw a catapult being fired for the first time and said, 'Oh Hercules, human martial valor is of no use any more!'"

"Damn straight, sir," said the Spartan. "It was a sorry day when we started using missiles to fight our battles instead of hand-to-hand weapons. Any coward can fire a gun or push a button."

"War is the handmaiden of progress, son," reasoned Garin. "The human race has had to evolve."

The Spartan wasn't letting this argument go. Particularly as it was one of his favorites. "Evolve into what, sir? Assassins creeping around in invisibility suits? Nimrods who rely on shadows instead of strength?"

"We either keep up or get left behind," said Garin. "Technology is a wolf we have by the ears. We can't stop it or let it go. We have no choice."

"Everyone has a choice, sir," said the Spartan firmly.

"Not everyone has your training or skill, soldier. Not everyone is ... well, 'Spartan'."

The Spartan merely grunted and returned to his coffee. He had no reply to that obvious point. Yet he sometimes felt exasperated that others could not see what he could see, that even boon companions such as the colonel and Vasquez did not agree with his point of view over the advancement of technology at the expense of man.

And people wondered why he didn't talk that much.

"The days of large standing armies duking it out among each other – with or without swords – is over, son," continued Garin. "Warfare will be increasingly asymmetrical now. Expect more of this sort of thing. It's a new Age."

"The Cowardly Age," muttered the Spartan.

"I prefer to the Cowardly Age to the Bronze Age." Garin held up his cup. "Better coffee."

"Good luck trying to change the Spartan's mind," said Vasquez with a smile.

"I'm American," said the Spartan, "I don't have to change my mind on anything."

With that, Garin got up. "Don't go changing, Spartan. We love you just the way you are. Anyway, I better head off. My increasingly poor life choices won't just make themselves. And the commander-in-chief calls. No doubt he'll also be wondering whether we've reached the point in human progress where we've started to lose control over our technology." Garin slipped over a piece of paper, then tapped it with his finger. "Go to this address. No one is going to find you in that Bermuda Triangle. Not even a ninja."

"Roger, sir," said the Spartan, throwing his commander a snappy salute.

Vasquez smiled at Garin. "Thanks for coming, sir."

"Bye guys – stay safe. We'll talk soon," said Garin as he left, followed by his other men.

Chapter 17

"Bullseye!"

Harmony, the President's secretary, turned away from her computer at the sudden movement.

"Throwing hats onto hatstands as you enter a room?" she observed in her Southern accent. "You're not James Bond, Colonel Garin."

"I AM James Bond."

"You better not be. Because he's a sexist, pale, British ass."

Garin leaned in next to her ear, his head touching his lover's lush blonde hair. "You look gorgeous. I want to tear off all of your clothes, cover you in honey and go at you right here and now."

Harmony laughed at the decadent imagery. "What is this, *50 Shades of Garin*? The President could have something to say about that if he found his secretary naked and covered in honey."

"I'm sure he's seen worse." Garin leant back and stared at Harmony. Blonde, blue-eyed, brainy ... she was an incredible woman. Not for the first time, he was amazed that she had chosen him. And no, he wasn't naïve enough to think that it had been his idea. Women always did the choosing.

"Take a picture, it'll last longer."

"Sorry. I was just lost in your beauty. So how is POTUS today?"

"He's in 'The Tent'."

"Again?"

"Yes. He's been in it all morning. Ever since he read the latest casualty reports."

"Oh dear." The Tent was a specially-made tent-like structure the President carried while travelling to conduct business without fear of electronic surveillance and eavesdropping. The fact that he was using The Tent inside the Oval Office itself – which already boasted state-of-the-art counter-surveillance technology – suggested that he was feeling extra paranoid. As if he feared people were listening in on his conversations and were out to get him.

Which, of course, they were.

As if reading Garin's mind, Harmony said: "I'm worried about him. He's getting to be like you, seeing enemies everywhere."

"That's because there *are* enemies everywhere. See you tonight?"

"Keep the champagne cool and the bed warm."

"Aye, aye, ma'am," said Garin, throwing her a salute and a wink as he entered the Oval Office. As Harmony had said, The Tent was indeed erected in the center of the room. It looked more like a camping accessory rather than a high-tech sanctuary for the Most Powerful Man in the Free World.

"Time to stop looking at naked ladies on your computer, sir," shouted Garin theatrically.

"That you, Garin?" said the President from inside The Tent, his voice slightly muffled. "Come on in. I've just finished updating my Tinder profile. Don't tell the wife." Chuckle, chuckle. Both men laughed because they knew just how devoted POTUS was to FLOTUS.

Garin opened the front flap. Inside was the President of the United States, working on a laptop.

"Good to see you, Mr President," said Garin, holding out his hand. POTUS shook it firmly.

"You're looking well, colonel. You never seem to age. What's your secret?"

"I'm on the 5/2 diet. I only shoot people five days of the week." Garin winked. POTUS chuckled.

"Take a seat," said the President, gesturing to a cushion opposite his own.

"It's like a secret clubhouse in here," said Garin, sitting down and folding his legs.

The Presidential Seal stood near the President's knees. Garin wondered if it was true that if it was ever knocked over that a team of Secret Service agents would rush through the door, guns out, in search of the threat. Part of him was tempted to knock it over to find out.

The President had taken a pile of paperwork into The Tent. Beside him were the latest satellite photos of troops massing around the various borders of Europe and Asia. Garin spotted a folded near the President's knees marked "Top Secret". Its title? "Mandatory population limits per country". *I must read that*, thought Garin.

"How are you today, Mr President?"

"Not good, Garin. Not good." He's looking stressed, thought Garin. His once-lustrous chestnut-brown hair was now completely grey. There were bags under the twinkling eyes that had charmed millions. Garin wondered how much sleep he was getting.

"Things are ... difficult, I admit, Mr President," said Garin, choosing his words carefully.

"And they're going to get worse before they get better, aren't they?"

"That's generally how these things work out."

The President sighed heavily. "Does it ever end?"

The question surprised Garin. He considered it carefully. "Not really, sir. You and I live in a world where it's always September 10. As the most powerful country on Earth, we will always attract enemies, just like lightning strikes the highest peaks. We're involved in a silent war, a war without an end ... a war without any frontlines."

The President's eyes went wide. "That sounds like a nightmare."

To some, such as the Spartan, the idea of an eternal war was a dream come true, thought Garin. He could picture the Spartan, *xiphos* in hand, happily sitting on top of a mountain of his slain enemies ... of which there were many. But to the President, he said: "Perhaps, sir. You either get used to that reality or you have a breakdown."

"Oh. It's almost too early in the morning to be having this discussion," said POTUS. "Particularly before my second coffee." The President pulled out a cigarette lighter and a cigarette. "Mind if I smoke?"

"Go ahead, sir." The President lit up and took a long, satisfying drag. The Tent was soon filled with fumes.

"God, that's good. All right. So, tell me what happened."

"Well, sir, a 'ninja' attacked my operative, Teresa Vasquez, in a Homeland safe house. Tried to poison her, then, when that failed, engaged her hand-to-hand. She fought the ninja off, who successfully escaped."

"Our enemies come at us in many strange forms." The President shook his head. "I didn't think ninjas existed any more outside of movies and cartoons."

"Oh no," said Garin with a knowing glint in his eye. "They're very much real. More common in the Orient than Stateside, though."

"Do we have any idea who this 'ninja' is?"

"We've examined her blood and the weapons she used, but no clues as yet."

"Great. Does it ever depress you just how many secret armies are out there, operating in the night?" sighed the President.

"Not exactly. Because some of those armies are ours … and we have the best soldiers in the world, sir."

"Of course, of course," said the President, waving his hand. "Please continue."

"The other disturbing aspect apart from the attack itself – apart from the attacker knowing where Vasquez was located – was the fact that the ninja was wearing an invisibility suit. Not one of our own, either. We only ever had one working model."

The President understood what that meant. "So it's happened then. Someone else has manufactured their own invisibility suits using our blueprints and Professor Eisenstein's expertise."

"We have to assume that, yes."

"The perfect assassin's tool, loose on the land. We face a clear and present danger in these invisibility suits."

"An *unclear* and present danger, I'd say, sir."

The President shot Garin an almost headmasterly look. "It's almost too early to be making jokes about this, Garin. Because finding ninjas is going to be hard enough, I imagine … let alone invisible ones."

"You are undoubtedly right, sir. Anyway, we'll be increasing our security at important facilities everywhere. We'll have to spread the word to VIPs about the suits themselves, what they can do. Plus your own security will naturally be increased."

"Good, good." The President grew pensive. "Imagine if the public heard about these suits. They'd be terrified."

"I agree, sir. Press silence is critical."

"And our own remaining suit?"

"Safe. I've instructed Vasquez to wear it at all times."

The President took another drag. "I think you'd better bring her in for a demonstration. I'll summon the Joint Chiefs of Staff, too. They'll want to see it."

That meant he'd be in the same room as the General, the Spartan's hated foe. Interesting. "Yes, sir. I'll invite the Spartan as well. I want him to be front and center for any counter-attack."

"He did a great job on the canister conspiracy. Too bad the bombs went off in Taiwan." The President had a sudden thought. "The Chinese Premier is coming here in a week's time. I wonder if …"

"I don't think that's a good idea, sir. At best the Chinese are our 'frenemies', at worst our enemies."

"That's a soldier's response, not a politician's." The President smiled wryly. "And you don't know what I was about to say."

"You were about to say, sir, that you should warn them about the missing invisibility technology. I would say no. Not even our allies are aware we possess the tech. Hell, not even the CIA knows. The fewer people that know, the better."

"Perhaps it was the Chinese who stole the technology."

"It's not beyond their capacities, sir, but I doubt it. Such a move would be considered too provocative."

"But who else could it be? A corporate entity? Terrorists? The Japanese?" The President pondered that last idea. "The Japanese are making disturbing noises about rewriting their constitution so they can go to war again. Plus, ninjutsu is a Japanese fighting art."

"I can't imagine why the Japanese would launch such an operation, considering they need our support against China's territorial ambitions more than ever. And just because someone practises ninjutsu doesn't mean they're Japanese. I know karate and that doesn't make me Chinese."

POTUS nodded. "Fair enough."

"I'm afraid the identity of the thieves is an 'unknown unknown'. That's what my Dungeon Master's Guide says." The President's computer pinged, alerting him to new emails. POTUS briefly looked at the screen, then turned back to Garin.

"How many of these suits could there be?"

"Hard to estimate. But considering the rarity of the 'unobtainium'" – chuckle, chuckle – "used in the suit's manufacture, I would say … no more than 50. Tops."

"Fifty!" shouted the President. "My lord, Garin! It's hard enough stopping just one person in one. And you say there could be *dozens* out there?"

Garin was never big on sugar-coating anything, much like his friend the Spartan. "I'm afraid so, Mr President."

"Hell, they could just waltz through the front door of the White House. There could be an assassin in this room right now and we'd never know it!"

Garin laughed, even as his eyes roamed the space looking for said ninja. "Doubtful, sir. This is one of the most secure buildings on the planet. Not even Vasquez could get in here with her suit and she's had more experience using the Ghost Armor than any person alive."

The President took another long drag of his cigarette. The nicotine seemed to calm him down. "So, what do we do about the Premier's visit? If anything happened to him while he was here, it could mean war. Things are *that* tense. And there's more than a few people on our side who want war, anyway."

"It's tempting to tell the Premier to stay home and watch some DVDs instead but I say we should proceed. A display of unity between the world's two great powers is something people would like to see right now."

"I hear that. The relationship between America and China will define the tenor of the 21st century. Everyone wants peace."

Do they, wondered Garin. But instead he said: "We'll offer some of our best people to help guard the Premier. Meanwhile, the Spartan and Vasquez will work with you and the Secret Service."

"Your Spartan does have 'a particular set of skills'."

"Nice movie reference, sir. But with any luck, we'll track down the perpetrators, neutralize them and retrieve the tech.

"In the meantime, I'll have a dossier prepared for you … and we'll arrange a demonstration of the Ghost Armor today." Garin got up and saluted. "Now if you don't mind, sir, I'll get right on it."

Garin gestured around the space. "And please try not to spend too much time cooped up in The Tent, Mr President. You're the President, not a Scout leader."

The President laughed. "It's not a Tent, it's a 'secure information facility'." Garin rose to his feet. "Thanks for coming. And colonel?"

"Yes, Mr President?"

"Could I please have that folder back?"

Garin sheepishly handed back the folder marked "Mandatory population limits per country" he had clandestinely stuffed under his arm. "Oops, sorry. An accident."

The President winked. "Of course. See you soon, colonel."

Chapter 18

The General had been summoned to the White House Situation Room, joining a select shortlist that included the other members of the Joint Chiefs of Staff, assorted generals and military luminaries plus the head of the CIA.

The summoning forced the General to skip lunch, but nevertheless piqued his interest. It wasn't often America's high priests of organised violence were gathered together at the Situation Room. Much to the disappointment of conspiracists everywhere, America's top generals seldom met in a group to discuss how to rule America and, by extension, the world. They all had their own various fiefdoms, their areas of interest, to manage, the secrets of which they jealously guarded from the others.

As his enemy the Spartan never appreciated, there was a strong political dimension to any top general's work. While a fellow general might be an ally on the battlefield, he was also a rival for promotions, appointments, responsibilities and even the President's ear.

If only the General's job was as easy as rocking up somewhere, pulling out a gun and shooting some busted-ass Third World terrorists, thought the General.

So such official invitations were infrequent and thus commanded commensurate respect. Apparently POTUS had pressing information to share about some amazing new technology. Technology which had, in fact, fallen into the hands of the enemy. Technology that was a major threat to national security.

It was bound to be an interesting meeting for several reasons. The relationship between the President and the Joint Chiefs of Staff was fraught. The President felt that the various wars conducted by the Pentagon cost him political capital and often embarrassed him with his liberal power base. For their part, the Joint Chiefs resented a civilian – even if he was technically Commander-In-Chief – telling them what to do or even threatening to withhold troops and resources. There was the widespread belief among the military that the current President simply didn't "get" the armed forces. The General had never had too much trouble with POTUS, but he knew others had.

As the General took a seat in the Situation Room near the front of the large rectangular table, he wondered if the announcement had anything to do with Colonel Garin's missing tech. If so, this could be a good opportunity to score some points against his old enemy.

Hungry, the General reviewed the titbits on offer on the table: fruit, tea, coffee and water. No pastries. Apparently the War on Carbs had now entered the White House, along with the War on Drugs and the War on Terror. And the War on Carbs was probably just as unwinnable, judging by the conditions of America's "foot soldiers" in the food courts of the country.

The General was almost last to arrive. General Regis was the last. The florid-faced Regis nodded to the room and then slowly to the General as he sat down. Regis was once described anonymously in a widely read article as a "Level 60 asshole". The General always remembered that quote – particularly as he had been the one who supplied it to the journalist. Heh.

Looking at Regis's piggish, close-set eyes, the General wondered what level of "asshole" Regis would describe him as. No less than Level 50, he would think.

But then the wondering ended as POTUS swept into the room.

"Gentlemen," said the tired-looking President, "thanks for coming. I know you're all very busy, but unfortunately this information couldn't wait." His eyes took in the men at the table. "No sign of the Vice President, then?"

The General thought he detected irritation in the President's voice. "No sir," he said.

"He'll have to catch up. Let's begin. I'll let Colonel Garin fill you in on the details." The President gestured to the open door. "Colonel, could you come in, please?"

The General watched as Colonel Garin swept into the room with his normal cocksure strut. Good old Garin, he thought sarcastically. Garin the fixer. Garin the feared man in the shadows who even generals knew not to cross.

Garin, Sir Francis Walsingham to the President's Queen Elizabeth.

Garin flashed a quick look of loathing towards the General – right back at ya, buddy – before stepping before the group. The President sat at the front of the table, settling in his chair with a soft, grateful sigh.

"Rare to see you during the daylight, colonel," said Regis. "Should we all be removing our SIM cards from our phones?"

There was chuckling at the reference to America's all-pervasive surveillance capabilities.

"Ask the CIA," joked Garin, glancing over to the CIA boss, who pretended to find the reference amusing. The CIA boss's hair was so well oiled and gelled, it looked like a Lego piece that had been strapped onto his head. His strange coiffure also featured in the unofficial nickname no one ever repeated to his face.

Then the Spartan also entered, like a Tier 1 rock star. All eyes swivelled in his direction, generals marvelling at this perfect specimen of war. Even the President's eyes seemed to shine as they took in the Congressional Medal of Honor shining on the Spartan's barrel-like chest.

No doubt they'd be hanging on the oaf's every monosyllable.

The General put two fingers on his pulse, feeling it rise. He hadn't been warned that his "hate interest" would be in attendance. Some subordinate would pay later.

He subconsciously crouched down in his chair, like a prey animal trying to make himself small and less obvious in the jungle. He was terrified by the Spartan's close presence and humiliated by the terror that he instilled in him.

Even more sinister was the fact that the Spartan noticed him, reversed direction and stood against the wall directly behind him. The Tier 1 terror didn't say a word, but gestured to his face just where his blade had cut the General. *Insolent bastard.*

Mouth dry, the General went to help himself to the carafe of water on the table.

"Let me pour that for you, General," said the Spartan, wrapping his hand around the General's as he grasped a glass. The General feared the Spartan would break the glass with a sudden, pythonesque squeeze. He pictured blood over all his maimed fingers.

Yet instead the Spartan slowly poured water into the glass.

"*Thank you,*" said the General acidly.

"My pleasure ... *sir.*"

The General couldn't help but notice the mockery in that "sir". His peers probably noticed it, too. He was about to say something, but then Garin began to talk. The General had to let the insult die on his tongue, turn away and pay attention.

"Good afternoon, gentlemen, Mr President," said Garin, standing in front of the table, hands behind his back, talking loudly so everyone in the room could clearly hear him. "I'll get straight to brass tacks. Several months ago, one of our research facilities was attacked by unknown parties. The guards and scientists inside were killed and the technology the scientists were working on was stolen. The lead scientist himself was also kidnapped." Garin looked around and read the mood of the room, which was shocked and disturbed.

Then he continued: "What the unidentified intruders stole were the building materials and blueprints for" – Garin stopped, as if pausing for some unseen record scratch – "the Mark 1 Ghost Armor. Also known as the world's first invisibility suit."

Garin paused, once again letting this even more alarming information circulate. The room went quiet. You could have heard a grenade pin drop.

"An invisibility suit?" asked General Regis. "That sounds like science fiction."

"Science fact now, sir," said Garin.

Indeed, it did sound like "science fact" to the General. He suddenly remembered the godless harpy who had materialised out of thin air to shoot at him during his last encounter with the Spartan. It was the sort of thing that was hard to forget, the subject of several sweaty nightmares.

"An invisibility suit … you couldn't make this shit up," said the General to murmurs of agreement.

"Colonel, before we talk more about the theft, would you mind explaining how the suit actually works?" asked the President, helping the dialogue along. To the General's mind, POTUS was calmer than he would have expected in this situation. Perhaps he had reserved his freak-out for when Garin initially delivered the information.

Garin nodded at the President, then continued. "The Ghost Armor is based on some pretty amazing technology. I could try to explain the tech behind it, but only one man can really fathom it – and he can remember 50 blackboards worth of equations in his head, so I'm not going to try to break down how the Ghost Armor works. I'll have my people send everyone here the Cliff Notes on the basic principles and how it is made.

"Suffice to say it's based on elements on the natural world, such as the camouflage abilities of creatures such as octopi and cuttlefish, quantum mechanics and a whole lot more.

"As to its practicalities, it allows the user to operate invisibly at a speed of approximately one foot a second. We had to sacrifice speed to make it work. The armor itself is your standard Kevlar-style issue, but incredibly light. Quite the miracle fabric.

"We've used the armor in many situations and found it invaluable. Particularly in combat situations that require undetected insertions.

"Since the dawn of history predators have been trying to perfect the art of stealth and camouflage. This suit goes a long way to meeting that need." The men in the room murmured among themselves, stimulated by the news.

"Truly, we live in a world of miracles," offered POTUS. "Does it turn people in Predator?" There were some polite chuckles at POTUS'S joke.

"Not quite, Mr President," replied Garin. "The Ghost Armor has more limitations. Once you fire your weapon or swing a blade you become visible. The user also becomes visible if they move too fast or collide with a solid object. And the suit can only work for 15 minutes or so before it needs recharging. It's extremely energy hungry.

"It was always envisioned as a rare, boutique tool. Special forces only. Not for mass use."

As if to pre-empt commentary as to why they should build such a dangerous thing in the first place, Garin added: "We're not the only ones with such a program. The Chinese, Japanese, French and South Koreans all have their own invisibility programs. We're just the first ones to make a functioning model."

There was more silence as Garin's disturbing news rippled around the room.

The President stared at the assorted luminaries, trying to gauge a reaction. "Questions, gentlemen?"

General Regis was the first to speak. "More like objections, Mr President," he said sternly, before turning to face Garin. "No one is dancing around in their underpants like Tom Cruise in *Risky Business* over this news, colonel. When it comes to security protocols, this changes everything."

The head of the CIA leaned forward. To the General's mind, the CIA head resembled a praying mantis about to strike. "Why didn't we hear about our own successful version?" he fumed. "Where was the Agency's heads-up?"

Good question, thought the General. Although it was understandable that Garin didn't tip off the "Christians In

Action". The CIA and the Pentagon had waged a decades-long war for influence over the White House, and the Pentagon had won. The CIA was the Pentagon's bitch now, and Garin, a former soldier, had as much Pentagon as Homeland Security in his DNA. The CIA had to be grateful for anything it got from the armed services.

But the General had questions of his own to ask Garin. He had his own agenda in this meeting apart from hurt professional feelings. "I agree … why are we only hearing about this now?" he said loudly.

Garin's left eye flickered in suppressed anger. "As I'm sure you'll understand, General, we needed to keep the Ghost Armor completely secret. People would have trouble processing this information. It's a … disturbing concept."

The General replied: "This should have come across our desks, Garin, even if in Cliff Notes form. I was unaware that there was a level of security clearance above top secret. Are you setting your own levels of secrecy, colonel? Victoria's Secret or something?"

"No, General," said Garin brusquely, jaw set. "There was a timeline in place to integrate this technology into the armed forces. We needed to figure out how to incorporate it with our current weapon systems before everyone was fully briefed."

"What has changed, then, apart from the theft?" said the General, feeling the Spartan's angry eyes burning a hole in his back.

"Other events have occurred that require us to spread knowledge of its existence."

"So you have even worse news apart from the break-in? Do tell," said the General drolly.

Garin nodded. "Last night, one of my operatives was attacked by a ninja wearing a copy of the armor. She survived to tell us about the attack.

"We must assume that our unknown enemy has started building copies of the armor, potentially to use to attack us. They must be well-supplied and equipped too, because the armor isn't something you just whip up on a 3D printer in the privacy of your own home.

"In short, they are serious people of the most dangerous stripe." Garin's statement hung in the air unchallenged for a few seconds.

"That's ... not good," offered General Archon, one of Garin's main supporters in the room. "This is like the Russians stealing the secrets of the atomic bomb. Our own weapon is being aimed back at us."

"That also means," said Regis, glancing back and forth at everyone, "that none of us are safe. These criminals could use these suits against anyone, from the lowest to the highest. We'll have to grow eyes in the backs of our heads." Regis paused, as if gripped by his own sense of drama. "And totally rethink our security details!"

"If our allies knew this technology was on the loose they'd do their nut," said the General. "Imagine the panic it would cause at the G20. What a fucking garbage fire." The General turned to Garin. "Who was responsible for security on the base?"

"I was, sir," said Garin, with just a hint of remorse. "Someone ordered my security away from the base before the attack. They were unaware of the base's contents."

"Are you making excuses, colonel?"

"No, General."

"Because that sounded like an excuse."

"No, sir," said Garin, staring ahead, "I take full responsibility."

"And so you should." The General leant back with a grin on his face. *Score one point for me,* he thought.

The General watched the infectious panic spread across the room. The generals were realising for the first time they were now personally vulnerable to assassination. There were angry murmurs. This was bad news. Terrible, actually. And Garin was caught in the center, a Dorothy flailing ineffectually amid the tornado.

"Gentlemen, we're not here to assign blame," said the President, raising his hands to invoke calm. "We're here the fix the problem."

General Regis folded his arms in scepticism. "You said something about a demonstration, Mr President. I'd like to 'see' this thing for myself."

The President turned to Garin. "Colonel?"

Garin nodded to a corner in the room. "OK, Vasquez, show yourself." Slowly, a figure in a body-hugging outfit became visible, one piece at a time like a white Cheshire Cat. In a few seconds, "Vasquez" had totally materialised in the room. Taa, daa.

Several of the generals got up out of their chairs. Garin smiled at the reaction, like a stage magician who had successfully made his comely assistant disappear, levitate across the stage or fly over the audience like a magical bird.

The General had a completely difficult reaction than awe.

"My God, it's her," he whispered, gripping the armrests on his chair tightly. The woman who had ambushed him in his torture bunker. The soldier who had rescued the Spartan from waterboarding. The Spartan's girlfriend. The sight of her stirred unwelcome memories – memories that involved him running from a room holding his bleeding, punctured stomach.

And what was that? Did she turn to him in recognition, a microexpression of disgust lurking under the mask, as if recalling the events of that day?

"Look familiar, General?" whispered the Spartan in the General's ear, almost forcing him to lose control of his bladder. The General tried to calm his mind. He imagined himself sitting under a tree, a cool stream beside him … and the Spartan's body floating through the stream. Yes. That relaxed him somewhat.

"Good afternoon, gentlemen," said Vasquez as she removed her mask, exposing her comely face and long, flowing hair. "My name is Teresa Vasquez. And this, as you can now see … is the Mark I Ghost Armor."

There was a second or two of silence as the room's occupants took in the marvel. And maybe a second extra to appreciate the attractive woman in their midst.

"Fire from Olympus," murmured the CIA chief.

"First stealth bombers, then stealth fighters, then stealth helicopters and now stealth humans," drawled General Archon. "Incredible."

"The incredible is only incredible until someone does it," said Garin.

"OMG," muttered the President, impressed, demonstrating the savvy use of net-speak that allowed him to capture the youth vote. "This is the first time I'm 'seeing' it too, fellas."

"All women turn invisible after a certain age," whispered a colleague into the General's ear, chuckling at his own sexism.

The CIA boss eyed the suit covetously. "What a perfect espionage tool. How much did this program cost, Garin?"

"Two hundred million."

The CIA boss smirked. "You could buy Detroit for $200 million. And you say the scientist who makes them has disappeared too?"

"Yes. We have his family in protective custody." The CIA boss nodded, no doubt filing away the information for future reference. The CIA's own covert ops program could benefit from owning a suit or two of Ghost Armor.

Meanwhile, General Regis eyed Vasquez warily. "Has Vasquez been in the room the whole time? We didn't notice her at all!"

"The suit can be very effective, sir," said Garin.

"Effective enough to use against us, Garin," growled the General, casting an angry glance at both Vasquez and then Garin. "Anyone who really matters. And now the enemy has them. An enemy, in fact, that you can't yet identify. Correct?"

"Correct, sir. There has been no contact with or from them. No negotiations or lists of demands."

"And you can't issue a Be On The Lookout For suspects you can't see," continued the General. "Find, Fix And Finish just doesn't work on invisible enemies." He gave Garin the cold shoulder as he turned to face POTUS. "Forgive me for speaking bluntly, Mr President, but just how many assholes with suits are out there, waiting to stab us all in the shadows?"

"I would say no more than a few dozen," said Garin.

"Just a few dozen!" raged the General, waving his hands. "One is more than enough!"

General Lynley was similarly vexed. He nodded towards Vasquez. "We're going to have to warn all our VIPs to be on the lookout for an attack by the Invisible Woman."

"The suit is unisex in its design," said Garin flatly.

"Invisible Men and Women, then," said General Lynley, irritated by Garin's footnote. "So what are we going to do now, colonel? What are we going to bloody well do?"

The General knew Garin's mannerisms well enough to tell he was unimpressed by the strain of cowardice in Lynley's voice.

But instead, Garin said: "We will seek out the thieves and deal with them. If they walk on this earth, if they breathe air, we can find them and kill them. We'll be laying some Ezekiel 25:17 on their asses. Have some faith in our abilities."

"Faith," snorted Regis.

"But for now, I've already got some ideas for countermeasures on how to neutralise the suit's advantages. We'll see if we can't 'Stuxnet' the thing somehow." Stuxnet being the computer virus that nobbled the Iranian nuclear centrifuges in 2007. "And we've got the world's most experienced operator," said Garin, now nodding to Vasquez, "for advice."

"I fail to find that completely comforting, colonel," said General Lynley. "Prevention is better than cure." Lynley stared at Vasquez. "No offence, soldier. I'm sure you're very effective in that suit."

"I think you've got too much on your plate, Garin, if you didn't foresee that this tech could escape the laboratory," said General Regis, turning to the President with an unctuous gleam in his eye. "You may require another level of oversight. A ... fresh set of eyes."

"Congress?" asked the President.

Regis shook his head. "Hell no, sir, pardon my French. I was more thinking someone from our offices."

"My office would like to take part as well," said the CIA chief with more than an interested gleam in his eye.

As Garin sat there holding his metaphorical manhood in his hands, unable to properly defend himself, his Invisible Woman standing there mutely, the General turned around to look at the Spartan ... and smiled.

The Spartan stared back angrily, unable to do anything in this arena to defend his precious colonel. He was impotent, despite all his brute strength. All the Spartan could do was respect the chain of command as Garin was verbally torn to bits. Wonderful. Worth the price of admission.

The General was filled with a blessed light of satisfaction. Garin clearly hadn't calculated that the first instincts of some of the generals wouldn't be how to save the country, but how to save themselves. And, once imperilled, they'd look for someone to blame. In this case, the good colonel himself, the deliverer of bad news. *A free lesson in the nature of man for the General's hated enemy.*

The General leant back, drank some of the excellent coffee on offer and watched as the Joint Chiefs of Staff got stuck into Garin. *You're in my world now, buddy.* Once word got out about Garin's blunder, he would no longer be the golden boy of Washington and Fort Bragg. The silver boy, perhaps. Or the copper boy. Perhaps even a baser metal.

Yes, thought the General, sipping his coffee as the Spartan scowled at him, a good day indeed.

Chapter 19

The Spartan did not like the way that meeting had gone. No, sir. Watching his commanding officer getting reamed by the top brass – instigated by the General, no less – had filled him with rage, rage he had nowhere to go with, no target for his angry, flexing hands.

Except for one possible location. One possible face.

The Spartan hung around after the meeting so that he could have a "friendly" chat with the General ... and to violently pass on his appreciation for the General's valuable contributions to the round table. He planned to lead the General towards a quiet corner or alcove and then apply some pain where it would do the most good.

For Garin was willing to take his side against anyone, no matter what the cost. The Spartan would do the same.

The General had remained to chat to General Regis. But it looked like that discussion was ending, Regis's body language suggesting he was about to leave. Yep, there he went. The General was bound to slither out any second, too.

As if sensing what the Spartan had in mind, the General threw a worried look over his shoulder as he left the room most ricky tick.

Unaware of the Spartan's intentions, Vasquez tried to get his attention. "Hey, did you see the faces on those generals when I became visible?" she said. "They looked as if the only Latina they expected to see in the White House would be a maid."

"Hunh," grunted the Spartan, still focusing on the General.

"It was rough on the colonel in there," added Vasquez. "No wonder he left like his *culo* was on fire."

"Hunh.

"Mr Eloquent here. Hey, while we're here, let's have some lunch. I hear the White House cooks are *amazing*. You can have some Greek, too. Do you remember the recipe for the Spartans's 'black broth'?"

"Maybe," said the Spartan as he pushed by.

"Hey!" heyed Vasquez.

The Spartan stomped down the hall. The General was just about to enter the elevator. He must have double-timed it, fearful of manhandling by his old enemy.

The Spartan dashed towards the elevator, pushing aside assorted and offended aides. He could hear a frantic tapping, as if the General was repeatedly pushing the "ground floor" button. Which he was.

Just as the Spartan was about to reach the elevator, the silver doors closed.

The last thing he saw was the General giving him the finger.

Chapter 20

The Vice President of the United States of America unplugged the smart TV in his room just in case anyone wanted to turn it into a listening device and hear his conversations – they'd been able to do that for some time, apparently.

And not just the people on his side.

He then removed the SIM card from his cell phone for very much the same reason.

Finally satisfied, he sat back in his impressively furnished hotel suite in downtown Chicago. Cool glass of apple juice in hand, he was taking a well-earned break after a gruelling breakfast fundraiser.

"Christ, those fundraisers are boring," he thought as he loosened his tie, put his feet up on the couch and sipped his juice. Ahhh.

In fact, he seemed to spend more time drumming up campaign funding than on any other issue. If someone had told him when he entered politics that his main activity would be ringing up rich, powerful, well-connected folk and begging them for campaign contributions, hitting the phones and coldcalling like a goddamn insurance salesman, he might have reconsidered his career choice altogether.

Then again, the thickening yet handsome VP was a people person, a one-on-one charmer, not a rocket scientist. What else was he going to do with his personal manner, perfect Kennedy-style hair and bedside manner? Sell used cars?

Hell no.

And fundraising pains aside, look at where he was now, he thought, as he scanned the deluxe room normally reserved for oil sheiks and rock stars. The VP of the United States of America. With a coterie of Secret Service bodyguards outside protecting his legendary behind. A man with a title that demanded respect everywhere in the real world, no matter how many smart-alec liberal TV shows made out otherwise.

Second to the Most Powerful Man in the Free World.

And the Most Powerful Man in the Free World was in trouble. The President was looking grey and tired and old, no longer the telegenic charmer of yesteryear. Voters were disenchanted. Even POTUS's own party was considering dumping him, particularly as millions of Americans had perished during his period in office. True, his administration did stop the canister conspiracy plot on US soil, but the Taiwan bombs had gone off, bringing the plague to the homeland. Someone had to be blamed apart from the terrorists. Unfortunately, the bubonic buck stopped with old POTUS.

Some on the other side of the House were even whispering impeachment.

And if the President was pushed or impeached, well, they would have to turn to the next man in line for the throne.

As much as he personally liked the President – hell, they had even been friends once, for real, not just "Washington" friends – the VP had ambitions of his own. He also had his own views on how to run the country.

The VP imagined himself being swept by the forces of history into the top slot, just like LBJ – only without the unfortunate assassination of his predecessor. A great man answering the call of destiny, as it were, humbly following the will of the people. Ready to serve his country in any way he was asked.

A tiny voice in his mind liked to remind him of the hypocrisy of his thoughts … but he wouldn't be where he was today if he listened to that voice very often.

His wife was completely behind him, too. Phyllis wanted to be First Lady: being Second Lady felt like winning second prize in a beauty contest. Besides, Phyllis hated the current title holder, a feeling that FLOTUS reciprocated with acid vigour.

Phyllis motivated him by emailing him daily "inspirational" quotes from the TV show *House of Cards*, starring Kevin Spacey as the conniving President Francis Underwood. Or "FU", as the wags called him.

Yes, Mr President … "FU".

The opposition had also put out feelers. They found the current POTUS too difficult to deal with. They welcomed someone more on their wavelength. "We'll even run fewer attack ads against you," chuckled one of their emissaries over cigars and brandy one fine Washington evening.

The VP had chuckled at that. And had been intrigued by the suggestion of secret backing.

Thus the jigsaw pieces were falling into place. All that was required now was the right … inciting incident.

So when the President's people had phoned his people, saying that the VP needed to attend a meeting with the Joint

Chiefs of Staff about a matter of urgent national security, he took it with a pillar of salt. Or whatever the fuck a pillar of salt looked like when it was at home. The VP had passed the point where he needed to drop everything and rush over whenever the President called. The bad news would have to wait. And after the plague attacks, just how bad could it be?

The VP smiled. Yes, let the President wait. It would give him an indication of the new balance of power.

"FU", Mr President.

The Vice President was broken out of his happy reverie by what sounded like screaming outside the room. His ears pricked up. Yes, that was shouting and screaming.

And then, a new, terrible sound.

Gunfire.

And it was right at his door.

He felt his chest instantly constrict.

His Secret Service detail were shouting. Then more commotion.

The Vice President heard the pistols carried by the Secret Service being emptied in rapid succession. It was a sound he had hoped and prayed he would never hear within his proximity.

The noise was answered by the shooting of silenced weapons. Bullets sprayed through the front door. The Vice President threw himself to the ground. *What on earth was happening?*

His mind urged escape. Yet there was no exit apart from the front door ... his security had insisted on a room with no windows. Should he hide in the bathroom? Phone the front desk, police or White House for help? Protocol demanded he stay put in a safe place until the Secret Service handled whatever was happening, but unfortunately he had no idea what that was. And as the battle continued, he wondered just how the Secret Service were coping with the mysterious threat. He had a 10-man team with him – surely that was enough to deal with any challenge?

He reached for his cell phone, trying to re-insert the SIM card with shaking hands. As he was almost done the front door flew open. It was Connor, loyal Connor, his white shirt covered with blood, holding a pistol in his hand.

"Sir, you've got to …"

Whatever Connor was about to say was cut short … because his head was severed from his shoulders in a single blow.

Connor's head rolled along the carpet towards him. The VP cried out, got to his feet and dodged the rolling skull, its eyelids still twitching horribly.

"Oh my God," he whispered. "Oh my God."

A tall, lithe man in a strange silver full-body outfit entered the room. He clutched a bloodied samurai sword before him.

"Oops," said the swordsman.

The figure removed his face gear to stare at the Vice President with undisguised hostility. The intruder had thin, hawk-like features, straight brown hair and, despite his stern demeanour, was coldly attractive. Handsome, even. Almost model handsome. He entered as casually as if he was attending a pool party, as if the Secret Service agent he had just beheaded had bothered him no more than swatting a fly.

Flanking him were two shorter, compact, masked men in similar, bizarre silver suits. Clutching machineguns, they closed the door as they entered. Their chests rose from their exertions outside. Yet their faces remained hidden.

The VP had gone from panic to terror in under 60 seconds. *This can't be happening*, his mind screamed.

The killers paused, as if politely waiting for him to speak.

"You murderers," uttered the Vice President in a thin voice he barely recognised as his own. "What have you done?"

"Your security detail has been … retired," stated the swordsman with cruel disdain. With a terrifyingly efficient gesture, he flicked the blood off his blade, some of the droplets landing on the VP's Hermes tie. The VP couldn't help but notice what a superb weapon the killer was holding and the familiarity in which he held it. The sword almost seemed part of him, like an extra limb or a prehensile tail on a jungle animal.

"They killed one of my own soldiers, despite our element of surprise," continued the swordsman, moving closer. "My compliments to their trainer." He looked the VP over with harsh, merciless eyes. "But, I wonder, was the prize they were guarding worth their lives?" The sword was now pointing straight at the VP, the tip straight at his throat. The VP moved aside. The sword point followed him almost imperceptibly.

Despite his terror, the VP tried to take control of an inherently uncontrollable situation.

"You're in a shitstorm of trouble, son," he bluffed. "Do you know who you're messing with? I'm the Vice President of the United States of America!"

"Yes," came the answer, "we are aware of that. It is you we seek."

The three intruders then said nothing, allowing the VP to fill the psychic space with his own terrible interpretations.

Who goes after the Vice President, the VP's mind screamed at him. No one entered the history books by gunning down the veep. It was the President that was the grand prize in the assassination game.

With all that in mind, the Vice President asked: "Who are you?"

"Your reckoning." The way the handsome killer said "reckoning" chilled the VP.

"Are you terrorists?"

"Don't be stupid," said the swordsman dismissively.

"Then … for pity's sake, what do you want?"

"Justice."

The VP's mouth went dry. "Justice? What justice? Whose justice?"

"History's justice. Now kneel." The swordsman moved closer. The VP backed away. The other two men slung their machineguns and grabbed the VP by each arm, firmly pushing him downwards.

"Kneel!"

"No!" One of the intruders muttered something and kicked the VP in the back of the legs, twice. He fell to his knees.

"Now," said the leader, now within sword reach of the Vice President, "apologize."

"What?"

"Apologize."

"What … what for? For being American? For being Vice President?"

"APOLOGIZE!"

The Vice President desperately wanted to live. Yet as he looked into the eyes of the killer in front of him, he sensed that he was trapped in a Kafka-esque nightmare: that no matter what he said, there would be no correct answer, no saving himself. No one was going to rescue him in the nick of time like in the movies. With his Secret Service detail all murdered, it would be precious minutes before any rescue was coming. Any apology would not stay the blade hovering above his head. He thought of his wife and family. Then he gritted his teeth and raised his chin.

"Screw you. I won't ever apologize, you bastard. Do your worst."

"Yes ... I will."

The leader rested his sword against the VP's neck.

"This is a samurai's weapon ... and the samurai were always judged by the quality and quantity of the heads they took. Your head would indeed be prized." The leader raised the Honjo Masamune up two-handed. "To die by this blade might be considered an honor. But that is not my intention."

The leader then swung the sword downward.

* * *

Later the leader went into Professor Eisenstein's locked living quarters and stood at the doorway. He said nothing. But his body language said everything.

So did the blood stains on his Ghost Armor.

"What have you done?" breathed Eisenstein. "What have you made me party to?"

The leader told him. In elaborate, bloody detail.

Stricken, the fruits of his genius used for murder, Eisenstein buried his head in his hands.

The leader smiled.

Chapter 21

If the news of the Ghost Armor's theft was like a panic attack in the halls of the White House, then the news of the assassination of the Vice President resembled an atom bomb going off. The knowledge that he was killed by some kind of edged weapon made it all the more baffling, intimate, ancient and terrifying.

Apart from the weapon used, it was precisely the sort of assassination scenario the Joint Chiefs had feared.

Security was doubled and then doubled again for anyone that mattered. Guards were told to shoot first and file reports later. Armored vehicles drove VIPs into secure locations. Police black-and-whites provided escorts. Others – including Garin's operatives – stepped up their efforts to locate the invisible menaces.

Not that the public knew about any of this. The Vice President's death was kept secret while a suitable cover story was invented. A car accident, perhaps. That usually worked. No one was about to admit that the veep had been assassinated by unknown agents employing next-generation stealth technology. Nor did the White House want the news that he'd actually had his head severed from his body getting out in the public domain.

The staff at the hotel had been forced to sign oaths of non-disclosure, which carried heavy penalties and even jail time if broken. Standard procedure. Garin's own people had sanitised the crime scene.

Meanwhile, Garin was sitting with the President in a heavily guarded, off-the-books pad in Washington, watching the security footage from the hotel.

They watched the attack on the relevant camera feeds – chilling, violent footage, but no shots of the VP's actual beheading – before the three assassins left via the hotel car park, machine-gunning a cleaner who happened upon the scene. Then the assassins got into a foreign car, carrying the dead body of one of their comrades, before driving off.

"See … one of them was killed, Mr President," said Garin as he gestured towards the screen. "They're not invincible. They're just men."

"But the price, Garin, the price. It took 10 Secret Service agents just to bring down one of them."

"The death toll was so large because the Secret Service agents were surprised, sir," said Garin as the footage finished.

"Surprised? I bet they were, if those assassins were wearing stolen Ghost Armor tech! And the Vice President! Jesus Christ! We haven't had such a high-level assassination since … since …"

"John Lennon?"

"I was thinking more in political terms." The President shook his head, then touched his neck without realising it. "Cutting off a man's head like that. It's barbaric!"

"There are worse ways to go, sir. Believe me. At least it was quick." At least we have a body to bury, thought Garin darkly.

"But to leave his head on the ground like that! The disrespect! The madness! This will not stand, Garin. This will not stand!"

"I completely agree sir." Garin paused, summoning his thoughts. "It's cartel-level violence, that's for sure, but I can't think of any particular Mafia that would be stupid or suicidal enough to do this. It must be something or someone … different."

The President nodded. He said: "What am I going to tell his wife? And his family …"

"The nation grieves along with them," said Garin automatically, reciting the rote words.

The President fixed Garin with a look: "I believe in open government. I want to be honest with the people. And yet … I don't think the nation is ready for this news, colonel. Particularly the circumstances of his death."

The room was silent, except for the sounds of freedom of the press flying out the window. "I concur, sir. We should maintain media silence."

There was a pause as POTUS scribbled down a note. "Why did they target him, colonel? Was he a target of opportunity or a number on a death list?"

"I don't know, sir," said Garin honestly. "But I have to assume that they may target you next. You're far more important, as a man and as a symbol." The President shivered a little at the news. But just a little.

"That's logical. Terrifying, but logical."

"This may have just been a dry run. Practice, if you will."

"Practice," repeated the President, shuddering. "I hate to think what they have in mind for real."

"I'm afraid it's going to get bloodier, sir. We're playing for all the marbles here."

"Since when were marbles bloody?"

"They are the way I play them, sir."

"Oh." Pause. "What do you advise, then?"

"For starters, I want to assign the Spartan and Vasquez to your security detail. The Spartan, because he will add valuable firepower to your team and he is one of the rare few people who can detect the presence of someone in the Ghost Armor. And secondly, Vasquez, because she knows all the strengths and weaknesses of the armor. Her advice will be invaluable on how best to counter their use."

The President nodded. "Agreed, colonel."

"I want you to have the best … no point having Billy Baldwin if you can get Alec Baldwin instead."

"Of course. Did you get anything from the crime scene?"

"Not really. Blood samples. Some shell casings. There was nothing special about their machine-guns. Custom-made jobs. We can try to trace them, but I wouldn't hold out for much there." Garin paused, mentally summoning up an interesting nugget of information. "However, one of my techs did discover slivers from a sword. The swordsman struck a wall. The techs say the metal dates back to the 13th century."

"Interesting. So the Ghost Armor isn't the only extraordinary equipment being used by the terrorists."

Garin nodded. "Yes. Still, I'm more of a gun man myself. Although the Spartan is quite fond of swords." Garin looked at his watch. "Speaking of whom, I'll contact him and Vasquez ASAP to join you, sir."

"Thank you, Garin." The President stared off into the distance, thinking unknown thoughts, before turning his attention back to Garin. "I don't need to tell you that we all need a swift resolution." Particularly with Garin's competency on the line after his chewing-out by the Joint Chiefs of Staff, was the unspoken implication.

Garin took the chance to rest his hand on the President's arm. "We'll get them, sir."

The President sighed, reaching for his packet of cigarettes as Garin got up to leave. "I hope so, colonel. For all our sakes."

Chapter 22

"So you're the Spartan," said Special Agent Tony Mancuso as he looked the prodigy up and down. "The President speaks highly of you. I've read your file. Impressive stuff. You've served your country well."

The older man, whose barrel-like body was clad in a grey suit with an American flag pinned to a lapel, stretched out a hand. "Tony."

The Spartan shook "Tony's" hand, but if Mancuso was expecting the Spartan to greet him by his first name as well, he was sorely disappointed. Instead, the Spartan stared at him, scrutinizing him as closely as a Spartan elder examining a newborn child for signs of weakness.

"How you doin'?" asked Mancuso eventually to break the silence.

"Good," replied the Spartan evenly.

To the Spartan's ears, Tony sounded like New Jersey native, even if he'd since hidden his accent with a clipped Washington tone.

As if he knew what the Spartan was thinking, Mancuso asked: "Where you from, Spartan?"

"Far, far away," he said.

"Ummm … right."

Vasquez saw Mancuso's discomfort and stepped forward. "Vasquez," she said as she shook Mancuso's callused mitt.

"Tony," said Mancuso with a friendly smile.

Once Colonel Garin had learnt of the Vice President's execution, he had dispatched Vasquez and the Spartan to guard the President.

"Are we going to save the world again, sir?" the Spartan asked the colonel.

"Save the President. Save the world," came the pithy reply. "The President's life is in your hands. No pressure, big guy."

And so here they were, ready to save POTUS and the world, standing outside the President's suite in a five-star hotel in Washington, being debriefed by their new friend, Special Agent Mancuso.

"So," said Mancuso amiably, "your boss says you've got form against these ninjas. Let's hope so. Welcome aboard."

"A pleasure," said Vasquez, with a slight smile. "I was sorry to hear about your men."

"We're all hurting over this one," said Mancuso, shaking his head. "Jesus … some asshole killing people while dressed in an invisible onesie. What a world we live in, eh?" Mancuso suddenly realized that Vasquez herself had an invisible "onesie". "No offence."

"None taken," she replied coolly.

"Anyway, we've never lost this many men in a single incident before. Who were these guys?"

"My bet is special forces," said the Spartan.

"Why?" said Mancuso, curious.

"Because I watched the videotape of the fight outside the VP's room. Your men were good … but not special forces good."

Mancuso gritted his teeth. "Pardon my French, but that's an insensitive fucking thing to say. The Secret Service are the best bodyguards in the world … Spartan. And protecting the President is the most important job there is. More important than whatever it is you do for a living." Mancuso attempted to bury a finger into the Spartan's chest. Mancuso was a big man, perhaps a line-backer in a previous life, and not particularly slow. But the Spartan caught the finger anyway. And held it.

"Maybe what you need here aren't bodyguards but battlefield units," replied the Spartan, his superior strength holding the finger in place. "The rumour is your men spend more time chasing counterfeiters than in combat."

"Is this the part where you tell me you eat Secret Service agents for breakfast?"

"No – too high in fat and sugar."

"Guys, please," said Vasquez, attempting to separate the two alpha males trying to establish who was top dog. "We're on the same side." Vasquez turned to Mancuso. "Don't mind my friend – he doesn't play well with others."

"I didn't request your help, Spartan," said Mancuso, pulling his finger away with effort. "I didn't ask for any 'military Viagra'."

"Hey, don't knock it until you've tried it," joked Vasquez.

"I didn't ask for your two-man 'surge'," continued Mancuso. "Just remember that."

"Why don't you remember it for me?" replied the Spartan coldly.

Mancuso's jacket opened slightly, revealing a pistol in a shoulder holster. "And you were ordered to help me, whether

I liked it or not. That was made abundantly clear. Just remember I'm in charge."

"I know who is in charge," said the Spartan ominously.

"I knew we should have checked first to see if Jack Bauer was available." Mancuso shook his head. "What am I going to do with this guy?"

"Chill, Mancuso," said Vasquez, throwing the Spartan a look. "We'll protect the President to the best of our abilities. We'll outfight anyone who comes our way. You can count on that."

Mancuso nodded, grateful that at least one of them was amenable. "I can see your partner isn't a 'people' person."

Vasquez smiled with the bittersweet memory of experience. "Maybe not. He gives every new person he meets a tough time. But there's no one better when the lead starts flying."

"That's the thing," said Mancuso. "You were right before, Spartan, about the Secret Service not being battlefield units. We're a subtle force. We serve and protect from the background. We want to prevent the lead from flying in the first place. The Secret Service identify and neutralize threats before any battle even begins. Before we have to draw our weapons."

"It's a good day when you don't have to pull out your AK?" quipped Vasquez.

Mancuso was pleased at Vasquez's observation. "Exactly. We tend to leave the macho shit for" – Mancuso glanced at the Spartan's direction – "others. It's not like being a soldier where you can just turn up, point and shoot. Nor should you. There is a constant surveillance element." Mancuso gave the Spartan an ocular once-over. "For instance, I'd stop a suspicious-looking dude like you getting within 10 feet of the President."

"You mean, you'd *try*."

Mancuso waved towards the Spartan's hands. "What's that you're carrying?"

"M249 Squad Automatic Weapon," said the Spartan, hefting the gun protectively.

"He calls it Fluffy," joked Vasquez.

"This is my SAW," said Mancuso, paraphrasing the Rifleman's Creed. "There are many like it, but this one is mine."

"There are not many like it," insisted the Spartan.

"I won't ask what you're trying to compensate for, carrying that cannon around. It is loaded?"

"Always."

"See … that's a battlefield weapon, like the Thompsons our grandfathers carried during World War II," said Mancuso. "We prefer pistols. More discreet … and you can better control where you send the bullets."

"The gun stays," insisted the Spartan in a tone that brooked no argument.

"What happens if you have to fire it in public?" asked Mancuso. "We don't want stray rounds flying everywhere. Particularly seeing how there's more than 200 Secret Service agents currently protecting the President. All those interlocking fields of fire. Remember: every bullet has a lawyer's name on it."

The Spartan had heard that battlefield bromide before. "I bet I'm a better shot with my SAW that you with your M4s and Glocks."

"And if I told you I didn't want you to bring it?"

The Spartan seemed to shrug. "I would say, 'opinion noted'."

A vein in Mancuso's head began to throb. "If you didn't come highly recommended I'd tell you to hit the road, Jack, and don't let the door hit your ass on the way out." Mancuso sighed again. "Can I at least ask you to cover it with a jacket or something when we're working crowds?"

"I can do that," said the Spartan.

Mancuso stared disapprovingly at the other weapon by the Spartan's side. "And for pity's sake, try to conceal that Arkansas toothpick."

"Spartan *xiphos*," corrected the Spartan.

"Whatever. We don't want the press thinking the President is protected by Freddy Krueger."

The Spartan was about to say something. Then he caught Vasquez's eye and nodded instead.

"What about your weapons?" asked Mancuso, turning to Vasquez.

"Silenced MP-5. Plus a knife. All stored on my back."

"And … one of these invisibility suits? The Mark 1 Ghost Armor? Because I'd like to see what we're up against."

Vasquez nodded. "I can arrange a demonstration for you and your men. Afterwards we can talk about tactics about how you can protect the President if a stealthed-up assassin enters the room."

"I'd appreciate that, Vasquez. Having those things loose makes our job that more difficult. I'll need some more details from the pair of you later, such as whether you have any special dietary, medical or religious requirements, but I think we can get started shortly." Mancuso turned to the Spartan. "See, Spartan? See how easy life can be when you co-operate with your teammates?"

The Spartan stared at Mancuso darkly. "The only easy day was yesterday. Something I think you're about to find out."

Chapter 23

"Spot anything?" said the Spartan into his throat mic as he walked through the crowd, SAW hidden under the dinner jacket in his hands.

"Negative," replied Vasquez. "Just you in the tux. Which you are rocking, by the way … even with the body armor underneath ruining the lining."

"The body armor stays."

"It wouldn't hurt you to dress up occasionally, lover." More than one of the female members of the President's security detail had cast admiring glances at the Spartan … not that he had noticed. She continued: "You forget that you're a handsome man, in a caveman kind of way."

"I'm not here to look good."

"Well, you do." Vasquez paused, then said: "You don't like this assignment, do you? You don't like being a bodyguard."

"I'm used to being a hunter … not being the hunted."

"I bet you are, my mighty hunter. Still, you're not wrong. Better to be the bull than the bullseye."

"Is that Mexican?"

"No, it's Vasquez. Speaking of being hunted, any sign of our shinobi?"

"Nothing so far." The Spartan shifted the SAW in his hands, making sure the diners didn't see it: Mancuso had stressed that he wasn't a fan of "open carry" when it came to machineguns.

He then made his way past two senior citizens in formal attire, gently pushing them aside.

"You should check those guys' toupees for concealed weapons," said Vasquez.

"That's a job for Special Agent Vidal Sassoon."

"Ha. You made a funny."

"You get one a day. That's your ration." The Spartan halted and performed a complete 360-degree awareness check of the room. There were more than 100 people inside, including guests, waiters and Secret Service agents. A large threat matrix, as the Spartan heard one Secret Service agent say. And there were too many people – and it was too bright inside – for thermal goggles to be of any use to spot potential tangos in invisibility suits.

"Still near 'Elvis'?" he said to Vasquez.

Vasquez laughed, a throaty, joyous laugh full of life. "That's not the correct code word for the President. But yes, I'm sitting in the empty chair. See if you can spot me."

The Spartan glanced towards the chair. There was indeed a seemingly empty seat beside the President – secretly occupied by an invisible Vasquez – at the ritzy dinner fundraising event at the Cathcart Hotel in Washington at 7.30pm. It was black tie, $5000 a head … and no press.

The Spartan thought he could detect Vasquez's presence, even if the other diners couldn't. (It was unlikely anyone from the Secret Service could, though. Vasquez had performed a dry run from Mancuso and his immediate circle. They had failed to spot her until she broke cover and tapped a tense-looking Mancuso on the shoulder. "You look like you're trying to stare through one of those old-fashioned X-ray specs," Vasquez had laughed.)

"Anyway, keep your head on a swivel," advised the Spartan.

"You too. And *try* to be nice to Mancuso. After all, he did spare us the standard polygraph and piss tests on the recommendation of the colonel."

The Spartan caught a glimpse of Mancuso in the corner. He stared back in a not-entirely friendly fashion. The Secret Service agent had paranoid eyes, constantly darting everywhere, looking for threats. "I didn't catch that last comment. You're breaking up."

"He already thinks you're some kind of throwback to a one-traffic light town."

"I'm a throwback to a no-traffic light town. Sparta."

"Don't I know it. And be careful with your SAW. Otherwise Mancuso won't get a 'I support the troops' tattoo on his back."

The Spartan stared at the diners tucking into their chicken parms, idly wondering how many had served their country in the armed forces. Probably not many. "Tough gig you've got, warming your ass on a chair."

"Any time you're ready, we can swap."

"A Spartan has no business wearing an invisibility suit." The Spartan briefly stared into the eyes of a waiter, who appeared to be watching him. Their eyes met, before the waiter quickly looked away. *Probably undercover Secret Service*, thought the Spartan.

"You're just afraid your ass is too fat to squeeze into one," joked Vasquez.

"Don't you mean my *culo*?"

Vasquez snickered. "So you've finally picked up some Spanish."

"Apart from the phrases I learnt from you, such as 'harder' and 'let's do it again'."

"In that case, I can recommend a few more when this is over. Anyway, enough grab-assing. Gotta get back to work. Out."

The Spartan and Vasquez had been assigned to guard duty only hours after talking to Mancuso. Tonight's brief: protect POTUS from assassins both visible and invisible. The Spartan would work the crowds. Vasquez would shadow the President himself. Jackson was outside guarding the Presidential limo.

Meanwhile, the Secret Service teams inside and outside the hotel were already briefed. They were stunned by the existence of the invisibility suits, but any complaints they had about working with someone wearing one would have to wait for later. Right now the Commander-in-Chief needed guarding. And they knew that any white ninja was on their side – any other color, including silver, was suspect.

Vasquez and Mancuso had conjured a rather cunning way of guarding the President. The large dining room had been divided into lines and sectors. Secret Security agents were tasked with regularly pacing along these lines and sectors. They moved so fast in an interlocking lattice than any invisible assassin would have little hope of crossing the distance without bumping into an agent and thereby becoming visible. Every square inch of the room had been accounted for. Vasquez had been impressed by how quickly the Secret Service had perfected their part in the plan.

The diners themselves, elite businessmen and women, political bigwigs, charitable worthies and One Per Centers, were becoming antsy at the constant movement, many curious glances being thrown in the direction of the moving agents. But the tactic was effective.

Vasquez doubted that she herself could have made it through the gauntlet.

"Looks like the President is getting up to speak," observed the Spartan.

"Yep. On it. Watch the room." POTUS got up out of his chair, waved to the clapping crowd and began to walk towards the podium. Vasquez carefully made her way up the podium beside him.

"You there, Vasquez?" whispered the President.

"Aye aye, sir," she whispered in return. "We've got your back. Knock 'em dead with your speech."

The President smiled, waved, waited for the applause to die down and made his way behind the podium. A bullet-proof shield protected him from any frontal assaults. The Spartan gripped his finger around the trigger of his SAW. If anything was going to happen, it was going to be soon.

"Ladies and gentlemen, thank you for coming," he said, eyes roaming over the crowd. "I'm very happy to see you all here tonight. As a nation, we have faced many difficulties lately … many obstacles to test us both individually and as a community. If you will indulge me, I'm reminded of a quote by Abraham Lincoln that I think is appropriate. He said …"

But the President didn't get to finish the rest of his sentence. Because something *did* happen.

* * *

All of a sudden the Spartan's gaze was drawn to the ceiling. His eyes were attracted to as-yet unspecified movement. He looked away to refresh his eyes, then refocused. Yes. Something felt wrong.

Ghost Armor wrong.

Then he saw it. A type of shimmer. An anomaly. A chameleon changing and masking its colors. High-tech trickery.

"Mancuso," ordered the Spartan, pulling out his SAW, "hit the power on the ceiling. There's a tango up there!"

Mancuso was quick on the uptake. "Roger!" he replied, gesturing to an unseen offsider.

At Vasquez and the Spartan's urging, Mancuso had had the ceiling of the dining room wired up, set to be electrified at a second's notice, just in case an intruder tried to crawl across it.

And such notice was now given.

Two figures in silver suits inching across the ceiling towards the President were now zapped with near-lethal current. They screamed as they became visible, lost their grip and plunged towards the tables, too stunned to perform any neat ninja acrobats to soften their fall.

The assassins crash-landed heavily on crowded tables, sending food, cutlery and crockery flying. There was more screaming as the horrified crowd beheld the strange intruders lying on the tables with their limbs askew.

Waiter, there's a ninja in my soup.

The Spartan was already in motion as the night warriors fell.

"Oh no you don't," said the Spartan as he slammed the butt of his SAW into a ninja's chin. It moaned yet still tried to get up, one hand up on the white tablecloth. The Spartan buttstroked the intruder even harder this time. The figure fell flat. The Spartan felt the ninja's pulse through the Ghost Armor. Yes. He was out. Alive, but out.

By now the President was being rushed out of the room, flanked by Secret Service agents and no doubt Vasquez. Meanwhile, the dinner guests were howling. This wasn't what they'd paid $5000 a head for. They wanted to press the flesh with the President – not have fried ninjas land in their food.

Some dived under tables. Others ran for the exit. Guns out, the Secret Service was doing its best to prevent a mass exodus and secure the room.

Meanwhile, at another table, five Secret Servicemen had seized the other ninja and wrestled it to the ground. Other Servicemen, including Mancuso, screamed orders as they pointed pistols around the room, searching for more hidden targets.

The Spartan hauled his unconscious captive towards Mancuso for disposal.

Meanwhile, the night warrior underneath the pack of Secret Service agents convulsed.

"Let him up! Let him breathe!" ordered Mancuso.

"What's happening?" shouted an agent.

"Damn, how do you open these suits?" shouted another.

The Spartan dropped his own ninja like a sack of deadly potatoes, pushed his way past and reached for the hidden zip on the cowl of the ninja's suit. He exposed the face of the ninja, who continued to thrash.

But it was too late. The ninja's mouth was covered by white foam. His eyes were rolled back. The shadow warrior convulsed once more and then lay still. Dead.

The Spartan stepped back from the body. "Suicide pill," he said.

"Fuck!" shouted Mancuso. "Shit!" An elderly woman screamed as she saw the body. The Spartan pulled the ninja's mask up over his face for decorum's sake.

"We still have one alive," said the Spartan, nodding towards his own unconscious captive. "Let's get him out of here and get the President to safety."

"Thank God for that, then," said Mancuso, relieved. He nodded towards some of the Secret Service agents. "You five, come with me. The rest of you lock this place down. I don't want anyone else coming or going." He nodded towards the dead ninja. "And someone get that body out of here."

Now it was just up to Vasquez and the other agents to get the President to safety.

Chapter 24

The leader couldn't take his eyes off the Spartan.

He had a front-seat view of his foe after smuggling himself into the Presidential dinner. Clad in a black suit, white shirt and red vest, the leader had assumed the identity of one of the waiters from the officially approved and vetted catering company.

The task had not been especially difficult: the art of disguise was a ninjutsu practitioner's meat and drink. Like all his elite shinobi, the leader was a master of *hensojutsu*, the ninja technique of disguise and impersonation. Contrary to Hollywood myth, the true art of the ninja was not dressing in black and climbing walls into impenetrable fortresses. No, it was hiding in plain sight, adopting another's identity, appearing to all and sundry to be anyone but who they really were.

He now looked exactly like the former – in all senses of the word – waiter. Neither his mother nor any facial recognition program would have recognised him.

Hiding in plain sight, the leader could observe the efforts of his other ninja, who were infiltrating the event with their invisibility suits. His choice of disguise meant that he had had to leave the mighty Honjo Masamune behind. However, his entire body was a weapon – his feet and hands deadly. He was never unable to defend himself.

Yet as he busied himself with the duties of a top-class waiter, pouring drinks and serving food, one eye on the crowd, the other on the well-guarded President of the United States, he came across a figure he instantly recognised from his group's stolen computer files.

The "Spartan".

This giant Tier 1 soldier featured prominently in the dossiers concerning the Mark 1 Ghost Armor. Evidently, this "Spartan" was the companion of the Ghost Armor's original owner, Teresa Vasquez. Much of his record had been classified, yet there was enough left within the redacted documents to suggest that this soldier with the unusual call sign was a formidable adversary.

Along with Vasquez, he was credited with foiling the Chinese canister conspiracy on North American soil. He personally defeated some of the so-called "Canister Six" in hand-to-hand combat, in particular the redoubtable figure known as the Monk. Truly, he was a warrior to be feared and respected.

As was Vasquez, who had battered his own companion during their recent encounter.

Looking at the Tier 1 soldier, the ninja fancied that the Spartan looked more Mongol than Spartan. There was something uncompromising in his stern features, something that reminded him of the horse-borne warriors that had plagued the ninja's homeland for so many decades. Yet the files did not explain why the Spartan had chosen that particular call sign.

The files contained something else about the Spartan. Something the leader had heard in whispers and half-traced conversations. Something that needed to be addressed. But that would have to come later.

The leader had also read that the Spartan had a penchant for blades: in particular, his Greek weapon, his *xiphos*. He wondered idly if he would get the chance to find out who was the better swordsman: he, with the Honjo Masamune, or the Spartan, with his *xiphos*. That would be a battle worthy of that legendary Japanese blade.

And a battle worthy of himself. Like the great Musashi of Japanese lore, the leader had been undefeated and undefeatable in swordplay from a very young age. Many of those battles had been deadly. The leader wondered if the Spartan would live up to his reputation in actual combat.

Sometimes the leader wondered if he lived in the right era. Maybe he would be better off living in the past, in the world of swords and honor. Perhaps even in Musashi's time. It was a thought he often returned to when facing the corruption and dishonor of his own era.

But now was not the time for such wool-gathering. He had a mission to complete.

As he served a corpulent businessman a cool beer, the fat tycoon roughly stuffed a $10 bill into the top of the leader's vest.

"Here ya go, pal," he sneered. "Go buy that Porsche you've always wanted." His companions laughed cruelly, their condescension for the lower classes echoing throughout the room.

And America liked to believe it was a classless society.

"Thank you, sir," replied the leader tonelessly, face blank. The ninja in him celebrated in the fact that the tycoon viewed him as a harmless wage slave – yet the warrior in him craved the respect that was every man's due.

For a second he indulged in the fantasy of striking the businessman's head from his body using the Honjo Masamune, sending a fountain of blood flying over the dog's companions. A pleasant thought. And certainly, honor would have demanded it.

Instead, he moved on to another table and its beckoning fingers, small women with big hair requiring refreshment. Then he locked his eyes onto the Spartan once again.

The leader found himself staring at the Spartan a little too long, a little too intently. This Spartan, he thought, seemed to possess a very old soul. The ninja felt a certain type of ultra-high frequency communication taking place between them, the silent dialogue of world-class warriors.

The leader remembered a line from the Spartan's file: "sugar is the downfall of America". He wasn't entirely wrong.

Then the American turned in his direction. That old soul regarded the leader harshly. The leader knew he had to act immediately to maintain his cover. Using all his mental skills of concealment, the leader compressed his *chi* to make himself appear insignificant, deferential, subservient. The Spartan stared a bit longer, as if he didn't quite believe this waiter was all he appeared to be … before finally turning away.

That was close, thought the leader.

The leader surveyed the dinner room once more. The one thing that stood out was the odd movement of the Secret Service. They were moving in a formulaic, almost mathematical manner. It did not follow their normal protocol. To see humans walking in such straight lines like machines seemed … unnatural.

Then it came to him. The agents had divided the room up into sectors and were rapidly moving through each grid reference, each checkpoint, as to deny any invisible walker passage. They had formulated their own defenses against Ghost Armor intrusions.

Any ninja attempting a ground assault was bound to collide with at least one agent. And any collision would instantly render the wearer visible.

Clever.

No doubt this Vasquez had helped concoct the plan.

Too bad she hadn't been slain right at the start.

The leader dared another look at the Spartan again, drawn to the other most dangerous man in the room. And his heart sank where he saw where the Spartan was looking. The roof. The ninjas' Plan B.

The Spartan said something into his throat microphone.

A few seconds later the two night warriors screamed and plummeted downward, landing heavily on tables. The leader watched, impotent, as the Spartan struck one of the ninjas with the butt of his machinegun, then again. The ninja went limp. The other ninja was seized by several Secret Service men.

Why had they fallen, wondered the leader. Had they been shocked by some unknown device?

By now the room was filled with screaming and agents with their guns out. The President was being rushed outside. Perhaps the other members of the strike team would have success. But it was time for the leader to leave. It grieved him to leave his men behind, but there was nothing he could do for them. They knew they would face 1000 dangers during their tour of duty, any one of them fatal, going into this almost suicidal mission with their eyes open.

Just as the leader walked rapidly towards the exit, the Secret Security agents swarmed towards the other ninja, who began convulsing. The ninja had chosen to take his L-Pill. The distraction bought the leader enough time to escape the dining room, carrying a silver tray in front of him.

However, he was soon stopped by two Secret Service agents with their guns out. But the barrels weren't pointing at him. Yet.

"We can't let anybody go past, sir," ordered the tallest. "Please return to the dining room."

"But people are dying in there!" the leader complained in faux terror.

"Sir, don't make us repeat ourselves," said the other agent brusquely. "This is a security lock-down. We ..."

Almost faster than the human eye could follow, the leader plucked two steak knives from the tray and plunged them straight into the agents' throats. The strikes were flawlessly fatal. As the agents gasped and fell, the leader caught the tray, lest the noise betray his presence.

Then, still carrying the tray, he escaped.

Chapter 25

Vasquez had done her homework for this scenario. She had scoped out the route where the President would be evacuated if the merde hit the fan and located the best place for any invisible ninjas to strike ... as well as her own counter position. Thus prepared, she had raced ahead of the Secret Service detail hustling the President out, climbed up to the ceiling, pulled out two blades, concealed them in her sleeves and straddled the walls in a starfish position.

Now, as invisible as a poor person in Tiffany's, she waited.

Soon she sensed movement below. There were two invisible bogeys coming along the corridor. She could even smell them. A foreign musk. Ghost Armor fabric and body odor. Vasquez waited until she guessed they were directly below her, then fell downwards.

One of her blades plunged into the neck of a silver ninja. The ninja immediately became visible, soaked with arterial blood. The other blade missed, Vasquez's arm stretching over the shoulder of the other ninja, which likewise lost its camouflage.

The stricken night warrior was out of the picture, Vasquez's blade strike true and deadly. But the second ninja wasn't waiting around for similar treatment. It grabbed Vasquez's wrist and firmly twisted the remaining blade out of her hand. Still holding her wrist, the ninja kicked Vasquez in the stomach, then the head, and threw her into the wall.

Ouch.

Vasquez moved aside as a fist came towards her face, hitting the wall instead. She blocked a backwards kick to her stomach, caught the foot as it came towards her face and swept the other leg out from under the ninja. She made to stomp on the ninja's throat, but the ninja dodged, span on its back, kicked Vasquez in the jaw, then flipped back onto its feet.

"You," hissed the ninja.

It was the same shadow warrior who had tried to poison Vasquez. The female phantom.

The *kunoichi.*

"Me, bitch," said Vasquez with equal venom. She stretched out her hands like monkey's paws.

The ninja launched a flurry of punches towards Vasquez's face and body. One by one, Vasquez blocked them. Then, remembering that she had shot the ninja the last time they had met, she slammed a fist into the ninja's wounded shoulder. Vasquez's efforts were rewarded as the *kunoichi* cried out in pain. This allowed Vasquez time to nail her with a flying knee to the head. The *kunoichi's* head snapped back.

Vasquez performed a handstand, grabbed the ninja's head between her legs, and pulled her whole body down to the ground. The ninja gasped as Vasquez applied inexorable pressure to the ninja's throat, her strong leg muscles choking the *kunoichi.* It was almost the perfect technique to render an opponent unconscious. Almost.

The ninja plucked a small blade from her costume and tried to strike Vasquez's femoral artery, where even the smallest nick could be fatal. Sensing danger, Vasquez allowed her leg grip to weaken as she reached down to grab the blade. The *kunoichi* seized the chance to kick Vasquez in the middle of her face, throwing her *chi* into the blow. The kick landed full force. Vasquez's left eye socket hummed in pain.

The *kunoichi* escaped the leg lock and flipped up onto her feet, standing over the stunned Vasquez. A cornucopia of unprotected vital points lay exposed to her trained hands. Yet before she could strike she could hear footsteps running down the hall. The Secret Service were almost upon her.

The *kunoichi* could attempt to kill Vasquez or escape, but not both.

With a curse in her native language, she chose escape.

Chapter 26

The Spartan and Vasquez were driving behind the Presidential motorcade after it had fled the hotel. The pair were in the back of the motorcade: the President's limo – nicknamed "The Beast" for its size and formidable array of protections and armor – was still visible down the road, flanked by multiple blacked-up SUVs, racing down the streets to a programmed sea of green lights.

Much had happened in the past 30 minutes. On the plus side of the ledger: an attempt on the President's life thwarted. One suspect in custody. Three Ghost Armor knock-offs recovered. The Spartan and Vasquez both safe.

And on the minus side? Two of the suspects were dead, one while in custody. Two more Secret Service men had been killed by an assailant disguised as a waiter, the murderer currently at large. Vasquez had taken a champion beating. And despite a huge security effort involving credential checks, sniffer dogs, sniper teams and men on the ground, the ninjas had still penetrated the President's inner sanctum. Without the Spartan's quick thinking and Vasquez's neutralizing of the second ninja team, it didn't bear thinking about.

Mancuso was also furious by the way Garin's men had treated him. After he had learned that they'd secured three of the Ghost Armor copies, Garin had sent a dozen heavily armed operatives to collect the suits. Mancuso had insisted that they were part of his evidence chain and had to remain with him, but Garin's men had insisted: even, somewhat ominously, cocking their machineguns.

Were they really about to fire on the Secret Service if they didn't get their way?

This had led to an angry stand-off, men snarling and bearing their teeth like baboons from a National Geographic documentary. The stand-off had gone all the way up to the President, who had sided with Garin. Saving his life was one thing, POTUS had said. But getting these suits off the streets was also vitally important. He was willing to defer to Garin in this case. The Secret Service had reluctantly handed over the Ghost Armors.

"Your boss comes across like he's everyone's favorite uncle, but he's as crazy as you are, Spartan!" Mancuso fumed over the phone.

"Don't insult my commanding officer," warned the Spartan as Vasquez drove. "And be grateful we were there to stop those ninjas. I even kept one alive for you … unlike your pals."

"Thanks. Now go stick a pineapple up your ass, Spartan." Then Mancuso hung up.

Moments later Garin called.

"Well done, comrades," Garin said. "I think it's safe to say you saved the President's life. And I know he's grateful. Spartan, nice work spotting those ninjas on the ceiling."

"Ninjas, sir? I thought they were mimes."

"Heh. And Vasquez, well done stopping the second team."

"Thank you sir," said the warrior in question.

"You say you faced the other ninja from before?"

"Yes, sir. I ended up with a few more bruises this time. I could do with an ice bath."

"What about Jackson?" said the Spartan. "Did he see any action?"

"Negative. POTUS is now safe in 'The Beast'. And that thing can withstand everything from a landmine to a RPG round." There was crackling over the phone as they ran over a speed bump. "Anything else we need to talk about?"

"No, sir."

"Vasquez?"

"No, colonel. All good. Apart from the bruises and the bruised ego."

"Then I'd better get off the horn. Stay with the President's team for now. He's one of the main targets – but something tells me he's not the only one. Hopefully we'll find out more from the suspect the Spartan brought in. And Spartan?

"Yes, sir?"

"Try not to aggravate Mancuso too much. He's already enough of a martyr."

"I'll try, sir."

"Good man. Garin out."

The Spartan waited a minute until after Garin hung up. Then he offered his own opinion on the situation.

"That's twice you've fought this ninja and she's still not dead," he noted with displeasure. "What's the matter?"

"Nothing's the matter," she replied, irritated that her competency was being challenged. "She's good. Special forces good – like you told Mancuso."

"She's too dangerous to live."

"Don't you think I know that?" said Vasquez archly, stealing a glance at him in the mirror.

"Just make sure to put her in the ground the next time."

Vasquez turned to the Spartan. "I don't recall giving you such a hard time when the Monk kicked your ass." The Spartan said nothing. "Got no comeback for that, have you?"

"I defeated the Monk in the end," he said eventually.

"After you had another shot. So give me one, lover." Vasquez swerved savagely around a corner. "She'll get more than a titty twister next time. Trust me."

Chapter 27

The leader and his lover were licking their assorted wounds in one of their many safe houses around the nation. They lay naked in bed in each other's arms. Outside, the leader's men busied themselves with training and research. Inside, the leader ruminated about their failure. Apparently, it wasn't an easy thing to kill a President.

"Curse them and their interference," said the leader.

His companion ran a finger over his muscular back and its many mystical tattoos. "You mean, Vasquez and this 'Spartan'?"

"Yes." The leader's back tensed up. His lover knew what was coming next. "If only you had killed Vasquez during your initial attack. We may have succeeded. They never would have come up with a plan to foil the Ghost Armor so quickly."

"We don't know that," said his No.2 cautiously.

"This Spartan would have been grieving over the loss of his love. He would never have been assigned to the President's security team, never would have spotted our men on the roof."

"We don't know that for sure, either," said the No.2, nestling deeper into the leader's chest despite being criticised. "And besides, the death of the President is only one part of the mosaic. The *gwailo* must suffer in other ways, too."

"Yes. The other plans are in motion. Fortunately, our missing brother doesn't know the details of those plans."

"Do you think he will talk?" asked the No.2.

The leader summoned an image of the captured shinobi. Yes, the ninja was fierce and exceptional, like all his team. Yet just because he was a ninja and a special forces operative, that didn't mean he was beyond the power and influence of the enemy.

"Possibly. Even a ninja can be made to speak. Every man has a breaking point." The leader seemed to sigh. "Still, our losses are below our projections for this stage of the plan."

"We fight with our hearts. We fight for our country."

"Yes." The leader paused, then said: "You have failed to kill this Vasquez twice now."

The No.2 got up on one elbow. "Are you officially reprimanding me?"

"Do I need to? Why have you not succeeded? Are you not up to the task? Must I remind you of the stakes involved?"

"That was unnecessary. Of course I know them."

"Is it because you were fighting a woman?"

"I find that question insulting."

"Then why have you failed again?"

"There is no why. She is an exceptional combatant, just like the dossiers said." The leader grunted sceptically, but she continued: "I had her on her back, wounded and ready to die. I had a choice: kill her and die at the hands of the Secret Service ... or escape to fight on."

"I see. Hunh."

The leader's grunting provoked his lover. "Why do you suddenly doubt me? You sound like my father … only he was angry because I never got married like a good traditional girl."

"You know I can't be seen to go easy on you. The men will suspect me of playing favorites."

"None of the 'men' would have done any better than I did."

The leader nodded. "I am aware of that."

The No.2 grabbed the leader's head and made him look into her eyes. "Would you have preferred that I died?"

"As your commander, I want you to do whatever is necessary without regard to your own life," he said. Then he pulled her close. "But as your lover, I am glad you chose escape. You know how important you are to … the team."

"Just so," said his No.2 with a soft smile, leaning back on his chest, listening to his unnaturally slow heartbeat. "I hope 'the team' knows I feel the same way."

"I suspect 'the team' does."

"Do you imagine that the Spartan and Vasquez are having this same discussion wherever they are?"

"Perhaps." The leader's eyes flickered to the Honjo Masamune, lying on a ceremonial dais nearby. "I hope to kill this Spartan himself. Not only for his meddling but for his past crimes. I now believe for sure he killed our master. He must be avenged."

"Yes," agreed his lover. "Let us make this pact: I will kill Vasquez and you will slay the Spartan. Then honor will be satisfied." She reached over to touch the silver cross hanging on his neck. "Have faith."

"Though my faith is sorely tested on occasion, it always returns."

"Just so." She reached over and brought his lips to hers. "Now come here."

Chapter 28

Homeland Security's Colonel Garin wasn't in charge of the interrogation of the would-be Presidential assassin. That had fallen under the purview of another security agency: an agency whose name, much like Lord Voldemort of the Harry Potter books, people didn't like to speak aloud in case it brought bad luck.

Such a decision was further proof that Garin's exclusive grip on the managing of the affair was slipping: blowback from the meeting at the White House Situation Room.

Still, Garin didn't object too strenuously. He found interrogation the least savory part of his job. Sometimes he wished he was still out there kicking asses and taking names like the old days in special forces: just like the Spartan was, unburdened by such problems as bureaucracy and accountability.

So Garin was just one of several faces peering through one-way glass into the bare room, watching the captured ninja being strapped to a bed.

The room opposite was wired for sound. Beside the captured ninja were various shiny medical instruments, plus a single chair.

And sitting in the chair was a man Garin had never met before. In fact, no one in the other room had.

A neon sign above Garin's head flickered on: "Room in use".

It was time for the game of truth to begin.

Interrogating the ninja proved to be a conundrum. Sure, they had quickly removed the ninja's suicide pill – but, judging by the fact that one of the ninja's accomplices had already used his own, it was a safe bet that this one would also attempt to commit suicide at the earliest convenience.

However, the very same acronym agency that was running the show had come up with an ingenious idea. An idea that didn't involve all the Guantanamo Bay trappings of shackles, ear plugs, blindfolds and adult diapers.

An idea Garin was most interested to see in action.

Garin watched through the glass as the ninja's Ghost Armor was removed, then carried away as delicately as if the carrier was clutching the Shroud of Turin.

"Their suits are just like ours, only silver," said a bloodless bureaucrat behind Garin. "You think they would have done something different."

"What, like put a fucking racing stripe down the side?" said Garin sarcastically.

The ninja's face now came into view. The shadow warrior was young, bruised and Chinese.

"A Chinese ninja?" said one voice.

"Is anybody really surprised by that after what happened last year?" said yet another.

This time Garin had to agree with the anonymous observation. If there was any silver lining to the current clusterfuck, it was that everyone's focus was back squarely on where it belonged – China. That country was going to be their main challenge for decades to come. The US and its allies had already wasted too much time and treasure dicking around in the Middle East. The future would be thrashed out in Asia. And that was where the US should be looking.

"Maybe they should play a bass solo," said a voice behind him.

"Why?"

"Because everyone talks during a bass solo."

Boom boom.

The colonel laughed despite himself, then turned his attention back to the interrogation. From what he could gather, the treatment of the ninja would be two-pronged. The first prong consisted of an IV full of a secret drug that was attached to the vein in his arm. The efficacy of this drug was supposedly enhanced by the electricity applied to the subject's brain via electrodes.

The ninja had not been allowed to regain consciousness after the Spartan's battering. Instead, he was kept in a state somewhere between consciousness and unconsciousness. It was in this twilight state that the drug would work its magic, making him talk as if he was addressing a friend or colleague.

The total effect had been likened to having a sound system attached to the subject's dreams.

Now the state was tapping people's very subconscious, thought Garin.

A phrase came to Garin's mind: "e-torture". *How very modern,* he thought sarcastically. He suddenly felt very old.

Garin watched as the first of the interrogators, sitting in the chair, began asking the ninja pre-prepared questions.

A ferret-faced man in a white coat observed Garin's baffled expression. "The aim is that one of our recruits will sound like one of the ninja's associates so he believes he's just having a normal conversation," he said. "The trick is getting the voice right in the first place. We have no idea what the ninja's friends sound like, so we have gathered what we hope is a wide sample. Let's see how they do."

Garin and the crowd watched as mostly Chinese-looking men filed in through the door, trying to hack the ninja's mind.

"I don't know you," said the ninja in Mandarin to the first voice, refusing to talk any further. Another volunteer was sent in.

"I have nothing to say to you," said the ninja to the second man.

"Go to hell, impostor," said the ninja to the third voice.

The ninja failed to react at all to the fourth or fifth voices.

"Hattori Hanzo," replied the ninja to the sixth man, who had dared to ask his name. Garin guffawed when he heard that, being the only man in the room to recognise the name of the legendary 16th-century ninja bad-ass who was also known as "the ninja's ninja".

There was a pause, as the interrogators tried to guess what part of China the ninja had come from.

"Increase the dose and the current," commanded a voice from behind the window.

It wasn't until the 10th man was sent in that they had luck. The ninja turned to face the voice.

"Here we go," said the "scientist", observing the positive reaction. "Now the ninja's subconscious will match the voice with a figure from its memory and create a narrative." He turned up the volume on a speaker on the wall. "Let's watch and listen."

"Ri? Is that you?" said the ninja, a note of hope in his slurred voice.

"Yes. We are safe. The President is dead."

"It is almost hard to believe. Killing such an important man." There was a pause. "The last thing I remember was being on the roof."

"The others gave their lives so we could escape."

"They died for the homeland."

"They died as heroes."

"The plan continues, then?"

"The plan continues."

"What does the leader want from us, then, now that our part is over?"

"He wants us to return home."

"Return home?" said the ninja, confused. "But we can't go back to China. We'd be executed immediately, for what we did in Taiwan."

The interrogator paused and raised a hand to his ear, receiving instructions from his handlers. "What we did in Taiwan was necessary."

"Yes. We had to make sure Commander Lee's plan succeeded." The ninja paused. "Wait ... what? Why are we talking about this? It is against orders. I ... I feel strange." The ninja suddenly went quiet. The men in the room opposite looked at each other, disturbed by the information that Commander Lee was involved.

But Garin was no longer in the room.

He'd run out soon as he'd heard the name Commander Lee.

Which meant the ninjas were the ones that let off the plague bombs in Taiwan. Which meant they were the second team that had never been accounted for.

Which meant, Garin thought with a rapid flash of paranoia, that his men were in danger.

"Get me a goddamn outside line!" he screamed.

Chapter 29

Thousands of miles away, in an off-the-books location overseas, the SEAL team Garin had used to hunt down and kill Commander Lee in China were relaxing in their living quarters. They were sweaty and tired, having just completed a five-mile run in full combat gear before poring over maps for tomorrow's op.

In less than 24 hours they would be hitting their targets during Operation Kingdom Come. But for now it was time to chill out and relax. It was beer and poker time.

Monkey, Whale and Puffer were on special assignment elsewhere, but the other remaining members of the team such as Dukey, Apache, Halen, Zero and Joker were in attendance. In all, seven men were in the living quarters.

Despite the plague, they hadn't been called to fulfil their primary mission: capture Pakistan's nuclear silos from trigger-happy extremists. But that didn't mean they hadn't been busy. They were busier than ever. The tempo of special operations was intense.

Dukey, Apache, Halen and Zero amused themselves with Texas Hold 'Em. Longbow and Backpack were taking naps.

Joker was on his laptop, looking at emails and pictures from home, replying with just enough information to satisfy his wife's curiosity but not enough to make her worry.

Joker, the team's unofficial leader, felt restless. He had received Colonel Garin's communique that the Ghost Armor technology was in the hands of secret enemies. He and his comrades had already "seen" how effective the armor could be during spec ops, courtesy of Teresa Vasquez. The thought that strange villains were out there using American tech against them – hiding in invisibility, waiting to strike – was disturbing.

He glanced around the room.

In theory, he and his men should be safe, fighting insurgents in a country where Americans weren't officially there. They weren't the only soldiers on the base, either. And they were special forces, bad-ass killers, the best of the best. Surely no one would fuck with them. Or even find them.

And yet ...

It was always the "and yet" that kept you awake at night. And kept you alive during a firefight.

For some reason Joker's eyes were drawn to the doorway.

And yet ...

"Hey, fellas, who left the door open?" he said. "We don't live in a barn." Leaving the door open was against regulations. It was a security risk. It was sloppy. It was a mistake waiting to happen.

"I bet it was Dukey," smirked the avuncular Apache. Dukey threw some poker chips at Apache. "Go on, you lazy fuck, close the door. And get me another beer." Apache grabbed an empty beer can, crushed it against his head, then tossed it at Dukey.

"Fuck you. It wasn't me. And I'm not your maid." The other men in the room laughed. Longbow and Backpack continued to sleep.

But Joker stared at his M4A1. It had "because karma takes too long" written on the barrel. Wise words and true.

And yet …

He went for his M4A1.

And then the shooting began.

The three ninjas who had snuck into the room became visible. They trained their silenced machineguns on the poker game, the location with the most targets. Dukey gasped as Apache's head exploded. That was the last thing he ever saw as rounds struck him in the chest.

Halen was shot in the back as he tried to dive for cover.

Backpack and Longbow never woke. They were gunned down in their beds.

Zero quick-drew a pistol and leapt to the side like Chow-Yun Fat. He shot a ninja in the shoulder and another in the side of the head. Yet it was a brief moment of heroism. The three ninja – including the one hit in the head, still up and moving in an amazing feat of strength – trained their weapons on Zero and ghosted him.

Joker raised his M4A1 and fired from cover, screaming all the while. His rounds found the head-shot ninja, putting him down for good.

The other ninjas rolled and flipped aside out of the way of his bullets. Outraged by the death of his friends, Joker continuing screaming and firing. Yet the shadow warriors evaded his rounds with stunning acrobatics.

Click. He was out.

As Joker reloaded, a ninja tossed a chained, sickle-like weapon at his gun hand. Before the Tier 1 soldier could react, the ninja drew the weapon back towards him, severing Joker's trigger finger and another next to it. Joker barely had time to glance at the space where his fingers used to be when the other ninjas shot him across the sternum.

Joker collapsed beside a bed.

The ninjas emerged from cover, nodded to each other and walked towards Joker. He was slumped face-down on the ground, blood pooling beneath him.

"It is done," said one in Mandarin, as alarms rang in the background.

"Three were missing," said the other.

"It does not matter. Their team is destroyed. Commander Lee is avenged."

Just then Joker rolled over. In his hands he held two fragmentation grenades with the pins pulled.

"See you in hell," he said.

The ninjas reeled back in shock.

Then the grenades went off.

* * *

The special forces soldier known as Monkey found the bodies first.

Seeing the ravaged corpses of his teammates, something in him snapped.

He decided three things on the spot.

First, those responsible must die.

Second, he would now pursue his secret desires, the ones he had held back for so long.

And thirdly, he would tell no one about his plans.

* * *

The General was at a black-tie special forces dinner in Washington when it happened.

Colonel Garin entered the room in his usual confident manner.

Someone booed. Loudly.

Garin stopped in his tracks, stunned.

Then another soldier booed. And another.

Word had spread. The special forces community had learnt that Garin had used Joker's team for an off-the-books attack on China. An attack that had resulted in blowback. An attack that had led to the deaths of Joker and his team by invisible, suited-up assassins.

More, they had heard that Garin was responsible for guarding the invisibility suits. Now formidable killers were murdering special forces soldiers using that very same technology. It was hunting season on America's best and bravest. All because of him. And as legendary as Garin was in that community, a Jedi Knight of bad-assery, his special forces peers weren't happy.

There was more jeering and bad vibes. Soon a third of the room was catcalling. Others tried to tell them to shut up, saying Joker and his team died doing their duty … but the catcallers weren't having it. Colonel Garin was about as popular in the room as "Hanoi Jane" Fonda.

For the first time ever in the General's experience, Garin looked distraught. The rejection of his precious special forces peers hurt Garin worse than any bullet.

Then, with the magic of paranoia, Garin's eyes found the General's.

The General smiled. And raised his glass to Garin.

This was the sweetest wine ever, he thought.

Chapter 30

Commander Lee had always had two teams.

The first, made up of his toughest soldiers. His tank units, as it were, led by the indomitable Monk.

And the second, his stealth units, his ninjutsu specialists, under the command of the leader.

Only one team would ever get the prized assignment of taking the plague canisters to the United States.

The other team would be sent to Taiwan instead.

Both teams were full of men who respected and admired Commander Lee and wanted to fulfil his mission.

Both teams wanted the American assignment.

Commander Lee told them to fight it out among each other.

In the end, it had come down to the Monk and the leader. One, a specialist in hand-to-hand combat, a master of the empty palm. The other, a master of edged weapons, in particular the Honjo Masamune.

The Monk had already broken many bones and fractured several skulls from the rival team.

The leader had rendered a number of the other team combat ineffective.

In the end, the commander had decided that their different specialties and high, deadly levels of expertise meant that the leader and the Monk couldn't literally fight it out. A true battle between the two men could lead to one of their deaths.

It was stalemate.

So Commander Lee went back and thought hard over which team to send.

It had insulted the leader's sense of pride that the Monk and his team were even being considered over his. The Monk was an orphan, even lower than a bastard. The leader's own heritage was illustrious: he could trace his lineage back to the heroes of the Boxer Rebellion and Mao's Long March. Who was this Monk, with all his Shaolin tricks and secret haughtiness, compared to him? He was an oddity without ancestors. The Monk reminded him of the rough, low peasant boys that tormented the leader as a youth, until the day he discovered his destiny by picking up a blade and making their blood run free.

Yet for some unfathomable reason, Commander Lee sent the Monk's team to America.

The leader was struck by a thought as old as time ... why him and not me?

Yet the Monk's team had failed in its mission.

The leader's team had succeeded.

And now the leader's team was left to continue Commander Lee's work. The commander had hoped that the plague would cripple America, but he had always left room for a Plan B.

This was to be the leader's mission.

And that mission had only just begun.

Many more would die before it was over.

Chapter 31

"What's the password?"

"You're an asshole."

"That's not correct," said the large, scowling Secret Service Agent.

"It's good enough," replied the Spartan. "You know who we are. You see anyone else around here dressed in black ops gear?"

"The password is 'liberty'," said Vasquez coolly.

"Thank you, Vasquez," said the agent. "You're cleared to continue." The agent and his armed partner walked past the Spartan and Vasquez, briefly touching their ears to receive new instructions from their comms.

Vasquez waited until the disgruntled duo were out of earshot, then said: "Was that necessary?"

"Necessary?" wondered the Spartan, holding his SAW in his hands as they patrolled the front of the house. "No. Enjoyable? Maybe."

"You shouldn't needle the Secret Service," said Vasquez, holding her MP-5 as they walked. "We're working for them."

"Working *with* them. They're our partners, not the other way around."

"What exactly is it about them that bugs you?"

The Spartan looked over his shoulder at the retreating agents. "Look at those suits and sensible shoes. They remind me of Boy Scouts."

Vasquez smiled, white teeth showing. "Boy Scouts that carry Glocks instead of cookies. I think we can both agree that we have the same goal in protecting the President. Yeah?"

The Spartan didn't say anything, just shifted the SAW in his hands. She could tell he wasn't particularly happy about being put on glorified guard duty.

"Think of this as just another chapter in our adventures. We're like a military version of Bonnie and Clyde. Well, maybe *Bonita* and Clyde."

The Spartan, Vasquez and Jackson had joined the retinue of Secret Service agents guarding the President at Mary's Lookout, a Spanish Mission meets Bauhaus meets money hotel that Jackson had called "upper-class cracker heaven". Mary's Lookout was once prominently featured on an episode of *Lifestyles of the Rich and Famous*, before that show was cancelled, possibly for fomenting anger among the 99 per cent at the decadent lifestyles that 1 per cent tended to live.

But the trio wasn't there to sample the award-winning wine, the meals from the cordon bleu chef or the lavish interiors. Odds were good that the ninjas would try to attack POTUS again, and Colonel Garin had wanted the three of them – the soldiers with the most experience in fighting the suited foes – there.

Fortunately, all the guests had been cleared, the frantic owner promised she would be compensated for her loss of revenue. There were no pain-in-the-ass civilians, which made it pretty much a free fire zone (assuming Uncle Sam was going to pick up the bill for any damages). It was just the Spartan, Vasquez, Jackson, the President of the United States of America, his wife, a cook, a maid and dozens of Secret Service agents.

Quite the little soiree.

Now it was just a question of whether the ninjas would RSVP.

"Do you think they saw the bait?" asked Vasquez.

"Probably. Stay tuned for another exciting instalment of *When Ninjas Attack.*"

The "bait" had consisted of carefully planted news items mentioning that the President would be staying in Martha's Vineyard. There had been accompanying footage of the hotel, along with the Spartan and Vasquez briefly appearing in several frames. If the ninjas had seen it, they would know where to strike next.

Where the Spartan and Vasquez would be waiting for them.

There were dozens of agents spread out over the surrounding acres. A first perimeter of guards out near the roads stretching out for a mile away. Then another ring within 500 feet of the hotel. Another ring was outside the hotel, with the Spartan and Vasquez patrolling there, and more Secret Service agents inside, joined by Jackson.

But not everyone was happy with the trio's presence. It was clear that the Secret Service didn't want them around. The Spartan had insulted their leader Mancuso. He had also "insulted" them by being the first to spot the ninjas on the ceiling, which should have been their job.

And their mere presence there was an insult, because it implied that they needed outsiders to do their job for them.

"Do you like this place?" asked Vasquez as they completed a circle and began again.

"Not an ideal location to defend. It's exposed on too many sides. I'm not sure how 'hardened' the structure is." The Spartan stared out at flat fields, with trees in the distances. "Plus, I think they should set up some mortars here. Good for defending the building."

"That's not what I meant. I was thinking we could stay here. We can spend some of the Spartan millions."

"There are no Spartan millions. The Spartans didn't believe in money. They made their currency so big and unwieldy no one would want it."

"I was kidding," said Vasquez with a smile. "Anyway, maybe they'd comp us after we're done here."

"Does this place have a gym? I didn't see one during our recce."

"No ... but it does have awesome guest rooms and amazing restaurants. I hear the amuse-bouches are out of this world."

The Spartan turned to Vasquez. "If you need me to amuse your bush, Vasquez, you only have to ask."

Vasquez groaned. "That joke is so bad it almost qualifies as an X-rated 'dad' joke." Vasquez suddenly had a curious look on her face. "One thing I've always wanted to ask you ..."

"Go ahead."

"You know how to make love. Quite well, actually."

"Thanks," said the Spartan, face a blank.

"I was surprised that first time. I expected you to be all thumbs. You didn't learn all that from special forces, did you?"

"If they taught that in special forces, I must have missed the class."

"So … someone clearly taught you how to please a woman."

"They did." The Spartan's face still wasn't giving anything away.

"And?"

"And what?"

"Who was it?"

Now the Spartan's lips almost curled into a smile. "That's a story for another time. A vacation story, perhaps."

"As long as we va-cay someplace with a gym, right?"

The Spartan nodded.

"Gotta keep that fitness up … otherwise you could get kicked out of Sparta for being overweight, right?"

The Spartan flashed her a half-amused look. "You've been hitting the history books again."

"Fancy publicly ridiculing in the streets citizens who were overweight," said Vasquez, shaking her head. "If they did that in America half of the country would be afraid to go outside."

"Maybe they should go outside every once in a while instead of sitting at computers all day."

"At least we don't have desk jobs," said Vasquez. "I like being outdoors." She glanced around at the scenery. "It's kind of pretty here."

"Pretty exposed. I would have preferred to put barbed wire around this whole place, dig some trenches. String up some Claymores."

"Do you really think that would stop our ninjas?"

"No."

Vasquez flicked a look over the Spartan's shoulder. "Great … here comes the third wheel."

Just then Jackson walked towards them from the house, making a show of zipping up his fly.

"That agent was a wildcat!" he said. "And a redhead. Something else to cross off the bucket list." Then, as if he was reminding himself of some important personal errand, he said: "Got to get me more of that Secret Service strange."

But if he thought his announcement was going to win him respect, kudos or even a high five, Jackson had chosen the wrong audience.

"We're supposed to be on guard duty, Jackson," said the Spartan coldly. "Where's your weapon?"

Jackson grabbed his crotch. "Right here."

"You're disgusting," said Vasquez.

Jackson laughed. He made a show of touching the tip of his nose with his tongue. "Hey, I give as good as I get."

"Enough," growled the Spartan. "You're on duty here. Cut the shit. Stop thinking with the 'little head'."

"There's nothing on me that's little, Spartan," crowed Jackson. Vasquez rolled her eyes. Jackson stood there, as if waiting for a retort from the Spartan. "Nice comeback," he said eventually.

The Spartan slowly extended his middle finger.

"Why are you even here?" said Vasquez. "I mean, did I miss seeing the Bat Signal over Commissioner Gordon's office or something?"

"He's here because the colonel ordered him to be here," said the Spartan dryly.

Now it was Jackson's turn to flip the bird.

Just then six Secret Service agents came down the driveway. They were a tight-knit group, huddled close together shoulder-to-shoulder in the manner of angry mobs everywhere. All that was missing were the flaming torches and pitchforks.

"Friends of yours, Jackson?" drawled the Spartan.

"Why do I get the feeling they're not about to ask us if we have any special dietary, medical or religious requirements?" said Vasquez dryly.

"Run," said Jackson in mock fright, "it's Five-O."

"Hey, you! Asshole!" said one.

"Looks like they're talking to you, Jackson," observed the Spartan. Black, white, Hispanic, Asian … Jackson had seemingly offended a veritable UN of Secret Service agents.

"Yes, you, Jackson," said the tallest and meanest looking as they came within 10 feet. And considering they were all tall and mean-looking and built like line-backers, that was quite a distinction. "What the hell do you think you were just doing in there?"

"None of your business," uttered Jackson.

"Fraternising with a Secret Service agent is forbidden within the ranks," insisted the ringleader. "That means it's doubly forbidden for the likes of you. Jesus wept … POTUS is in the building. Our Commander-in-Chief. I can't tell you how *wrong* what you just did was. Show some goddamn respect."

"Hey, it's not like I boned the First Lady," taunted Jackson. His face took on a cunning look. "Besides, don't try to pretend the Secret Service have never been bad boys before. We all know they have been. I read the papers."

But no one was touching that one. Not even the ringleader.

Instead, he turned to the Spartan and pointed. "Don't think we approve of you, either, Scotsman."

"Scotsman … heh," snickered Jackson.

"My name is *Spartan*."

"I know, guy," said the agent, pulling a face. "We heard what you said about our men being pussies. What a helpful thing to say from an alleged ally. They died as heroes protecting the Vice President, asshole."

"You're pushing it," said the Spartan laconically.

But the agent wasn't finished. "What did you say, 'They weren't special forces'? I hear a bunch of your guys got aired out by the ninjas as well. And they were your *precious* special forces. So what was *their* excuse? Weren't they *special* enough?"

The Spartan's face froze. Something cold came over his eyes. He saw red, black, purple and all the other colors of combat. His huge hands became fists.

Jackson gazed at the Spartan's bunched-up mitts. "*Now* you've done it. Don't you know he's like the Hulk? You shouldn't make him angry. You won't like him when he's angry." Jackson stared at the Spartan again. "Well, you'll like him *less* when he's angry."

Sensing danger, or maybe just heeding Jackson's warning, the Secret Service men fanned out. If they knew they'd just said the wrong thing, they weren't about to apologize. The bad blood had been brewing between the Spartan's retinue and the Secret Service. Now it was coming to a boil, no matter what their superiors had to say about it.

Jackson cracked his neck from side to side. "What we have here is a failure to communicate."

"So we're doing this?" said Vasquez as she looked at the Spartan for confirmation.

The Spartan lowered his SAW and pulled his combat gloves tight. "Correct."

"They're the Secret Service, Spartan," she warned.

"So what?" answered Jackson.

"Uhh, they protect the President," explained Vasquez. "They're the good guys."

"We need to have this discussion first to clear the air," said the Spartan, watching the men around him move into position. "Plus they insulted special forces. There's special forces and there's everyone else. And *they're* everyone else."

"Go on, come at us with that overrated *Karate Kid* shit," taunted one agent. "We're trained to deal with assholes like you."

"No ... you're *not*," insisted the Spartan.

Yet there was another dynamic at play here, one not necessarily apparent to the Spartan's colleagues. In his mind, one had to defend one's honor whatever the cost. Whatever the circumstances. Whatever the inconvenience. Whatever the odds.

Even, sometimes, against one's "allies".

"*Chingalo*," Vasquez finally said. *Fuck it.*

The Spartan nodded as he finished adjusting his combat gloves. "Let's do this, then. But no casualties." The Spartan gave Jackson the eye. "And no brass knucks."

Three of the agents flicked out extendable batons. The other three trusted their hands. "Prepare to be embarrassed," said one.

It was on like King Kong.

As a baton swung towards the Spartan's legs, he raised his leg, then struck it down again, pinning the agent's baton. As the surprised agent struggled the Spartan punched him square in the face. Newly liberated teeth went flying. The Spartan tossed the agent to the ground over his hip with a judo throw. He held the agent's hair as he sank his fist into the agent's face again and again. Stunned, the agent wasn't putting up much of a defense.

In the background, Vasquez launched a flying kick against an attacking S-Man. Not to be left out, Jackson grabbed an agent's tie, pulled the man towards him and used the momentum to deliver a powerful right hook.

"Never wear a tie to a fight," counselled Jackson, ruthlessly pummelling his opponent while still holding the tie. Then Jackson was crashtackled to the ground, still grinning.

The Spartan's opponent seized one of his fists to stop the vicious attack. Another agent grabbed a baton in both hands, raised it from behind over the Spartan's neck and began choking him. It was the type of chokehold that made headlines whenever the LAPD used it. The Spartan was dragged to his feet, his hands automatically grabbing for the baton.

Given an appropriate breather, the agent on the ground rallied and slammed heavy punches into the Spartan's rock-hard stomach.

"Bastard!" he said as he punched, voice different thanks to his newly missing teeth.

The Spartan kicked the agent in front of him in the balls. As the agent winced and bent over, the Spartan introduced the sole of his boot to his temple. The agent sprawled down on the ground. He was neutralized.

However, the Spartan was still being choked out by his angry, baton-clutching friend. The Tier 1 soldier blacked out for a second. A scene from special forces training flashed back into his head.

"Most of you will fail this course," said the grim-faced instructor. "We only want the best of the best."

And that was what he was. The best of the best.

The Spartan kicked backwards with his heel, striking his foe's groin. If a strike to the nuts was good enough for his partner, it was good enough for him. The agent grunted but held his grip.

"Nice ... try," uttered the agent.

The Spartan slammed his head backwards against the Secret Service man's face. He felt bone and cartilage give way.

He did it again. Same effect. The agent was beginning to wilt. The Spartan felt hot blood against his hair.

Only problem was, the baton was still choking him.

The Spartan grabbed a baton off the ground and struck over his shoulder. The agent screamed. The Spartan had hit an eye. Finally, he managed to break free of the chokehold. As the agent clutched his bloody eye, the Spartan whipped at his legs again and again until the agent eventually fell to his knees.

The Spartan delivered a final hardy kick to the jaw. The agent wasn't getting up any time soon. Two down.

Panting, he took in the scene. One of Vasquez's foes was already face down in the grass. She was engaging the other in hand-to-hand. Whoever this agent was, he was skilled. The pair went back and forth like fighters at an elite dojo.

Meanwhile, Jackson was enjoying himself. His face was bloody, but he was smiling as he traded blows with the Secret Service men. Jackson always liked a good brawl.

Seeing the Spartan's interest, he grabbed one of the agents and hurled one towards the Spartan.

"Here, Spartan, catch!" he shouted.

As the dazed agent came towards him, the Spartan extended his right arm, clotheslining his opponent. The agent's feet came clean off the ground. His entire body hit the ground with a thud. Then the Spartan hit him in just the right place, hard. And it was over.

Jackson stuck his fingers into the nose of his last opponent. The agent was so shocked by the strange move that he dropped his defenses and grabbed his violated nose. Jackson fustigated him with his club-like hands.

Jackson wasn't fighting any more – he was just playing with his food.

"Goddamit, Jackson, finish it!" ordered the Spartan.

"Killjoy," said Jackson, before he removed his fingers and knocked the agent to the ground with a right cross.

All the President's men lay on the ground, moaning and groaning. Their shirts were stained with blood, their souls stained by the shame of defeat. It was safe to say this drubbing wouldn't be appearing in the monthly Secret Service newsletter.

"Hey, look," said Jackson, pointing in the air. "We're on TV."

A small drone, little bigger than a toy helicopter, was watching them.

Jackson gave it the finger.

The Spartan made his way towards Vasquez. She had the last combat effective agent on the ground, hand twisted behind his back. The agent swore in language that would make a sailor blush … then watched as two pairs of boots walked near his head. The agent stopped struggling.

The Spartan bent down on one knee.

"I think we've made our point," said the Spartan ominously. "Take your friends and get out of here. You do your job and we'll do ours. And never the twain shall meet."

The agent simply stared wordlessly into the Spartan's fearful blue eyes.

"Now fuck off and go get your asthma inhalers," added Jackson.

The Spartan grabbed the agent's tie and pulled his head towards his face.

"What he said. And don't you ever let me hear you bad-mouth special forces again or I won't be so gentle next time."

Chapter 32

You can do a lot if you have access to an invisibility suit. Like use it to hijack an aircraft. Then fly that aircraft tens of thousands of feet over Martha's Vineyard. Then ignore the angry radio warnings about crossing restricted airspace, set the plane on autopilot, HALO jump out of the aircraft with five more of your special forces ninjas, freefall at terminal velocity and descend through the air upon Martha's Vineyard in the dead of night, machinegun in hand, in search of a President you want to kill.

And so, Martha's Vineyard would run red tonight. But not with wine.

* * *

The six night warriors knew that everything had to be perfect.

They had to land in just the right place. They had to immediately neutralize any nearby opposition without raising the alarm. And, in any event, the ninjas had only precious minutes to achieve their plan. The window for killing the President was ultra-slim.

And, as each of them knew, it was a suicide mission in any case.

As the six ninjas swooped down in their parachutes, the eight Secret Service men failed to look up until it was too late. The ninjas methodically wiped them out using silenced submachineguns. Only two agents managed to lift their weapons up before a hail of rounds silenced them, their last sight one of the ninjas floating ever downwards, backlit by a half-moon. Death from above, all the way from Communist China.

The agents' blood appeared quite black by the light of the moon.

The ninjas landed heavily next to the dead agents, knees bending, boots on gravel. One landed awkwardly, ankle twisting badly. He stifled his cry of pain. Another felt slightly ill, as if suffering from the effects of hypoxia or decompression from the HALO jump. Yet like his comrade, he kept his complaints to himself.

The group waited a second to see if the alarm had been raised. Nothing. The ninjas still had complete surprise. For now.

They seized the limp and bleeding bodies of the agents, stashed them along with their deactivated radios in nearby hedges and covered them over with their HALO chutes and oxygen tanks. A basic disguise, but adequate. The ninjas took a final moment to check their weapons, both custom-made (machineguns) and exotic (shurikens, ninjato short swords, knives), and that everything was strapped down tight so it wouldn't make a noise when they moved.

Their ancestors had been invading keeps and castles and assassinating warlords for centuries. Now it was their turn.

Four of the night warriors took cover by the kitchen door, two on each side. Another guarded a ninja as his companion used an electronic device that quickly dialled through all possible frequencies to open the electronic lock. Contrary to ancient myth, walking through solid walls and doors was beyond the formidable powers of even the most skilled ninja. Fortunately, the intruders' high-tech electronic device worked. The door beeped softly. They were in.

Two Secret Service agents turned as the door opened. At the sight of the silver-suited shinobi, one raised a walkie talkie to his mouth, finger on the talk button, words trapped on his next breath. He was immediately shot in the head, along with his partner. They slithered to the ground. The lead ninja dived and grabbed the walkie-talkie before it could strike the floor and make a noise.

They paused again. So far, so good. Their cover remained. They still retained the element of surprise.

The ninjas dragged the dead agents towards the door.

Just then a chef holding a large silver bowl full of vegetables entered from a wooden side door.

He froze in place when he saw the ninjas and the dead agents. "Please don't do this," the chef whispered.

A ninja raised a lone finger to his lips. "Shh."

The terrified chef remained rooted to the spot. The ninja slowly walked up, took the bowl from the cook's nerveless fingers, raised his weapon and fired.

The chef's body was added to the pile like so many stock cubes. Then the pile was stuffed into the surprisingly large walk-in pantry.

They knew what they had to do now. The ninjas had all studied the floor plans. Each would become invisible in turn and comb through the building, wiping out opposition in designated areas, before regrouping at the spot where the President was most likely to be sleeping. They would have to rely on trust, instinct and training, unable to communicate via hand signals or squeeze a comrade's back to let them know they were there.

"There must be no errors," said the unit leader, Kopo, in Mandarin. "Control the shadows."

Kopo, mysterious Kopo, mighty Kopo, favorite of the leader, steeped in the darkest and most eldritch of ninja arts.

The ninjas nodded to each other, reloaded mags, waited the requisite 15 seconds, then became invisible.

Now the hunt for the President could begin.

* * *

"Are you there?" whispered a voice in Mandarin.

"Yes."

"In position," said a third voice.

Three of them were gathered before the hallway.

Ahead lay at least six Secret Service agents.

And beyond that, the bedroom of the President of the United States.

"I'll take the ones on the left," whispered Kopo. "You two take the ones on the right. Fire on three, two, one …"

Even from a distance of 20 feet their accuracy was deadly, head shots all round. The agents slumped to the ground, dead before they could even point and shoot.

The ninjas because visible.

But then, so did something else. One of the agents had been standing behind a Vulcan M61 cannon, connected to a metal base and plugged into the wall. One of the downed agents must have been holding a dead man's switch. Suddenly the motion-detecting cannon swivelled their way. And fired.

Two of the ninjas sprang into movement, leaping high and to the left and right.

The third was too slow. He was shredded by 20mm rounds.

Kopo and his remaining colleague raced down the hall, backflipping, bouncing off walls and dancing around as if they were in a parkour video. Their actions confused the cannon: just when it was about to lock onto one of the ninjas, another would dance and distract its sensors, forcing it to re-acquire its target.

By their skilful team effort, and despite several near-misses, they reached the cannon.

Kopo unplugged the troublesome machine, which seemed to sigh as it was deactivated.

The other ninja kicked down the door.

They expected to find the President of the United States of America.

Instead facing them was Jackson, holding his Remington shotgun.

To quote Admiral Akbar from *Star Wars*: "It's a trap!"

Jackson pointed the barrel towards the ninja.

"Howdy," he said.

Then he fired.

* * *

Kopo entered just as his ninja comrade was shot in the face by a figure who was clearly not the President.

He raised his machinegun and fired at the African-American, who ducked behind a bed and fired shotgun rounds in his direction, forcing him to cartwheel out of the way.

Suddenly he was crashtackled to the floor. A large white bruiser had him pinned. Or so the soldier thought.

Kopo was an expert in the "dim mak", the infamous martial arts blow also known as the Touch of Death.

Delivered by a skilled practitioner, its vibrations could be deadly, either instantaneously or over a period of weeks.

Kopo was such a skilled practitioner. And his *chi* energy was fresh, unused. He had power to deliver.

And so he delivered the power of the dim mak into the Caucasian soldier's chest.

He watched with satisfaction as the soldier's face lit up in shock. Then the American fell face first on the ground.

* * *

"Is that it?" asked a voice.

The Spartan found himself sitting beside an oddly-cold fire in a dark cave. He was dressed in black special forces night ops gear. Beside him was his SAW, barrel warm from recent use.

And besides that was a being with an ancient-looking face but the body of a muscular young man, wearing a white loincloth.

The Spartan realized he had met this disturbing being before in his dreams.

"You again," said the Spartan.

"I repeat," said the figure in his cold, supernatural voice, "is that it? Are you done?"

"Am I done what?"

"You have just been hit by the 'dim mak', the so-called touch of death," said the disturbing figure. "A death sentence for most men. So here you are ... on the brink of death."

"What do you expect me to say?" growled the Spartan. "Do you want me to beg for my life? Because I won't do that."

"I wouldn't expect you to," said the odd being. "But you're on the cusp here. Things could go either way. I just wanted to know … are you ready to put down your sword and shield yet? Are you ready to step over to the other side and see what's next?"

The Spartan stared into the being's eyes. He thought he saw stars there … along with images of possible alternative futures featuring himself as something other than a Tier 1 soldier. The visions were hypnotic. He felt a strange pull sweep over his soul. But it only lasted for a moment. Then it disappeared.

"No. Fuck no." He stood and grabbed his SAW. "Put me back into the fight, weirdo."

The figure smiled an angular smile impossible to perform on a human face.

"That's the spirit. Go now. You won't remember this conversation. Step into the light, young man."

The Spartan stared hard at the figure, then headed towards the illuminated cave entrance.

"Goodbye, Spartan. We will meet again. Perhaps sooner than you think."

Then the Spartan opened his eyes.

The Spartan awoke to an incredible pain in his chest. He'd never been struck that painfully before. On a scale of one to 10, 10 being a gunshot wound/piercing dental pain/childbirth, this felt like an 11. Special forces and his own nature had trained him to deal with pain, but this was something else.

He tried to move, only to be weighed down by the intense agony.

He'd often told Vasquez that "pain was merely the opening and closing of a synapse". Yet it was one thing to wax lyrical about the chimerical nature of an electrical signal, another to experience its burning urgency first-hand. Still, he did his best to push the pain aside into a part of his brain that wouldn't impair his combat efficiency.

He willed himself to his feet. He refused to stop. Refused to quit. He was the master of his body. He forced it to obey him, despite the pain.

Slowly, he made it up.

He could hear gunfire outside. The battle royale had begun.

Meanwhile, the night warrior that had struck him so fiercely was trying to feed Jackson his Remington. The pair wrestled over the weapon, but Jackson, looking worse for wear, was losing the fight. Maybe he'd been hit by the same sort of hoodoo the ninja had used on the Spartan. In a second or two Jackson was in danger of being killed by his own shotgun.

The Spartan drew his *xiphos* and slashed down on the exceptional ninja's shoulder, the sharp blade slicing through armor and into bone. The ninja's scream was muffled by his mask. Yet the wound was bad enough to allow Jackson to rally. Jackson redoubled his efforts with the shotgun, reversed the direction of the barrel and fired into the ninja's centre mass.

The ninja silently fell to the ground. Yet he was still twitching.

"Those suits are armored," said the Spartan, sheathing his *xiphos*. "Hit him again."

Jackson fired again. And again. And once more to the knees just in case he turned zombie or something.

High-tech suit or not, few suits of armor win a game of "Rock, Paper, Shotgun" at close range. Nor did this armor. The night warrior lay still.

"Goddamn," said Jackson, panting, as he looked at the bloody ruin of the downed ninja.

"Yeah."

"Shit, look at us killing together," joked Jackson. "It's like 'ebony and ivory'." He then checked the Spartan for injuries. "That dude had some wicked moves. I thought he killed you."

"I thought that myself for a second," said the Spartan, mind grasping at some half-remembered dream. The Spartan grabbed his SAW. "Come on. Let's go help the others."

Chapter 33

Depending on your viewpoint, the battle between the shinobi and the Secret Service was either stunning or ghastly. Stunning, if you had no personal skin in the game, and you enjoyed watching some of the world's best combatants trading bullets, fighting hand-to-hand, and, in the case of the ninjas, disappearing, only to reappear at the backs of the Secret Service agents.

Ghastly, if you were sensitive about all the bloodshed and were dismayed by the large casualties the Secret Service were taking in defense of their President, who was holed up in a room guarded by half a dozen agents.

It was deadlier than a Westeros wedding inside Mary's Lookout.

In ordinary circumstances, the massed agents would have seen off the ninja threat. They would have corralled the invaders into crucial choke points and used their superior firepower to end them. But the Ghost Armor tech gave the ninjas a critical advantage, allowing the shinobi to deliver sneak attacks from the flanks, from on top of the ceiling, or from wherever the agents didn't expect them to be.

Nor were the night warriors just using guns. They employed shuriken, knives, poison darts, stun grenades and even segmented chains to lethal effect. Agent Mancuso had watched, barely believing his eyes, as a chain had come out of nowhere, wrapped itself around an agent's neck, then snapped it, the agent's body pulled backwards. Another ninja had jumped from a bannister, skewered an agent to the ground with a sword like a child skewering a bug, then danced away from furious return fire.

By now the Secret Service agents were grabbing their wounded comrades and pulling them out of harm's way, then applying tourniquets and basic first aid.

Guarding the President's front door, Mancuso was doing his best to co-ordinate the defense amid the fog of war. While the odds favored the agents, it would only take one determined ninja to get to the President. The question was whether the ninjas could be fended off for long enough for the Secret Service's superior numbers to turn the tide.

The ninjas fired in tight, accurate bursts, covering each other as they moved. They were hard to hit, even without taking the invisibility suits into account. If any of the Secret Service agents had any doubts about the usefulness of ninjutsu in the modern world, they were now stone-cold believers.

Vasquez had climbed on top of the staircase, trying to guess where the ninjas would appear next. She thought she detected a pattern in one shinobi's movements, that the night warrior used a particular hallway for ratholing and stealthing up. She also observed something else ... that their Mark II Ghost Armors were recharging faster than the Mark I. It was perhaps by a second or two, but you could kill someone in a second or two.

The Chinese had upgraded their model.

Bullets continued to fly in all directions of the compass. Vasquez was disturbed by the risk of being shot by her own side. Yet when her target ninja re-appeared and darted off down a hallway, she struck. She drew a garrotte, silently dropped down behind him and wrapped it around the ninja's neck.

One of the ninjas tossed a smoke grenade in their direction. Both the ninjas and the agents were now afraid to shoot in case they struck an ally. It was now a duel between Vasquez and her opponent.

Vasquez kicked the ninja's legs, making him kneel and giving her more leverage for the garrotting. She put all her strength into it. The ninja thrashed back and forth before slamming her against the wall, hoping to trap Vasquez there, but she leapt up on top of his shoulders. However, her grip was now loosened. The ninja flipped around, dislodged Vasquez from his shoulders and kicked her in the sternum, knocking her against the wall.

Now they were both in smoke, fighting an enemy they couldn't see. Vasquez ducked as a punch flew over her head, then tried to sweep the ninja's legs. She felt her foot brush the ninja's armor as he leapt over her feet.

The ninja's speed was incredible.

She felt a sudden movement in the smoke and a stinging in her left arm. A shuriken was buried there, while another flew past her shoulder. Then she was buffeted by an unseen kick to the stomach and a tiger's paw punch to the face. She removed the shuriken, hoping it wasn't poisoned, and hurled it back towards the ninja, to no apparent effect.

Fighting in the smoke, unable to see her opponent, reminded her of her martial arts training when her sensei forced her to wear a blindfold as the class attacked her.

Fortunately, the ninja was equally baffled. The pair ran into each other mid-move. Vasquez did the splits, grabbed the ninja's nuts and squeeze hard. The ninja coughed. Actually, he more like yodelled. No amount of kung fu or qi gong could make a blow to the balls feel painless.

The ninja quickly rallied. A kick to the shoulder forced Vasquez to release her grip. She flipped back onto her feet and batted away one, then two punches. Vasquez missed with a side kick but connected with a roundhouse kick, her foot landing home hard.

Vasquez danced back, expecting a foot or a fist in return. Instead, she felt a blade slice her side. The cut was small yet deep. Had the ninja drawn a sword?

As her hand went to the site of the injury, she felt the outline of another weapon contained in her webbing. A weapon the Spartan had often derided as more fitting for an '80s street mugging than an elite battle.

She pulled the 1980s weapon, took a wild surmise as to where the ninja might move next, then squeezed the trigger.

An anguished cry proved that she had scored a direct hit.

She had just maced a ninja.

As the smoke slowly began to clear, Vasquez saw her opponent hold his hands up to his face, unable to escape the mace soaked into his mask. Vasquez shoulder-charged him and knocked him to the floor. She drew her own sharp knife and stabbed the ninja in the vulnerable, unguarded spot between the chest and neck armor. The blade penetrated deep and true.

The night warrior died without making a sound.

Vasquez stared at the body. "No one beats the Wiz," she said.

Chapter 34

"Yo, Yojimbo, where you at?" said Jackson as he fired his Remington shotgun. He felt he had a bead on one of the last two ninjas. His experience fighting the invisible Vasquez last year gave him insights as to how someone in the Ghost Armor might fight.

Jackson had switched to special buckshot rounds. The custom-made rounds were less lethal, but had a wider dispersal area. One hit – even a glancing wound – should be enough to disrupt the Ghost Armor's operation and make Mr Yojimbo show himself.

Jackson ducked as interlocking fire from the Secret Service almost hit him, bullets knocking stuffing out of the couch he was concealed behind.

"Check your fire, asshole," he shouted.

A Secret Service agent with a black eye hunkered down next to him.

As Jackson continued sending rounds down range, he noticed the Secret Service agent he'd had sex with in a bathroom stall. She was only a few feet away, shooting two-handed with a Glock.

Noticing Jackson's attention, she couldn't help but smile back.

Suddenly the ninja became visible. Jackson's buckshot had winged him.

The ninja took a bead on the female agent.

Without thinking, Jackson grabbed the agent beside him and hurled him in front of her.

The agent took the machinegun blast meant for Jackson's friend, pulping the agent's upper torso.

Even the ninja appeared shocked by Jackson's callous actions.

Then a Secret Service agent crashtackled the ninja to the ground.

The rest of the agents rushed over and began kicking the ninja to death.

* * *

The lone surviving night warrior saw what was happening. He was now the last. There was nothing for it but a suicide run straight towards the President.

He seized his remaining smoke grenades, flashbangs and incendiary tear gas canisters and threw them around him in a wide arc. A last gasp of theatricality and deception.

Secret Service agents choked and staggered about.

The ninja drew his ninjato, then bounced off one wall with his foot, then another, and somersaulted in the air. On the way down he struck the head straight off the body of one Secret Service agent. Now on his feet, he sliced across the stomach of a second agent, gutted a third, stepped forward, grabbed the hand of the final agent as the agent attempted to shoot him, then, with one hand, thrust the point of the ninjato under the agent's armor and into his heart.

The ninja had slain four men in barely six seconds.

Now the President's door lay before him.

The ninja ran down the hall. Then stopped.

Now visible out of the swirling smoke was a big American, holding a short, sharp sword in his hand.

The American looked potent. And angry.

"You want the President, you have to go through me first," he declared.

* * *

Front foot out, the ninja held his ninjato in front of him two-handed. The ninja's answer to the samurai's katana, the ninjato was a short weapon not unlike the Spartan's own *xiphos*. It was also lethally sharp. However, the ninjato, like the katana, was more of a slashing weapon: his *xiphos* was best for stabbing.

One way or another, thought the Spartan, this fight was going to be over fast.

The Spartan and the night warrior raced towards each other. At the last moment, the ninja flipped into the air, struck at the Spartan with the ninjato and landed. If it hadn't been for his helmet, the Spartan might have been scalped. As it was, the ninjato bit into the helmet strap and then into the Spartan's head, causing the helmet to fall off and his head to bleed.

I should have been faster than that, thought the Spartan. The burning pain in his chest reminded him that he was still wounded from before.

But any triumphalism on the ninja's part was halted as he touched his side, realising the Spartan had stabbed him during the exchange.

"Now we're even," said the Spartan.

The ninja came at the Spartan, striking two-handed down at the Spartan's head. The Spartan blocked, deflected another blow aimed at his shoulder and leant backwards at the ninja tried to impale him in the neck. Now overextended, the ninja attempted to pull his arms back, but not before the Spartan sliced deep into his underarm. That wound was going to be a bleeder. Every second was going to cost the shinobi strength. If the ninja didn't have a clock on him, he did now.

The ninja snarled and launched into a sophisticated attack consisting of eight strikes, ranging from the head to the stomach, and even at one point the Spartan's hamstrings, a two-handed blow delivered on one knee. Only one got through, the ninjato running along the Spartan's ribcage, while another was caught by his body armor. Yet the ninja received two strikes in return, one under the armpit and one on the right shoulder. If the ninja was hoping the blow to the Spartan's head would help him he was disappointed as the blood streamed down the side of his face rather than into his eyes.

The ninja attempted acrobatics again. He bounced off a wall and thrust both feet towards the Spartan's chest. The Spartan pivoted and performed a sidekick into the ninja's chest. The shinobi fell to the ground, but rolled out of the way as the Spartan attempted to impale him. In barely a second he was attacking the Spartan with his ninjato again.

Their blades clashed several more times before the Spartan shoved his opponent back. The Spartan was aware that four Secret Service agents were nearby, pistols raised, about to make their move. He had to wrap this up, one way of another.

The ninja realized that there was only one way this was going to end, too.

But the Spartan was ready.

As soon as he sensed the ninja had made his decision to swallow his suicide pill he let his *xiphos* fall to the ground, grabbed the ninja by both shoulders and headbutted him. Then again. And again.

The Spartan's bones were as strong and dense as a Neanderthal's.

The ninja, built for speed rather than density, wasn't so blessed.

The ninja crumpled in his arms.

The Spartan let the conquered shinobi fall to the ground.

"He's all yours, boys," he told the Secret Service. They swarmed the ninja, fishing the pill out of the false tooth in his mouth and binding his arms.

The Spartan's head was bloody, but unbowed. The attack was over. It had failed. The President was safe.

For now.

Chapter 35

"All the ninjas dead?" asked Jackson as he stood in the background. "Damn … I wanted to see one of them jump backwards up a tree or some shit."

The Spartan, standing next to a bloody Agent Mancuso on the driveway, glanced at Jackson coldly, hoping that Mancuso wasn't paying attention. He wasn't. The Secret Service man was still gathering his wits.

"This is a slaughterhouse," said Mancuso, pained. "We've lost at least two dozen agents, not including the wounded. My colleagues. My friends. Men and women with families."

Such butchery was a shock to the Secret Service agent. But the Spartan had seen such scenes all too many times.

Mancuso stared at the house again, watching the first responders, medical staff and the clean-up crew do their work. The first of the black bags was brought out of the doors. Bags containing his men. "This is the single biggest disaster the service has ever faced. The only consolation is that we did our job. We kept the President out of harm's way."

"Yes," said the Spartan. Mancuso turned to him, glancing at the fresh bandage on the Spartan's head from the sword wound.

"Is this what you love, Spartan? This bloodshed? This … carnage?"

The Spartan looked away from Mancuso. Part of him knew the answer was true, that he welcomed the combat. He welcomed skilled foes that used swords. He welcomed the challenge of being pushed to the very edge. Instead, he said: "We will avenge your men. I promise."

"That won't bring them back." Mancuso stared at the house again. Then he turned back to the Spartan, hostility in his eyes. "You have my gratitude for protecting the President." Mancuso paused again. The Spartan realized that in some way they had humiliated Mancuso, that Mancuso had had to turn to outsiders to do his job. He had unintentionally emasculated him. "But right now, get the fuck out of my sight," he continued. "I don't want to see you around. You or your friend there."

The Spartan nodded, then walked away with Jackson.

Yes, the trio had saved the President. Yes, they had killed six more ninjas, which meant six more Ghost Armors recovered.

But not everyone was pleased.

Mancuso was unhappy because of the death toll. The Secret Service boss has also heard that Jackson had pushed one of his agents into the way of gunfire, apparently to protect a Secret Service agent he had enjoyed bathroom sex with. The male agent who had been the recipient of Jackson's "romantic" gesture had died. Mancuso was talking loudly about having Jackson charged with manslaughter.

Then there were the President's missing cufflinks. Mancuso had accused the trio of stealing them.

Upon hearing the accusation, the Spartan stared wordlessly at Jackson.

"That's racial profiling," said Jackson. "Does this mean I'm not going to get to shake the President's hand?"

But the cufflinks were small potatoes, marginalia in some dusty official report, compared with the charge that the trio had indulged in fisticuffs with the Secret Service only hours before the ninja attack. That last nugget of info had drawn Garin's ire.

"For fuck's sake, Spartan, why did you have to beat up the Secret Service?" said Garin over the speaker phone.

"They insulted special forces, sir," replied the Spartan.

"Ever heard of turning the other cheek, son?"

"No."

The Spartan could just picture Garin shaking his head. "And from what I hear, you instigated the brawl. I didn't expect you to be all plaiting each other's hair, but I did expect more co-operation. I'm disappointed with you, son."

"They got in our faces," insisted Jackson, leaning in to be heard.

"After you were caught having sex with a Secret Service agent," insisted Garin tartly.

"We were always going to get into it with them, sir," came the Spartan's reply. "We just don't get along. Different mindset. Different mission."

"Yeah ... they protect fuckers, we waste them," added Jackson.

"I don't think you can equate America's political elite with insurgents, terrorists and al-Qaeda, Jackson ... even if certain individuals among them might qualify as 'fuckers'," said Garin.

"They're just ... they're just too clean-shaven, sir," said Spartan. The Spartan's words had their effect. All three men were instantly taken back to black ops in the Middle East and Afghanistan, where it was commonplace for Tier 1 operatives to grow beards to disguise their identities and blend in. Bearded and often covered with mud and/or blood, their appearance and attire were a far cry from the neat, clean suits and polished shoes of the Secret Service.

"Yeah," said Garin, no doubt picturing the Middle East in his mind.

"I get it," said Jackson, who had been on many of those same dusty missions himself.

"Is this some sort of guy thing?" interjected Vasquez. "Because I feel out of the loop here."

"You'd have to have been there to understand, Vasquez," explained Garin. "And by there, I mean the Middle East. But anyway, Vasquez, what's your take on the situation?"

"I stand behind my team 100 per cent, sir," she said. "Yes, we behaved at times in an unorthodox manner ..."

"You can never get through a special forces meeting without someone using the phrase 'unorthodox manner'," breezed Jackson. "They should make a drinking game out of it."

"... but, if I may *finish*, we performed our primary mission, sir: saving the President. And I joined in on the lawn brawl. Willingly."

Garin went silent for a few seconds. Then he said: "Right. Right." There was another pause as Garin presumably weighed up what he was going to say next. "Well, you're all off the Presidential detail in any case. The Secret Service don't want you there, and the President has agreed. I tried to talk him out of it, but he said the relationship between the Secret Service and the President was too important to jeopardize, even in the face of danger. After you're no longer around he'll still have to deal with them daily. His office and theirs have a bond that goes back centuries." Garin took in a deep breath. "As for me personally – apart from your other *shocking* behavior – well done in protecting the President. They'll be more work to do with the ninjas, believe me."

"We're ready to serve, sir," said the Spartan, glad that Garin needed him.

"As for now, Spartan, Vasquez, you can go back to my apartment in Little Belgium and await further instructions. Mind the store for me. Meanwhile, Jackson, you regroup at your own pad. Orders will follow shortly as we clarify the situation. And watch out for ninjas. They're invisible now."

"Sir, yes, sir!" said one and all. Even Jackson.

"Garin out."

Chapter 36

Professor Eisenstein sat in front of the small television in his cell, watching the daily news with the leader. The scientist stared with no small amount of satisfaction as the President held a press conference in Martha's Vineyard, talking up the Chinese Premier's upcoming visit.

As POTUS spoke, Eisenstein turned to the leader.

"The President lives," he said, unable to hide his satisfaction. "Your killers failed. So much for your regime decapitation."

In response, the leader drew the Honjo Masamune and held it at Eisenstein's unshaved throat. The blade drew a tiny trickle of blood.

"Don't be too smug. I can still have you killed at any time. Think of your family." Eisenstein gave the leader a look that was both stubborn and afraid.

"I think about them all the time."

"Good. Focus on your problems and not on those of others." The leader quickly withdrew the sword and sheathed it. "Anyway, the odds were always against my men. It is no easy thing to kill a President, even one as decadent as yours."

"He's not my President. I was born and raised in Russia."

The leader couldn't help but laugh. "Russia. Of course you were. How silly of me to forget." The leader paused, summoning old thoughts. "Once we were in awe of our mighty Communist comrades from the north. The only force powerful enough to stand up to America. Now we are the only force powerful enough to stand up to the United States. And then … supplant it."

Eisenstein stared back at the face of the living President. "Then you'll have to do better than that. Your failure is all over TV."

The leader favored Eisenstein with a smile that chilled the scientist. "Yes. But I suspect our next success will be all over TV, too. Our next mission – at least the one I choose to make visible – shall be a multimedia event. And I shall play the starring role." The leader looked over his shoulder at a puzzled Eisenstein. "Stay tuned to this channel."

Then he left the room.

Chapter 37

Organised crime in the US changed forever thanks to events in the sleepy hamlet of Apalachin, New York on November 14, 1957. Suspicious about the number of expensive, out-of-town vehicles turning up to the home of alleged mobster Joe Barbara, police raided the house, only to find dozens of possible mafioso ensconced therein.

Police detained dozens of alleged mobsters ... shattering the image that America had no organised crime problem forever. A red-faced FBI director J. Edgar Hoover was forced to admit that the Mafia existed after all.

Thus, the FBI launched a decades-long crusade against the Italian Mafia that led to the arrest of many of the members of New York's Five Families. Cosa Nostra was reduced to a shadow of its former self in the US (although its Calabrian cousin, the 'Ndrangheta, was still thriving, considered to be one of the most powerful crime groups in the world).

The Apalachin disaster was a singular warning to organised crime not to gather in large numbers at any one venue.

However, like any other large corporation, regular meetings of the Mafia still took place – even meetings between the various crime gangs of America.

Marchenko, former Russian sleeper agent, Red Mafia boss and friend of Colonel Garin, was at one such inter-group meeting. Cigar in hand, glass of vodka at his elbow, he was sitting with representatives from some of the biggest crime organizations in America. The summit was a Racketeer Influenced and Corrupt Organizations Act prosecutor's dream.

The Santini family had taken responsibility for hosting this summit in their Nevada hotel. The Santinis had had to personally vet everyone in the hotel before any of the other crime bosses would step inside.

No one wanted another Apalachin.

Marchenko knew a few of the gangsters here, either by face or by reputation.

Marchenko wasn't overly popular among the group – the Russian Mafia were more feared than liked. Some "patriotic" gangsters also hadn't forgotten the Cold War, resenting the "Communist" in their presence. The Italians tended to "bust his balls", bitter that the criminal empire they had painstakingly build over generations was now being eaten away by upstarts like the Russians.

However, as long as the other gang leaders continued to fear him in general, he could live without their bonhomie.

Across the table was Mr Choi from the Lonely Dragons, who he had met last year. The triad elder had been instrumental in the death of Commander Lee, the madman behind the canister conspiracy. Their transaction had been mutually beneficial. Marchenko had wanted Lee dead, too, after Lee had tried to have him killed for murdering his son.

Marchenko and Choi nodded to each other.

Also in the large conference room were representatives from the Colombians, the Jamaicans, the Japanese ... and the new, all-powerful kids on the block, the Mexican cartels. Between them, the men and the organizations they represented had infiltrated just about every facet of American life.

The group was into hour three of the crime summit. They had already dealt with their semi-legitimate concerns. Accountants, bankers and lawyers had already discussed everything from new police powers to tax laws, in some cases using PowerPoint presentations.

Then the "banksters" had left the room so the gangsters could discuss more "hands-on" business.

At the moment, a wiry, expensively dressed older man from the Mexican cartels known as the Jaguar had the floor. The Jaguar had the unnerving habit of never blinking. He had deep grooves in his face, as if he was angry often. Which he probably was.

Yet right now he was trying to be civility itself. The Jaguar was saying that the cartels wanted to expand into San Francisco. They wanted a taste of its huge methamphetamine market. The Lonely Dragons, who considered San Francisco their own turf, a tradition stretching right back to the gold-rush days when the tongs joined the Chinese coolies on the gold fields, objected.

If the Jaguar looked like a man who was angry often, Choi was almost the opposite. Choi's calm face reminded Marchenko of the Zen master who, falsely accused of impregnating a beautiful young woman, merely answered, "Is that so?" Then, after his reputation had been ruined, only for the girl to later recant, merely replied again, "Is that so?"

In this instance, Choi listened to what the Jaguar had to say – news of similarly shocking import to that received by the Zen master – then lit his cigarette slowly, gathering his thoughts.

"We respect what the Jaguar is saying," said Choi smoothly, before exhaling smoke. "We understand that the cartels want to expand. The Lonely Dragons have no problem with that. We are all businessmen here."

There were murmurs of approval around the room. Many gangsters liked to believe they were really "businessmen" instead of murderers.

"But San Francisco has been our uncontested terrain for many years," continued Choi. "We have long earned the right to it. This has long been understood."

"We understand, Mr Choi," said the Jaguar, opening his hands in what he no doubt assumed was a friendly gesture. "We just want some room in the marketplace. To whet our beaks a little."

"And more than that, San Francisco has special historical importance to us," said Choi, as if he had not heard what the Jaguar had just said. The Jaguar was about to interject, but Choi was on a roll. "It is also my home. Thus you might understand our reluctance to share."

The room turned to the Jaguar to see his reaction. The Mexican took in all this information soberly, no reaction on his weathered face.

"That is why we have come here in the spirit of friendship, to figure out ways we can work together," said the Jaguar, a false smile on his lips. "So we can avoid … unnecessary complications."

The room went quiet. Everyone understood the subtext of the Jaguar's words. If the Lonely Dragons didn't share with the cartels, there would be bloodshed. And the cartels were dangerous people to say no to. They had the money, the endless personnel and the will to take on just about anyone.

Fortunately, the cartels didn't maintain the stranglehold of the North American market that they did in Mexico. Nor did they have the US police bribed, afraid or neutralized. Maybe other gangs could be coaxed into a coalition with the Lonely Dragons to limit the cartels' power in North America. No one wanted to see the cartels get any stronger.

Including Marchenko and his Russians.

All things Choi knew full well.

"No one wants bloodshed," said Choi evenly.

"Perhaps we can discuss this further, at another time," said the Jaguar coolly.

"I look forward to it," lied Choi.

The two men smiled at each other with the sincerity of perfume salesmen.

It was then that Marchenko knew that they would probably try to kill each other.

There was another pause. It seemed that that discussion had come to its natural conclusion.

"There's something else that I want to say," said the excitable and talkative Santini capo. "We're having problems with …"

The Jaguar raised his hand. "One moment, my friend. I want to discuss the thing we spoke about before."

"Oh, *that*," said the Santini capo, who relaxed back in his chair. "Sure, let's get to it."

The Jaguar pulled two photos out of a folder and passed them around the table. Curious hands grabbed at them. "These two *pinche* scum have caused us … problems," said the Jaguar with studied distaste. "This man and this woman have murdered my people both here and in Mexico. More recently, they assaulted one of our headquarters in Juarez, leading to the deaths of many of our soldiers … as well as one of my own protégés, may he rest in peace." The Jaguar made the Sign of the Cross over his chest.

"These fucks killed a whole bunch of our guys last year, too," raged the fleshy-faced Santini capo. He rested a thick finger on the photo of the man. "From what the cops told us, this bastard wasted more than a dozen made men like he was Rambo in *First Blood*."

"In *First Blood* Rambo doesn't actually kill anybody," Marchenko said. "I think you mean *Rambo II*."

The Santini capo's eyes boggled at Marchenko's odd yet accurate trivia. "Who gives a shit? Point is, we want these *pezzonovantes* dead."

"So do we," said the Jaguar, watching as the crime bosses in the room examined the pictures with curiosity. "The cartels do not forget."

Marchenko smiled to himself. If there was one thing all the men around the table shared, it was an almost pathological inability to forget past grievances. Organised crime was like a pack of elephants that way.

A pack of psychotic elephants, perhaps.

"So what's the problem?" said the head of the Jamaicans, pushing the pictures away with a decided lack of interest. "Kill them already."

"It is not that simple," explained the Jaguar diplomatically. He intercepted one of the pictures as it spun around the table, then held it up. It was a grainy photo of a big Caucasian man dressed in a military uniform and armed with a Squad Automatic Weapon machinegun. "This individual, who calls himself the Spartan, is a US special forces soldier. Tier 1. His death will be noticed. That's why we thought to bring it up here at this forum."

Marchenko understood the need for revenge, the appeal of the vendetta, but wondered if the Jaguar really knew what it was like to go against special forces. Particularly American special forces. They were a breed apart. Their speed, skill and ferocity were unlike anything else on Earth.

Marchenko knew how good special forces soldiers could be from his own training in Russia. He'd passed the gruelling training course of the Spetsnaz, Russia's own feared special forces. Staring around the room, looking at the assembled gangsters and their various physiques, he doubted many of them would qualify.

The Jaguar grabbed the second photo and held it up for all to see. It featured an attractive brunette Latina wearing odd white body armor. "And this ... *specimen* ... is Teresa Vasquez. She is a former Juarez policewoman who we believe is working with this 'Spartan'. She killed the cartel boss I mentioned. In a knife fight, no less. Which makes the manner of his death even more personal."

Marchenko got it. To have a cartel boss killed by a cop – and a woman – was humiliating to the cartels. And history had proven that men could endure just about anything – pain, torture, starvation – except humiliation, the sting that kept stinging, the pain that never really went away.

"A chick iced one of your boss dudes?" snickered the head of the Bronx Fierce Boys. "Shit." There were a few more chuckles. There was always bad blood between the Mexican and African-American gangs in America.

The Jaguar's eyes grew large, revealing the killer within. The Mexican had humiliated himself slightly by revealing that information. Not in Marchenko's eyes – the Russians were early adopters in using women in combat – but the rest of the gangs remained macho bastions that didn't properly appreciate the skills of the opposite sex. More fool them.

The Jaguar chose to ignore the previous comment. "So … as you can now see, gentlemen, this isn't a simple contract. There might be complications. Mostly from your side of the border. After all, no one is going to miss another dead cop from Juarez."

"May I see those pictures?" asked Choi.

"Certainly." The Jaguar pushed them towards Choi, their fingers briefly touching. The Lonely Dragons capo stared at the images for a while, then said: "We had a similar incident last year. We lost many men. These two resemble those responsible."

"Our needs meet as one, then," said the Jaguar, no doubt intending this as a sweetener all along.

"Show me those pictures," ordered Marchenko. Choi briskly passed them over.

"Do you know these scum?" asked the Jaguar, suspicious, as Marchenko silently examined the images.

"Never seen them before," mumbled Marchenko. But he thought he recognised this "Spartan". And he even remembered his friend Garin talking about an indomitable soldier in his ranks who had that call sign. This felt like more than a coincidence.

And coincidences make an "ass" out of "u" and "me".

He kept his face blank as he pushed the pictures away. "I don't think anyone has ever greenlit an active US special forces soldier before. This could be risky."

"We're willing to take that risk," said the Jaguar firmly.

"And everyone else is fine with this?" said Marchenko, staring around the room.

"I thought you Russians didn't have a problem killing cops," said a voice at the back.

"We're talking about special forces here," he replied. "Big difference." He noticed Choi and the Jaguar watching him intently. He addressed his next comment to them. "If you kill one and get caught, you'd be labelled a terrorist. And the last thing you want is to be labelled a terrorist by the US Government. You'll get very different levels of treatment, believe me."

"I understand your caution, Mr Marchenko," said Choi, meeting Marchenko's gaze. "But I must agree with the Jaguar. We can't let the word spread that outsiders can kill our men. Whatever the short-term cost, the long-term lesson will be invaluable. Even for special forces soldiers … who should be out chasing 'terrorists' rather than organised crime."

"Hey, from what I here, they're too busy chasing up their missing camouflage technology," said the Santini boss, laughing.

"*What* missing camouflage technology?" said Marchenko. The Jaguar flashed the Santini boss an angry look. Someone had spoken out of school.

"It is just a rumour, nothing more," said the Jaguar, waving his hand as if the matter was beneath him. "Probably all lies. Let us return to the issue at hand."

Marchenko stared at the Jaguar one final time. He felt that the Mexican gangster wasn't telling the entire truth – that, in fact, he was crying crocodile tears and putting on a show for his audience.

"OK, fuck me with a horse's cock, what do I care?" he said, pretending to be suddenly bored of that matter, although he was anything but. "I've said my two roubles worth. Do whatever you have to."

"I must also caution against this," said the yakuza representative suddenly. "I agree with Mr Marchenko. I don't think it's wise targeting the American special forces. They are not like the police. They are well-funded and battle-hardened. You can't predict how their superiors will react."

Choi seemed irritated by the Japanese gangster's interjection. Just like with the Mexicans and the African-Americans, there was bad blood between the Chinese triads and the Japanese yakuza, bad blood stretching back to the history between their two homelands.

But it was the Jaguar who answered him.

"That's providing they find out about the contract the first place. And I'm sure no one in this room is about to talk, are they? Are we not all men of exquisite silence?" There was a fraught silence.

Marchenko looked at the yakuza man's fingers as he drummed them on the table, unhappy with the plan yet bound by the unspoken consensus in the room.

Finally, he lay back in his chair.

The Jaguar had won the argument.

"So, unless anyone else has any further objections, we will advertise the contract tomorrow on the dark net," said the Jaguar. The dark net being the secret internet criminal groups used when they wanted to talk to each other. "The Santinis and the cartels have both agreed to put up $5 million each."

Marchenko whistled. "That's a lot of macaroni and cheese."

"The price is an indication of how seriously we take the matter, the potential risk and how quickly we want it concluded," continued the Jaguar. "Whoever successfully completes the assignment will have to retire from professional life forever."

The Jaguar paused as his eyes took on a particularly unsavory, almost salacious gleam. "Plus there will be bonus if Vasquez is captured alive for … special treatment." Everyone knew what that "special treatment" would be. "And you can let your own operatives and freelancers know there's work to be had."

"A $10 million dollar hit?" said the cartel man from Colombia. "Every hitman south of Texas will want that contract."

"And probably the ones north of it, too," smiled the Santini capo.

"Good," said the Jaguar, satisfied. "So it's settled. We will kill this Spartan and Vasquez. The rest of you need not concern yourself with the practicalities. And now, onto other business."

The meeting continued apace. Afterwards the Santinis laid out a drugs-and-hookers buffet: stress relief for all the boys in "waste disposal management". But Marchenko was keen to bounce. He needed to call his friend Garin and warn him.

And to ask him about this missing "camouflage technology".

* * *

There were few phones in the world that had the technology to foil any attempt at electronic surveillance. Marchenko owned one such device.

And so did the bullet catcher he was now calling – Colonel Garin.

"Speak to me," said Garin brusquely.

"What sort of greeting is that?"

There was a beat as Garin recognised the other voice. "I thought that passed for friendly in Russia."

"Your mother passes for 'friendly' in Russia."

"I see you're still full of old, lame jokes."

"I've got all-new lame jokes." Marchenko exhaled loudly. "Have we finished with the ritual exchange of insults?"

"I believe we have."

"Then be quiet and listen," Marchenko insisted. "I have important news to share. There's a hit order out on your friend the Spartan."

They both listened to their hissing phones for a second. "Wait. Stop. Rewind. Now play again."

"I've just come from a meeting of my 'associates'. The Santinis and the Mexican cartels claim your friend killed many of their soldiers last year."

"So?" said Garin, unimpressed.

"So ... they want revenge."

"Really. How badly?"

"Ten million dollars badly."

Garin breathed in. "That's a big contract. Juicy. Lots of honey for the flies."

"*Da*. There will be many interested parties."

"They don't know who they're fucking with," growled Garin.

"You ... or the Spartan?"

"Both."

"No, they don't. I did try to warn them. But fuck their eyes if they don't take advice. Do you also know a 'Vasquez'?"

"Affirmative. She's partners with the Spartan. Comrades in arms. Lovers."

"They want her dead, too. Something about killing one of the cartel bosses."

Garin's stomach suddenly complained. He wondered if he was developing an ulcer. He'd read the latest research saying that ulcers were caused by bacteria and not stress, but he wasn't sure if he believed it. Eventually, he said: "Jesus … more blowback. It's not like I don't have enough on my plate. And I need the pair of the Spartan and Vasquez to deal with what is already on my plate."

"Sorry, my friend. I thought I should warn you."

"And I'm grateful, Marchenko," said Garin sincerely. "I know you won't go to the cops with things like this, only to me … a fellow soldier in the life, as you say."

"That's all I know. The contract will be advertised on the dark net tomorrow. Good luck, Garin."

"Thanks." Garin paused. "My friend … do you ever think that …"

"Things are spiralling beyond our control? Every day, *tovarisch*. Every day."

"You, too? Maybe it has something to do with getting old."

Marchenko paused. "From what I see of the young folk, they have the same problem. The world is getting more complex."

"Tell me about it," sighed Garin.

"We'll share a vodka and talk about it soon." Marchenko paused. "There was one other thing … there was talk of missing 'camouflage technology'. Do you know anything about that?"

Garin breathed in deeply. "That's a whole other conversation right there. The conversation of the day, as it were."

"Because the subject of 'camouflage technology' rings a bell from my old days in the KGB. I would like to acquire any such technology."

"I can't talk to you about that right now, Marchenko. That's a conversation we'll have to have face-to-face sometime. But I would appreciate it if you hear anything more on the subject. They'll be something in it for you."

"I don't work for money, Garin," said Marchenko, sounding a little insulted.

"I know. But you would have my appreciation and gratitude."

"Where would you be if you didn't have your old friend Marchenko to bail your ass out of the fire?"

"Maybe I'd have a burnt ass."

"If I learn anything more on either subject I will let you know. Now quit whining and take care of business," said Marchenko, pronouncing "business" with at least one zed.

"Yes, mom."

Click.

***

It wasn't long before Garin got wind of the first plot against the Spartan and Vasquez. And it came from US Marines, no less.

Four scumbags dishonorably discharged after shooting civilians in Afghanistan – tried, but acquitted through lack of evidence; steroid use had eventually gotten them shitcanned – had heard talk of the contract on the Spartan. They'd been seen in bars near Fort Bragg, asking for information about the Spartan's whereabouts. The leathernecks wanted to meet Jackson just to catch up and shoot the shit, they claimed.

Garin knew better. He knew the gang of four had already been accepting hits stateside. He phoned Jackson and gave him the deets.

"Ten million?" said Jackson, whistling. "For that amount of money I'm tempted to take up the contract myself."

"It'd be your funeral," said Garin. Then: "I want you to

meet these assassins and sell your soul to them. Tell them you hate the Spartan and you know where he might be."

"And then?"

"I'll leave it to your discretion."

Jackson snorted. "Bullshit. I know what you want me to do."

"Then do it."

"Asking me to whack American citizens because they want to whack your boy? And you're sure we're not gangsters?"

"Are you using a sanitised phone?"

"Of course."

"Good. I don't want you to ever use the phrase 'American citizens' over a phone line again."

"Fine. What's in it for me if I take the job?"

"My gratitude. Plus the usual conditions apply." The usual conditions being that Jackson got to keep any valuables he found on or around them. Garin wasn't too fussy about collecting evidence.

"Oh, and Jackson? No bar-room fighting."

"Heh. Roger, colonel."

And so Jackson met the four ex-Marines. We've been kicked out of the service, they said. But there's plenty of dough to be made on the private circuit, they said. We hear there's bad blood between you and the Spartan, they said. There's money on his head, they said. You can have some of it, they said. There's 50 large in it for you if you can tell us where he is, they said.

"I *might* be able to help you," said Jackson. "Meet me around the back."

The four ex-Marines got into their car.

Jackson drove up in his Jeep and wound down the window.

"I've changed my mind, boys," he said. "No one gets to

kill the Spartan except for me."

He drove away, looking at their puzzled expressions in his rear-view mirror.

Then he detonated the mine he had attached to the bottom of their car.

Chapter 38

In the event China went to war with the United States, the Chinese military had prepared a list of American targets it called "the irreplaceables". These "irreplaceables" were the best of the best of their enemy: brilliant men and women whose genius-level talent and brainpower could potentially sway any conflict.

Sourced from all races, colors and creeds, "the irreplaceables" had the ability to win battles, create entire industries from scratch, plan trillion-dollar economies, out-think the world's smartest people, imagine the future and forge the technology and circumstances to bring a country there.

They were once-in-a-generation types, the flukes of nature that sprang up at random, the prodigies that even China – with its own gene pool of 1 billion-plus very smart, very hard-working people – feared. They were the Isaac Newtons of their eras, the Einsteins, the Marie Curies. They were threats to China's future hegemony.

Their skills and abilities were so impressive that they would be impossible to replace: hence the name.

America would bleed if the irreplaceables bled.

The leader had seen some of the names of the irreplaceables.

Now, equipped with the Ghost Armor suits and his ninjas, he decided to act against them.

* * *

It was widely tipped that US biogeneticist Indira Kumar would win next year's Nobel Prize for medicine. Her knowledge of the human genome – and her pioneering techniques for altering the genes of humans – were like something out of science fiction.

And that was only the techniques out in the public sector. Her private work for the US military was something else altogether. Her projects made the Six Million Dollar Man look like a Ken Doll. Kumar's research was set to revolutionise the American fighting man. She had discovered some very remarkable things about the human body – and how to upgrade it. Something the military was very keen to explore.

And yet, she thought as she stood on the train platform, she liked to imagine that she was actually working for all of mankind. True, her research would be first used by the military, but she imagined that it would filter through to the general public. After all, look at GPS and the internet ... military programs now enjoyed by billions. Many would live happier, healthier, more vital lives thanks to her research.

The thought that she was working for the betterment of humanity filled her with a sense of satisfaction.

She still retained this sense of satisfaction when she was pushed by an unseen hand in front of the 8.49am train.

No one saw a thing.

* * *

Clyde Moore was known as "Mr Gadget" in engineering circles. And yet that seemingly harmless, almost patronising nickname did little to reflect the vastness of his brain. Nor did it seem a fitting moniker for a CEO who ran a multi-billion-dollar industrial empire.

Still, it was a nickname Moore didn't mind. He'd been able to fix things and invent gadgets even since he was a child, growing up alone and with a lot of time to kill in the orphanage. Only now instead of building ham radios and simple computers he was building road networks, weapons systems and the robots of the future.

Building things just came easy to him. And his fertile mind continued to invent and invent. His "gadgets" had the potential to disturb the world's balance of power and disrupt many industries. The military loved him, but the private sector – and his rivals, staring obsolescence in the face – weren't so sure.

That was why he had a small army of guards distributed throughout his penthouse, former elite soldiers and ex-special forces all. Not that there were any in here, thought the 50-year-old as he took off his robe and dived into his pool. Moore was a keen swimmer. The guards knew well to leave him alone when he took his dips.

But just as Moore was beginning to enjoy the swim, something seized his leg and held him under. Staring down, desperately searching for what held him, he could see nothing there. He gasped and gurgled and lost air.

Alarmed, he tried to swim to the surface. The invisible force held him still. Moore thrashed and thrashed, fingers just breaking the surface of the water, but whatever he tried, the force refused to let him go.

That beautiful brain flooded him with panic, sensing its own demise.

Eventually, the thrashing slowed down. Then stopped.

Moore floated on the surface of the water.

And something else stepped out of it.

* * *

"Man, I just crushed that," said billionaire IT genius Zack Johnson, raising his palm in the air. "Give me five."

One of his giant bodyguards performed a reluctant high-five. *Slap*.

Zack crashed back into one of the soft chair in the green room of the *Roger Cormorant Show*. Yes, he had indeed just crushed his performance on the high-rating late-night comedy program. The jokes his staff had written for him went down a bomb. His PR and media team would be happy. He had been funny, clever, self-deprecating ... *human*. For a brief moment the public would be cheering with him, rather than envying his vast wealth and resenting the fact that someone so young had the President on speed-dial.

Zack looked in the mini-bar. "They don't have my soda. Hey, Lurch, duck out and get me one. You know what I want. And some Skittles."

Whether the other huge bodyguard objected to being called Lurch was unknown, because he left the room without complaint in search of said soda. Certainly, the vast sums of money he was being paid would be enough to soothe the former Marine's ego.

Sometimes his bodyguards reminded the small, thin Zack of the sporting meatheads who bullied him at school. Humiliating athletic types gave him a certain amount of pleasure. So did the knowledge that he was now a billionaire who dated supermodels, while his erstwhile high school tormentors were probably working on minimum wage as janitors or in a lumberyard or something. Whatever it was geniuses didn't do for a living.

Zack helped himself to a handful of M&Ms in a bowl. He felt like making a joke about how he wanted them all in blue – and to send the remaining bodyguard to get him some – but decided not to. That would seem petty if someone leaked it to the press. Even if it would be funny.

As the world's richest 22-year-old and creator/CEO of Brainplant, the leading social media company, he was aware that his wealth attracted enemies. The ultrarich had to take care of themselves. Kidnapping was always a possibility. Otherwise he would have ditched Lurch and co long ago.

"Get a bodyguard," a fellow billionaire had advised him. "Hell, get 10. We're not popular out there."

He reflexively touched the slight bump on his thin left arm. Implanted inside was a tracking chip. He hadn't wanted a tracker, but his security people had insisted. All the best people had tracking chips, apparently.

Anyone worth kidnapping, that is.

That same billionaire had told him to get the chip, too.

So had the US military because of all the work he was doing with the Daedalus program. But he didn't like to think about that work too much or the grim-faced people he worked with. Talk of death and destruction bummed him out. Plus, if his fans knew he was working for the military, they'd think he sold out. And Zack enjoyed all the hero-worship from the IT fanboys and girls.

He nervously drummed his fingers on the chair. He was still surfing the adrenalin rush from being on TV. Zack enjoyed his fame and the adulation his power in the tech world brought him. It was almost too much for someone his age to handle – a billionaire before the age of 25! The numbers of world leaders on his smartphone! But Zack thought he was handling it. *Crushing it, even.*

And anyone who thought otherwise was a douche.

Zack was aware that his remaining bodyguard was watching him carefully. The ex-Marine was paid to watch him closely, but still, he felt like a little privacy. Online privacy might be dead, but that didn't mean he wanted to have someone physically hovering over him every second of the day.

He scarfed down another handful of M&Ms. Yes, Lurch No.2 would have to leave. He could wait outside with the rest of the security team. Zack wanted to luxuriate in the pride of his TV performance. He swallowed the rest of the M&Ms and opened his mouth to issue a new order.

But he didn't get the chance.

A sword suddenly swung through the neck of his bodyguard.

The bodyguard's head landed in Zack's lap.

Before Zack could scream a foot collided into his face.

Then he felt another blow.

Then blackness.

Zack knew he was in trouble when he came to. He tried to move, but found himself unable to budge. His head aching, he glanced down to discover that his arms and legs were tied with rope to a chair. Zack looked up again to see that all the walls in the small room were covered in white canvas.

The IT billionaire felt the beginnings of a cold shiver run down his spine.

There was more. Directly in front of Zack was a video camera, the red light on the top blinking to denote that it was recording.

And behind that stood a tall, supple man dressed in a strange, all-over silver suit. A horror holding an unsheathed samurai sword.

"You're awake," said the masked figure in a voice rich with command. "Good. We can begin."

Zack stared around, breathing hard. There was no air in this tiny space. "Where am I?"

"Somewhere where we won't be disturbed."

Zack stared at his restraints again, as if having trouble believing they were really there. "Who ... who are you?"

"Now that would be telling."

"Is this a kidnapping?" Zack's eyes went to his arm and the small, fresh cut there.

"No, this is not a kidnapping," said the figure, standing completely still. "And yes, I have removed your tracking device. I don't want to be interrupted during our ... conversation."

Zack's stomach churned. He was a genius – by his own estimation and that of others – but fear was clouding his higher brain functions. He took a deep breath and tried to remember his kidnap training. The young billionaire recalled a PowerPoint presentation. "Step one: open a dialogue."

"What do you want? Talk to me, man. Whatever it is, we can make a deal. Everything's negotiable."

"Everything's negotiable. That hasn't been true in my experience." Zack imagined the figure smiling behind the silver mask. "You have nothing to offer me ... except for one thing."

"Just name it, dude! My people will deliver the money! Just let me go!"

"I fear you will be reluctant to pay this price," came the slow, deliberate reply. The swordsman slowly walked up to him. He moved differently to Zack's bodyguards, his movements terrifyingly lithe and precise, no energy wasted. The man roughly grabbed Zack's chin in his hand. "Zack Johnson, captain of industry. Only you're no captain I'd like to salute." He suddenly held Zack's face towards the camera. "Is this the face of a man trying to 'build a better world'?" he asked savagely.

Zack said nothing. But he began breathing heavily, gulping in air.

"Gah … it disgusts me to think that someone so young has so much wealth while his elders starve. In any other age you would have been trampled into the ground. In another time your head would be on a pike for the world to see." The tall man waved his hand towards the camera. "But where are my manners? Say hello to your online audience."

Zack glanced back towards the camera. "What?"

"Yes. You have an audience of millions. The people who have made you so rich and powerful. This is streaming live to the internet." The horror turned towards the camera. "Give Zack a warm welcome, people. He's feeling a little shy."

Then he turned back to Zack. "Just imagine how many 'likes' this is getting. I wonder how many people are secretly enjoying your predicament. You're not the most popular person, Zack. I hope you don't mind me saying that. And if you do mind, I don't care." The masked face tilted in thought. "Hmmm … it's a shame I didn't bring my phone. We could have posed for a 'selfie' together."

A sliver of hope sprang up in Zack's breast at the thought of having an online audience. "Go on," said the kidnapper mockingly. "Get it out of the way. You know you want to."

"Help! Help!" shouted Zack, thrashing ineffectually in his chair. "Some mad fucker's kidnapped me! If you're seeing this, track down the IP address and help me!"

There was a pause. The room was silent except for the sounds of Zack struggling in his seat. After a few seconds, his abductor asked, with disdain, "Are you finished?"

But Zack wasn't. "Hellpppp!" he screamed, even louder this time.

"This signal is being bounced off so many satellites you might as well be screaming on the moon," said the kidnapper calmly. "There will be no rescue, no matter how loudly you caterwaul. You're only embarrassing yourself now."

"Fuck! Fuck!" Zack knew that such a technological feat could be possible. Immediate rescue was unlikely.

"Shall we wait a little longer? I think I can almost hear the rescue choppers."

"Jesus, what do you want? Say it!"

"I want you to apologize," intoned the figure in silver gravely.

"Huh?"

"Apologize. I want you to apologize."

Zack felt his face become wet with perspiration. "I don't get it. Apologize for what?"

"For your greed. For your country. For everything."

"I don't understand." His captor brought the edge of the sword to Zack's neck. Zack felt his blood flow.

"Apologize! Sincerely! Now!"

Zack's mind raced. Surely there was some rational way of talking himself out of this death trap. An apology could be a good start. Give the crazy man something and maybe he'd take the sword away from his neck. Step two in the anti-kidnapping guide: establish common ground with your captor.

Besides, they were just words.

"Jesus, I apologize! I apologize for whatever the fuck you want me to apologize for! I apologize! There! I said it! OK?"

The masked man quickly withdrew the sword, the blade slicing the air with a whooshing sound. "Good, good," he murmured. He paused, then stood behind Zack. "Your Vice President refused to apologize. He knew it wouldn't save him. I have to admire that."

Zack's tormentor raised the sword. "He's dead now," he said, staring straight down the barrel of the camera. "That's right, America. Dead. Killed by this very sword. Sadly, your media has failed to report it. I suspect your government has suppressed the information ... just as it has suppressed other truths in your recent past." The swordsman turned to the camera conspiratorially. "You might want to ask why."

"You ... you killed the Vice President?" asked Zack in a tiny, scared voice.

"Yes. He was a symbol of your country. Much as you are." There was no remorse in the strange figure's voice over his crimes ... just chilling purpose. He raised his sword. "To die by this blade might be considered an honor. But that is not the intention." The kidnapper paused. "Remember what I said before about having your head on a pike?"

Zack screamed. The camera caught it all.

"Perfect, Zack. And that's a wrap."

The sword descended.

Chapter 39

Governments worldwide battled mightily to pull the footage of Zack's execution off the internet and airwaves, but in today's multiconnected new world, even a second's hesitation was too late.

Within minutes the footage had been shared to the nth degree around the globe. Millions in the First World had already seen it and commented on it on social media platforms. It wasn't like the old days where you could lean on a newspaper or TV proprietor to stop them publishing something embarrassing. Once it was on the net, it was impossible to stop despite the best efforts of an army of social media "scrubbers".

In a cruel irony, the late Zack himself had written algorithms that permitted ultra-fast encrypted sharing of information. Now he was being hoisted (or "posted") on his own petard.

Even the Chinese, those masters of internet control with their Great Wall of Censorship, couldn't halt its viral spread.

Within hours the video clip was one of the most-watched social media video clips (non-cat category) of all time.

Reactions varied. Many were horrified by the sheer brutality of the killing. The public had been kept from the reality of war for decades, so such a public execution harkened back to the days of the Vietnam war, where you could watch Vietcong being executed in the streets of Saigon while you ate your TV dinner.

Yet others weren't particularly sad that one of the One Percenters had met such a violent end. In a world increasingly divided into the haves and have-nots, the death of one of the ultra-rich "haves" was greeted with almost jubilation in chat rooms.

Some even thought the executioner had a certain level of dark charisma.

The media was overdosing on the spectacle, tut-tutting at the crime while spreading it as far and wide as they could.

The story was running 24/7 now, the public insatiable in its need to know all aspects of the snuff film. Who was the masked man with the sword? Had Zack's body been found? Was his head really decorating a pike somewhere?

And more still – was the claim that the assassin had also killed the Vice President true?

There were few answers to be had.

And none of them did a damn bit of good to calm the situation.

* * *

The Spartan and Vasquez watched the execution on a laptop, the Spartan sitting down, Vasquez peering over his shoulder.

"It's like a scene from Mexico's drug wars," said Vasquez. "Gross. And that guy with the sword? What a psycho."

The Spartan nodded. But he also thought something else.

That the killer held the weapon like a man born to swordwork.

And such a man was dangerous.

Chapter 40

Shintaro turned off his plasma TV set after watching the footage of the execution. He had studied the bloody scenes for more than an hour, comparing the images with those he held in his mind. Eventually, he unfolded an intricate, faded drawing, held it close to the screen, froze the image, and carefully compared the drawing with the image on TV.

At last, he was satisfied.

It was true. The fine detailing on the weapon was the same. The length, the breadth, the handle were all correct. The executioner had used the Honjo Masamune to murder the unfortunate American billionaire.

The Honjo Masamune, the sacred sword Shintaro had been searching for for more than 30 years.

The blessed blade had finally been sighted. And more than that – the Japanese agent had a good idea who had been wielding it.

Shintaro and his team had been searching for the Honjo Masamune for more than 30 years. It had travelled through various countries and had fallen into many renegade hands over those decades, but had always remained with the Chinese.

Shintaro and his 10-man team had been tasked with recovering the sword – and not to return to Japan until they did. He and his men had wandered the earth like Far Eastern knights, endlessly searching for their Grail, facing many challenges of strength and faith.

They had exerted themselves hard, but their adversaries had been clever and similarly determined. There had been much bloodshed on both sides, a secret war hidden from its host country.

But Shintaro was not dissuaded. He was a disciple of bushido, descended from samurai. And the way of the samurai was death.

So Shintaro had persevered over the years, when the prize seemed far from his grasp, when others would have given up and returned to the bosom of their families. Duty and honor kept him going, sustaining him long after most would have surrendered.

He had seen his family four times in the past 20 years. His son had grown from a boy into a nervous teenager who didn't recognise or respect him. His wife and daughter were almost strangers. His wife supported his cause, but his children could only pretend to understand it. Nor could he tell them when his mission might end, if ever.

Meanwhile, the Japan he had grown up in had changed immeasurably ... he sensed that not everyone in the new generation would respect his quest or even care about some missing old sword. Everything the new generation worshipped was economic or electric.

Certainly he could not imagine his son, a virtual shut-in more interested in videogames and the internet, a weak-willed, sexless "herbivore man", ever taking on such a responsibility.

Shintaro was aware that he was caught between two cultures: a Japan that had irrevocably changed and an America he could never be fully part of. He was a warrior with a mission but nowhere to call home.

Reading his reports, Tokyo had sensed his growing despair. It had dispatched a geisha to the US to console him.

After a week he sent her away. Her company, her sympathy and her body were unwelcome, her faux concern grating.

He started drinking more heavily. Yet *sake* could only do so much to dull such pain ... and the shame of failing to complete his mission.

Some nights, when he almost reached the limits of doubt, he hit the *sake* too hard. Cold noodles, rice wine and regret were his fare on many evenings.

Of Shintaro's team, he was the only one left alive. The last had died in his arms, perishing from some vile fish toxin used by the enemy. Employing poison struck him as the height of dishonor. Poison was a ninja's weapon, one he would never stoop to use.

He had been badly wounded on several occasions, his body covered in scars, both from blades and bullets. The Japanese agent was missing a finger on his left hand, as if he had been a yakuza punished for failure. He had personally killed many Chinese, but their ranks had always been replenished. Few had talked – and those that had had supplied him with outdated information.

He had even been captured once: by a determined American who somehow knew of his mission. Rather than turn him in, the special forces soldier had been amused and fascinated by his operation, and had let him go with a warning never to endanger American lives during his quest.

It was an instruction he had kept – along with an unusual friendship with the American.

Yet Shintaro now had the best opportunity in years within his sword reach. He had tracked the enemy to six possible safe houses around the US. Analysts back in Japan were calculating the odds of which one the enemy would use.

Shintaro stood to his full height. At five and a half feet, Shintaro was small for the men of this era, but his body was as hard as stone, with barely an ounce of fat. He drew his samurai sword and examined the blade by the room light. His deadly katana had its own illustrious history, dating back to the time of the shoguns.

Yes, Shintaro was descended from true samurai. Not like the pretender, who wielded the Honjo Masamune yet carried himself in the manner of a ninja. It disgusted him that the noble blade was in the hands of such a dishonorable foe. A ninja, no less ... the eternal foe of the samurai, the night warriors who struck from behind rather than face an enemy head on. The Honjo Masamune belonged in the hands of shoguns, not shinobi.

Samurai and ninjas hated each other with the lethal passion cats reserved for dogs.

But Shintaro could not underestimate this ninja foe again. The Chinese agent was a master of the blade, something two of his soldiers had learnt to their ultimate regret, their essence spilling onto the cold floor of a hastily abandoned warehouse.

And while Shintaro's will was as strong as ever, he was no longer a young man. He had begun his quest as a 25-year-old ... and that was 30 years ago. The pretender had youth, speed, stamina and, yes, a dauntless spirit on his side. It was possible Shintaro could slay him in single combat, but he could not take the chance that he might die in the struggle and that the Honjo Masamune would be lost for yet another generation.

The ninjas themselves had also become harder to track. It was as if they had begun to disappear from view as Shintaro followed them. Impossible ... and yet, how else to explain their sudden, new-found stealth abilities? Unless he had become careless. Or the enemy had become more careful.

So Shintaro would have to exercise extreme care. He glanced at the armor resting on a stand nearby. Yes. It was time to wear it again and make his ancestors proud. He would complete his mission for his own sense of honor and for his country, which badly needed good news after a prolonged economic recession, the calamity of Fukushima and being supplanted by China as the world's No.2 economy.

Shintaro knew there was one other person could contact for support and reinforcement. An old friend who knew of his mission ... and approved. A fierce American who fully understood the warrior code and matters of honor.

He would call Colonel Garin.

Shintaro reached for his phone.

Chapter 41

The leader watched his lover in the shower. Standing invisibly in a corner, he took the opportunity to admire her perfect, supple body – a field of sweet flesh he knew all too well. Her form was almost perfect, her face most comely.

He felt his urges rise. Yes – he would have her. Now. And she would have him. If she would take him.

As he moved closer he collided with something out of thin air. Another night warrior appeared in front of him, gasping with shock. One of his men had had the same idea, to spy on the lone female in the group as she performed her ablutions. It was to be expected that his men would miss the company of women after so many months without the touch of a female.

But this was *his* woman. And the leader was outraged.

He would punish the offender now.

* * *

His lover stopped soaping herself, stunned by the sight of two ninjas outside the cubicle.

With a snarl on his lips, the leader drew the Honjo Masamune and swung it down towards the man's neck. The other ninja barely had time to raise his hands in defense – or to plead for his life – before the blade severed his head, slicing straight through the ninja's Ghost Armor.

The body collapsed to the ground.

His lover noted the gesture and deciphered its meaning. She nodded in approval. Her body was for him alone.

"Take off the suit and come here," she said, beckoning with a spare hand.

He obliged her.

* * *

Later, the leader took both parts of the Ghost Armor and tossed them on Eisenstein's work station.

"Fix this," he said bluntly.

Eisenstein eyed the pieces of garment, noting the blood and the almost surgical precision with which they had been separated.

"What happened?" he asked, holding the pieces up.

"One of my men disappointed me." The leader fixed Eisenstein with a cruel, unforgiving stare. "Pray you do not do the same."

Eisenstein swallowed hard.

Chapter 42

Every assassin had their own speciality. Some liked knives. Some preferred the intimacy and tradition of the garrotte. Some killers preferred to shoot their victims up close, while others sniped from rooftops half a mile away. There were those who dabbled in poisons, some who arranged "perfect accidents" and the odd assassin who liked to run over his victims in cars.

Salvatore DiCaprio (no relation) was known as the "car boot killer" in his native Sicily. His speciality was secreting himself in the trunks of cars, following his victims to their place of rest, and then quietly assassinating them with a silenced pistol as they slept. Not only did his victims take care of all the transportation, they also supplied him with a getaway car.

Salvatore thought there was a neat elegancy to that equation. He disliked showy assassinations: he had no desire for spectacular deaths like his colleagues, blowing up bridges and entire entourages just to get to one wayward judge. His method had never failed him, mostly because it was simple and discreet.

The long hours hiding in car boots never bothered Salvatore. He was used to enclosed spaces from his many years in solitary confinement in prison in Sicily.

It also helped that he was a small man ... a small, grey, anonymous-looking man few would remember if they saw him on the street.

Yet he was getting on in years: particularly in "assassin" years, where every year after 40 might as well have been five. It was approaching the time to return to some quaint, rustic Italian village where he could drink the local wine and fuck middle-aged American women going through mid-life crises.

Salvatore had done much wetwork for the Santini crime family in Italy. They had lured him to the States with the promise of their $10 million-dollar contract. Such money was bound to attract the best – plus half the underworld would have spotters out, keen to gain a commission for locating the target.

One such freelancer had located the primary targets near Martha's Vineyard. The freelancer had followed the Spartan and Vasquez, tipped Salvatore off en route, and allowed the Sicilian to follow their trail.

Salvatore had arranged for the freelancer to be paid, waited until the targets answered the call of nature at a gas station, the big man going to the bathroom, the comely Latina buying gas and snacks, before he let himself into their car boot. He was familiar with their brand of American-made four-door sedan, often favored by the government. He knew its locks well. Within seconds he was in.

He curled his body up into a ball, made himself as comfortable as he could, took two amphetamine pills to keep him sharp and awake, and prepared to wait until his targets turned in for the night at some motel or other location. It was already dark and the pair looked tired.

Then he would make his move.

He felt the car slump as the big man entered, followed by the woman who took the wheel. He thought about which of them he would take first. He wondered if it would be the woman. The European counter-terrorist police had a saying – "shoot the women first" – because to survive in a male-dominated terrorist world the women had to be more ruthless than the men. He did get a dangerous vibe from this "Vasquez". But the big American also looked deadly. Perhaps he would just play it by ear.

The car started.

Salvatore smiled. He wondered what he was going to do with all that $10 million dollars.

* * *

Vasquez drove. By mutual agreement, Vasquez usually drove. One, the Spartan hated driving, and two, when he drove, it was like he was racing through a war zone, the vehicle being peppered by bullets. And when he parked, it was like he was trying to crash the car.

More than that, he disagreed with the absolutism of road instructions such as "right lane must run right". Sometimes, he believed, just like on the bad roads of Afghanistan and Iraq, "the right lane" could do whatever the hell it wanted.

So ... Vasquez usually drove. Like now.

"We've picked up a tail," said Vasquez, staring in the rear-view mirror.

The Spartan followed her eyes with his own. "You mean the pair of Suzuki Hayabusas? They've been following us since the gas station."

"Longer," said Vasquez, her eyes flicking between the road and the mirror. "Pissed off anyone lately I should know about?"

The list of people the Spartan had pissed off was long. But he replied: "Nope."

"You think they could be after the $10 million bounty the colonel warned us about?"

"That much money is bound to attract all the scumbags."

"I guess you're thinking about sticking your SAW out of the window and shooting them."

The Spartan flashed back to the suicide car bomber that had come almost too close for comfort in Iraq. "Our rules of engagement state we can't do anything until they do something threatening," said the Spartan. "Just in case they really are extreme sports enthusiasts rather than killers on motorbikes."

"A rare display of restraint, lover," smirked Vasquez. "It feels like a cartel hit to me. They're *sicarios*."

"What?"

"Hired assassins. More Spanish for you to remember." One of the Hayabusas accelerated straight past their sedan, swerving in front of the vehicle. "There. I've seen this before. Been *part* of it before. It's a cartel sandwich. The one ahead sets the trap. The one behind pushes us into it."

You may use deadly force to defend yourself from serious injury or death, flashed the warning from the Spartan's Rules Of Engagement card in his mind. The Spartan grabbed his SAW. "Let me take care of your *sicarios*. I'll disable their vehicles first. Deny them transportation."

"I have a better idea. But first, we need one of those bikes." Vasquez put her foot on the gas. The nimble Hayabusa behind them sped up. Vasquez increased her speed. The bike kept pace.

"Hold on," shouted Vasquez. She slammed on the brakes just as the rider was drawing a machinegun from his leather jacket. The rider let loose with a burst into the trunk before he crashed into the back of the car. He flew over the roof and bonnet before landing awkwardly onto the road. The Hayabusa skidded to the side. Its tyres spun before the engine cut out.

"Let's brace him," said Vasquez as she pulled over and quickly exited the vehicle, followed by the Spartan with his SAW. Fortunately, the road was relatively deserted. And if anyone saw what was going on, no good Samaritan was about to stop.

Or a bad Samaritan.

The biker moaned as Vasquez tore off his helmet. The rider was young, Latino, his face bloody.

He looked like a sexy Jesus.

Vasquez put her pistol against his head. "Who do you work for?"

"I need medical attention," he gasped.

"Don't make me ask again, *pendejo*. Who do you work for?"

"Talk, or we'll kill you," warned the Spartan.

Looking at their grim faces, the *sicario* didn't need to be told a fourth time to talk. "The Jaguar."

Vasquez recalled the mocking message she had been sent by "The Jaguar", thanking her for killing Fighting Dog. The cartel kingpin's gratitude evidently had an expiry date.

Vasquez pushed the gun more firmly against the *sicario's* head. "I've heard of him. So has half of Mexico. And you're chasing the $10 million-dollar bounty?"

"Si," said the *sicario* weakly.

"Why is the bounty so high?" asked Vasquez.

"Because whoever takes the contract will have to quit the profession because of the heat," said the rider, eyes darting around, afraid. "You killed Fighting Dog with a knife. The cartels feel humiliated that one of their own was killed by a ... a ... a woman."

"Good," said Vasquez with satisfaction.

"I've heard enough," said the Spartan, raising his SAW.

"Wait, wait!" said the *sicario*, holding his gloved hands in front of his face. "I can help you. I have something I can trade for my life!"

The Spartan held his SAW aside. "It's a trick."

Vasquez lifted her Beretta away from the rider's head. "OK, I'm listening. Make it good."

"We were set to place a radio-controlled mine on the road," said the rider rapidly.

"I figured something like that," said Vasquez. "I worked in Juarez. Full of tricky scumbags like you." Vasquez reapplied her weapon to his temple. "That's not enough to buy my mercy." The *sicario* raised his gloved hands.

"Wait! Wait! I have more! The ... the Jaguar was the one who ordered Fighting Dog to kill your family."

Vasquez froze. "What?"

"It was The Jaguar all along. That's worth something, right?"

"Yes," said Vasquez, now steely-eyed. "It's worth this." Without hesitation, she stepped back and shot him in the temple. The gunshot echoed over the traffic noise. Vasquez stared at the Spartan. "If it's true what he said, my revenge isn't over."

"We'll find out later," insisted the Spartan. "Drag the body towards the side of the road. I've got to take care of something else." The Spartan glanced back at Vasquez's pistol. "Still using the Beretta? I can get you better."

"It's not the size of the gun, it's how you use it," smirked Vasquez. "And I don't recall any complaints from you so far."

The Spartan smiled despite himself. He found himself smiling more ever since he'd met Vasquez.

As Vasquez pulled the dead cartel hitman to the side of the road, the Spartan went to the back of the car, raised his SAW and fired into the boot.

"What *are* you doing?"

"Thought I heard something." The Spartan flung upon the boot, then stepped aside, weapon up. Inside, a critically injured middle-aged stranger groaned. The stowaway had been shot twice – once by the cartel rider, and a second time by the Spartan. He was bleeding from several wounds, stretching all the way from his legs to his stomach, the latter clutched in a feeble attempt to stem the bleeding.

"We had a hitchhiker," stated the Spartan. He hauled the olive-skinned man outside of the boot. "Thought I heard a groan when the trunk was shot up."

"That sneaky bastard!" shouted Vasquez. She stared at the ruined back of the car. "Guess we won't be getting that car deposit back."

"No." The Spartan held the unarmored intruder by the lapels. "It's name, rank and serial number time, asshole. Who are you? Who do you work for?"

"Fuck … you," uttered the stowaway. His eyed blazed with the passion of a true psychopath. Then he said something in Italian. The Spartan dropped him to the ground in response. The stowaway crumpled.

"Why don't you follow your *own* suggestion," he said.

The Italian clicked his foot against the ground. A knife sprang out of the point of his boot. He swung it towards the

Spartan's leg. The Spartan stepped away, then stomped down on the blade, snapping it at the base.

Then the Spartan put his knee on the man's head. "Nice try. That's some real Bond villain stuff right there. Unfortunately, you're as superfluous as Scaramanga's third nipple." The Spartan pressed harder. "So ... you work for the Santinis or something? I don't think I've pissed off any other Romans recently." The assassin said nothing, just twitched in pain. The Spartan prodded him with his SAW. "Talk."

"He's not going to make it," said Vasquez. She looked back up the road. "And if we want to catch the other rider, we have to move." Vasquez had already donned the dead biker's leathers and helmet. She nodded, her face now hidden under the visor.

"Finish it. Give him the whole nine yards."

There was a time when the former cop in Vasquez might have tried to talk me out of shooting him, thought the Spartan. He said: "You heard the lady."

The Santini killer cursed in Italian, some vile peasant vitriol. "The Spartan," he said. "A stupid name. I've been to Sparta. There's nothing left."

"*I'm* what's left."

The Spartan raised the SAW and fired, holding down the trigger for a good three seconds. The killer twitched and jerked as the bullets went home. Then the assassin lay still.

"See you down the road," said Vasquez, then rode off on the Hayabusa, dirt flying up beside her tyres.

The Spartan dragged the car boot killer to the side of the road beside the cartel assassin, got into the car and drove off.

* * *

Vasquez accelerated as fast as she could on the Hayabusa, zooming down the highway looking for the likely assassination point. In a few fraught seconds, she saw what she was searching for: a bridge on top of the highway, with a convenient lurking spot for a *sicario* with a radio transmitter. A classic cartel ambush point.

Sure enough, as she came closer, she spied a helmeted rider on a Hayabusa lurking in the shadows, holding something in a gloved hand. Vasquez guessed it was the mine trigger.

She rode up and tapped the front of her helmet with her own gloved hand, indicating that she wanted to talk. It was dark and from a distance it would look like she was the small Mexican hitman she had just shot. They had the same lean body shape ... and Vasquez could ride a motorbike with the best of them.

As she came to a stop right next to the other rider, sending dirt and gravel flying, the rider lifted his visor.

"What's wrong?" he said in Spanish, leaning forward on his Hayabusa. "And where is the car?"

Before the rider could figure out it wasn't his partner, Vasquez had her Beretta out. She shot him in the forehead as he fumbled for his pistol. The rider fell back, along with his bike.

All done, she thought, staring down at the dead man and the fresh, neat hole in his head. Now to locate the mine on the road.

Then she would have to think some more about the revelation that the cartel boss behind her family's killing was still alive.

Chapter 43

The General smirked as he leant back in his expensive, ergonomic Swedish chair in his office, regarding the journalist sitting in the chair opposite.

For many, a meet-and-greet with this Pulitzer Prize winner would be considered an honor. For many, this tall, well-preserved gent was the very epitome of an investigative journalist, a towering figure who made the corrupt and powerful quiver in their shoes.

The General was not one of the many.

The General had read the journalist's award-winning articles and watched him many times on TV as he fought for truth, liberty, open government and democracy. This silver-haired interrogator had brought former Presidents and business leaders to their metaphorical knees with his sharp, incisive questioning. His syndicated columns were read by millions. His radio spots held the attention of the ears of the nation. More than once he had been described as "the Cronkite of his generation".

He had even won a Peabody.

He was also, the General thought, smiling again, *his bitch*.

"I only have 10 minutes to spare," said the journalist, his mellifluous voice rich with arrogance.

"You have as long as I want you to have … Brett," said the General harshly. He pointed a finger at "Brett". "Don't forget that. And don't forget what I have on you."

What the General had on the prince of print and titan of TV was knowledge of a scandal far greater than some commonplace money or sex crime. No, Brett was guilty of the worst crime possible for a journalist – plagiarism. Plagiarism was akin to being found guilty of treason in the world of the hack. Journalists could and did survive drug, fraud and sex scandals, but once they were convicted of plagiarism in the court of press opinion their careers were over.

The General took a moment to reflect on the hypocrisy and double standards of the world. A military commander might be forgiven for ordering a missile strike on a village that killed dozens of innocent people – "shit happens" – yet a journalist was hung out to dry for clicking "cut and paste" one time too often. "Control C, Control V" had destroyed many a career.

Go figure.

But the young Brett had gone further than clicking "cut and paste". In his early twenties, he was also guilty of making up quotes, inventing fictitious interview subjects, even inventing facts to sex up a story.

The fact that it had happened decades ago, when the journalist had been a mere intern trying to make his way up the competitive Washington career ladder, would be no excuse. But, living in a less curious, less suspicious age, Brett had gotten away with it, climbing to the very top of his profession. There would be no tell-all midday telemovie about

Brett's crimes, no bestselling memoir where Brett tearfully tried to explain his side of the story to the public and Oprah.

Unless, of course, the General made it so. Which Brett knew all too well.

The General possessed a dossier of Brett's misdeeds, hanging onto the information for decades until he decided to pull the trigger.

Like now.

Which was why Brett's head was bowed under the weight of the knowledge that the other man had him on toast.

"Cheer up," the General told Brett. "I'm going to give you a big story. Huge."

Brett head snapped back up at the mention of a huge story. "What is it? Bigger than the death of the Vice President?"

"Let's just say it's part of the same story. A subset, if you will."

"Speaking of the Vice President ... I can't get anyone to confirm he's dead," said Brett, reaching into his bag for a notepad. The General leaned forward and slapped it out of his hands.

"No notes, dickhead," he said. "Not until I give your permission."

"Ow," said the journalist, rubbing his wrist. "That's assault."

The General laughed, subconsciously touching the scar on his face given to him by the Spartan. "My friend, you have no idea what being assaulted really means."

Brett scowled and rubbed his wrist. *Pussy.*

"But I can confirm that the VP is indeed dead. That weirdo you saw on TV killing that young fool Zack was responsible." No great loss there, thought the General. Particularly as the VP had come between the General and his revenge against the Spartan last year.

"Christ," breathed Brett.

"Christ indeed. Cut his head right off. Snicker-snack, went the vorpal sword. Killed about a dozen Secret Service agents in the process. I've seen the pics. They had to carry the VP out in two bags."

"My God."

"Are all your exclamations religious?"

"Sorry. I went to a Catholic high school." He paused. "Who is the man in silver?"

"We don't know yet. But his colleagues are Chinese. Chinese ninjas, of all things." *Those assholes escaped from the History Channel, just like the Spartan*, thought the General.

"Ninjas plural? There's more than one?"

"Yes. And they're deadlier than a Texan rattlesnake. Plus they're still at large killing people."

Brett's eyes went wide as he lapped up the juicy deets. "Do we know why they're killing A-list Americans?"

"Because it's fun. Kidding. No. No idea. Except that they clearly hate the United States." The General was going to add, they hate our freedoms, except he was afraid he would laugh at the cliché, used by every social-climbing asshole in Washington.

Brett nodded, clearly savoring the information. "Hating the United States is a pretty big club. So that's the story you wanted me to print?"

"Part of it. I also want to help you place the blame at the appropriate doorstep." The General paused, folding his fingers into the shape of a steeple. "Let's just say a ... missing technology is responsible for the ease in which the assassins have completed their job. Technology that was the responsibility of a certain colonel." The General nodded towards Brett's pen. "*Now* you may begin to take notes."

Brett's pen was poised above his notepad. "Does this colonel have a name?"

The General automatically shook his head. "Are you kidding? I won't give you that. Let's just call him … 'Colonel X'."

"Catchy."

"Would look good in a headline, too. If our Mr X done his job right, the technology wouldn't have been stolen, the Vice President would probably still be alive and you wouldn't be seeing live executions on the internet."

Brett breathed in deeply, savoring the dirt. "The plot thickens. So … can you tell me what the missing technology is and who it belongs to? Army, navy, air force, Marines?"

"No." The General swivelled in his chair. "And I'd be careful about digging into that if I were you. Or even trying to find out the colonel's name. Not everyone is … as friendly to the press as I am. And this colonel is one mean, slippery bastard."

"Despite dropping the ball on the missing tech."

"Despite that. My advice to you is to run with what I've given you. Confirmation that the Vice President is dead alone is enough to make you the star of the evening news. Enough to bump the Chinese President's visit from prime position."

"I need to have someone else confirm this information before I run it. I need a secondary source."

"No, you don't," said the General angrily. "Have I ever lied to you?"

"Well … no. But why do I suspect you've got it in for this colonel? How do I know you're not using me in some political game?"

A Shakespearean quote sprang to the General's mind: "He that filches from me my good name/Robs me of that which not enriches him/And makes me poor indeed." But only an asshole quoted Shakespeare when a brusque slap down was what was required.

"You don't know if I'm using you in some game," insisted the General coldly. "Just be grateful I'm using you at all." The General could see Brett was working himself up to make the kind of witty rebuttal that made him the darling of the left-wing media. But the General wasn't in the mood to hear the wisdom of a eunuch.

"And need I remind you, you're not in some episode of Aaron Sorkin's *The Newsroom*," he scolded. "We both know exactly what kind of man you are. Or were. A pretty speech about the freedom of the press isn't going to save you if the truth about your past plagiarism gets out."

The General tapped his folder. "You have the same choice as the cartels give their enemies. Silver or lead. Or ink or lead, really. Take the gift – which in this case, is the biggest story going – or take the lead, which is that your news story is replaced with another big story, involving plagiarism and worse by one of the biggest stars on the Hill." The General snickered. "Try getting a sit-down with the President after the latter story hits the interwebs."

The General watched Brett squirm in his chair. He could see the torment behind those telegenic brown eyes. But the General knew his man. Our lion of the Fourth Estate had too much to lose – money, power, prestige, the company of comely, educated, star-struck women – to throw it all away at this stage in his career over a fit of conscience. Swallowing his pride was easier than becoming a non-entity.

"Time for your offering of earth and water," crowed the General.

This was the part of power the General enjoyed, the bending of men to his will, the breaking of their spirit and resistance. It was surprising just how many individuals failed to make even the most token resistance in the face of authority. In the General's experience, only the rarest crooked nail refused to be hammered down. Only the most stubborn, sturdy nail withstood the hammer blows, dreaming of the chance of retaliation.

And Brett was no brave, crooked nail.

"All right," uttered the defeated journalist. "Damn you, all right. How do you want me to quote you?"

"As an 'top-ranking Pentagon source'. Yes, that sounds about right."

"Fine," answered Brett huffily. "But we're not done, even with your caveats. You've just given me the skeleton of a story here. I need to add meat to it. I have more questions I have to ask to round out the piece."

The General smiled and leant back in his chair, satisfied he had gotten his way. "Of course. I'm always happy to help a member of our fearless press. Ask away."

Chapter 44

The leader leant in the doorway as Professor Eisenstein toiled over a damaged set of Ghost Armor.

"Did you like my little show with Zack?" said the leader, voice muffled underneath his mask.

"You're a monster," came the cold reply.

"An effective monster. Zack's execution has spread all manner of chaos. Now everyone from a Vice President to a billionaire knows he's not safe. This Ghost Armor is a great leveller of men." The masked head tilted slightly. "Almost … democratic."

"Listen to you," said Eisenstein, still refusing to look up. "Do you think this is a game?"

"What, like Blind Man's Bluff, Professor?" said the leader gaily. "Or Murder In The Dark? Yes … perhaps it is a game. A bloody game."

"How much blood will make you happy?"

The leader regarded Eisenstein with amusement. "For a man who builds armor that turns soldiers into invisible killing machines, you are surprisingly squeamish, professor."

"But what is your end game? What do you hope to achieve?"

"You're an intelligent man. You figure it out. Let us just say that power, like nature, abhors a vacuum."

"And you and your kind hope to create and then fill that vacuum?"

The leader said nothing.

Eisenstein gestured to the TV set in the corner, his one luxury during his imprisonment. "I see the Chinese Premier is coming to America in two days. Is that timing coincidental?"

"Few things are coincidental." The leader adopted an odd pose. "We shall push the world until it groans 'enough'. And then we shall push some more."

Professor Eisenstein gritted his teeth. "You're insane."

"I am perfectly rational. Something you should continue to count on for your own fortunes."

"How are my family?"

"They are safe. For now."

"I want to talk to them." Professor Eisenstein's voice sounded pained. "Why won't you let me talk to them?"

"You don't need to talk to them. Concentrate on your work at hand."

Professor Eisenstein stared at the movement of the leader's face underneath his mask. Then something struck him.

It was an interesting fact in theater that masks worn by actors could be frighteningly effective in communicating the emotions of the actor underneath. Even though the ridges and contours of the mask were fixed, they could somehow take on an almost magical ability to transmit everything from joy to misery.

It was then – only then – that Professor Eisenstein figured it out. Watching the leader's bare face outside of the Ghost

Armor, he had been unable to detect falsehood when the ninja claimed that he had his children.

Now, with the leader's face masked, Professor Eisenstein knew for sure that the leader was lying.

The leader didn't have his wife and children. And what's more, he sensed that the leader never had.

He now knew that he had to resist.

"The equipment and resources you've left me aren't enough," he said. "If you want continued maintenance and upgrades, I'll need access to the internet."

"I would advise you of the consequences of deception," said the leader.

"All the scientific research I need is stored on the net. It's the way of the future."

"So Zack would say. And look what happened to him."

Eisenstein's blood ran cold at the threat. But he pressed on. "You want the best out of me, I need net access. Plus new materials."

In a flash, the leader drew the Honjo Masamune and rested it against Eisenstein's neck. The razor-sharp blade drew blood ... blood that dripped down the scientist's neck and onto his white coat. Eisenstein held his ground.

Finally, the ninja said: "I will grant you limited access. Under supervision. But you can forget any thoughts about begging for help. We can't be tracked. Just as I told the late Zack."

"I heard you the first time," said Eisenstein, brushing the blood off his neck, his hand coming away red.

The leader withdrew the Honjo Masamune. "Your wish will be granted. We are not barbarians." The leader half-turned, then paused in the doorway. "And cheer up, professor ... we are almost at the end."

The leader then left the room.
Professor Eisenstein cursed him in Russian.
But he now knew what he had to do.

Chapter 45

"Nicely done, sir," cried Harmony as Garin rolled off her, both having loudly reached the moment of completion. "A command performance. You live up to your reputation."

"Reputation?" said Garin. He reached over to his bedside table and lit a cigarette, used the burning end to light another, and passed it to Harmony.

"Girls talk, Garin. Your reputation as a champion cocksman – and a sufferer of restless penis syndrome – precedes you."

"I didn't know the medical establishment had accepted restless penis syndrome as a genuine condition, but I aim to please."

"You know what your women call you?"

"Tell me."

"The Rainmaker."

"Why?

"Because you know how to make us wet." As if to punctuate the statement, Harmony took Garin's hand and put it between her legs.

"Rainmaker," said Garin, trying out the word. "I like that." Garin took his hand away and sat up on the side of the bed. "For a while I thought you weren't going to come."

"Couldn't you tell I did? I thought you were an expert at that sort of thing. What did you call yourself – 'the Columbo of the clitoris'?"

"That's not what I meant. I meant you showing up at my place."

"Oh." Harmony studied Garin's face. "Why would you think that?"

"Because I'm not exactly flavor of the month in Washington."

"Nobody tells me who I can or can't see," said Harmony, nostrils slightly flaring at the thought of having her private life dictated to her by the whims of popular opinion.

"Good to hear." The colonel took the opportunity to admire Harmony's naked body. He had so little opportunity to admire beauty in his job, he took every chance in his private life to admire it he could get.

Harmony raised an eyebrow at his scrutiny. But something else was concerning her. "These doubts are unlike you, Garin," she said. "You fuck – and from everything I've heard – kill like a man half your age. So why the worries?"

Garin stared at the wall. "Maybe I'm having a senior moment. Maybe I'm just getting old." Garin flexed his right arm, as if to see he still had strength in it.

"To me it seems like you never age at all," said Harmony, studying Garin's scarred and bare form. "I wish I knew your diet secrets." Harmony stretched like a cat. "You should do me next to an airfield sometime. I like making love with the planes flying overhead."

"Hey, I'm a soldier, not a flyboy. But I can arrange some tanks to trundle past the window next time."

"Not quite as romantic," sniffed Harmony.

"So you want romance. How about this?" Garin plucked a bottle of champagne from a nearby ice bucket. Then in one swift gesture he pulled out a cavalry sword and ran it along the bottle until it reached the neck, neatly slicing off the cork and the neck. "Taa daa!"

Harmony clapped. "Nice party trick."

Garin poured Harmony and himself a glass each.

"It's called sabrage. Goes back to old Napoleon's time. This is the real stuff, from the French region of Champagne. Not that sparkling white wine shit. It's not legally allowed to be called Champagne if it doesn't come from there."

Harmony raised an eyebrow. "So if I have a Philly cheesesteak, it has to be served from a greasy spoon in Philadelphia to qualify? Goddamn." Harmony clinked her glass with Garin's. "Cheers. Here's to good times."

"I'm going to drain the dragon," said Garin romantically.

"A bit Too Much Information there, sir." Harmony reached down under the bed and pulled out a folder. "By the way, speaking of credit … you know that plan of yours where you planned to seduce me so I'd pass on secret information from the White House?"

"Yep."

"Looks like it's paid off. Sort of. The President said you wanted to read this file. You still have at least one fan in DC." Harmony handed Garin a manila folder titled "Mandatory Population Limits Per Country". "I recommended you read it while three sheets to the wind, because afterwards you'll be completely sober."

"You've read it, then?" said Garin, surprised.

"Yes. Are you going to have me shot now?"

"Maybe we'll both be shot." Garin accepted the folder eagerly. "Thanks. I was curious about that file."

"He knew you were. Now go use the bathroom. I'm going to watch TV for a bit before we make love again. And don't wait so long next time to call me. Whatever you soldiers like to think, happiness isn't a warm gun ... happiness is a warm woman."

"Heh." Garin put the folder in his leather valise, then busied himself in the bathroom for a few minutes. Then he heard Harmony calling him.

"Garin, you better get out here."

"Hold your horses." He got out just in time to see the shape of a man's head on TV. Above it was the headline: "Who is Colonel 'X'?"

Harmony turned to him. "I think they're talking about you," she said.

Garin gaped at the screen.

"Christ."

* * *

As it so happened, Vasquez was also watching the footage, which was running on multiple channels. She turned to the Spartan, concerned.

"Are they talking about Garin?"

"Who else?" growled the Spartan. He should have known that his old enemy might strike out at someone close to him. And here it was. A media hatchet job instead of a hit squad.

Seeing the look of understanding in the Spartan's eyes, Vasquez asked: "So who would leak this information? Who would stand to benefit?"

The Spartan curled his hand into an angry fist. "The General."

* * *

Jackson's reaction was considerably different.

"Turn that shit up," he told the bartender in Harlem.

He immediately suspected who this "Colonel X" might be. And he knew all about the missing technology. Had fought folk wearing it, actually.

One drunk raised a finger to object to the game being taken off the TV. One glare from Jackson instantly silenced him.

Jackson returned to the screen, watching the news item with keen relish. He thought the scoop might represent an opportunity to be free of Garin at last. A disgraced colonel was a powerless colonel, one who no longer commanded men. And Jackson was reaching the stage in his life where he didn't want any commanding officer – even a good one.

Sorry, Garin.

Jackson rested his arms on the bar, the President's newly-acquired cufflinks gleaming on his jacket. "Bartender, the next round's on me!" he exclaimed to the cheering crowd.

Chapter 46

"Have you read the morning news, professor?" said the leader as he entered the de facto mess hall where his men and Professor Eisenstein were eating breakfast. The leader opened his mask and helped himself to jam on toast, then picked up the newspaper beside Eisenstein.

"Who is Colonel X?" he said, reading the headline. "How amusing. Page one, too … right next to the article about the Chinese Premier's visit. A nice splash." The leader didn't wait for Eisenstein's reply. "Yes, who is 'Colonel X'? Maybe I should thank him for letting me have access to the Ghost Armor technology." The leader affected an American accent: "He sure humped the dawg, buddy. Dang."

The leader laughed and tossed the paper aside. "It's very Western, to think just one man is to blame. There are many men to blame.

"But if your adopted country wishes to believe in the narrative that one person is solely responsible, more fool them. Let them indulge in finger pointing rather than try to address the root cause of their problems."

The leader ate more toast. Crunch, crunch. "Although … if one man was to blame, surely it would be you, Professor Eisenstein. You are the creator of the Ghost Armor. Only you fully understand its secrets. Without you, none of this would be possible. Your Vice President might even be still alive." As Eisenstein stared at him with loathing in his eyes, the leader added: "How does it feel … to know that all this blood is on your hands?"

"You should ask the same question of yourself," said the professor grimly. "You have made a fetish of killing. You have turned the armor into an executioner's shroud."

The leader regarded Eisenstein with a wry smile. "Is your imagination so limited you think we are just using this suit to kill? For a brilliant man, that shows a certain naiveté.

"Again … it is a very Western idea to believe that you can simply kill to achieve all your objectives. That if you somehow shoot all the 'terrorists' – all the 'bad guys' – no more will spring up to take their place. Look at your country's efforts around the world and tell me how that has worked out."

Eisenstein glared at the leader as the ninja poured himself a cup of coffee. The other night warriors at the table were studiously ignoring the pair, choosing to dine in silence. But there was the occasional shy stare, as if the ninjas were curious as to why their leader spent so much time talking to the thin, odd foreign scientist. Not that they would dare voice their concerns … the leader had ensured himself extra obedience by the murder of the peeping ninja at the shower cubicle, an execution he had subsequently explained to his soldiers. (The dead ninja wasn't greatly missed. An outsider even among outsiders, there was talk he was actually part Korean.)

A ninja wearing Ghost Armor with the hood down whispered into the leader's ear, then handed him an envelope.

"A case in point, professor," said the leader, holding up the envelope. "Having the power to kill your enemies is important, but sometimes the best missions are the ones where you never have to pull out your weapon.

"Information is power, too. And we have been busy amassing information.

"You armor is the perfect infiltration tool. Several of my ninja have already penetrated some of America's most important buildings undetected.

"My compliments to your work, professor. We're sifting through the data they stole now." The leader stared at Eisenstein. "Sadly, none of it will be accessible from your computer. But much of it is very interesting. Your country has been very … wicked."

"So you've become common spies now?" said Eisenstein scornfully.

"We're not just anyone one thing. We have all embraced a certain duality. Such is the way of the ninja."

"I bet you pulled the wings off flies as a child."

The leader laughed, then got up. "I *do* enjoy our conversations, Professor. You make me smile. Not something many Westerners can intentionally make me do." He glanced at the newspaper again. "However, I have planned something that should push your 'Colonel X' from the front pages. I'm hoping it will happen today. Watch this space."

Then he left as Eisenstein's eyes burnt into his back with hatred.

* * *

The ninja entered the top-secret drone warfare command center in Las Vegas.

The ninja entered the backdoor program into the computer network.

The ninja exited the command center, undetected.

Because what the leader had told Professor Eisenstein was right. Sometimes the mission wasn't about killing at all.

Sometimes it was about the future.

Chapter 47

The Spartan slept. As usual, he dreamt of war. He dreamt of standing with his Spartan shieldmates on the field of battle during the ancient age of heroes.

His shieldmates stood firm as the enemy charged, swords up, screaming war cries. As shield clashed against shield and man pushed against man, the Spartan struck out with his long spear, his dory. He took the first foe in the eye. The enemy howled and went down. Another took his place. The Spartan struck him through his open mouth. Again, the foe crumpled, disappearing under the mad melee of feet and bodies. And yet another took his place.

The Spartan ducked, parried, took a sword blow on his shield and struck again. His dory made its way past the foe's armor and buried itself in the man's stomach, effortlessly entering flesh.

Yet as the Spartan tried to pull the dory away, the enraged soldier seized the shaft, preventing the Spartan from pulling it away. With insane strength he bent the shaft, then used his strong hands to strangle the Spartan.

The Spartan headbutted him with the crest of his helmet, sending the foe backwards, then drew his *xiphos*. He buried the blade into the enemy's thick neck. Finally the soldier went down in a fountain of crimson.

Another wave of the enemy approached. The Spartan duelled with a further foe, deflecting a sword with the hilt of his *xiphos*, before burying his blade into the man's ribcage and beyond.

He ducked another attack and slashed the tendons of an enemy, then rose in time to fight off two more foes. His *xiphos* found the heart of the figure opposite, but he received a nasty slash on his left forearm in return. The Spartan kicked straight out, knocking the man off his feet, then, as the ancient soldier fell among the mud and blood and bodies, he thrust his *xiphos* into his heart.

As the Spartan rose, observing the conflict for a second, he realized with terrible suddenness that something was wrong. He wasn't fighting in the noble battles of Thermopylae or Plataea, coming to grips with the hated Persians.

No ... he was battling his fellow Greeks. The armor, the swords, the faces were all unmistakably Greek.

And further – he realized exactly where and when he was fighting.

He was reliving the battle of Leuctra.

Leuctra, the battle where the Spartan army was defeated by the Thebans.

Leuctra, the battle that shattered the image of Spartan invincibility forever.

He watched in anguish as his shieldmates were cut down one by one. The Spartan fought on with cold fury, dealing death all around him, pushing through endless lines of men, but for every enemy he killed, two of the crack Sacred Band of

Thebes took their place. He raised his *xiphos*, trying to rally his comrades, but the tide had turned against the Spartans.

Yet still he swung on. He felt a blade caress his back. Then an armored foot kicked his knee from behind, forcing him to the ground. A hand made to grab for his arm. He cut it off. However, another hand seized his sword arm. More hands grabbed his other arm.

He roared as strong men pinned him down.

A tall Theban stood above him, raising a sword. The Spartan screamed in anger and thwarted rage. And then …

"Wake up, Spartan!" shouted Vasquez, shaking the Spartan.

The Spartan sat bolt upright in bed.

"You OK? You were screaming."

"In anger," said the Spartan, wiping the sweat off his forehead.

"Bad dream?"

"Never had one like that before."

Vasquez gently touched his face. "Want to talk about it?"

"No." He helped himself to a glass of water beside the bed.

"As you were, then," said Vasquez, rolling over again. "Never heard you scream in your sleep before, though."

"Forget about it," said the Spartan, pulling the blankets back up to his chin. "Go back to sleep, Vasquez. We'll be busy tomorrow."

Soon the Spartan could hear Vasquez's gentle breathing as she drifted off. It was good that she was sleeping properly again. Ever since she had discovered the truth about the Jaguar's role in the death of her family she had been imbued with renewed vigor as well as sound sleep, as if her body had been waiting to be called back to war and its familiar rhythms all along.

But he couldn't sleep. Because he remembered what he was dreaming about … and the fateful battle of Leuctra.

The Spartan didn't believe in omens. Yet he still hoped his dream of Leuctra wasn't one.

Chapter 48

The General's secretary, a young, attractive, ambitious blonde in a pink pencil skirt, popped her head into the door of his office. "It's Colonel Garin on the phone for you again, sir. That's the third time today. He says it's urgent."

"Urgent for him perhaps," muttered the General.

'What was that, sir?"

"Nothing. Just thinking aloud, Cyndi."

"He keeps saying you've poked the bear," said Cyndi, baffled.

That news pleased him. "Of course he is. Take a message."

Cyndi went off to take Garin's message. A message the General would never bother to read.

The General's cell phone rang. "Unknown caller," read the screen. The General suspected it was Garin. Certainly, Garin had the ability to evade caller ID. He clicked his phone shut.

"Better get used to people not talking your calls, 'Colonel X'," the General said aloud.

He sipped his sweet coffee and looked at the newspapers again. *What wonderful coverage*, he thought. Washington's elite would be giving Garin a wide berth, afraid of guilt by association. The General had wounded his enemy nicely. The press did have their uses after all.

Garin had lost his faith in God long ago. Maybe he would now also lose his faith as a player and powerbroker in Washington. That would be good, too.

The General luxuriated back in his chair. For a moment he felt like a Bond villain. He imagined himself stroking a white cat in his lap and giving his secretary a double entendre nickname like Pussy Galore.

Ah, fun and games.

Still, the General would be carefully checking the brakes of his car the next time he drove. Garin was bound to retaliate in some way, in the way all cornered, wounded animals did. Maybe the car-brake concept was too hardcore, though. Perhaps Garin would launch some psy op against the General instead, much in the same way the General had with his own "Colonel X" campaign.

Yet the risk was worth it to see Garin squirm. He imagined Garin like a duck, seemingly composed on the water's surface but paddling frantically underneath to keep afloat. Maybe with a few duck hunters lurking in the reeds to pop a cap in his feathered ass. Heh.

The General texted his tame hack Brett. "Keep up the pressure on Colonel X," he typed. "Hit the talk shows. Work things into a righteous lather. The public NEEDS to hear this story."

The General grabbed his laptop. With Garin distracted, it was time to deal with the other threat, the true threat: the Spartan. Only the General wouldn't be employing anything as subtle as a media smear campaign.

No, sir. The Spartan deserved a more direct response.

The General opened his web browser. His boffins assured him that no one could track his internet movements on this computer. And the site he was about to visit had its own formidable protections, its own methods of anonymity. More than once he had heard law enforcement lament how uncrackable it was.

Entering the dark net, the General clicked onto the site. He then located the relevant posting, which contained the names of freelance hitters interested in the $10 million-dollar contract for killing the Spartan and Vasquez. The General wondered who was brave – or crazy – enough to put a hit on a Tier 1 operative like the Spartan. They had a major reckoning in their future. The special forces community would come down on them like a hammer from heaven.

Yet the General hoped to exploit the contract long before that.

He scrolled down. A finder's fee was being offered for anyone who had information about the duo's location. The General wasn't interested in any blood money: but he was interested in helping these captains of private industry find the Spartan. He'd failed to eliminate the Spartan using Jackson and his special forces team last year. Perhaps the private sector could succeed where the bloated public sector had failed.

He looked at the avatar of one particularly popular "contractor". The contractor's rating on the site was 95 per cent. Apparently, hitmen could be ranked just like any other supplier of a product or service. "Fast and efficient," claimed one happy customer. "They never see him coming," beamed another. "No one expects someone like him to be a killer, which makes him the perfect choice," read one more. "My organization is very happy with his service."

"We have a winner," muttered the General.

This worthy had more than two dozen glowing recommendations from the world of crime. He was available for assignments anywhere in North America and Europe. His only restriction? "No woman or children."

And his avatar? "Surfer Dude". A blond man holding a long surfboard.

He sounded like a hippie asshole, thought the General with some amusement.

He laughed. The Spartan would hate being killed by a New Age murderer. Almost as humiliating as being killed by, say, a hairdresser. It was too delicious not to try.

He entered in some details.

There, he thought.

Now all the General had to do was wait for "Surfer Dude" to reply.

* * *

The General had to kill a few hours before he received a reply. He busied himself with enjoying some of Cyndi's Costa Rican coffee as he scrolled through the internet reaction over the "Colonel X" story. Both the coffee and the net trolling were delightful.

Three hours later he saw "Surfer Dude's" icon appear on his computer desktop.

The General clicked the link.

"I don't think I know you, Area 51," came a distorted electronic voice through his speakers: Area 51 being the General's own handle, complete with flying UFO. The General activated his own voice app.

"First-time customer," he typed. He added: "Are you really a surfer?"

"Totally, dude," came the unsurfer-like computer voice. "Is that a problem?"

"Not if your success rate is accurate."

"It is ... dude." The General wondered if he had just added the extra "dude" to annoy him. "But like I said, I don't know you. This is a tricky business, based word-of-mouth referrals. A closed community, if you like. How can I trust you? How do I know you're not Johnny Law?"

The General gritted his teeth. He was used to having his orders obeyed without question. Such was the peril with dealing with the private sector. But he was prepared for such defiance. "I'm sending you a package of information now. It contains photos and the sort of detail no outsider would possibly possess. And no cop would hand over."

There was a pause as the General sent his information.

"Information received," came the voice through the speakers. Perhaps it was just the General's imagination, but the electronic voice sounded pleased. "Hang back for 15."

Precisely 15 minutes later, Surfer Dude returned.

"Your information looks legit. This is great for background, but I need a location. Can you help, Area 51?"

"Yes. The target is very peripatetic ..."

"Peri-what?"

"Moves around a lot. Never in one place for long. But there is a place the target likes to hang out. You can hit him there. His guard will be down."

"Music to my ears, Area 51. If your information is correct, there's a finder's fee coming your way. Payment on successful completion of the mission, of course."

"You can keep the money," typed the General.

There was a long pause.

"So what's your motivation, Area 51? Why do you want to harsh his mellow?"

"He stole my wave once," typed in the General.

"LOL," came the reply. "I'm not going to complain. Helpful citizens like yourself make my job all the easier. I've read your dossiers. Thanks for that. But you can only tell so much from words. What sort of man is this Spartan?"

That was a question you could fill a whole book trying to answer, thought the General.

Instead, he typed: "He's out to lunch. He's in the *Twilight Zone*. Don't worry about what kind of man he is. The only thing you need to know is that he is extremely dangerous. Many have failed before you. He's a Charles Lindbergh of violence … he just keeps going and going, beyond the point of reason and sanity. So don't give him any chances."

"I don't intend to. Particularly if he really is special forces."

"If you really do look like a surfer you might be able to get the drop on him. He'll view you with contempt. He won't regard you as a threat."

"That's the general idea, Area 51. My unique selling proposition." There was a pause. "And Vasquez? Do you have any information on her?"

"Negative. She may or may not be with him. Don't underestimate her, either. She's deadly." The General recalled his own encounter with Vasquez, who saved the Spartan from his torture chamber. Yes, she was dangerous, too.

"That's probably why the bounty is so high. But I won't kill her if she's there. I don't kill women or children."

"So I gather."

"Or animals."

"Animals?"

"You'd be surprised how often than comes up."

"Not much surprises me any more, Surfer Dude." Not since he'd seen his own guts spill out over his stomach, courtesy of the Spartan's blade. "I'm sending you the address now."

There was a pause. "New York's Little Belgium. I'll say hello to Poirot while I'm there."

"You do that."

"You sure you don't want any dough for this?" Left unsaid was, *it's easier to trust – and understand – people who just want money.*

"I said no the first time," typed in the General. "After this exchange you will be unable to contact me again. Don't fail me, Surfer Dude. You wouldn't want a bad review." The General severed the connection.

He had just surfed over the Rubicon. Now the General just had to wait to see if this assassin lived up to his reputation.

Chapter 49

Unbeknownst to either party, the exchange between Surfer Dude and the General was reported shortly afterwards to cartel leader the Jaguar. He had ordered his IT people to monitor the progress on the internet of the contract to kill Vasquez and the Spartan. The Jaguar's highly paid IT professionals had been unable to determine the true identities of the pair discussing the contract, but they had managed to supply the text of their conversation as well as the information exchanged.

This "Surfer Dude" had an excellent record in completing contracts. Yet the Jaguar thought he would send his own operatives instead.

He decided to send in the South Africans.

These former state-sanctioned killers had carved out a solid reputation ever since the fall of apartheid, where they were no longer needed to kill or suppress the black population. As a man of color, the Jaguar naturally despised the South Africans' former racist profession, but he had to admit they were very good.

Over the years the original team of 12 had been whittled down to six – no great loss as far as the Jaguar was concerned, the fewer racist white men around the world, the better – but they still continued to take high-risk assignments, jobs they fulfilled in a brutally efficient manner.

With the presumed death of Jaguar's two *sicarios* – they had failed to make their last four phone checks – he decided not to risk any more of his people. The Jaguar was old enough to remember when Mexicans had been regarded as a "disposable people". They were anything but now. Particularly the cartels.

So the six South Africans it was, then.

It was always a tricky question as to how many trigger men to send on a hit. Send one, and the target may survive. Send 10, and the target – or the police – may be tipped off before the assassins even got into range.

Sending large teams to operate on US soil was always dangerous, anyway. To the Jaguar's mind, the American security forces seemed to love violence and gunfights. For the cartels, such violence was largely business: but for the Yankees, brought up on a diet of Westerns and shoot 'em ups and with easy access to firearms, such bloodshed was almost enjoyable.

But yes, as for the hit, let the South Africans take the risk. If "Surfer Dude" was caught in the crossfire, he cared not. As long as this Spartan was taken care of … preferably taken alive first so he could divulge the location of the hated Vasquez.

Yes, it was for her that his rage burned. Women weren't supposed to be part of the cartels' game: they were supposed to stay home and cook and clean and bear children. Vasquez had to be made an example of. That one of their own had been killed by a woman would remain a stain, a shame, until the death was avenged.

And so the Jaguar picked up the phone to make the call.

Chapter 50

"Bitch!" screamed Cody as he weaved his Jeep through New York traffic, one trembling hand on the wheel, the other on the half-empty bottle of Wild Turkey.

Cody, a pudgy, middle-aged store manager from Queens, had just learnt that his wife was leaving him for another man, taking their two sons with her.

Now he was drinking and driving.

And screaming.

"Screw you, Estelle!" he howled as he narrowly missed a small truck. "I'm a good father! A good man!"

Yes, he was a good man. If he told himself that enough, maybe it would make it true.

Cody had known things had been bad between them for a long time. Yet he'd hoped that their family surviving the Taiwan Plague would be a fresh start for them. But once the pressures of survival had subsided, the same issues that had drove them apart resurfaced. Particularly Cody's out-of-control drinking and gambling. Neither was his fault. Society was to blame, according to his AA sponsor. At least, that was the message he took away from all those meetings.

Evidently Estelle had reached her breaking point.

"I thought I'd married a winner," she screamed. And, of course, that was the worst crime an American could commit – not to be a winner.

To be, in fact, a loser.

Perhaps she was right. But to take his sons, too?

That was going too far.

He knew where the bastard Estelle was sleeping with lived, address programmed into the Jeep's onboard GPS. There was a loaded pistol in the glove compartment. Cody could already imagine its reassuring grip in his hand. He wanted to see what would happen when he pointed it at the man sharing his wife's bed.

Maybe the gun might go off.

Guns did that.

Cody glanced out of the side of the window, aware than he was passing an important government building.

Damn government, he thought woozily, not fully appreciating that he was already going at more than 80 miles per hour towards an empty pedestrian crossing.

Still, he was surprised when his Jeep collided with a solid object. He saw a human shape bounce up upon his bonnet and then the windshield, its head smashing the glass.

"What the fuck?" he thought for a second before the Jeep collided into a nearby street sign.

Cody slumped over the wheel, unconscious, his car horn blaring ... completely unaware that he had just hit one of the most wanted men in America and accomplished the greatest achievement in his life.

And provided the authorities with one hell of a lead.

Chapter 51

New York's "burnt-over district" had earned its title in the 19th century as a religious hotspot, a Mecca of zeal and holy fervor. One writer had quipped that there were so many holy rollers and chosen folk around central and western New York that there was no unconverted people left to "burn" or "convert". Everyone living there, it seemed, was some kind of believer ... or on their way to becoming one.

One could argue that even the ninjas ensconced in the seemingly harmless warehouse in today's burnt-over district were believers of the most powerful stripe.

Two pieces of information had led to the fortuitous discovery of the ninja HQ. The first was the news that a drunk driver had accidentally killed a ninja crossing the road in activated Ghost Armor.

Another reminder, to Colonel Garin at least, that there was one god to which all men must bow: Chaos.

The ninja's corpse was a clue in itself. It stood to reason that the ninja had to be within reasonable walking distance of his base. Luck, once again, was on Colonel Garin's side.

The second piece of information lay inside the head of Shintaro, a Japanese secret agent, soldier, modern-day samurai and deep-cover operative.

Shintaro wanted the Honjo Masamune, now in the hands of the head-harvesting ninja in silver; and Garin wanted said headhunter and his whole crew.

Having hunted the night warriors for years, Shintaro had a list of many of their potential hideouts in the US. Now, with the dead ninja on the road to complete the puzzle, the pair had narrowed that list down to one likely location.

Instead of playing ninja Whack A Mole as before, they had the chance to hit them all in the one place.

Which is where all of Garin's people were now.

The list of "all" included the Spartan, Vasquez, Jackson, two dozen special forces soldiers, Garin and his friend, the Far Eastern knight Shintaro, plus other sundry support staff. More forces maintained a four-block perimeter around the building. A veritable ring of steel surrounded the suspect structure.

Delta, Rangers, SEALs: all the big forces were represented. They had come from around the world, faces tanned from the Middle East standing next to the pale complexions of warriors based stateside. The special forces soldiers had a grudge to settle: the death of the team that escorted Garin to China to take out Commander Lee.

Naturally, the three surviving members of the slain team – Puffer, Whale and Monkey – were also present. They wanted payback the most. Particularly Monkey. Monkey practically vibrated rage.

If there were any men in the world that the Spartan could call brother, it was these brave, proud soldiers.

Various operators nodded in appreciation when they saw the Spartan. Even among the elite of the elite, the best of the best, there were stand-outs such as the Spartan. The Spartan's rep went a long way, the deciding factor for some of whether to take the mission when Garin had reached out. "Colonel X" was currently in doubt – blamed for the loss of the Ghost Armor suits and the death of Monkey's team – but the Spartan's credit was still good, as was Vasquez's as a fully blooded, proven operative and the only female war fighter in the gathered group.

In a quiet corner, some of the more religious operatives prayed. Seeing this, the Spartan thought, "Let's hope God is on our side." He glanced around at the soldiers preparing for combat, knowing that some might not make it back. How many times had he seen such a gathering? Been *part* of it?

He had lost count.

Dressed in full battle gear, the Spartan marched up to Garin. He was busy talking to an unknown Japanese man who was clad in lacquered red armor. Judging by Garin's body language, the Spartan could tell the colonel thought the armored man was important. A soldier, perhaps. Definitely some kind of fighter. Perhaps even Garin's friend.

The Japanese man regarded him with shrewd eyes. The Spartan towered over the stranger by almost a foot, but he could tell the man wasn't cowed. In fact, judging by his eyes, his frame and general demeanor, he looked as hard as a railway spike.

Garin nodded at his star recruit. "Spartan."

"Sir." The Spartan hefted his SAW over his shoulder. "Is it true the ninja HQ used to be a Blockbuster warehouse?"

"That's classified, soldier. And possibly funny."

The Spartan simply stood there, staring at the Japanese man, as if to say to Garin "introduce us".

"Spartan, this is Shintaro," said Garin, his voice almost formal.

Shintaro bowed deeply, the sword on his left-hand side swinging. The Spartan returned the bow.

"Your reputation proceeds you, Spartan-san," said Shintaro politely.

He decided he would return the stranger's politeness. "I like your armor. Is it old?"

"Very."

"It's pretty … but would it stop a bullet?"

"A bullet fired before the Meiji Restoration, perhaps," said Shintaro dryly.

The Spartan was impressed that Shintaro would enter gunfights in only semi-bulletproof armor. "Samurai armor is an interesting choice of gear to fight ninjas. Because ninjutsu is designed to take down a samurai in armor."

"Or a Spartan," observed Shintaro.

Touché.

"I've fought these ninjas. They're good, but they fall just like any other man."

Shintaro nodded. "But they fall hard, yes? They are men of stone who don't believe in screams. And forgive my impoliteness, Spartan-san, but that cut on your head seems new. Did a ninjato cause it?"

The Spartan's fingers touched the wound. "You know your blades. The pyjama man who did it regretted it quickly enough, though."

"Good," said Shintaro, pleased. "Ninjas lack the honor of the samurai and your own tribe. I have made it my mission to bring their types low. And to return what they have stolen."

Garin took this as a cue to talk. "They have a blade that belongs to Japan. A priceless sword they bought at a yard sale in the US, if you would believe."

"The Honjo Masamune," said Shintaro, with more than a little awe.

"I've heard of it," said the Spartan, hand going to the *xiphos* on his hip. "Nice sword. I thought it was supposed to be lost after World War II."

"For a long time I almost believed the same," said Shintaro, almost wistfully. "But the ninja used it on live TV to execute that IT child. Another taunt in a long list of insults. Almost as if he doesn't care that we know he has the sword."

The Spartan sensed history and bad blood behind those remarks. "What's your role in this?" He looked over Shintaro. "And where's your weapons? I don't see any gun. Just that katana on your side."

"You fight with guns, I will fight with swords."

"You're taking a sword to a gunfight?"

"Yes," said Shintaro, without vanity.

"Do you have a death wish?"

Shintaro's eyed danced with mischief. "As you Americans say, 'Look who's talking.'"

"He's got you there, Spartan," said Garin, a smile curling on his lips.

The Spartan grunted in approval. He was beginning to like Shintaro. In some ways, Shintaro reminded him of Garin, a fit yet aging soldier kept going long past special forces retirement age largely through sheer force of will.

Was that to be his destiny too one day?

"And what of that sword by your side?" said Shintaro, nodding to his *xiphos*. "Do you ever use it in battle?"

"Surprisingly often."

"Perhaps we have more in common than it appears. We're both after the ninjas. But I want the Honjo Masamune."

Garin re-entered the conversation. "So, Shintaro will be joining the teams during the insertion. Don't worry about him – he can handle himself." Shintaro nodded in appreciation at Garin's confidence.

"There is just one thing, Spartan-san," said Shintaro, eyes now fierce. "Do not under any circumstances harm the Honjo Masamune."

The Spartan went quiet for a moment. He disliked caveats and added complications before going into combat. "This ninja has tried to kill my girlfriend twice. If I get him in my gunsights I'm going to take the shot."

"We know that, Spartan," placated Garin. "We just want you to do your best to avoid damaging the sword. Japan is very keen on its return."

"I hit what I aim at, sir. Besides, shooting weapons out of people's hands is for the movies."

"Correct," said Shintaro, mollified.

"Maybe he won't even use it when we bust in there," said the Spartan.

Shintaro stared at the Spartan closely. "Don't be surprised if he does. I could tell by the way he held it in that execution video that he's fond of it." Then he looked down at the Spartan's *xiphos*. "And don't be surprised if you must whet your own blade, too. In my experience, swordsmen are automatically drawn to other swordsmen on the battlefield."

"You know my thoughts on duels, son," said Garin. "I don't want another repeat of the Monk."

"Understood, sir," replied the Spartan.

Shintaro turned to Garin. "The Monk?"

"Long story," stated Garin.

"And don't shoot the Honjo Masamune," warned Shintaro. "You would make a lot of people angry."

The Spartan turned to face Shintaro. "Like your ancestors?"

"*Hai*. And yours, too, Spartan."

Shintaro pulled the mask of his samurai armor over his head. His face now resembled that of an angry, flaming demon.

The Spartan smiled a rare smile.

Chapter 52

"Alert! Alert! Enemy attack imminent!"

The loud klaxon inside the ninja HQ alerted its residents to the American forces outside. The leader hefted the Honjo Masamune as his *genin* – his foot soldiers – got into their prepared positions. They had always planned for such an attack. It was inevitable that the Americans would find them with all their resources. Still, the leader was surprised just how stealthily the Americans had gotten their people into position. He had barely minutes to prepare.

Judging by the security camera footage, he estimated they were facing a force of no less than two dozen. Perhaps the Spartan and Vasquez would be among them. He assumed as much.

Hoped for it, actually.

"We shall stage a fighting withdrawal," said the leader to Professor Eisenstein, grabbing the professor's skinny arm. "Grab your notes and your laptop, professor. You're coming with me."

The leader glanced around the warehouse as his men got into position and faded into view.

"Your rescuers are walking straight into our trap," said the leader, slipping his face mask on. "Every inch of this building has been prepared for battle." The leader dragged Eisenstein up to the top of a walkway for a better view. "Here. I want to see this before we leave." The leader turned to Eisenstein. "Enjoy the show, professor."

Chapter 53

"You ready?" said the Spartan to Vasquez as he stood outside the wall of the HQ, SAW in hand, clad in black combat armor.

"Affirmative," said Vasquez, clutching her own MP-5 and wearing her unactivated Ghost Armor. "This is going to be hairy, isn't it?"

"Reckon so."

Stacking up shoulder-to-shoulder with his special forces comrades felt very familiar to the Spartan. In a way, it almost felt like home. Even if he knew this mission was going to be red-star bad.

The Spartan glanced over to the other side of the HQ entrance, where Shintaro was camped, wearing his odd armor, sword out. He wondered how Shintaro would fare in the coming melee.

The gathered soldiers were grimly quiet. If they had any doubts about performing a black op on American soil, they kept it to themselves. There was no time for thoughts, anyway. Now was the time for action.

"Breaching on three, two, one," said a soldier as he slapped a timed, shaped charge to the large entrance.

Kaboom.

The charge had done its work.

The way into the HQ was open.

The soldiers rushed through the space, weapons up.

"See you in Sparta," said Vasquez, turning to face him, then running forward.

Let the adagio of aggression begin.

Chapter 54

Yet there was a third factor at play in the battle.

Professor Eisenstein.

At great personal risk, Eisenstein had secreted a small object near the entrance. He planned to activate it when it would do the most good.

Like now.

Eisenstein clicked the detonator in his hand just as the charge on the front door went off. There was a fizzing explosion as ripples of energy flew around the ninja HQ. To their surprise, all the ninjas within the area suddenly became visible. Electromagnetic pulse energy even washed over the leader, bringing him into the visible spectrum.

The ninjas had lost the advantage of invisibility.

And those first few seconds in battle were crucial.

The shinobi were far too taciturn to vocalise their feelings, but Eisenstein fancied he felt a great collective wave of regret pass through the warehouse as the ninjas' advantage was removed. More fool them for not watching more carefully what he had been up to on the internet: that Russian website catering for big-breast fetishists was actually a spec ops site which included instructions on how to make a micro EMP grenade. The dour ninja watching over his shoulder had been filled with disgust rather than curiosity as Eisenstein had clicked through those enormous bosoms, secretly noting the coded instructions in the captions below.

The leader swore in Mandarin. He grabbed Eisenstein's hand and tore the detonator away.

"Very clever, professor," he said. "Let me reward you." The leader thrust the edge of the Honjo Masamune through the sole of Eisenstein's shoe and into his big left toe. Then twisted it.

Eisenstein screamed. Blood flowed.

"We will discuss this later, traitor," said the leader as the special forces soldiers burst into the area. "But for now, let's move."

Chapter 55

The special forces teams threw grenades, smoke canisters and flashbangs before them as they entered the warehouse. In normal circumstances, such measures would have brought them precious seconds to get into position and neutralise the enemy. Unfortunately, they were assaulting a position where the enemy had already dug in. And were waiting for them, weapons hot.

The Spartan flinched as a soldier beside him went down, struck in the upper torso. As he dove for cover, him going one way, Vasquez the other, the Spartan spied silver ninjas all over the warehouse, taking cover behind pallets and boxes, lurking behind walls, even strafing as they ran. Fortunately, all were visible, despite their Ghost Armors. That last fact was a great advantage.

Another special forces soldier screamed as what appeared to be an engine block fell from the ceiling, crushing him. Two of his comrades immediately used the large engine block for cover. Others tried to extract the wounded soldier. The Spartan kept firing his SAW and moving from cover to cover.

There were more surprises from the ceiling. A ninja slid down a rope to land immediately inside a tight-knit group of operatives. As heads and guns swivelled his way, the shinobi slashed out with his ninjato, striking two special forces men across the chest and back, a whirlwind of energy.

Without pausing, he attacked the Spartan, aiming a two-handed blow straight for his face.

The Spartan raised his SAW and caught the blade along its barrel. The ninja was surprised. The Spartan kicked him in the chest, sending him backwards, then raised his SAW and ghosted him.

Not for the first time, the Spartan noted that the ninjas didn't die like normal men. They went to the beyond with regret in their hearts but barely a sound on their lips. Very manly. Almost … Spartan.

As the Spartan continued to move, he heard a loud boom. Two ninjas were hurled into the air as their position in cover was destroyed.

The soldier known as Puffer was armed with "The Punisher", the XM-25 grenade launcher that exploded precisely above opponents and made a mockery of cover. A perfect weapon for such an op. Maybe it was even the weapon rescued from the late Fighting Dog.

The Spartan took cover behind a pallet and let loose with his SAW, trying to kill a cartwheeling ninja. The foe was too quick, dodging and then sending his own fusillade that made the Spartan retreat into cover.

A flash of red caught his attention. Shintaro in his red samurai armor was engaging a ninja mere feet away. Had the ninja been trying to sneak up on the Spartan? He made to give assistance, then moved back. His concern was unwarranted. Shintaro blocked two blows from the ninja's weapon with his own katana and slashed the ninja diagonally from shoulder to groin. Shintaro's swordwork was intuitive, superb, almost Zen. The Japanese agent then delivered the coup de grace with a strike through the neck.

The Spartan turned back towards the front. Vasquez was firing upon the ninja that had the Spartan pinned. As the ninja turned to deal with this second front, the Spartan raced forward and shot him with a six-round burst. The ninja fell, weapon falling out of nerveless fingers. The Spartan nodded towards Vasquez, who was still visible. She nodded back.

The battle scene was bloody chaos, carbines, rifles and submachine guns dealing death in small, tight bursts. There were grave casualties on both sides, but the Spartan sensed the fight was slowly going their way. They would clear the warehouse and then push on towards the figure behind the whole conspiracy, the slayer of the Vice President, the elusive "leader", the boss ninja, the *jonin*.

The Spartan sensed more movement nearby. Two ninjas stood before him, swords out, unafraid. One waved towards him with its blade, as if to say "come on". He raised his SAW, staring down the iron sights, then stopped. His personal sense of honor – his desire not to shoot an enemy offering an open invitation to sword combat – pulled at his soul.

He kept them covered. Yet still they waved him forward, even as they slowly inched backwards, one foot over the other.

The Spartan moved closer, keeping his SAW trained on them. Once he was within *xiphos* range, he would …

But the Spartan never got to finish that thought. A trap door opened directly below him, sending him plummeting downwards.

* * *

The Spartan fell down the small shaft, ready to thrust his arms against the sides if he was about to land on spikes or worse. Seeing that the concrete below was clear, he landed. Then immediately rolled as a sword swung towards him. The Spartan came up, *xiphos* in his hand. Yet the ninjato strike had merely intended to separate him from his SAW. The blade had slashed through the strap that held it to his body, sending the gun clattering on the floor.

The Spartan quickly took in his surroundings, glancing from side to side. Within striking distance were five compact ninjas in Ghost Armor. They were armed, too, holding everything from swords and spear-like naginatas to the knives on ropes known as kyoketsu-shoge.

For a second the Spartan glanced at his SAW. Spotting this, the night warriors maintained a semi-circle around him, blocking access to the weapon. He now faced cold steel wherever he turned. He pointed his *xiphos's* edge towards them, ready for their attack.

Yet of most interest was the tall, panther-like ninja hanging back, his handsome, angular face exposed. He stared at the Spartan with undisguised malevolence. It seemed as if the boss ninja, the *jonin*, knew him already.

Unlike the armor of his fellow ninjas, which showed signs of being damaged and then repaired, the Ghost Armor of this shinobi was pristine, as if no one had ever laid a scratch on him.

Beside him was the scientist known as Professor Eisenstein, scared and bleeding from the foot.

And in the tall ninja's hand – the Honjo Masamune.

Shintaro's precious prize.

"Look at him, comrades," declared the *jonin*. "Look at this 'Spartan'. This is the arrogant American who murdered Commander Lee."

The *genin* said nothing, but he could feel their hatred from behind their masks.

"And you must be the scumbag who killed the Vice President," the Spartan fired back.

"Do you think that makes us even?" said the *jonin* scornfully. "Commander Lee was worth 10 of him."

"Commander Lee said he wanted revenge, too – right before I shot him," said the Spartan. The Spartan sensed the distress the news caused in his audience. The atmosphere in the room because even more grim, if that was possible.

"What do you want?" asked the Spartan after a beat.

The *jonin* smiled. "Revenge for our master. Then for China to rise and replace your decadent country as the world's leading power. And other things I doubt you'd understand."

"Try me." *Garin would want to know this asshole's motivation.*

"Very well. There are too many people in the world. There are not enough resources to go around. The Chinese people must have their rightful share. Their future must be … assured. And it can be assured better if there isn't a hungry America eating more than its fair share."

"I thought our two countries had a relationship."

"For now. You think that the gold we give you makes you rich. But it only weighs you down. It makes the sacks that you carry on your backs heavier."

"So you've stolen the Ghost Armor and targeted us," said the Spartan, keeping his eyes on the ninjas.

"In my eyes, all Americans are legitimate targets," intoned the *jonin*. "And yes, I hate your country. I hate your countrymen, with their greedy hearts and dead souls. So this is much pleasure as it is duty.

"But you … I hate you most of all."

"Sounds like someone didn't buy you a pony as a child," said the Spartan, waving his *xiphos* like a firebrand to keep the circling ninjas at bay. "But I understand you better than you think. You worship death. So come get yours."

The *jonin* smiled, showing white teeth. "Of course. Where are my manners?" He clicked his fingers. "Take him," he commanded.

His *genin* sprang into action. The knife-rope came for the Spartan first. But the Spartan was ready. He allowed the knife to flick towards him, permitting the rope and the blade to wrap around his forearm. Then, pulling the rope and its surprised ninja towards him, he slashed through the ninja's bicep, before burying his *xiphos* into the assassin's stomach.

The ninja crumpled and kissed the floor.

The *jonin* laughed and clapped.

"You have some skill after all," he crowed. "Excellent. Maybe this will be worthwhile."

The ninja with the naginata came next, along with his fellow wielding a gleaming ninjato. The Spartan moved out of the way as the point of the naginata flashed by his stomach. However, the ninja quickly reversed it in his hands so the wooden pommel struck the Spartan in the chin. Dazed, he barely parried one, no, two sword strikes, before he felt pain in his left leg. The last ninja had stuck the point of his sai there. As the ninja twisted the sai, the Spartan grabbed his arm and threw him into the others, buying himself a few seconds. He plucked the sai out of his leg and hurled it back at the ninja ... who caught it effortlessly in mid-air. Impressive.

But then the *jonin* entered the fray, slashing and slicing with furious energy, the Spartan scrabbling to catch its edge on his *xiphos*. The *jonin's* skill with the Honjo Masamune was dazzling. The Spartan had never faced a warrior so quick, so assured with the blade. It was like he had made the Honjo Masamune an extension of his own body, a third, deadly arm.

The *jonin* struck the Spartan on the shoulder in a blow that his armor only partially deflected. The Spartan flinched. As expected, the Honjo Masamune was razor sharp. The Spartan slashed out wildly, aiming for the *jonin*'s head, but his enemy had already stepped out of the way, dodging the blow with ease and scorn. He returned to his position beside Eisenstein.

Then the other four ninja were on him again. He parried sword blows and sais, uncomfortably aware how the fight was going. The pained look on Eisenstein's face said it all, the professor's savior quickly turning into quarry.

Mathematics was against the Spartan. A master swordsman could fight many swordsmen of lesser skill ... but fighting three or more true experts was a challenge even for a master. And these ninjas were indeed true experts. It wasn't like in the movies where Conan or Zorro or The Three Musketeers could fend off dozens of bladesmen with ease. Because that only happened in the movies.

Thus, the real-life, non-movie thing happened. The Spartan felt a cut to his arm. Soon followed by a slice on his back. And a kick that sent him spinning towards one of the walls. In the background, the *jonin* seemed set to attack again. With a flash of insight, the Spartan realized what his ninjas were doing. The rest of the pack was chasing down the prey so the alpha male could claim his prize.

But a Spartan – and a US Tier 1 soldier – was no man's prize.

As the ninja with the naginata thought to pin him against the wall with the point of his weapon, the Spartan blocked the blade with his *xiphos*. As they wrestled, he smashed down on the wooden handle with his elbow, breaking the naginata in half. The ninja was momentarily shocked by the Spartan's skill. The Tier 1 soldier seized the pointed tip as it fell to the ground and thrust the jagged wooden edge into the ninja's throat straight through the Ghost Armor. He gurgled and fell to the floor, the wood still in place.

The Spartan heard a cry of frustration from the front. Evidently the *jonin's* plans for revenge weren't working out as planned. Or, perhaps, the battle was taking too long, the booming from above becoming louder and more urgent. The *jonin* re-entered the fray, the Honjo Masamune a terrifying weapon as it thrust and slashed towards the Spartan's face and body. It collided loudly and heavily against his *xiphos*, the clang the sound of the clash of two ancient civilisations. The Spartan leant back as the sword came so close to his face he had an intimate view of the blade's artwork. Pretty and deadly.

Again the Spartan, as expert a swordsman as he was, had trouble keeping up. It took all his skill to bat away the Honjo Masamune – which was almost twice as long as his *xiphos* – let alone face three other ninjas armed with swords and sais. He deflected the Honjo Masamune and dealt minor counter-thrusts to the other ninjas, but it was clear he was being overwhelmed. He fought on with even more frenzied energy than ever.

The gods of war favored the Spartan for a moment as he found a gap in the *jonin's* defense and struck downwards. Alarmed, the *jonin* raised his forearm. The Spartan's *xiphos* crashed into the forearm with a ringing sound. The Spartan realized the ninja was equipped with iron sleeves, metal rods inside the Ghost Armor that could deflect a blade strike. The impact would bruise the *jonin* but he would keep his arm. The Spartan would have to resort to stabbing strikes instead.

"You focus your attention on too many styles," said the *jonin* between swings. "Your energies are divided between swords, guns and fists. Whereas I have perfected just one style."

"You talk too much," said the Spartan.

Yet if the Spartan was hoping the *jonin* was going to dash away and let his men take him on as before, he was disappointed. This time the *jonin* remained with his soldiers.

The frantic battle continued, loud, aggressive and fast.

The Spartan remained desperately outnumbered.

The Spartan took the eye out of one ninja with a thumb gouge and almost slashed straight through the hamstring of another, but the fight was only going one way. A foot kicked him one way. Then he was kicked in another. His knees were kicked out from under him. He fought hard, roaring, but strong hands grabbed each of his arms, forcing him to his knees and wrenching the *xiphos* out of his grasp.

It was just like his dream. It was just like Leuctra.

The *jonin* held the edge of the Honjo Masamune to the Spartan's exposed neck.

"You fought well," he said, triumph in his voice. "It would have been interesting to face you alone. But my men deserved their revenge, too." The *jonin* rose the blade up two-handed. "To die by this blade could be considered an honor. And in your case, you could consider it so, despite your crimes."

Just as the *jonin* was about to swing downwards, a voice rang out before them, full of authority and command.

"Let the boy go and face me," insisted Shintaro, magnificent in his armor, samurai sword wet from the blood of his foes.

The *jonin* smiled.

***

The Spartan didn't hesitate. He grasped the arms holding his, then, with an almighty tug, pulled the two ninjas holding them towards each other. Their heads collided with a most satisfactory thud. He kicked free of the hands holding his legs and rolled out of the way as the Honjo Masamune came towards his neck, striking concrete instead.

The Spartan seized his *xiphos* just as Shintaro moved forward. The *jonin* nodded towards his two stunned compatriots, who peeled off to face the Spartan. One more ninja remained at the boss ninja's side.

Dust fell from the ceiling as an explosion went off above.

"Is that you, Shintaro?" said the *jonin*.

"Surrender the Honjo Masamune and you may yet live," came the fearless reply, voice distorted by the mask.

"Kill him," the *jonin* instructed his associate. The ninja charged at Shintaro, blade held high and two-handed. Without even stopping, and with almost effortless contempt, Shintaro ducked the blow and slashed the ninja shoulder to groin. The ninja collapsed, severely injured, quivering hand clutching the gaping wound.

The *jonin* prepared the Honjo Masamune in defense.

"You are chasing your death, old man," he said as they circled each other.

In reply, Shintaro swung his sharp, long weapon towards the *jonin*. The enmity between them was almost palpable. Samurai versus ninja? Japanese agent versus Chinese agent? Talk about your epic grudge match.

The furious battle began, sharp swords seeking out flesh. Their blades clashed for many seconds as they blocked, parried, feinted and sought gaps in the other's defenses. The *jonin* was young and extremely fast. Yet Shintaro had experience on his side. They were evenly matched for a moment.

Eisenstein watched for the corner of the room, clearly terrified.

Meanwhile, the Spartan engaged the other two ninjas. One was the stocky ninja with the sais, while the other fought with a ninjato that had already tasted his blood.

Yet the ninja with the sais had already lost an eye to the Spartan. The Spartan decided to focus on him first. He moved around in a seemingly erratic yet deliberate manner, making the most of the wounded ninja's impaired vision and lack of depth perception. The Spartan struck the ninja once on the ribs, slashed his back as they both parted and attempted to strike his neck. Instead his *xiphos* tore a hole in the ninja's Ghost Armor around his mouth.

The other ninja performed a series of aggressive strikes, crying out with *chi* energy with the last blow, forcing the Spartan back as he blocked. The shinobi took to the air and leapt at his head, trying to capture the Spartan's head between his legs and twist savagely. The Spartan ducked. The ninja landed on his feet and flipped backwards across the room. The Spartan tracked him and, when he was vertical once more, slugged him extremely hard in the jaw.

He was going to follow up with a deadly blow when the sai wielder thrust both sais straight at the Spartan's face. He caught the sais with his *xiphos* just in time. But now his blade was caught between the sais' guards. He wrestled with the ninja, trying to reclaim his weapon.

The ninja spat something from his mouth, aiming for the Spartan's own mouth. Instead the small object hit the Spartan's cheek and fell to the ground.

The Spartan realized with disgust that the ninja had attempted to spit his suicide pill into his mouth. A vile trick. But a clever one.

As the Spartan wrestled, he kicked the prone ninja in the jaw – hearing a satisfying crack that told him everything he needed to know – then shoulder-charged the sai ninja. The Spartan's extra weight and strength gave him the advantage, and, placing one leg behind the ninja's foot, he used the extra force and leverage to get his opponent on the ground. The ninja crashed to the concrete, exhaling as the Spartan's weight collapsed on him. The Spartan slammed the shinobi's head against the concrete, then, raising onto his knees, got his strong arms around the ninja's neck. The ninja was built for speed and athleticism, not for brawn. His hands flapped around the Spartan's bicep, but the struggle was short. With a final effort, the Spartan ended him.

He rose to his feet, grimly determined.

So much for the *genin*.

Now for the *jonin*.

Chapter 56

This was not going how I imagined, thought the *jonin* as he battled for his life.

Firstly, he had anticipated killing the Spartan with the Honjo Masamune, delivering the death blow once the Tier 1 soldier had been lured down into the space, slashed and battered by his fellow ninjas, and finally presented at his feet. The Spartan's execution for the crime of slaying Commander Lee had been well prepared. Despite the loss of men, it had all gone to plan. Until God or the genie of fate had decided to laugh at the *jonin's* plan.

The sudden appearance of Shintaro was something he could not have possibly expected (yes, the *jonin* knew his name, gleaned from the dying lips of one of his operatives many years ago). What on earth was that Japanese gadfly doing here? Now? And why was he clearly working with the Americans?

The *jonin* batted away Shintaro's blade before attempting to impale him through the chest. Shintaro twisted so the Honjo Masamune went through thin air and swung his weapon backhanded at the leader's face. The *jonin* stepped away from the blow with the relaxed ease of a master bladesman. Still, he was far from relaxed. Their fight had lasted a mere 20 seconds, but most combatants who faced the *jonin* one-on-one would have been dead in half the time. And time was something the *jonin* just didn't have.

The Spartan wasn't helping the situation, either. The *jonin* had underestimated the Tier 1 soldier's talent for fighting and survival – a talent which he could see over Shintaro's shoulder he was using with devastating effect on his remaining ninjas. He would have to act soon or face a similar predicament as the Spartan mere seconds ago, outnumbered and facing overwhelming force.

First he had to deal with Shintaro. And he knew he could. The Japanese agent was good with a sword – excellent, even – but the *jonin* was, well, magic. He had skill and youth and reach on his side. Shintaro had dealt only minor blows to the ninja, while the *jonin* in return was slowly turning Shintaro's body into a red ruin.

And yet, Shintaro did not flinch as the Honjo Masamune cut through his armor and into his flesh. In fact, if the *jonin* didn't know any better, he would have sworn that Shintaro felt honored every time the Honjo Masamune bit into his body.

Nor did Shintaro allow his sword to parry the Honjo Masamune full on, merely knocking it aside in defense as if he was also afraid of damaging the sacred blade.

Strange.

The *jonin* cried out as he delivered a two-handed blow to Shintaro's mask. The mask absorbed and deflected most of the strike, yet a single eye was now exposed. An eye that blazed with rage.

"Surrender what you have stolen," said Shintaro in an unnerving voice, swinging his katana viciously at the *jonin's* torso.

"Come get it, 'samurai'," came the reply as the *jonin* parried the attack and hacked at Shintaro's hands, scoring a light blow that sent armor flying.

In his mind, he was already preparing a complicated 10-strike attack that would lead in Shintaro's downfall. After that, he would take care of the Spartan.

Just then he heard a woman's cry from above. He recognised the pained voice. It was his No.2. His lover. And she had yelled out in extreme pain. He had only ever heard her cry out like that once ... and that was during training in China when her left leg had been broken by an instructor's kick.

He was distraught and distracted for a millisecond. His elaborate *kata* was interrupted.

That was enough for Shintaro. He brought his katana two-handed up against the *jonin's* chest. It was only the *jonin's* extreme speed and reflexes that saved him from being cut in twain. Nevertheless, the katana scored a deep cut across his chest, slicing open his Ghost Armor and the flesh beneath it.

The *jonin* howled.

Yet despite the agony, he could see that Shintaro's swing had left him overextended and open.

"You want the Honjo Masamune," he cried as he thrust it into Shintaro's stomach, past armor and into flesh, "Take it!"

The *jonin* expected Shintaro to fall from the critical strike. Instead, Shintaro dropped his sword and grasped the Honjo Masamune with both hands.

"Give ... me ... the sword," he repeated, grasping the razor-sharp metal with unnatural strength. Horrified, the *jonin* tried to pull the blade away, only succeeding in pulling it back slightly and slicing Shintaro's fingers. The two men were stuck in a ghastly tug of war. The *jonin* yanked again with all his strength. Still Shintaro held the blade with lethal might, his single exposed eye staring in reproach and hatred.

The stalemate held for a bloody couple of seconds.

Then the Spartan had dispatched his last foe and turned his head towards them. With the strength of desperation, the *jonin* kicked out at Shintaro, pushing the agent's chest back while using his last reserves to pull at the Honjo Masamune. Success. The blade was free.

"Stop!" ordered the Spartan.

Shintaro tottered, yet reached down for his blade. "Get ... him," he managed.

The *jonin* plucked an egg-shaped device from his pouch and flung it towards Shintaro. The Spartan tackled Shintaro so the device missed Shintaro's head and its acid started eating into the concrete.

Before the pair could get up, the *jonin* grabbed the trembling Professor Eisenstein and raced out of the door. The Spartan and Shintaro were still coming. The *jonin* detonated the charge above the door. Stone and rubble fell, blocking off the door. He heard a cry of frustration. His pursuers wouldn't be getting through all that stone in a hurry. He had expected the best yet nevertheless prepared for the worst, as all serious men must.

You can't catch me, I'm the Gingerbread Man, he thought.

"Time to go, Professor," insisted the *jonin* as he dragged the scientist down the corridor and to the secret passage that would allow them to escape.

Chapter 57

There was nothing quite as exciting – or terrifying – as having someone shoot at you and miss, thought Vasquez as she dodged a volley of bullets. Twisting behind the corner of a crate, she brought her MP-5 up and fired at the direction of the fusillade. She couldn't tell if she hit anything as she was forced to retreat again due to withering return fire. Her amygdala was screaming at her, sensing stress and danger all around.

Two doughty special forces soldiers joined her at her hidey-hole. Together they sent more rounds down range, searching out elusive, nimble targets.

Just then there was an almighty explosion in front of her, forcing her to blink. Puffer had wasted her targets with a shot from the X-25. She turned around and nodded in his direction. He smiled and nodded back.

Time to move.

Vasquez and the two special forces soldiers advanced. It was chaos in the warehouse, the noise almost deafening. Bodies fell on both sides. Men were screaming. Some screamed for medics. Others just screamed, from rage or from pain.

Vasquez's armor had already been hit by ricochets. Fortunately, the Kevlar saved her from serious injury.

But perhaps she thought too soon. A bullet grazed her exposed cheek, making her duck. Her companions were too slow. She heard the sickening wet impact behind her, heard them fall to the floor. They weren't making any noise.

She looked back. They were *gone*.

Bullets kept flying towards her, delivered by a disturbingly proficient shooter.

I'm feeling very attacked right now, she thought. Vasquez ducked around a concrete barrier, fired and retreated. Her opponent did the same, her virtual mirror.

Vasquez caught a quick glimpse at her shooter. And immediately knew who it was, despite the disguise.

It was the *kunoichi*.

Yet Vasquez had thought this might happen. And she was ready.

With incredible speed, Vasquez slapped in a special magazine into her MP-5 and aimed at the *kunoichi*. She shot the ninja's own MP-5 out of her hands, bullets striking gloved fingers. Vasquez heard a yelp. But she wasn't finished. Advancing rapidly, Vasquez went full automatic on the ninja, peppering her all over the body with her bullets. The *kunoichi* cried out even more, defenseless against the onslaught. Yet none of the rounds were fatal – only extremely painful. Vasquez had come equipped with a mag of rubber bullets. She wanted to take the *kunoichi* alive.

And now she was right above the writhing female shinobi. She kicked her full on in the face, boot landing with a pleasing crack. She imagined more than a few teeth were loosened. The ninja's head snapped to the side. Yet without hesitation she kicked Vasquez in the groin. Payback from their first fight.

Vasquez groaned and stepped back. The *kunoichi* attempted a leg sweep. Vasquez evaded the move, but it nevertheless bought her opponent time to get to her feet with a quick flip.

Now they stood in front of each other, hands extended out, as the battle raged around them.

"This time we finish it," vowed Vasquez.

She aimed a punch at the ninja's head. The *kunoichi* grabbed the arm as it sailed past, then came closer and kneed Vasquez in the stomach. Vasquez responded with a wicked head butt. The ninja came off worse in the exchange, tottering back.

The pair traded a rapid series of punches and kicks. Vasquez landed a firm elbow to the face, while the *kunoichi* delivered a strong kick to the chest. The ninja expected Vasquez to go spinning back, yet the Mexican remained on her feet, a determined look on her face. The *kunoichi* paused, surprised.

"You're different," she said.

She's right, thought Vasquez as she rained blow after blow on the ninja, wearing her opponent down. The realization that there remained another person responsible for her family's slaying had filled her with new, dark energy ... energy to continue the fight.

Energy she was now directing straight at the *kunoichi*.

Vasquez delivered a cruel backhanded blow to the *kunoichi's* mouth. There was now blood visible underneath the ninja's mask. Vasquez dodged two punches and a kick in return, ninja limbs striking mere air. She struck the *kunoichi's* stomach, slammed her elbow into the ninja's face and gasped as the ninja stabbed her in the neck with fierce, rigid fingers.

She bit back the pain and located the spot at the *kunoichi's* right knee where she had shot her with rubber bullets.

Vasquez now capitalized on her previous work by delivering a devastating kick to the kneecap.

There was a horrible, ungainly noise. The *kunoichi* screamed, her agony audible even over the din of battle.

The mighty kick had shattered the kneecap.

But Vasquez didn't pause to gloat. She grabbed the ninja's head, turned it around and slammed it down onto the concrete.

Then again.

And again.

The ninja went limp in her hands.

Vasquez did it again, sensing correctly that the ninja was faking it.

This time was the charm.

The *kunoichi* was out.

Vasquez allowed herself a moment of triumph. It had taken three fraught battles, but she had downed the strange, powerful woman. And brought her in alive, just like she used to do on the beat as a cop in Juarez.

It was a victory for her as significant as any of the Spartan's duels. The *kunoichi* was as relentless an opponent as any of the Canister Six she fought last year.

Vasquez felt like she should say some catchphrase, like "there's no crying in baseball" or "you forgot your boarding pass".

Instead, she said softly: "Fuck you."

On a whim, she tore off the *kunoichi*'s facemask. The face underneath was pretty, elegant, pained.

Vasquez reached down and tied plastic cuffs to the ninja's arms and legs.

There. Done.

The Spartan would be satisfied that she had bested her foe.

Garin would be pleased that someone who had dared attempt to assassinate his people was defeated.

And now they had a new captive.

Chapter 58

They say a man can drown in an inch of water.

The same can be true for an inch of blood.

The special forces soldier known as Monkey was finding out that truth as he held a wounded ninja face down in a pool of its own blood. Despite being wounded himself in half a dozen places, Monkey's strength was inexorable, undeniable. It could almost be described as that of a man driven mad by grief.

"You killed my friends! You killed my friends!" he screamed, voice hoarse, as he held the thrashing ninja down. Shrapnel struck Monkey on the face, but he cared not, lost in the moment.

What the ninja thought of Monkey's accusation no one would know. Monkey's dark task was soon accomplished. The ninja's feet stopped their frantic beating on the ground. Monkey released his grip, panting.

But there was indeed method to Monkey's madness. Casting a glance around him, he dragged the ninja into a darkened corner of the warehouse and stripped his kill of his suit. He checked to see that no one was watching, then stuffed the suit in his backpack. Warriors traditionally took strange trophies from their fallen enemies – everything from a beating heart to a severed ear – but few had the chance to claim such a miraculous, high-tech prize.

The special forces soldier had selected this ninja because he was short and wiry, just like Monkey. Physically, they could have almost been twins. Twins that shared the same wardrobe. Monkey had selected his quarry well.

Yes, Monkey had plans for this set of Ghost Armor. Plans for the future. Plans that his comrades were not privy to.

Monkey plucked two high-explosive grenades from his webbing and tossed them towards the dead ninja. He planned to confuse his combat crime scene more by leaving a mangled body. Maybe this ninja never had a suit in the first place, he imagined the post-mortem investigators saying. Who would be able to tell otherwise from the bloody mess left behind?

Monkey ran back towards the fight as the grenades went off, stolen Ghost Armor safe in his possession.

Chapter 59

Jackson felt like he had been sent to the naughty corner. Colonel Garin had instructed Jackson to hang back in his HQ in case of counter-attacks. But the huge African-American soldier wasn't happy. He shifted his Mossberg 500 pump-action shotgun in his hands uncomfortably.

This is some back of the bus bullshit, he thought as he watched Garin barking out orders before the live feed from the attack on the giant TV screen.

The Tier 1 soldier would've preferred to have been in there in the action, not babysitting his commanding officer. It was yet another reminder of how Jackson was tired of taking orders from anyone but himself.

Not that it wasn't dangerous in the warehouse, judging by the screens. Both the ninjas and the special forces folk were taking large casualties. The close-quarters combat was as fierce as anything Jackson had seen or experienced.

Frankly, it looked like a house party at Vlad the Impaler's castle.

Jackson couldn't help noticing that Monkey was throwing himself into the fray like a madman.

Plus some Japanese geezer in red armor was killing people with a sword. What the fuck was that about?

Jackson sighed. Sitting still didn't suit him.

Fuck Garin again for putting him on guard duty.

Garin screamed into his microphone as he lost radio contact with the Spartan. The colonel barked to the techs to get him back in contact. Running to do Garin's bidding was the thin, twitchy, brilliant Sorensen, back from an extended leave.

Thus Jackson was the only one in the room paying attention and ready to rock and roll when a ninja killed the two guards at the door with a silenced submachinegun. The mid-sized but muscular shinobi then turned his weapon towards Garin. Apparently, the other side had also decided to try to take out the enemy's command post. A decapitation strike. Smart.

Things seemed to slow down to a crawl. Time dilation, the head shrinkers called it. Happened all the time in combat.

Jackson could see Garin half-turned, his mouth open in an "o", reaching for a pistol at his side, too slow by half.

He could see the stunned expressions of the technical support team, too scared to move.

And then he could see himself.

Jackson experienced a moment of perfect clarity. All he had to do to free himself from Garin's command was let the ninja shoot Garin, then kill the ninja in turn. No one could reprimand him for failing to act quickly enough. And no one would be able to prove anything otherwise.

Fate danced on a coin.

Then muscle memory and training and duty kicked in. He raised the Mossberg and fired. The range was extremely close.

The ninja was ratatouille.

The tech support team cried out as they were spattered with blood. Sorensen looked like a dog in one of those "I can't handle this right now" internet memes.

Garin stood there, gun in hand, gaping. He stared hard at Jackson. It seemed as if he realized the conundrum Jackson had faced. That he'd had the chance to get rid of his boss but had elected to save his life anyway. Garin's face grew thoughtful. He nodded to Jackson.

"Thank you, soldier," he sombrely.

"Hey, no problem, colonel," replied Jackson, resting the warm barrel of the Mossberg on his shoulder.

So he'd saved Garin after all. He had surprised even himself.

But now Jackson figured that his debt to Garin was pretty much paid in full.

Chapter 60

American special forces soldiers tended not to die in large numbers ... not in combat, anyway. They were too exceptional. Which made the action in the warehouse atypical in the annals of special forces. Seven elite warriors had been killed in the fighting. And everyone had been wounded in some way.

It was a steep butcher's bill. A high price to pay for avenging the deaths of Joker and his team.

Yet if the Americans had suffered, the ninjas had suffered worse. Seventeen had been eliminated, with three severely wounded. Thus, the mission had been a qualified success. Special forces honor had been satisfied and avenged.

Garin's people had also snatched up the scientists and engineers working on the Chinese version of the suits. They were the brains rather than the brawn behind the operation and surrendered without too much fuss, saving their energy to ask for lawyers. There would be no more Ghost Armor knock-offs for the time being, from that team at least.

And one semi-conscious shinobi had even been taken alive – Vasquez's ninja bête noir, a high prize indeed, close to the Ace of Spades on their most-wanted playing cards.

"I want to be there when you interrogate her," Vasquez told Colonel Garin, "she's my collar."

"Done," agreed Garin.

The *material* side of the ledger was also good. The search through the ninja base had garnered 19 sets of Ghost Armor. More good news for Garin and the President. The one missing set was viewed as an anomaly. Maybe not every ninja got a suit. Maybe they just ran out of materials. Maybe one ninja had thought it was "casual Friday".

Sadly, the ninja's leader had pulled an Amelia Earhart and vanished without a trace.

Meanwhile, the Spartan sat on a bench in Garin's ad hoc HQ, stripped down to his underwear, while medics worked on him.

He roughly pushed away the small cup holding pain pills being proffered. He would bear the pain. It was a point of Spartan pride.

Garin came up to him.

"Nice work in there. You've done a man's job, sir."

"Thanks, sir."

"But I hear the leader got away."

"Correct."

"With Eisenstein."

"Affirmative."

"The assholes you meet on the job," sighed Garin. "Why didn't you kill the head ninja, son?"

"I tried. He was amazing with the sword. A real prodigy. Best I've ever fought."

"That's ... disappointing. How the whole thing played out and all."

"Is there a problem, sir?"

"Tell me again how it went down," drawled Garin.

"The Vice President's killer led me into a trap. I was almost down for good until Shintaro reinforced me. In the ensuing duel Shintaro was impaled by the Honjo Masamune." Indeed, Shintaro had been rushed to hospital and was being operated on as they spoke. "What's the word on Shintaro?"

"Touch and go. Still, he's a fighter."

"Make sure he gets the best possible treatment, sir. He saved my life."

"Will do, son."

The Spartan nodded. He wanted Shintaro to live. He owed him.

"But let's get back to the duel, Spartan," said Garin, sensing the Spartan's distraction. "Because that's the part I'm having trouble with."

"Why is that, sir?" said the soldier in question. "Careful," he told one of the medics working on the sai wound on his leg.

"Because you have history with going on mission-endangering duels. Remember that nonsense with the Monk?"

"That was not nonsense, sir," said the Spartan, "that was …

"A matter of honor?" said Garin sharply. "Did history repeat itself in that warehouse? Did you encourage this duel and jeopardize the mission? Because duels are for assholes. Remember what happened to Alexander Hamilton?"

"With respect, sir, Hamilton was a Founding Father, not a member of special forces." Garin flashed the Spartan a disappointed look, regarding the comment either as perverse or unpatriotic. The Spartan continued: "I didn't even know where the leader was. He set this all up himself. He wanted revenge for his master, Commander Lee. So, it seems, did his ninjas."

Commander Lee, the madman whose crazed scheme had resulted in plague canisters being unleashed in Taiwan, with the effects spreading around the world.

"But you still ended up getting into a swordfight with him," said Garin, staring at the Spartan's bloody wounds. "Pretty strange during a major gunfight."

"As I said, sir," said the Spartan, irritated that his word was being questioned, "the ninjas slashed the strap holding my SAW as soon as I landed in the room."

"Because otherwise you just would have put three rounds into the leader's head as soon as you had seen him? Sent him to the Other Place, right?"

"Correct."

"Uh-hmmm." Garin sighed. "I guess I'll just have to believe you, Spartan. But still …"

"'But still' could be summed up as the history of warfare, sir."

"Tell me this, then – if the leader had been standing there alone, not reinforced, Honjo Masamune in hand, goading you on to fight him one on one … would you have accepted?

The Spartan considered the question. "Possibly. But that's a hypothetical, sir. The facts on the ground were different."

"I repeat: uh-hmmmm."

Just then Vasquez appeared, the hood of her Ghost Armor peeking out of the top near the collar. She looked at the wounded Spartan.

"Treat him well, boys," he told the medics. "I have a vested interest in that body." She touched the Spartan on the shoulder. "Hey."

"Hey."

"You OK?"

"Good enough. What about you?"

Vasquez felt her jaw, which was aching. "Good enough. What's going on?"

"The colonel is wondering whether I jeopardized the mission by getting into a swordfight with the lead scumbag."

"Did you?"

"See?" crowed the colonel. "You have form, Spartan."

"No, I didn't deliberately seek him out," he said. Seeing Vasquez's sceptical glance, he added: "Hand to God."

"I believe him," said Vasquez.

Garin seemed to shrug. "Fine."

"So you brought your stalker down, I hear," said the Spartan. "Nice work."

"Thanks," said Vasquez with a smile. She thought she could detect relief in the Spartan's voice that she had survived the battle. "I heard you had your own close encounter, sir," said Vasquez, turning to Colonel Garin.

"Who told you that?" he said, as if surprised.

"I did," said Jackson, poking his head into the triangle. He stood there, grinning.

"Right," said Garin, seemingly embarrassed.

Jackson faced the Spartan. "A ninja assassin had him dead to rights. I took him out before he could make the colonel deader than Archduke Ferdinand. Ain't no thing."

Garin said nothing, lips pursed. It was uncomfortable knowing that you owed another man your life.

"It *is* a thing," replied the Spartan. "I owe you one."

"Yeah, you do," said Jackson, smiling.

"I'm ... grateful," said the Spartan with effort.

"Well, shit. Bet that was hard to say. Bet those words stuck in your throat."

The Spartan stuck out his big hand. Jackson shook it, still grinning. Garin's eyebrows raised almost imperceptibly.

"Get a room, you two," said Vasquez.

"I'm going to bounce," announced Jackson. "Find gainful employment as a private contractor. Maybe I'll go back to Iraq. I hear the money's still good there."

"War Is A Racket, eh?" said Garin slyly.

Jackson slowly nodded to Garin. "War Is A Racket, colonel. Always. See you round the firing range."

"Jackson," said Garin neutrally.

"We'll meet again," said the Spartan.

"Count on it," said Jackson over his shoulder.

As Jackson left, Vasquez said, "Any of you want to tell me what the hell that was all about?"

"Forget about it," said Garin dismissively. "We've broken the back of the leader's army, but he's still a ninja, and ninjas work best as solitary animals.

"Vasquez, come with me to interrogate the *kunoichi*. And Spartan, I want you to return to my apartment and await further instructions. Because you just know this isn't finished."

Chapter 61

Surfer Dude felt a familiar itch at the back of his neck. It was the itch he got whenever someone was about to steal his wave ... or steal his contract. Standing on the street outside the target apartment in Little Belgium, he put his surfboard against a post, bent down to adjust his flip-flops and peeked over his shoulder. Surfer Dude saw the reflection of a gunsight on the roof of the building across the road.

Suddenly the gunsight vanished from view.

Surfer Dude pretended not to notice. Yet inside he was livid. He knew it wasn't the police: there were still barely enough of them alive after the plague. Which meant other assassins were here for the Spartan contract. He wondered if "Area 51" had been shopping information around to other parties. He had assumed he had received the information exclusively. If that was not the case, Area 51 would regret his actions.

Still carrying the giant longboard – an item that was both prop and tool – he sauntered over to a street vendor and ordered some disgusting meat on a stick thing. Surfer Dude was largely vegetarian and took care of his body, yet he gingerly ate the meat to blend in – his stomach no doubt paying for it later – and to give himself time to think.

He couldn't afford to leave enemies at his back. There was nothing for it: he would have to infiltrate the building and deal with the opposition.

He was in full character now: Hawaiian shirt, board shorts, flip-flops, surfboard. His disguise had fooled many people, allowed him access to many places. No one feared a surfer.

Yet the Latino street vendor gave Surfer Dude a doubtful glance. Yes, the poor, undocumented and working class sometimes saw through his disguise to detect the predator within. To be powerless in America was always to be on the lookout for danger no matter what guise it took.

That was why Surfer Dude liked to prey on the rich (and not just because he was poor as a child). They imagined Mafioso-style killers with bent noses coming after them, not beach bums with ripped abs.

Sometimes snobbery could get you killed.

Vile snack finished, Surfer Dude threw the stick into the garbage, crossed the road and stood outside the building where his rivals had taken camp. It was similarly upmarket to the target location and lacked a concierge. Good. Surfer Dude didn't want to answer any awkward questions.

He mashed all the buttons on the security door.

"Yes?" asked a voice, old, male, entitled, probably Caucasian.

"Package for ..." – Surfer Dude checked the mail slot – "Mr Durkheim, sir."

"Can't you leave it in his slot?" said Mr White Privilege.

"It needs a signature, sir." He emphasized the word "sir" to make the other man feel important. The door buzzed open. Apparently, the man on the other end *did* like to feel important.

Surfer Dude took the elevator and made his way to the roof door. Two large, salty-looking dudes blocked the way. They were wearing blue uniforms from an electrical repair company, but Surfer Dude had never seen electricians that were so muscular. Nor did they look like tradesmen who spent most of their time indoors fixing electrical circuits: their faces seemed weather-beaten and brown from too much time in the sun.

One had a scar near his left eye, which was slightly cloudy, as if it had undergone some extreme trauma.

In short, they looked ex-military.

He knew the look. He was ex-military, too.

Surfer Dude sauntered up.

"Hey, dudes, what's happening?" he said easily.

"Electrical repairs on the roof," said Scarface gruffly. "Turn around and go back." Scarface's accent was wrong, a non-native mimicking an American accent. Both he and his partner looked wrong. Sounded wrong. Smelt wrong.

"The super didn't say anything about repairs."

"Last-minute call," said Scarface.

Surfer Dude had of course never spoken to him. Now he knew they were lying.

"Now fuck off, retard," added his friend, pushing him back with a hand to the chest.

Surfer Dude *hated* people who used the word retard. One of his favorite cousins was mentally handicapped, a delightful boy full of love.

That settled it.

He pulled out a joint from his shirt. "OK. No harm, no foul. Want to split a jay?" Surfer Dude pulled out a lighter and lit the joint. The two unhappy customers looked disgusted.

Scarface again reached forward to push Surfer Dude away, crossing the path of his partner. It was time to act. Things would happen quickly now.

Surfer Dude flicked the burning joint into Scarface's eye. Scarface howled and shut his eyes, yet still threw out a blind punch. Surfer Dude seized the hand, twisted it, broke the wrist, and pushed Scarface's face hard into the wall, hopefully adding a fresh scar.

His partner gaped and went to move … just as Surfer Dude grabbed his surfboard and swung it into his stomach. Ooof. Then, with muscles honed both in the water and in the gym, Surfer Dude buried the sharpened steel fin of the board into his head. The fugazi repairman fell soundlessly, blood pouring out of his head. Yet for a moment Surfer Dude fancied he saw bafflement in the man's eyes as he fell, as if he couldn't believe he was being killed by a surfboard.

By now Scarface was beginning to recover. Eyes open, he reached for a pistol in his suit, struggling to seize it with his unbroken hand. Surfer Dude attempted to strike Scarface in the throat but missed. The pistol was now facing him, a finger curling on the trigger. Surfer Dude kicked the gun from the man's hand, the pistol hitting the wall.

As Surfer Dude threw a loping punch, Scarface ducked and pummelled Surfer Dude's stomach. Yet Surfer Dude's stomach was as firm as a brick wall. He had an eight-pack to die for.

Scarface had been suckered.

Surfer Dude brought his knee up into the man's face. He continued striking with both fists and feet until Scarface was flat on the ground, stretched out like a bug. He picked him up, held him in a headlock, then finished him. The man voided his bowels and lay still.

Surfer Dude stared down at the dead man's blue suit. Its logo read "Zhapp Electrical". And indeed its owner had been zapped.

Surfer Dude paused for a second, catching his breath. He really didn't know what waited for him once he stepped through the door.

He opened a compartment in his surfboard and withdrew a silenced pistol. A custom job, it contained 12 armor-piercing rounds. He wasn't particularly fond of guns, but he felt one may be called for.

He then lay the board against the wall.

He felt the handle of the door. It was unlocked. As slowly as he could, he eased it open. The metal door gave way with barely a sound.

Stealthily moving forward on his flip-flops, silenced pistol in his left hand, he spotted three men at the edge of the roof. Each wore the blue suit of Zhapp Electrical.

One – the spotter – had binoculars trained on the building opposite. Another was staring through the scope of a sniper rifle. And a third was on the phone.

Surfer Dude briefly wondered why no one had sought to question why so many electricians had been needed to fix an "electrical fault". Perhaps the electricians had come in two by two, just like in the Ark, and no one could tell the difference between them. Perhaps the super was getting his drunk on. Or, more likely as was the wont of the world, no one had given a shit.

He crept closer.

Unfortunately for the other men, their crouched positions presented their heads up as if they were in a carnival shooting gallery. And Surfer Dude was always a dead shot at those carnivals as a kid.

Surfer Dude breathed in. *Aim, fire and move on. Aim, fire and move on.*

His first two rounds took the sniper in the head. The sniper collapsed back, fortunately still clutching his rifle and not dropping it off the roof. Surfer Dude's next three rounds took the spotter in the upper torso. Again, the would-be killer flopped back like a duck shot at a carnival.

Aim, fire and move on.

The third man was surprisingly fast. He brought up a silenced submachinegun and fired at Surfer Dude. The blond assassin rolled to the side, dodging the bullets and continuing to shoot until he heard a groan. He had tagged the last man in the stomach. He was wearing Kevlar but the round had nevertheless penetrated. A lucky shot to the side. The shock of the wound had forced the assassin to lose his weapon, which clattered along the ground from his outstretched hand.

Surfer Dude ran up as his target drew a knife from his belt. He grabbed the knifeman's wrist and kneed him in the head. The knifeman dropped his weapon yet continued to struggle, so Surfer Dude delivered a kick to his freshly injured stomach.

The knifeman screamed.

Surfer Dude kept going with the foot vibe. He had particularly powerful legs from years of surfing. He stomped on the man's head until his flip-flops became all bloody.

Eventually Surfer Dude stopped and took a deep breath. His opponents were down. His gun-fu had been strong.

A lot of people had died just so he could get to one man. It was like that movie *Saving Private Ryan*. Well, *Killing Private Ryan*, maybe.

Looking at his handiwork, he realized he would have to call in "the cleaners" to dispose of these bodies. Another expense. He didn't enjoy killing people when he wasn't going to be paid. "Freebies" were for psychopaths.

Suddenly another Zhapp man came out at him from behind a roof vent, armed with a pistol. Yet he was too close – and too slow – for his own good. Or maybe he was just caught out by Surfer Dude's surprising speed. Surfer Dude caught the man's wrist, threw a knee into his groin, twisted the gun out of his hand, threw his opponent to the ground and kicked him in the head. It was a solid kick. The would-be assassin moaned, barely conscious.

Surfer Dude flipped him over. Up close Surfer Dude noticed that he had a scar that almost neatly divided his face in half. He looked vaguely Orcish.

"God damn," said Orcface in a thick foreign accent. "I'm …"

"Wounded? Aren't we all?" Surfer Dude surveyed his prey. "So, who are you, dude? Because you don't sound like you're from around these parts."

"I'm … we're from South Africa," he managed, glaring balefully at Surfer Dude.

"*Seth Afreca*. Long way from home, bro."

"Never should have left. So who … cough, cough … the hell are you?"

"Same as you, dude. Same as you. A hitter. A mechanic. A merc."

"You … look like Matthew McConaughey."

Surfer Dude preened a little. "Hey, thanks. I try."

"I …"

"… can't believe a surfer took out my entire team? Yeah, I get that a lot. No one expects a surfer to be violent." Surfer Dude stared at the bodies on the roof. "But humans have fucked up the world. They're a virus, man. That's why I don't mind killing men. Good for the environment. Good for Mother Earth. Good for my karma."

"That's … why you kill?"

"Who else am I going to tell my tragic backstory to … a therapist?" Surfer Dude stared at the other dead men. "So who sent you to steal my contract, bro?"

"The cartels." Two words that demanded immediate attention and respect.

Surfer Dude paused. "That's … inconvenient."

"They'll kill you for this."

"Unless we're both after the same target, which we are." Surfer Dude stared down at the bleeding man. "Besides, you don't look very Mexican to me. Which means to them you're expendable. I've dealt with them before, too. I'm taking it was the cartels your friend was on the phone with. So … thanks for the tip. Appreciate it."

"Guess you're going to let me go now."

Surfer Dude guffawed. "Yeah. And Santa Claus is real." He got up and stretched to his full length. "Are you ready?"

The other man nodded weakly.

"You don't want to say any last words or anything? A prayer?"

"No. Get on with it, you freak."

Surfer Dude raised his foot. "Okey dokey."

The foot descended.

Chapter 62

The Spartan rode the elevator up to Garin's apartment. Normally he would have taken the stairs, but he was tired. Wary of overexerting himself to the point of combat inefficiency, he had this once chosen the easy, modern electrical option.

He held his SAW in a duffel bag in his left hand, feeling its weight. The Spartan decided he would soon reload his weapon and give it a post-combat check over. He flicked his eyes to the other weapon at his side. He would sharpen and shine his *xiphos*, too. Its edge was still sharp, its metal still firm despite recently hacking through flesh and bone.

To his irritation, the elevator stopped. A tall, blond surfer in board shorts and flip-flops stepped in.

"Room for one more, bra?" he said cheerily.

The pair danced around as the surfer brought a large surfboard into the small space.

"Sorry ... my bad," said the stranger as he entered, forcing the Spartan to move sideways.

The surfer, a handsome, cheery oaf with arms the size of tinned hams, grinned. The Spartan scowled and dismissed him for a pleasure-loving civilian fool.

The Spartan didn't surf.

It's not over until we get a fix on the ninja with the Honjo Masamune, thought the Spartan as the pair travelled upwards. *Next time we meet I'll put him in the ground, whatever sword he's using.*

The elevator pinged. They had reached the floor of Garin's apartment.

The Spartan suddenly smelt something underneath the surfer's aroma of coconut oil, Sex Wax and sweat. Gunpowder. The surfer had recently fired a weapon. He was more than he appeared. The Spartan had been so fixated on spotting invisible ninjas, he failed to spot a monster hiding in plain sight.

The Spartan dropped his bag to free up his hands.

The doors of the elevator opened.

The surfer smiled and took cover behind his surfboard. "Surf's up," he said.

An explosion slammed the Spartan into the back of the elevator, the concussive energy knocking him off his feet. It was a strange explosion, more raw energy than pyrotechnics, designed to disorientate rather than destroy. The Spartan was stunned. Yet the suspicious stranger was still on his feet, his board protecting him from the blast.

The surfer slammed his board into the back of the Spartan's head. The Spartan tried to lift himself up with one hand, but the surfer struck him with the board again.

And, finally, again.

The Spartan lost consciousness.

* * *

He awoke to a triumphant voice crowing near his ear.

"I must say I'm kind of disappointed, big guy. You had this killer reputation. I was expecting more of a struggle. Something ... well, epic." Hands on his hips, the odd surfer stood over his prey. The Spartan was lying sideways on the floor of Garin's apartment, immobile.

Helpless.

With great effort, the Spartan lifted his head. "Fuck ... you," he slurred.

"Got some fight left in you? Bravo." The Spartan followed the surfer's glance down to a fresh pinprick in his arm. An empty syringe lay nearby. "The drug's Russian, you know. Those guys are animals. I ask you, when was the last time Russia produced a world surfing champion? World champion assholes they've got plenty of. But surfers? Nada. That's why I don't work with them."

The surfer nodded at the Spartan's hands and feet. They were bound with zip cords. "Still, I hogtied you just the same. Just in case there really was something to your reputation."

The Spartan opened his mouth. Nothing came out.

"I am grateful to you, though. With the money I collect on you, I'll be able to retire." The assassin stared past him for a second, as if recalling a distant memory or his "greatest hits" reel. "Because someone eventually isn't going to buy my act and come out blasting, am I right? Now chill for a bit while I take care of business." The assassin paused, then turned back. "The Spartan, hey? How many times have you seen *that* movie?"

The Spartan knew what movie he was referring to. If he could have been bothered wasting his strength, he would have rolled his eyes.

The assholes you meet on the job.

"I like your sword," said the surfer as he slipped it off the Spartan's waist. "I think I'll keep it."

The surfer took a final look at the Spartan, as if to confirm to himself that his Russian drug had rendered the Spartan immobile, then grabbed a cell phone and walked into Garin's kitchen.

The Spartan knew which drug the surfer had used. The Tier 1 soldier had been trained in drug and poison resistance just like a ninja, taking smaller doses until he had become immune to the toxins. Garin had insisted: he didn't want the Spartan to be immobilised by some underhanded venom.

It was only this resistance that allowed the Spartan the barest of movements. He felt like he had two tonnes of concrete weighing him down, but he had to act. And soon. He refused to quit. Refused to let this fuckwad send him to the afterlife. The ghosts of his ancestors would never give him peace for such an ignoble end, to be struck down by a coward's blow delivered by a buffoon.

Moving his hands with the greatest of efforts, he brought them down over his shoelaces. The metal-like material was designed to saw through restraints. The Spartan began to saw through the plastic cuffs.

Meanwhile, the surfer was on the phone, having placed the Spartan's *xiphos* on the counter.

"Hello? Who is this?" Pause. "Right. And you're with? You won't say? Uh huh. Uh huh. OK, I'll go first. You don't know me ... well, you may have heard of my work name. Surfer Dude." Pause. "Yes, the one from the bulletin boards."

The Spartan made his way through his arm restraints, which popped off silently. Now he began on the restraints on his feet. He tugged hard. The effort required was extraordinary. But he had no choice. No one else was coming. Not even Garin's neighbors, who were terrified of the colonel and wouldn't leave their apartments to investigate anything less than an atomic bomb going off. He had to free himself or die.

"Where did I get this number? The answer's wrapped up in what we need to talk about." The Spartan heard the fridge being opened. He imagined the surfer inspecting its contents. Then the fridge closed again. Maybe Garin didn't have this guy's brand of tofu.

"Those hombres you sent to take care of this Spartan guy? They got in the way. That's why I have their phone." There was a pause. The surfer opened a can of beer. The thought that the scumbag was enjoying a cold brew while the Spartan was seemingly helpless – no longer a threat of any kind – insulted him.

"What do I mean, 'got in the way'? The South Africans were going to poach my contract. Maybe even kill me. So ... I had to remove them." There was another pause. "Yeah, permanently. And yes, all of them."

The Spartan tried taking the bearings of Garin's apartment. There had to be something he could use as a weapon. He knew that the colonel had a gun cabinet in his bedroom, but to get to that he would have to make his way past the killer surfer, who would spot him immediately. He would never be able to reach his *xiphos*, either. So he had to rely on something close. Something lethal.

"Calm down, dude. *Calm* down. Can I just ... can I ... can I just say it wasn't like I woke up and planned any of this? They were just *there*."

There. The Spartan saw it on the wall. A ridiculous weapon, but the closest one he could see that might do the job. The Spartan began to crawl towards it.

"No, I'm not trying to be cute. Yes, I know what you do to people who think they're cute. The entire world does. So let's try and put it behind us … and focus on what I can offer you. Because we can both win here."

The Spartan made his way to the wall. Pushing himself against it with his shoulder, he reached up towards the gun cabinet. His first attempt failed. His drugged body slumped back to the ground. He girded himself for another attempt.

"I have this 'Spartan' with me. The underworld's most wanted. He's not going anywhere unless I want him to. Or *you* want him to." Pause. The surfer hurled the now-empty beer can into a corner. "Ahh, I thought that might make you happy. I'm willing to hand him over. And take a haircut on the bounty for killing your mercs, too. Say – 25 per cent?"

The Spartan made another grab at the case. This time it opened. With trembling hands, he removed the duelling pistol and the assorted equipment. He hunkered down again and assembled the equipment in his hands. Now he just had to remember how Colonel Garin had loaded the thing. And hope that the centuries-year-old weapon would work again.

"Good. Groovy. Vasquez? No … no sign of her. He came alone." Long pause. "No. I won't accept that contract. I don't kill women or children. Bad karma." Further pause. "Forget her. Let's return to the Spartan. Tell me where you want him and I'll deliver him up like hot pizza. Dead or alive. You choose." There was another long pause as instructions for the delivery of the Spartan were delivered.

The Spartan cocked the old pistol. Poured gunpowder into the barrel. Rammed in a ball with the ram rod. One of the balls fell to the floor, making a noise.

"What was that? Sorry, can you hold for a second?"

The Spartan kept going. He poured more powder on the frizzen pan as the surfer came around the corner.

"What are you doing there, bro? Don't you know it's pointless to resist?"

The Spartan still had his back to the surfer. He felt the man lean down and put a strong hand on his shoulder.

"You're just being foolish now."

The Spartan fully cocked the pistol. Then he turned to face the surfer.

"Oh," said the other man.

The duelling pistol was mere inches from his eye.

The Spartan pulled the trigger.

With a loud bang, the pistol's ball buried itself into the assassin's eye.

He went down.

So did the Spartan, as spent as the pistol.

Chapter 63

"Come on, *come on* ... the Spartan's not answering his phone," said Vasquez, flicking her hair with irritation as she snapped her mobile shut.

"Forget about him for now," said Garin. "We're about to start."

Vasquez looked at the *kunoichi*, who was now strapped to a table with an IV in her arm and electrodes on her head. A slender Chinese-American man sat in a chair beside her, holding her hand. The ninja appeared unconscious.

"How does this work again?" asked Vasquez. Garin explained the procedure. Vasquez looked appropriately appalled. "That's ... utterly horrible." She stared at the captured *kunoichi*. "This isn't who we are. And if it is, it shouldn't be."

"The procedure leaves no marks. She won't even know it took place."

"Beating the truth out of her would be more honest."

"I also have a certain ... distaste for the procedure," admitted Garin. "But it works. Let's listen."

The interrogation began.

"Where … am I?" said the *kunoichi* weakly.

"You are safe," soothed the slender man as he held her hand, who as far as the ninja knew was her *jonin*.

"I feel strange."

"You have been wounded."

"The last thing I remember is fighting the Vasquez woman," said the *kunoichi* in a dazed voice. "What happened next?"

"You killed her. We fled. Now it is time for the next attack." The interrogator paused for effect. "Do you remember your role?"

"Yes."

"Tell it to me. Where are we to strike tomorrow?"

"You told me never to repeat the location."

"We are alone. Answer the question."

"Is this a test?"

"No. Name the next target."

"I'm … I'm tired."

"Why isn't she answering?" Garin bellowed to a tech in the observation room.

"I don't know," he replied. "We're using the correct doses."

"Increase them," insisted Garin.

More drugs and electrical current were applied.

"Ahhh," moaned the *kunoichi* in pain, either from her existing wounds or the procedure.

"Answer me," insisted the interrogator, harsher this time. "Where are we going to attack next?"

The *kunoichi* paused for a long time. "It's never going to happen, is it?"

"What are you talking about?"

"Us, I mean. As a couple. As a husband and wife. We will never be free of duty. We will never settle down in my village and live a normal life. I will never bear your children. It was all a mirage. A deceitful dream."

"What? I ..."

A single tear ran down the *kunoichi's* cheek. "There is only death before us."

"Holy cow, this is dark," said Garin, shaking his head. "I didn't expect this." Vasquez appeared stricken, as if the *kunoichi* might have been speaking about her and the Spartan.

The interrogator gently squeezed her hand, like a lover might. "Once we complete this final mission, we will leave together. I promise."

"A promise written on running water," said the ninja sadly. "Now let me rest. I will talk no more."

"We are not finished here," insisted the interrogator. "Talk to me!"

But the *kunoichi* had gone silent.

Chapter 64

Half a world away, the ninja known simply as Chen clutched his chest as he stood over the submarine controls. Around him lay the dead crew of the Chinese sub, victims of the poison gas he had introduced into the air supply. His costume was soaked with blood, courtesy of the bullets of the late commander, who had drawn his pistol and shot him when one of his comrades had fallen upon Chen, rending him visible.

But it mattered not. Chen had never expected to survive. He had but one goal – a goal he was now about to accomplish.

Chen adjusted the submarine's targeting system so it locked onto the US aircraft carrier in the waters of the South China Sea. The sub remained undetected – just as Chen had been, safe in his invisibility suit, until moments ago – but would become visible as soon as Chen pushed the missile launch button.

Which he did now.

Chen's actions were now sending a missile known as an "Assassin's Mace" towards the U.S.S. Abraham Lincoln. Packed with enough explosive power to sink a large ship, the missile was equipped with advanced scrambling technology that broadcast thousands of signals, making it seem as if it was coming from many directions at once. By the time the enemy figured out which was the correct course as the missile leapt from the surface to the air, it would be too late.

And Chen had just launched four of them.

Within seconds the screen told him that two of the missiles had scored direct hits.

He paused, a rush of exhilaration running through him. He had succeeded. The U.S.S. Abraham Lincoln was, for all intents and purposes, destroyed, the wreck sinking, any survivors now scrambling for safety.

He grabbed the controls and directed the submarine towards the bottom of the South China Sea. Chen hadn't expected to escape, either.

He sat down in the commander's chair as the sub dove. The ninja didn't have long to wait for a response, either. The radar lit up with warnings of incoming missiles. Whether they were American or Chinese retaliatory responses, he had no idea.

They slammed into the submarine's hull, unhindered.

Then there was nothing.

Chapter 65

"Are you all right, young man?"

The Spartan awoke to see a blonde, smartly dressed angel hovering over him. Actually, scratch that – it was no angel: it was the President's secretary.

"I repeat, are you all right? Do you require medical assistance? Should I call someone?"

The Spartan was sore and shaky, but he knew it was nothing critical. Nothing broken. Nothing that couldn't wait. "Not right now, ma'am."

"I see." Pause. "If you were a cat, I'd say you just lost one of your nine lives."

"If I was a cat, ma'am, I might even agree with you."

"Well, you're better off than your friend there." The Spartan glanced over: the surfer assassin was definitely dead, a starfish-shaped wound over his left eye. Do Not Pass Go, Do Not Collect $200. The once-placid visage was now pained. Good.

"Let me give you a hand-up," said the secretary, eying the Spartan cautiously. The Spartan wasn't too proud to accept the hand. Her grip was surprisingly strong. "You're a big one, aren't you," she said, taking in the Spartan's full size as she hauled him up.

"Thank you, ma'am." He rested one hand against the wall, still woozy from the drugs and his injuries. His mouth tasted like cotton. He had failed to pay attention to the danger this surfer had represented … and in combat that usually meant death.

But he was now up on his feet. That was the main thing.

"I recognise you, don't I?" said the Spartan. "The President's secretary."

"Harmony," she replied, fixing him with cool eyes. "And you're the Spartan."

"Affirmative. What are you doing here, ma'am?"

"I was here to see Colonel Garin."

"Right." The Spartan wondered if they were lovers, but decided not to ask. That was none of his business. Nor was it relevant.

"What happened here?" she asked, staring at the dead body. She was pretty cool for a civilian who had just come across an unconscious man lying next to a dead body. A woman of substance, then.

"Some freak assassin," replied the Spartan, eyeing the strange surfer. "Tried to kill me. Came off second-best."

"Evidently. Looks like violence *does* solve problems. Good thing you live up to your namesake." It seems as if Garin had mentioned him to Harmony, which suggested more close bonds. Garin didn't talk shop to just anybody.

Harmony stared over towards the kitchen. "What's that surfboard doing here?"

The Spartan looked at the board, lying next to the bag holding his SAW. "He hit me with it."

"Very strange."

"Brained by a surfboard. A definite first." The Spartan went to the kitchen sink and splashed water on his face. He had nearly been murdered. The first time he had almost been killed, he was flushed with adrenalin and felt like puking. He could handle it better now, but his system was still full of an edgy type of energy.

The Spartan then took a second to return and kick the surfer in the head. Not only for the attempt on his life, but for violating this sanctuary that the Spartan and Garin had spent so much time talking in. More than that, it was the place he had first encountered his lover Vasquez. Now it was no longer secure. Garin would probably have to move. Screw the surfer for that.

The visitor said nothing about the Spartan's sudden violence. The Spartan sensed that she may have even understood it.

Harmony continued looking around the apartment. "I wonder how he knew to come here."

"I'd like to know that, too," replied the Spartan, rubbing his head again.

"That might have to wait," said Harmony. "Something has happened. Look at this." She walked over to Garin's large-screen plasma TV and turned it on. The station instantly lit up with the image of a sunken US aircraft carrier. The U.S.S. Abraham Lincoln, sunk by the Chinese in the South China Sea. The official death toll was in the hundreds, if not thousands.

The Spartan stared at the images.

"Do you have any idea what this means?" said Harmony, eyeing the screen and then the Spartan.

"Yes, ma'am," he said. "War."

Chapter 66

"The Chinese say the missile attack wasn't their idea," an anxious President told the Joint Chiefs of Staff in the Situation Room. "They say one of their submarines launched the missile, but they claim the attack wasn't authorized by either the government or the military. For now, I believe them."

"One of Garin's bogeys, perhaps," observed the General.

"My thoughts, too," said the President. "Both us and China have been very careful not to escalate the situation in the South China Sea. We sent our ships through to maintain freedom of maritime trade and they continue to build their bases there despite the objections of their neighbors. But so far we've both kept our hands to ourselves." He paused to pour himself a glass of water, an old trick to give himself time to gather his thoughts. He took a sip, then said: "Well, it's a disaster either way. What is our response, gentlemen?"

"Daedalus," said the General. The other Joint Chiefs in the room seemed to murmur in agreement.

"Daedalus," repeated the President. Daedalus, America's orbital weapons system, capable of hurling virtually unbreakable metal rods at hyper-speed down to Earth at a moment's notice. A rail gun in space. An irresistible force never fired in anger … yet.

Invoking its name brought silence to the room as everyone considered the implications of its use.

"We've just lost an aircraft carrier," said the General. "It's all over the news. We must retaliate immediately and decisively. The navy has sunk the sub responsible, but that's not enough. No, sir."

Admiral Raeger nodded in approval at the General's observation. "One submarine is not … proportional. Not with an aircraft carrier down and hundreds of souls lost. We need something more. Bigger." Raeger turned to look at the screens revealing the satellite feed of the South China Sea. It seemed as if half the Chinese navy had suddenly arrived. "Something that reminds the world never to screw with us."

"So Daedalus is perfect," said the General, crossing his arms.

"We should go all the goddamn way and retake Taiwan while we're there," growled General Regis.

"That's not proportional, either," chided Raeger. "Not at this stage."

The President stared at the screens. "I wonder what Colonel Garin would say."

"With respect, sir, the boys and I want you to leave Garin out of it," said the General, waving his hand. "We agree with your earlier assessment. We can imagine a scenario where one or more of these invisible ninjas captured the sub and used it to fire against us. It does seem highly unlikely that a Chinese submarine commander would unilaterally take it upon himself to start World War III."

"After all, none of the Soviet sub commanders did so after decades of Cold War tension," General Regis informed the room.

The General nodded soberly, then continued: "That being the case, Garin must accept some of the blame after losing the suits. We want him as far away from this as possible."

"The whole 'Colonel X' thing in the media isn't helping things either," said General Regis, not without a small undercurrent of glee. "Garin is … politically embarrassing at the moment. We think that a vacation is in order for the good colonel." Regis continued: "Think of what his actions – or inactions – have cost us. Have cost *you*, Mr President."

"Colonel Garin is a stand-up guy," offered the President.

"He seems to have fallen down on this one, sir," said the aging but highly respected Admiral Creacy, chairman of the Joint Chiefs of Staff, speaking for the first time.

And speaking for the room, it appeared.

The President paused, thinking. He liked Garin, but POTUS was still a political animal. And Garin was in bad odor. Particularly after the sinking of the aircraft carrier, something that hadn't happened since World War II and was a definite blow to American prestige. The President had little political capital to spare to fight Garin's corner – he needed whatever was left to save himself. His already-low poll rating would be even lower after this disaster.

And none of Garin's supporters were speaking up in support of the colonel. The images on the screen said everything that needed to be said. Any favors or debts the men in the room owed Garin were conveniently forgotten. They were all too busy washing their hands of the inconvenient colonel, Pontius Pilate style.

Scratch that: there was a late entry. General Archon. "For the record, I think we should still keep Garin in the loop. He's invaluable in times like these. A canny fighter and strategist. And in my opinion, he can't be faulted for the initial loss of the suits."

There was an awkward hush in the Situation Room. No one else was going to speak up for Garin as he was thrown under the metaphorical bus. The other Joint Chiefs were probably wondering why Archon had stuck his neck out for Garin. Did he owe him something? Was it fear? Or something else? Friendship?

Either way, the President shook his head.

"Opinion noted, General Archon," said the President, almost absent-mindedly. POTUS paused, waiting to see if anyone else had anything to add. They didn't.

The President didn't mention Garin again. It was now understood by all that he'd be left on the sidelines.

Instead, the President asked: "And we have a target for Daedalus?"

"Yes, Mr President," said the General. "China's biggest and most advanced aircraft carrier. They're very proud of it. Apparently, it's the first and only one that's come close to being as powerful as one of our own."

"And Daedalus is ready?"

"Yes, Mr President. It is already armed and locked on target. We just need you to give the order."

"Do we know what happens when we open this door, gentlemen? Do we know what's behind it?"

"We know it's not Narnia, Mr President," said the General archly.

"It's a risk we're willing to take," offered General Archon. "In this we are of one mind."

The President absorbed the information in silence. There was a pause.

Then he nodded.

** * **

Within minutes Daedalus swung into action. High above the Earth the war satellite readied a thick, long rod, constructed of some of the hardest metals known to man. Cameras more powerful than any in existence zoomed in on the centre of the Chinese aircraft carrier. Another second passed before the rod descended a tunnel, propelled by electromagnetic coils, and hurtled earthward towards the Sun Wu.

The speed at which the rod raced towards its target was staggering. Yet even more staggering was the sheer destructive power the rod threatened to unleash. It was estimated that a mile-wide asteroid colliding with the planet might be enough to destroy all life on Earth. Scientists had assured the President that Daedalus was not about to cause the destruction of mankind ... but whatever it was fired at, it would most assuredly obliterate.

It was just the type of button-pushing missile weapon the Spartan despised. Yet unfortunately for the honor of the US military, the Spartan wasn't manning the controls that day.

The Daedalus rod appeared as a blip on the radar of the Sun Wu for a mere moment – not enough time for its automatic defense systems to craft a response. Not that it could.

And so the rod struck the centre of the Sun Wu with a force that could only be described as Old Testament, Wrath of God Awesome.

The kinetic energy it delivered was immense. The aircraft carrier virtually snapped in two as if was a building block tormented by a huge child.

An invisible shockwave stretched out from ground zero, striking the vessels near the carrier.

Within that dread radius there were no survivors.

***

"Do you want war?" yelled the Chinese Premier down the phone to the President of the United States. "Because wars have been started over far, far less!"

"With respect, Mr Premier, we had no choice but to respond after *your* sub sunk the Abraham Lincoln," replied POTUS. "You had to expect a response with the whole world watching."

"Bah! With *greater* respect, Mr President, I already told you that we didn't initiate that attack," replied the Premier, shifting uncomfortably on the chair in his luxury hotel room in Manhattan. "Why would we? What would there be to be gained? If we haven't responded to your other provocations in the South China Sea, why would we now?"

"The missile came from one of your hunter-killers," said POTUS, emotions in check. "That is an unmistakable fact."

"A submarine you also sunk, which puts you ahead in casualty stakes."

"It's more helpful if we don't think of things in those terms, Mr Premier."

Which, thought the Premier, *was an easy thing for the person with fewer casualties to say.* "In any case, we think the sub missile was launched by one of those ninjas running loose."

"Chinese ninjas, by all accounts. Trained by your military."

"*Alleged* Chinese ninjas."

"Alleged, then." Both men had an archness in the voices, unaccustomed as they were to being so directly challenged.

POTUS continued: "I'm sorry, Mr Premier, but I have to answer to my people and my military. Action was required."

"That action was unjust," said the Premier, still angry. "Many other ships were destroyed besides the Sun Wu." The Premier recalled the scene of the wreckage, now being played side-by-side on the world's TVs with the footage of the downed American carrier. The images enraged him – how *dare* the Americans kill his people? – but the death toll and the mysterious manner in which the Chinese aircraft carrier was destroyed produced in him not a little awe.

In the end, perhaps death was the only thing not overrated in life.

But back to the duplicitous American on the other end of the phone.

The Premier continued: "Now I have to answer to MY people. They're furious, too. Our national prestige has been assaulted. There's an angry mob outside your embassy in Beijing."

"Matched by an equally angry mob outside your embassy in New York. But to answer your previous question, no, we don't want war. I want to do everything possible to avoid that."

"Attacking our navy is a poor way to start, then." The Premier glanced over at the armed bodyguards in the room. "What exactly did you use, anyway? God's own gun?"

His people had told him the attack had come from space, which is why the Chinese military was readying its anti-satellite missiles and searching for a target. The Premier had heard that the Americans had cancelled Project Thor, their secret project to deliver a kinetic orbital strike from space ... but maybe they had mothballed Thor to create a newer, better weapon. So much for the Outer Space Treaty banning weapons of mass destruction from space.

But the US President wasn't giving anything away. "The weapon system is classified, Mr Premier. What is not classified is my sincere desire to sit down with you and talk this over."

The Premier paused and leant back in his chair, thinking furiously. He was already ensconced in his hotel ahead of tomorrow's UN meeting when they had learnt of the sinking of the aircraft carrier. He was now in enemy territory. His security people had quickly taken over all the floors of the hotel – rudely evicting VIPs from the top floor – and turned the building into a fortress. A fortress filled with giant TVs and marble spa baths, but a fortress still.

More armed Chinese agents were outside, maintaining a wide perimeter around the hotel.

The Americans let it happen, maintaining a respectful distance. Such efforts had been anticipated by the home forces.

For now, there was an uneasy stalemate.

And it was going to take a lot more than the ritualistic exchange of pandas to solve this political problem.

The Premier hadn't lied. The Chinese people were demanding a response. His military wanted to respond as well, anxious to shake off the "peace disease" that had afflicted and weakened their ranks. Escalation was in the air. The US and Chinese navies were facing each other, commanders with fingers on triggers waiting for the order to fire. Rival jets were flying so close to each other it was a miracle none had collided. Citizens both East and West were baying for each other's blood, humiliated by the blows to their national prestige.

"Why should I meet with you tomorrow? How do I know you don't have more outrages planned?"

"Because the criminals behind this are pushing us towards conflict ... conflict neither of us really want. The world is holding its breath, just like it did during the Cuban Missile Crisis. Mr Premier, this is *our* Cuban Missile Crisis. A show of unity at the UN would be the best way to show everyone that we're jointly determined not to be cowed or coerced by terrorism."

"By all rights, I should just leave. Your actions prove you are a poor host."

"I implore you to stay, Mr Premier," said POTUS, soundly deeply sincere. "This is a time for unity. For diplomacy. Not for leaving the negotiating table. We need to unclench our hands." *And our sphincters, perhaps*, thought the Premier. Then the other man added: "I can guarantee your safety."

For a moment the US President sounded like a Mafia godfather, guaranteeing a rival's security at a sit-down where the rival would be assassinated.

The Chinese Premier paused for a long time. Many thoughts swirled through his head. The sinking of the carrier. His own domestic political situation. The military posture of the Americans. The risk of his own assassination, just like that of the American Vice President, a secret his security forces had winkled out. The possible repercussions if he did leave.

What was the right thing to do? What would be gained by staying? Was "POTUS" planning further attacks?

The American President was supposedly a "good" and "honest" man. But how "good" could any leader that sent men to their deaths be? And how "honest" was any leader who would give the order to suddenly blow an aircraft carrier out of the water with a secret, undeclared weapon?

The Chinese Premier often found the Americans inconsistent. Whereas the Chinese stated their intentions and kept their word – the benefits, perhaps of having a one-party system – American policy and intentions sometimes varied between Presidents and administrations. That made them unpredictable, prone to about-turns and policy changes based on personality and public opinion.

And they called the Chinese inscrutable.

But POTUS wasn't completely off the mark. They had both lost aircraft carriers. There was a delicate balance of sorts as the two navies stared down at each other on the South China Sea.

"Mr Premier?" prompted POTUS.

The Chinese Premier paused again. He needed to make the right decision here, particularly after the early "retirement" of his predecessor. The stakes for him – personally – were high. Perhaps he needed to play for time. Perhaps staying put was the wise move.

And above all else he needed to make the wise move. His predecessor had made "unwise" moves. And look what had happened to him.

And so the Chinese Premier eventually said: "I will stay, Mr President. But there had better be no more surprises. No more sunken ships or death from above. Because then we might be faced with circumstances neither of us will be able to control."

Chapter 67

The *jonin's* hands shook as he reached for the opium pipe. He had been unable to control his nerves ever since escaping from the warehouse. Yet it wasn't the death of his men that caused his angst – nor the knowledge that the Spartan had escaped, or that the American authorities had somehow managed to track him down.

No ... it was the realization that his lover, who had been captured by the Americans, was lost to him forever. He felt it in his bones. He felt it in his soul.

The thought that he would never see her face again – nor craft a future together with her – filled him with the type of anxiety he hadn't experienced in decades. And all his meditations and ninja tricks were failing to alleviate that terror.

He was trained to climb mountains with 40 pounds on rocks on his back. He could hold his breath for minutes and cling to window ledges with just the tips of his fingers for seemingly hours. He could withstand heat and pain and hunger. There was not a man alive who scared him.

But he was not trained to deal with the loss of the love of his life. Nor had he ever expected to. This wasn't something he could pray to the Carpenter God for or Zen away.

Even the idea that he had successfully completed many of his mission parameters – from sending on vital information to cripple America in times of war, to the theft of the Ghost Armor technology, to the assassination list of America's most vital people he had prepared – failed to calm his soul.

His lover had been … sacrificed … for the cause. It was a sacrifice he was unwilling to accept.

Such was his psychic pain, he barely noticed the throbbing agony caused by the chest wound inflicted by the Japanese hunter's sword. That wound would heal. The other would not.

He needed relief. He needed to hack his brain's very operating centres. He needed to tranquilise the biological machine that was his body so it was fit to perform again. And so, he returned to the opium pipe.

The *jonin* would occasionally use the pipe when he completed a successful mission or assassination. Despite the strictures of being a ninja – and the official condemnation of any Chinese agent using drugs – he felt entitled to reward himself with a bowl now and then. Such usage hardly impaired his abilities. And the idea that ninjas should have no pleasure in their lives at all went against his instincts, as well as the latest studies in neuroscience regarding motivation and reward in humans.

But now he was just using it to dull the pain. In his arrogance, he had not truly expected his lover to be among the mission's casualties. He now realized it was a sacrifice he was unwilling to make for the sake of the mission. A ninja was taught to fear only the failure of his mission – yet one could also add to that the failure of his future, the loss of the woman who would sire his children and walk with him along the road of life.

He took a drag on the pipe. *All the things he should have said to her. All the plans they had. Now gone.*

He blamed this ... Spartan. The American stood at the centre of it all, stood between him and complete victory. The dog had killed his mentor Commander Lee. Now he played a part in taking away his woman.

The Spartan did not deserve to live. The *jonin* would see to that.

Perhaps he would be made to apologize before he died.

Then there was that other figure of hate, Professor Eisenstein, who watched him as the *jonin* smoked on the pipe. He stared at Eisenstein properly now. He thought he detected a sliver of contempt among the fear. He imagined Eisenstein thinking, "All Russians know misery. And now you know it, too."

The *jonin* then stared at his *genin*. The other ninjas were in various state of injury. They would be of little use to him now, more liabilities than assets. All were combat ineffective, only suited for guard duty or delivering first aid.

The room smelled of opium and death.

The *jonin* lay down as the opium took effect, resting the Honjo Masamune at his side. He was no use to anyone at this moment. A fearful ninja was an ineffective ninja.

He was very close to his next location. He would get his head straight before moving into position ... and then take the Spartan's head for himself.

And maybe he would also do something about that expression on Eisenstein's face.

* * *

The General learnt of the failed hit on the Spartan from one of his underlings. He greeted the news like someone had just told him he had a bug in his ear. According to the report, the contractor had wounded the Spartan – possibly seriously – only to be killed by the Spartan in Garin's apartment.

The General was deeply disappointed. He had allowed himself the audacity of hope when "Surfer Dude" had taken on the contract. But yet again the Spartan had proven himself unkillable – proven himself both lucky and formidable.

Now the surfing community would have to light a candle for the late, lamented Surfer Dude.

At least Garin's apartment had been violated. The General would have loved to have seen the hated colonel's face when he heard of that invasion of privacy.

However, he had to finally admit that there was more than luck on the Spartan's side. The soldier truly was a prodigy of violence. The General had no intention of giving up his quest to remove the Spartan from the board ... but for now he had to blend back into the shadows and think of some other way to do it.

And if he had learnt anything from the experience, it was this: never shoot a large-caliber man with a small-caliber bullet.

Chapter 68

Colonel Garin was drunk. He was sitting in the lounge room of his lover Harmony, shoes up on his coffee table, glass of Scotch in hand. A half-drained bottle of 20-year-old Chivas Regal rested on the coffee table next to his combat boots.

Opposite him, regarding the colonel with quizzical eyes, was Harmony.

And she was angry.

"This is not what I had in mind when I invited you over to my house."

"You said you would comfort me."

"I meant, y'know, that we'd have sex. Not that you'd get drunk." Harmony's eyes went to the bottle on the table, regarding it with disdain. "On my husband's hideously expensive Scotch, no less. You're already enjoying his wife … enjoying his alcohol seems like an excessive liberty."

"It seemed like the appropriate response," said Garin, sipping more of the fiery liquid. "The President refuses to talk to me. A hitman almost killed my best soldier in my apartment … an apartment, I might add, I can now never return to because it's been compromised. The word is out that I'm too radioactive to be around. I've been sent on unofficial 'gardening leave'." Garin took another sip. "And I don't even *have* a garden."

"And so you decided to behave like Prohibition was coming back?"

"Sure, why not?" Garin took another sip.

The colonel thought of the advice a drill sergeant had once given him: "If you're having doubts about your job, wear boots one size too small. The pain will distract you from your doubts."

Garin had never taken the sergeant's advice. Otherwise maybe he'd be bitching about his tight boots instead.

"This display of self-pity isn't exactly a turn-on, you know." Harmony decided to pour herself some Scotch. She sniffed the glass, had a taste, then put it back down.

"Good?"

"Disgusting. It burns the throat."

"But in a *good* way." Garin fiddled with his phone, his hands all thumbs. "I've been phoning the President all afternoon. No reply. And there's no answer to my texts."

Harmony raised a perfect eyebrow. "He won't reply. Texts have a way of finding their way into the press. And the media is having a field day with the whole 'Colonel X' thing."

Colonel X himself frowned. "So … has the President said anything about me?"

Harmony laughed at hearing Garin talk like a shy schoolgirl asking whether her crush had expressed interest in her. "I get the feeling he hasn't given up on you."

"He has a funny way of showing it."

"It's … political."

"Pffff. Politics."

"I'm here, aren't I?" said Harmony in a softer voice, placing a hand on Garin's shoulder. "His secretary. Don't think he doesn't know about that."

Garin went for the bottle of Scotch. Harmony grabbed it instead. "Hey!"

"You're cut off." Harmony left the room and put the bottle in the kitchen. Garin heard her turn something on. Then she returned.

"You know the President's life is still in danger," said Garin. "The leader of those ninjas is still out there with that ancient meat cleaver of his."

"So ... what are you going to do about it?"

Garin shrugged. "What can I do?"

"Enough with the self-pity, soldier. I believe in you. So does the President. You know what he once called you?"

"An asshole?"

"The Vince Lombardi of special forces. The coach the combat experts come to for advice. So quit feeling sorry for yourself, Vince, and do your job."

Garin felt moved by Harmony's impassioned words. The old warrior spirit swelled up inside of him, mixing deliciously with the alcohol. He smiled a lazy, drunken smile. "Yes, ma'am."

"That's better. Now I'm going to pour some coffee down your throat while you come up with a plan." Harmony left for the kitchen. "There must still be someone you can rely on," she shouted over the noise of the coffee machine. "People of unquestionable loyalty and skill. Soldiers who will obey you regardless of the prevailing winds of Washington."

Garin smiled again, head now in the game. "There are. And I can think of two of them right now."

* * *

"Spartan, are you there, son?"

"Yes, colonel," answered the Spartan on his cell phone. It sounded to him as if the colonel had been drinking, but he hid it well.

"Where are you?"

"Close, sir. Twenty minutes as the drone flies."

"Vasquez with you?"

"Affirmative."

"Hi, colonel," said Vasquez from what sounded like a car.

"Let me put you on speakerphone, sir." The sound from the phone changed. "Done."

"What are you doing?"

"Just got rid of the body of the intruder in your apartment. He's with your people for ID."

"An assassin with a surfboard. Incredible. Yet the perfect cover, if you come to think of it."

"Just so, sir. Which is why he got the drop on me."

"It's too late in the game to start being careless, Spartan."

"Yes, sir." The Spartan paused as he internalised Garin's caring reprimand. "Moving on, I've just received a call from 'the teams' to check in." The "teams" being the special forces teams.

"Can I ask you to hold off on that?"

"Of course, sir. What do you need?"

"I've been cut out of the loop and the President won't talk to me. But he still needs protection. Those damn ninjas are still in the wind, and there's no one else I can trust more to take them down than you two."

"I'm ready to serve, sir," replied the Spartan without hesitation.

"This is … unofficial, son."

"Official or unofficial, I'll always have your back, sir." Like Delta Force said: once in, never out.

"Me, too," chimed in Vasquez. "Point the way, colonel."

"Your willingness to serve – both of you – touches me. Only here's the onion: I can't exactly point the way for the two of you. We don't know where they will strike next. I have no intel. Nothing to go on. We must assume it's soon, though. Do either of you have any thoughts?"

The Spartan paused. Normally he was never asked to play sleuth. He turned up where the boffins and spies told him to go.

Yet he had a flash of insight. Something the colonel had said a few days before. *The connections we forge with people can make all the difference in life.*

He thought of the letter the Monk had left him after their fight at the Spartan's farm. It was still with him. In his top pocket. Unopened. Gaining potency. After all these months.

Now was the time to open it.

"*Now* you open that letter," said Vasquez.

Inside with a piece of white paper with a phone number written on it in black ink.

"I might have something to go on, sir. Just let me make a call."

Chapter 69

In a remote village far from China's bustling, polluted major cities lived The Man In The Cave. According to the village legend, The Man In The Cave had arrived several months ago in the dead of night and quietly made his home in the village's vast cave network. It would be weeks before he made his presence known to the proud, poor folk who had little but wanted to keep what little they had.

Few had ever gotten a good look at the shy visitor, but those that did said the big Chinese man had a large scar on his face, as if he had been seriously wounded. Perhaps he had gone to the cave to heal. Perhaps he was hiding from someone. Yet the villagers sensed he meant them no harm, and so they were content to leave him be, curious to see what he would do next.

It didn't take long to find out what that was.

Word spread that The Man In The Cave was open for business. And that business was … justice. He was offering his services to solve disputes where the innocent and the powerless and the humble had been wronged.

Petitioners were required to leave details of their woes in a nook outside the cave. No contact was to be had in person with The Man In The Cave. Nor would he accept money or gifts for his services. And not every request was accepted.

And yet, over time, things did happen. For instance, the son of a local party boss had run over a local village woman in his Maserati, killing her. Drunk at the time, the teenager was never punished, forgiven by indulgent police afraid to anger the Communist Party elite. Worst still, the boy expressed no remorse, boasting that the bitch should never have gotten in his way ... and crowing to all who listened that he was untouchable thanks to his father's connections.

Two weeks after a petition had been left outside of the cave, the teenager was found in the middle of town, quite dead, trapped in the wreckage of his mangled Maserati. Perhaps he had driving while under the influence again. Perhaps it was a mere accident.

Or perhaps it was justice meted out by The Man In The Cave.

There was more to come. Prompted by a secret hand, bosses decided to clean up factories that polluted the local rivers and streams. Land barons halted plans to illegally acquire property from villagers. Extortionists were found dead. Goons hired to stop petitioners making their complaints to the court woke up in the middle of the village square with their legs broken.

In public, the rich and powerful began to treat the villagers with more care and respect, taking their grievances to heart.

In private, they were furious that the natural order of things had been upended by an outsider. They hired thugs, police and eventually skilled assassins to deal with this "Man In The Cave". Armed with knives, clubs, guns and explosives, the paid villains made their pilgrimage to the cave, sometimes in broad daylight, sometimes in the dead of night, all with the same mission.

The thugs returned with broken bones and whispered warnings to pass on. The police were beaten to within an inch of their lives, their weapons smashed to pieces on rocks.

The assassins were found dead by the hillside hundreds of feet from the cave entrance.

For now, the villagers were delighted. For now, the unjust were stuck in stalemate. For now, neither bullet nor fist nor blade could dislodge The Man In The Cave.

For now, the man once known as The Monk was content to serve his countrymen in this capacity.

Then he received the phone call he had been waiting for.

* * *

"I have waited a long time to hear from you."

The Spartan recognised the rasp of the war fighter on the other end. "Your voice is different ... but it is you."

"Yes," said The Monk calmly.

The Monk, the leader of the canister conspiracy. The superb soldier who almost killed the Spartan twice, only to fall during single combat against him on the Spartan's farm.

"I thought I killed you."

"You did. But I'm better now."

"How did you get off my farm?"

"That I will not tell you, my friend."

"Are we friends?" asked the Spartan, though not without a certain pleasure at the thought.

"Of course we are. Despite our differences. Despite the separation of oceans, countries and ideologies. After all, you only turn to a friend for help."

"How do you know I need help?"

"Don't you?" asked the Monk impishly.

"Yes."

"Then you have learnt an important lesson, Spartan. It does not undo a man to ask for help. No man is an island. Not even a Spartan. So, tell me how I can assist you."

"We've come under attack. Chinese ninjas. Wondered if you could shed some light. Because they feel like special forces soldiers. Fight like them, too."

"The ones that killed your Vice President."

The Spartan was surprised. "Would it do me any good to ask how you know that?"

"You have answered your own question. You know who I was. People talk to me. Do you think I live in a cave?"

"Judging by the reception, it sounds like you're talking from one. The ninjas are after the President, too. Tried to kill him twice now."

"That was part of the plan."

"The plan?"

"Yes, Spartan. The plan to cripple your country, one way or another. The path to war. Commander Lee always had two teams. One, led by me. And another, led by a ninja. Tell me … have you fought him yet?"

"He almost killed me," said the Spartan, not without due respect.

"That is a small club," said the Monk. "He fights with the Honjo Masamune, does he not?"

"You know of it too, then. So you know him? What can you tell me about this *jonin*?"

"You fought him. There is no better way to know a man than to fight him."

"He was fast and arrogant. Good with a blade. Expert."

"That is true. And how do you plan to defeat him?"

"I thought the usual way – a bullet or a blade in all the major orifices."

"One cannot see one's reflection in boiling water."

"What is that supposed to mean?"

"That you won't beat him through aggression and rage. You will require discipline. A plan."

"And any advice on his fighting technique you can share."

"You shall have it. But what you really want to know is where he will strike next."

"Yes."

"Isn't it obvious, Spartan? It will be at the UN."

"And how will he do it?"

"In person. And he will have other people in place, too."

"We've wiped out just about all his crew."

"Not these ones, Spartan. Not only would they be in place … but they've been there for a long time."

The Spartan paused. These were the sort of details he needed to hear.

Then he uttered: "Tell me more."

Chapter 70

By the time he was fully enlightened by The Monk, the Spartan and Vasquez had arrived at their safe house. As Vasquez got her equipment ready, the Spartan reached for the phone again. He had one more call to make. One that was unlikely to be as pleasant and personally satisfying as the last.

But it needed to be done. He wanted to be the hunter again. The Spartan wanted to be reacting less and acting more. So he dialled.

"Hello, who is this?" said the voice.

"The Spartan."

"What the fuck are you doing calling me, Spartan?" shouted Secret Service Agent Mancuso. "Don't you know you're dead to me? Don't answer that. It's rhetorical. And why are you calling me now? I'm balls deep in arranging security for the President's visit to the UN in the morning."

"I have new information about a plot against his life."

"The Spartan. Big tough guy. I thought you didn't give a shit about anything. That you didn't care."

"Of course I care, Mancuso."

"Then tell me what you know. And make it quick. I'm busy. It's like Grand Central Station in here. "

The Spartan paused. "No. It's part of a package deal. You have to do something for me first."

"Screw that. Give me the information or stop wasting my time. Just talking to you is giving me *agita*."

"You still need help fighting those ninjas. Vasquez and I can help you."

"Yo, Mancuso," said Vasquez in the background.

"Look, Spartan, after what happened last time, I'd be crazy to let you anywhere near the President."

"You mean after the last time when we saved him?"

"You left out the part where you decked my men."

"They were asking for it."

"I'm about to hang up."

"Listen to me, Mancuso," said the Spartan urgently. "If there's one thing we both agree on, it's about protecting the President. And you have to agree that Vasquez and I have form in stopping those ninjas."

"You're not in my chain of command. I don't have to admit anything."

"We want access to the UN building."

"Didn't you hear? Colonel Garin doesn't have the President's ear any more. Which means Mr Spartan doesn't always get what he wants."

"What Mr Spartan wants is to take down those ninjas. They tried to kill me. They targeted my girlfriend. They *cut* me. That makes it personal."

Mancuso exhaled loudly. "That's what I'm worried about. I repeat, give me your information or hang up. Because I won't work with you again."

"Why?"

"Because you're about as popular with my men as a fart in a Jacuzzi. Because I believe in law and order … and from what I've seen, you believe you're a law unto yourself."

The Spartan had no response to that.

Vasquez gestured impatiently with her hand. "Give me the phone."

The Spartan handed it over. "*You* talk some sense into him."

"Mancuso, this is Vasquez."

"Hey, Vasquez. Don't think I'm not angry at you either."

"I know you are. But you do need our help."

"I don't need two hotheads out for revenge. I understand revenge, believe me – my people originally come from Sicily – but it's not a valid motive for a government operative. It's not an emotion I want to see in someone working with me."

"I hear you, Mancuso. We can keep out emotions in check. Trust me. We're professionals."

"I don't know, Vasquez. You I can work with. I get you. You're a former cop. But your partner …"

"Will be on his best behavior. At least towards your men. He'll save his aggression for the ninjas."

There was a pause. "I'll make my decision after I hear what you have to say. Your information better be worth it."

"It is," said Vasquez. "Trust me."

* * *

"So that's that," said Vasquez once she and Mancuso had come to an agreement. "It's on."

The Spartan nodded and grabbed his SAW. "Outstanding."

"Slow down, cowboy. Put down your weapon. It will take Mancuso at least an hour to get us squared away and it's Zero Dark Thirty here. So there's something we have to do first."

"Which is?"

Vasquez responded with a sweet, gentle kiss on his lips. "Take off your clothes and get into bed."

"What? Now? Do we have time?"

Vasquez allowed her clothes to fall to the floor, exposing her firm, bare body. "We'll make time."

Chapter 71

One of the joystick jockeys at the drone warfare command center in Las Vegas noted an anomaly on his computer screen. The air force pilot drank some diet soda through a straw, then turned to his fellow "cubicle warrior".

"I didn't know we had any missions scheduled," he said, pointing to his screen. "Did you power up the drones?"

"Nah," shot back his colleague, not bothering to turn around. "Not on the roster."

The pilot was irritated that the other man wasn't taking him seriously. "Because they're getting ready to take off."

Now his colleague was turning around. "Which ones?"

The air force pilot stared at his screen, scarcely believing what he was seeing. "*All* of them."

"That's … impossible," said the other "pilot" – a civilian, not a trained air force pilot – as he stared at his blinking computer. His gaze then turned to the massive overhead screens. Indeed, dozens of drones – the most advanced models in the US arsenal – were heading down the runways. "Oh God, look at that." He typed in some commands. "Hell, I'm locked out."

"Me, too," cursed his colleague.

Other voices beside them now also claimed that had been kicked out of the network. A murmur of fear spread around the cubicles.

The pair stared at the overhead screens in disbelief.

The air force pilot had never liked the drones, ever since he'd been benched from actual flying and told to man a desk instead of a cockpit ... ever since he'd been forced to become, as the still-flying pilots referring to them as, a "cubicle warrior".

They might as well have ripped the lieutenant bars from his shoulders.

God's Angry Man? The pilot was that. He was also God's Redundant Man ... God's Outsourced Man.

The pilot felt it had lessened him, to be informed that some machine was more of a flyer than he was. In some Luddite way, he had always mistrusted the unmanned hunter-killers, mistrusted the lack of human supervision over them apart from that of a keyboard and a joystick.

Sometimes he had even fantasized about crashing one into the side of a mountain and blaming it on mechanical error.

But now he was faced with error of an entirely different nature.

He said: "This is bad. Very bad." Unmanned drones armed with cannons and missiles under someone else's control, capable of flying at more than 1500 miles an hour? Yes, bad was the least of it.

"You're telling me," said his colleague, a single bead of sweat trickling down his pasty face. "So who's controlling them?"

"I don't know. My computer's completely frozen."

"Mine, too." Static and wavy lines danced across the terminals.

"What do we do now? Call IT?" A lone voice said "not to panic", which, of course, made everyone instantly panic.

Dozens of eyes watched as the first of the drones took off into the skies.

"Hit the kill switches," said the commanding voice of their supervisor.

The room watched as more drones took off one by one.

"Nothing," swore the supervisor. "Shit!"

So much for the kill switches.

For some reason the air force pilot thought about that commercial airliner that had been hacked via its in-flight entertainment system. Surely such a scenario was impossible here? "If we're not in control of them, then who is?"

Then he had another, equally chilling thought.

"Wait a minute. Don't we have some of those XT-51s here?" The XT-51s being the air force's above-top-secret new drones, both invisible to radar and possessing basic AI technology that allowed them to make combat decisions independent of human command. They were as much jet fighter as drone. Perhaps more so. Like the upgraded Reapers, the XT-51s could fly faster than the speed of sound, travelling at speeds no human pilot could easily stomach.

Their combat suites were the combination of battle tactics gleaned from thousands of flight hours from America's finest pilots plus more thousands of man hours from America's finest IT minds. They were also equipped with the latest in frequency-jamming equipment, something that could be used in both a defensive and an offensive capacity. Their creation had led to earnest articles about a new "military artificial intelligence arms race".

"Look," cried a voice.

Everyone turned.

Coming towards the screen were three XT-51s. All of which were equipped with bunker-busting bombs.

Just the thing to bust the very bunker the drone pilots were now in.

"They wouldn't," breathed the air force pilot. He stared at a photo of his wife and child on the console, his hand touching the photo's glass cover.

But he knew they would.

The drones had benched him. They had unmanned him. And now they had come to take away the rest of him.

All he could do now was watch the screen as the bombs flew towards them.

Chapter 72

"Here we go again … trying to find ninjas in a haystack," said Vasquez as she and the Spartan approached the headquarters of the United Nations several hours later.

Together they passed through the first Secret Service cordon, their passage permitted by Mancuso's advanced warning.

Mancuso wasn't wrong about the UN HQ being busier than Grand Central Station. There was massive security outside – private guards, Secret Service, cops, dogs, snipers and counter-snipers – and that was before you even got through the front door.

Cars filled the nearby streets, most security vehicles, with the occasional limo dropping off various dignitaries, the tiny flags of foreign countries flapping on the black vehicles' hoods.

Inside you could expect more guards, the world's diplomatic elite, their various entourages, presidents, prime ministers, the press and more. Imagine that number of people spread out over 39 floors.

That was a big security assignment for even the world's finest.

The Spartan estimated that any ninja intrusion team would be small. Anything larger would be conspicuous and counter-productive. Yet as he and Vasquez had personally discovered, any one of them could be deadly.

And it only took one man – or woman – to kill a President.

The Spartan's pulse thrilled at the prospect of imminent battle.

Vasquez gave the HQ an appreciative once-over as they walked closer. She stared up at the roof.

"Tall building. I half-expect to see Don Draper falling from the top in slow-motion."

"Who?"

Vasquez smiled. "Never mind, culture buff. Speaking of culture, did you want to get a selfie in front of the Knotted Gun?" The "Knotted Gun" being the famous sculpture of a revolver with its barrel knotted and rendered unfireable in a poignant pro-peace, anti-violence statement. "It's what people usually do at the UN."

"Civilians, you mean. I'll pass."

"You want to give war a chance, don't you?"

The Spartan's lips threatened to break out into a smile.

"Spoilsport," said Vasquez. "At least they stopped the public tours for the day. No pain-in-the-ass civilians to watch out for. Still … a hell of a place to stage an assassination."

"With the world's press watching? Correct. This place hasn't seen as much action since Khrushchev banged his shoe on a table at the General Assembly." And it was about to see more, thought the Spartan. He curled his fist. He knew the *jonin* was inside somewhere. He could *feel* it.

A 12-man security team quickly walked past the pair. Vasquez noted the mass of bodies. "Having this amount of security around is almost a disadvantage. Too many warm bodies for thermals. Too many innocents for a firefight."

"We'll have to be more ... surgical," said the Spartan, glancing down at his *xiphos* sheathed under his jacket. "Precise."

"Maybe that's why Mancuso said we couldn't bring the heavy artillery this time." The Secret Service boss had forbidden the Spartan to bring his SAW. Instead, the Spartan was armed with only a Glock 17, his *xiphos* and some flashbangs. Vasquez had her knife and her MP-5 strapped to her back, under her shirt and next to her own Ghost Armor.

"I'm not going to need the SAW," said the Spartan. "I have a feeling it's going to come down to close-quarters combat."

Vasquez favored him with a smirk. "With you, it usually does."

They went silent for a spell as they were forced to wait in a queue at the front.

"Report in, soldier ... how are you going?" asked Vasquez, eyeing him head to toe. "In the past 48 hours you've been drugged, beaten and stabbed."

"The mind surrenders before the body."

"That's not an answer."

"I'm combat ready. Besides, your lovemaking last night was the most painful ordeal."

"That would explain the screaming."

"I don't recall you being too quiet either."

Vasquez smiled. "Two jokes in one day ... I'm starting to get worried about you, Spartan."

"Be worried about our enemies instead. Because this is the day I end the *jonin*." The Spartan paused. He could feel the eyes of Secret Service agents burning against his neck. He ignored it. "And how are you, Vasquez?"

"The Mexican cartels have put a price on our heads, our boss has been disgraced and we're trying to stop ninjas from killing the President," said Vasquez. Then she slipped some sunglasses on her face. "And we're looking good while doing it."

"You always look good, Vasquez."

"Can I quote you on that?"

"Sure, go nuts. Anyway, let's get into character and go wraith chasing. The mission has officially begun. Everyone we see from now on is a suspect." The Spartan scanned the crowd with hard eyes, as if expecting to spot ninjas.

The world's deadliest game of hide and seek had begun.

The pair looked almost indistinguishable from the other Secret Service agents milling around the entrance. The Spartan was clad in the standard Secret Service garb of a black suit, white shirt and black shoes. Only his shoes were heavier and thicker than the typical Secret Service issue. They were combat shoes built for urban battle. One kick and the recipient would be in a world of pain.

Vasquez was wearing a black pantsuit, white shirt, black, slightly more stylish combat shoes and her sunglasses. Light make-up covered the facial bruises incurred during her battles with the *kunoichi*.

Together they were a daunting pair.

"They're with me," said Agent Mancuso as he met them at the front entrance, waving away agents about to accost them.

Mancuso looked tense. He looked pissed. He looked determined.

Just the sort of look you'd want to see on a man tasked to protect the President.

"So you're here," he said, looking them over.

"Thanks for the invite," said Vasquez, because she knew the Spartan wasn't going to.

Mancuso tossed the Tier 1 soldier a glance. "Spartan."

"Mancuso."

"I see you've left the SAW at home. Good. We've got more than enough firepower here. We need your eyes, not your trigger fingers."

"We've brought all four of them," said Vasquez. She gestured towards the entrance. "Shall we?"

Mancuso nodded. "Don't be surprised if the building looks different to what you've seen in the tourist brochures. There's been a lot of changes to it since 9/11. Lot of things the public knows nothing about."

"Changes a ninja could exploit?" questioned the Spartan.

"Perhaps," mused Mancuso. "They have been pretty good at exploiting everything else, wouldn't you say?" Mancuso stared at Vasquez. "Including your Ghost Armor."

"Blame the tailor," replied Vasquez. "I'm just the store model."

Together they made their way through the security gates. Vasquez dropped her MP-5, her ammunition and her knife into a plastic container as she made her way through the metal detector. The Spartan did the same with his Glock and *xiphos*.

A guard who clearly pumped iron on his days off waved a wand over Vasquez's body. The wand squealed loudly. The guard turned to Mancuso.

"Damn, there go my prosthetic limbs," joked Vasquez.

"It's fine," said Mancuso. "She's wearing special armor."

"I'll have to pat her down, sir," the guard replied. As the guard put his hands on Vasquez's shoulders, en route to the rest of her body, the Spartan moved forward.

"Relax, tiger," Vasquez said. "Let the man do his job."

The guard quickly did so, hands probing Vasquez's body, one eye on the Spartan just in case. It was over in seconds.

"Feels like armor," said the guard. "Not Kevlar, but something else."

"It's custom-made," said Vasquez, smiling to put the man at ease. Which it did.

"You're clear to pass. Next."

The Spartan stepped forward. The guard waved the wand. His own armor – lighter than what he usually wore, with no protective plates guarding chest and back – didn't set it off.

"Sir?" said the guard sitting down at the X-ray machine as he noted that someone was trying to bring a sword through security.

"He's with me, too … for my sins," said Mancuso, waving the Spartan through. He personally handed the Spartan back his *xiphos*. "I *can* trust you to behave, can't I?"

"I'm saving my misbehavior for the ninjas," said the Spartan dryly.

"Don't make me regret this."

"You won't, Mancuso," said Vasquez as she re-attached the MP-5 to her back. "So … where do we start?"

"We've just had word that the security camera system is off-line," said Mancuso. "Happened about five minutes ago. Pretty suspicious timing. I was just about to go over there."

"We'll tag along," insisted the Spartan.

"In the meantime, take these," said Mancuso, handing each of them radio ear-pieces. "I'll be able to hear anything you say. Not that I'm particularly fond of the things the Spartan says."

Another burly guard appeared at Mancuso's shoulder. He was Caucasian, brown-haired, mid-30s, fit-looking, sharp-eyed, smiling. Clearly one of the more high-end guards. There was a Glock at his waist, next to keys and a walkie-talkie. His little nametag said "Jeremy".

Jeremy handed each of them two walkie-talkies. "Set to the Special Service frequency," Mancuso added.

"I can talk them through the security camera system, sir," Jeremy said in a pleasant voice. "You can stay here if you like. I know you've got a million things to do."

"Thanks. Guys, this is Jeremy. He's part of the in-house security team. Listen to what he says."

"Hey there," sang the man himself in a possibly over-caffeinated voice.

The Spartan stared hard at Jeremy. The security guard returned the look calmly, seemingly undaunted by the Spartan's size and demeanor. Vasquez stared at the Spartan, as if wondering what was suddenly going through her partner's mind.

The Spartan's left hand found its way to the hilt of his *xiphos* for a second. Then it re-emerged from the suit.

"Lead the way, Jeremy," ordered the Spartan.

Chapter 73

Vasquez immediately knew that something was wrong. The Spartan was talking to Jeremy. All casual-like. He was chatty, even.

The Spartan never just *chatted* to people. Particularly strangers.

"Loquacious" was not an adjective that belonged anywhere adjacent to him.

So what was her lover doing conversing with this guard like they were old pals? She'd barely heard him use so many words in one sitting. At first, she thought the Spartan had begun talking to interrupt Jeremy's walking travelogue about the building, how it had been the official HQ of the UN since its completion in 1952, boasting important structures such as the General Assembly Hall, which has just had a major renovation yadda yadda yadda.

But now she realized it was something else.

And all she could do was follow behind and wait to see what happened next.

"Have you always wanted to be a security guard, Jeremy?" asked the Spartan.

"I sort of fell into it," said Jeremy as they walked. A slight Southern twang to his voice made Jeremy's words seem more agreeable. "I served in Afghanistan and Iraq. Joined right after 9–11. When I saw those towers go down I knew I wanted to do my part, so I signed up with the Marines."

Jeremy pulled up his left sleeve to reveal a tattoo that said "semper fi". Then he pulled it down again.

"Once my tour was over I looked for other work. I thought about the police, but guard work at the UN pays better. Good hours, too." Jeremy's eyes swivelled to take in the sight of the British Prime Minister walking past with his entourage.

"So you went from war – the father and king of us all – to protecting diplomats," asked the Spartan, his face still not giving anything away. "How did you like it over there in Iraq?"

"Eye-Raq?" Jeremy's face flashed a certain doubt. "It was OK."

"I preferred Afghanistan myself. No one smiles over there. And if they do, it means they're about to light you up. You have to watch the smilers."

Jeremy smiled.

"Looks like you're a smiler too, Jeremy."

Jeremy immediately stopped smiling.

"So you said things were OK in Iraq. Elaborate on 'OK'."

"Things got pretty hairy."

"So you saw people die. Your comrades. Fellow soldiers."

"He might not want to talk about that, Spartan," said Vasquez diplomatically, placing a soft hand on his. After all, she didn't want to talk about her police colleagues killed in Juarez. It was a rule among soldiers both serving and retired that you didn't ask people to describe their time "in country" – it was up to them to volunteer the information.

Even the Spartan, as insensitive as he could be with strangers, knew that.

Hence her continued bafflement.

"No, that's all right, Vasquez," placated Jeremy, palms open. "I'm not offended, ma'am." To the Spartan, he said: "Yes, I did, sir. More than one. IEDs mostly, but the occasional sniper attack, too."

The Spartan nodded. "That sort of thing can make a man question himself, can't it, when you have to drag a gunshot colleague to safety? Make him question what he's doing … make him question what his country is doing there in the first place. Make him wonder whether it's all worth it.

"Hell, the sort of sights a soldier might see – experiences he must endure – could even make him wonder whether he should be working for someone else. Someone who *appreciates* him more."

To Vasquez's trained police eyes, Jeremy seemed to freeze. But only for a second. He gestured down the hall. "We'll be at the security room in about a minute or so."

"Bear with me, Jeremy," said the Spartan, nodding to Vasquez as she scowled at him. "Because I'm just trying to figure out a few things." The Spartan paused. "I had a friend give me some advice before I came here today. He told me to watch out for friendly strangers. Strangers who might want me out of the way. Strangers who could lead me into a trap."

Jeremy appeared nervous. "I don't know what you're talking about, sir. Anyway, the security room's just down here."

"Thanks, Jeremy. You're very helpful. Maybe you can help me some more. What do you know about ninjas?"

Jeremy forced out a laugh. "Just what I see on the TV. Funny-looking men running around in pyjamas. Japanese fellas."

The Spartan kept walking towards the door. "They're not that funny-looking, Jeremy. Not when you fight them. Not when they're doing their damndest to kill you. And they're not always Japanese now, are they? Why, sometimes they're even American."

Jeremy ignored the question. "Just through that door, sir."

Vasquez had stopped scowling. Now she was plain intrigued.

"I guess I'm just wondering what might make a soldier betray his country. Because it can't just be about the money. There must be some emotional motivation, too. Some deep private grudge that won't go away. An itch you can't scratch."

Jeremy said nothing, but Vasquez, former cop that she was, could tell Jeremy was disturbed by the line of questioning.

"And now it's just too late to walk away," concluded the Spartan ominously.

Vasquez felt a thrill of adrenalin course through her.

The Spartan went to grab the handle – then stopped and looked over his shoulder at Jeremy.

"What will I find through that door, Jeremy? Some of your friends? A flashbang or a grenade strapped to the door? I'm thinking the latter. And then each of us gets a bullet in the head."

"You've been watching too many Joe Pesci movies," joked Jeremy. But the joke went flat.

The Spartan continued: "Later you can blame it on the ninjas. Who will know any difference? And I right?"

Jeremy said nothing. But his face went dark. Something previously hidden jumped up behind his eyes, swirling like an angry tornado.

"Vasquez, grab him!" shouted the Spartan.

Vasquez seized his arm with both hands just as Jeremy attempted to draw his pistol. Jeremy elbowed Vasquez hard in the face. He was a strong man, yet still she clutched his arm. Jeremy pulled the trigger. Rounds flew by Vasquez's face to embed themselves in the fancy walls.

"A little help here!" she yelled.

But the Spartan was already on it. He seized Jeremy's other arm by the wrist, two-handed. The Spartan used his entire strength as he wrenched Jeremy's arm. He kept at it until he had dislocated Jeremy's left shoulder.

Jeremy howled.

In the distance, Secret Service agents saw the fracas and began bolting towards them.

Jeremy fell to the ground. He tried to bring his gun arm around, but the Spartan pinned it with his foot. Then he raised his foot and seized the impostor's wrist two-handed.

"And now for the other one," he said. Once again he pulled until Jeremy screamed and the other shoulder was dislocated.

The Spartan examined his handiwork. "He won't be dancing the funky gibbon any time soon."

By now the Secret Service agents were upon them, guns aimed at Jeremy.

"You, sir, are an angry, angry man," commented Vasquez as "Jeremy" squirmed on the ground, snarling and spitting, arms all useless.

"That's not the first time I've heard that."

"A heads-up would've been appreciated."

"He might have sensed trouble. And I knew you'd react in time." To the Secret Service agents, he said: "He's one of them. Take him to Mancuso."

"No more surprises like that," said Vasquez as they watched the struggling Jeremy being led away.

"That was the low-hanging fruit. It'll get harder from here on."

"Are we going to go through that door?"

"No point. The Secret Service will tell us if there's anything interesting inside."

Five minutes later the Secret Service reported in. The room was full of unconscious IT dudes.

Plus one flashbang strapped to the door.

But no ninjas.

Chapter 74

The drone squadrons made their way across the United States.

Many queried exactly what they were doing – "is this real world or exercise?" was the question of the day – but there was no answer from Las Vegas.

Civil aviation authorities were baffled. They asked the military for clarification.

No answers were forthcoming.

Yet not every military commander was so sanguine about the thought of armed drones flying thousands of feet above mainland America. Like dragonflies, drones typically flew alone, not in groups. This behavior was suspicious. If anything, they should have been flying out to sea, not over suburbia.

Two F-22 Raptors caught up with the squadrons over Nebraska. Just in case they were looking at another 9/11 – and with still no answers from Las Vegas – the pilots started shooting down the drones with 20mm Vulcan cannons.

They gunned down an upgraded Reaper and a Predator drone apiece. Drone metal plunged earthward, hopefully to land on an empty field or remote forest rather than a school.

The squadrons continued, as if failing to notice the sudden loss of two of their members.

"Should we continue?" asked one Raptor pilot to the other.

"Affirmative."

Their fingers paused on the cannon triggers.

Yet neither got to fire another round – because the AI-enhanced XT-51s swooped down from 10,000 feet, targeted them with missiles and blew them from the skies.

Chapter 75

"Control the middle ground," the Monk had told the Spartan.

Apparently it was some type of Sun Tzu wisdom. But fortunately, it translated into something simple: set the dogs loose on level 20.

So they did. Fortified with a sniff of a swatch of Ghost Armor fabric, taken from a captured ninja, the highly trained dogs went to work.

The Spartan and Vasquez got there just in time to watch the German Shepherds attack thin air.

A thrashing ninja became visible in that thin air.

Furious at the attempt at invisible trickery, the German Shepherds redoubled their efforts, each selecting a limb and dragging the night warrior to the ground.

The Secret Service pounced like they were part German Shepherd, too.

The Spartan had to admit it was a beautiful sight.

Chapter 76

By the time the drone squadrons reached Indianapolis they had lost more than a third of their strength.

Yet still the XT-51s, equipped with combat suites and blessed with reaction times beyond those of even the best human combat pilot, protected the other drones, shooting down planes and incoming missiles.

And still the squadrons, in the control of unknown parties, made their way eastward.

Chapter 77

The Spartan heard the walkie-talkie at his side crackle. He reached for it.

"So you've taken Jeremy," said a cool voice. "You are wiser than I expected."

"Who is this?"

"If you want to know, step away from Vasquez. Do it now."

The voice sounded familiar. Vasquez looked at him with surprise as he stepped away. The Spartan held up a hand as Vasquez attempted to close the distance between them.

"I repeat, identify yourself."

"Have you forgotten the touch of the Honjo Masamune so quickly?" The Spartan had a sudden vision of the ultra-sharp samurai sword coming at him … and the face of the *jonin* who wielded it so expertly.

"So you're here. What do you want?"

"I have called to grant you … a boon. Now that we have fought, Spartan, I believe I understand you. You crave war. Any war. You live to fight men one-on-one for reasons even you don't understand."

Whether he agreed or not, the Spartan continued to listen.

"So why not fight me again?" coaxed the voice. "You know I'm the main danger to the President. Eliminate me, and you succeed in your mission goals – both the real goal and your secret undeclared goal."

"Why should I waste my time on a duel?"

"Because every fiber of your being is screaming at you to do it." There was a pause. "Do you not trust your comrades to foil my plot? Where is your faith in American prowess?"

"Don't try to play me, asshole."

"I'm not trying to play you, Spartan, I'm trying to fight you. Because you murdered my commander. And you cost me my woman. And either way, my part in this is finished. Events will roll on with or without me." There was a short pause. "But make your decision quickly. This, as your nauseating television commercials say, is a one-time offer … act now without delay."

The Spartan considered the offer. Yes, he wanted the fight. Was that selfish of him? Probably. And yet, part of what the *jonin* was saying was true. The ninja remained the main danger to the President, both for his fearsome fighting ability and his clear leadership position in the plot. The President – indeed the country – wouldn't be safe until he was dead.

Maybe the Spartan was merely rationalizing his own desires. Maybe he was, as someone had once called him when the barracks had all been in their cups, a "battle junkie".

Either way, the decision was made.

"Fists or swords?" asked the Spartan.

"Swords. Your *xiphos* versus my Honjo Masamune."

The answer pleased the Spartan. Yet he asked: "How do I know you'll even remain at large by the time I get to you?"

"Because everyone will be too busy dealing with what is about to come."

"I can't imagine a swordfight in the UN building going unnoticed."

"Trust me, that will be the last thing on anyone's minds."

"How do I know that this isn't another trap?"

"You don't. Besides, you have the advantage of numbers here, not me." Another pause. "So … do we have a deal? Or will you die never knowing who was the better warrior?"

"I already know the answer to that question. When do we meet?"

"You will know when."

"Give me the details, dead man."

The Spartan listened as the *jonin* filled in the gaps.

Chapter 78

The drones were now approaching New York.

So far, the hunter-killers had failed to fire on anything: the only opposition came from the XT-51s, which only seemed to be defending the squadrons and themselves, shooting down any opposition before resuming their guard duty.

No one wanted to provoke the drones – or whoever was controlling them – into suddenly firing on the civilians below. The thought of drone strikes occurring on US soil was unthinkable. Not to mention the risk of drone wreckage landing on people and property.

There were already news reports starting to come in about that.

With news from Las Vegas still sketchy at best – there were reports of an explosion there, complete with casualties – the response to the drones continued to be ad hoc. Technical experts struggled to figure out who was controlling the drones.

The Texans, as paranoid as ever, wondered if the President – or the UN – was trying to stage a coup.

The drones had been reduced to 25 thanks to a combination of anti-aircraft missile defenses and F-16 and F-22 sorties. The human-piloted jets had been shot down by the XT-51s, but not before bringing down several drones each. One XT-51 had been destroyed by a particularly skilled pilot, seconds before missiles slammed into his own jet, leaving him mere moments to eject.

The F-16 pilots fared worse. The humans behind the controls were no match for the XT-51s. They'd already lost a dozen jets – and five pilots who failed to eject in time – to the AI-enhanced machines.

Again, no one could be sure whether the XT-51s were merely following their programming and defending themselves from a perceived threat. If the squadrons were left alone, perhaps they would continue to fly out to sea, where they could be dealt with far away from the public and the media.

It was all happening very fast. Terrifyingly fast. And no one wanted to call it wrong.

Now, with a breakthrough on who was controlling the drones and from where, the word came from the President's people. Don't allow the drones to enter New York air space.

Shoot them down. All of them.

Chapter 79

The Chinese Premier was informed that there had been "disturbances" at the UN HQ.

He was asked by the Americans whether he wanted to abort his visit.

The Chinese Premier said no.

He was coming in by the front door – like a real leader.

Along with 50 heavily armed, Olympic-level killers.

The US President was also asked by the Secret Service whether he wanted to abort.

Assassins had been found on the premises – and no one was sure that they were the only ones.

Then there was the drone situation.

Yet like the Chinese Premier, he said no. The world needed to see the reassuring handshake between POTUS and the Premier, to see the show of unity between East and West.

Only POTUS was prudent enough to arrive through the underground basement.

Alone with dozens of heavily armed, Olympic-level protectors.

Chapter 80

The missiles were flying and the jets were in the air, but it was too late. The drone squadrons had reached New York. Their numbers were further depleted to under a dozen, but still they made their way onwards, protected by the vigilant XT-51s.

They had been built to survive. Built to evade the enemy. Built to stop at nothing.

They had done all that.

Only now they were attacking, not just defending.

The drones were now firing on American targets.

On American people.

Rockefeller Center, the Museum of Modern Art, Penn Station, Grand Central Terminal and everywhere in between ... the bullets were raining down. Bullets intended for anywhere except the homeland.

Oh God, one imagined the city screaming, *not again*.

Yes, replied the world, *again*.

Cars blew up. Glass flew like flying daggers. Civilians were torn to shreds indiscriminately, whether they dived for cover or tried to film the spectacle with their iPhones. There was blood, panic and chaos.

A path of carnage all the way between the drones and their final target.

Chapter 81

The collision of military metal against civilian glass and steel felt like a tremor to those in the UN HQ.

"Whiskey Tango Foxtrot?" gasped Vasquez. *What the fuck?*

Vasquez and the Spartan rushed to the windows and looked below. On the ground appeared to be the remains of a plane.

The Spartan grimly examined the flaming, smoking wreckage. He peered closer at a tail fin that bore a manufacturer's logo. "It looks like … a Reaper drone."

"I repeat … what the fuck?" Perhaps foolhardily, others below rushed towards the wreckage. "I can't believe that just happened."

"I can," said the Spartan. This was his warning. His sign. His call to arms. "It's time to regroup with Mancuso."

"Roger that."

"And stay away from the windows."

"No shit." Vasquez continued to gape at the site. "What type of attack is this?" she eventually said, turning around to face the Spartan.

But the Spartan was gone.

Chapter 82

The Spartan ran towards the UN General Assembly Hall. The *jonin's* reference to a sign had been unmistakable: drones slamming into the side of the building had to be it. And from the sights and sounds of things, the attack was ongoing. The building continued to rock and shudder as if struck by bullets and possibly missiles.

Who knew how long the building would and could stand?

Everyone the Spartan passed was rushing in the other direction, downwards and towards the exits. The Spartan had to duck for cover as high-caliber rounds crashed through the windows and struck down a politician and his security entourage. He heard screams and cries, but he had no time to tarry or lend assistance. The fact that the *jonin* had prior knowledge of – and, for all the Spartan knew, had somehow arranged – this drone attack, meant he was too dangerous for everyone's sake to be allowed to run free.

The Spartan had to kill him. Now.

He felt bad about abandoning Vasquez and going it alone. Two is one and one is none, as the SEALs liked to say – one of anything could always fail and it was always smart to have back-up.

Yet some things you just had to do yourself.

Still, he had faith in her abilities, including her ability to survive. If anyone could help protect the President, it was her. He hoped she would later understand what he did.

There was something else nagging him as he ran. The *jonin's* skill with a blade was incredible. Could the Spartan actually defeat him? Would his ghost be forced to sing: "Go, tell the Spartans, thou who passest by/That here obedient to their laws we lie"?

No, he told himself. *No time for doubts now. Only duty.*

Still running, he made his way into the Assembly Hall, feeling a powerful sense of climax on its threshold. Its wide doors were already open, beckoning him to enter.

A trap, perhaps.

He drew his Glock from its holster and stood at the doorway. He stopped, performed a 360-degree awareness check just in case an invisible ninja was about to drop from the ceiling and impale him, then stepped forward, checking the corners as he did so.

There was only one figure in the room, who was dressed as a security guard and out of shape.

And yet, in his hand, lay the Honjo Masamune.

Those cold, unmistakable eyes added further proof. It was him.

The *jonin.*

The disguised ninja clapped.

"You made it despite the drones," said the *jonin* as he inched closer. "Good. I didn't want a machine doing what a man should."

The Spartan holstered his Glock and instead drew his *xiphos.* "Nice disguise," he said, putting one foot slowly in front of the other, the point of his *xiphos* aimed at the *jonin's* head.

"Disguise is a ninja's métier," said the *jonin*. "As is borrowing another man's face. But you want to know what the real secret to this disguise is? The fact that I am overweight." The *jonin* tapped his stomach with the Honjo Masamune. "To be fat in America is the equivalent of being invisible. No one takes you seriously. No one see you as a threat."

The *jonin* added: "But I can't complain. The false stomach helped conceal the cut your friend Shintaro gave me. It allowed me to get through the strip search."

There was no point asking about the man the *jonin* had "doubled". He was clearly dead. "And the sword? How did you get that through security?"

The *jonin* smiled. "A true ninja does not share all his tricks."

"What about the drones? How did you arrange that?"

The *jonin* smirked again. "The drones make such wonderful theater, don't you think?" he said, not answering the question. "Now let me ask *you* something. Where is my lover? Is she alive?"

It took a second for the Spartan to realize he was talking about the captured *kunoichi*. "I don't know where she is. She's alive, that's all I know."

"Thank you," said the *jonin* sincerely.

The building shook again as it was struck by something … something that had no right to do so.

"Listen to that," said the *jonin*. "What a magnificent sight it must be. To be outside and watch the missiles strikes, to see the golden decline of Western power illuminated in the Hellfire's glare." He suddenly raised the Honjo Masamune. "But enough. Let us fight. Any last words?"

The Spartan scrutinized his enemy. He respected the ninja's fighting skills, but he felt no kinship with him as he had with his last deadly enemy, the Monk. There was no connecting tissue between this *jonin* and The Monk.

The Spartan just wanted him dead.

And yet, what would the Spartan do if someone killed his commander officer, Colonel Garin, as he himself had slain Commander Lee and set the *jonin* on his heels? How far would he be willing to go in the name of revenge? How many people would he be willing to kill? How many temples would he tear down around his ears?

So perhaps, in the end, he understood the *jonin* just a little.

"I fight for the past," uttered the Spartan, his words coming from deep within. "I am Spartan."

The stark words seemed to move the ninja opposite, who paused, and then said: "I fight for the future ... for the future of my people." The *jonin* tilted the Honjo Masamune in an open invitation. The Spartan could see his face reflected on the blade. "Shall we begin?"

Without waiting for a response, *the jonin* charged towards the Spartan.

The Honjo Masamune came straight towards the Spartan's head.

The Spartan's *xiphos* met its edge on its handle.

It had begun.

Chapter 83

Vasquez had seen some incredible things in her adventure-filled life. Ninjas. Cartel hits. Invisibility suits. Stealth attacks on China. A Tier 1 soldier who took on all comers, who later became her lover.

But this recent development threatened to top them all.

If someone had told her this morning that she'd be hunkered down on the ground floor of the UN HQ, engaged in a gunfight with the protection services of more than one foreign leader – including the most powerful of all, those of the Chinese Premier – as drones shot at the building and the unfortunates outside, she'd have accused them of lying.

And yet, that was exactly what had happened.

The first drone attack had forced all the security teams in the building to draw their weapons, searching for targets to shoot. Then, when those teams came across other protection teams – all full of men and women with itchy trigger fingers, trying to lead their charges to safety – it only took one wrong word or gesture to ignite the tinderbox.

Or at least until someone fired first.

Which they did.

Hence the pandemonium.

No doubt Taylor Swift had written a song that covered this exact situation.

Vasquez, Mancuso and his Secret Service team were engaged in a heated firefight with the security service guarding the Chinese Premier. She didn't remember who fired the first shot, but it didn't matter. Dozens of fighters were now going at each other hammer and tongs with ballistic weapons.

Fighting for her life, Vasquez was too busy to be annoyed at the Spartan for ditching her. Vasquez knew the Spartan would never leave her for another woman ... but he would temporarily leave her for another battle.

The furious Chinese agents were as good a shot with their pistols and submachine guns as the American Secret Service, their accuracy uncanny and scary. Bullets of many calibers spread their fearful, deadly geometry around the room.

It was hard to tell what was obscener: that this temple of international diplomacy dedicated to peace had been turned into a war zone or the rapidly escalating casualties from both drone attack and man-held weapons.

A few fighters like Mancuso were trying to shout above the din for calm, but no one was listening.

The US President was somewhere else, possibly in danger.

Vasquez fired her MP-5 at a Chinese agent, striking him in the legs and forcing him to the floor like a holy penitent. She was shooting to wound rather than kill. The agent screamed in pain and pawed at his legs. Another Chinese agent dragged him away by the shoulders.

"We've got to break this deadlock!" shouted Mancuso in her ear. "Vasquez, I need you to do something!"

Before Vasquez could turn around Mancuso groaned and fell to the side. A bullet had struck him in the shoulder. And perhaps elsewhere, too.

He collapsed, yet still held something up in his hand. A cell phone.

"The President is on the line," said Mancuso weakly, his face instantly going pale. "I need you to use your suit and get this in the hands of the Chinese Premier. The front exit is blocked. Unless we stop this quickly unknown numbers will die."

A Secret Service agent rushed over to tend to Mancuso. "Please, Vasquez," uttered the stricken man.

Vasquez nodded and took the cell phone.

"Vasquez, it's the President," said a firm, familiar voice. Vasquez felt a thrill at having THE President on the other line.

"I'm here, Mr President. Command me."

"I need you to put me in touch with the Premier, Vasquez. We've discovered that these drone attacks are being coordinated from China. We must shut them down. Otherwise we'll have to bomb the sites ourselves ... and we sure as hell don't want to do that. So, Vasquez ... can you help?"

"Yes, Mr President," she replied.

Then she looked over to where the Premier was located.

There were dozens of gunmen there, ready to shoot down anyone who came close.

Just how the hell was she going to complete Mancuso's mission?

Chapter 84

The *jonin* seem to come at the Spartan from all directions. The ninja slashed straight down towards the Spartan's head, then struck on either side of his neck as the Spartan quickly parried the first blow with his *xiphos*.

As before, the *jonin's* speed and skill were incredible. The Spartan was relying purely on instinct, training and muscle memory as the Honjo Masamune came at him again and again. The samurai sword gave the ninja an edge on length, but the size slowed him down compared to the quickness with which the Spartan could deploy his smaller *xiphos*.

As for skill, that had yet to be determined.

It wasn't until seven sword strokes in that the Spartan saw a gap in the *jonin's* defense. He stabbed at the *jonin's* stomach – the *xiphos* was best suited as a stabbing weapon – only for the *jonin* to lazily slap the blow downwards and slash at the Spartan's neck. The Spartan danced back, but still the Honjo Masamune left a burning slash on his check.

"First blood to …"

The Spartan punched the *jonin* square in the face, no doubt loosening more than a few teeth and cutting his crowing short.

The *jonin* frowned and touched his cheek. "That won't happen again," he said.

The Spartan didn't waste his time with words. He thrust at all the *jonin's* vital points, starting with the neck and the heart and finishing with the groin and thighs. In a display of reckless arrogance, the *jonin* dodged each blow rather than bother to block them with the Honjo Masamune.

The two combatants paused as the building was rocked by a loud explosion.

The *jonin* resumed his assault. He again struck two-handed down towards the Spartan's head. The Spartan blocked the attack. For a moment, there was a battle of strength, the *jonin* trying to push the Honjo Masamune down, the Spartan pushing upwards, their feet moving back and forth, before the *jonin* realized the Spartan was stronger and broke off the encounter.

The Spartan's eyes flicked towards the edge of the *xiphos*. The Honjo Masamune had left a contact mark on its edge.

There was no such mark on the Honjo Masamune.

The Spartan scowled.

His opponent grinned.

The *jonin* cried out as he attacked the Spartan's torso, following with an upward strike that nicked the Spartan's right ear. The *jonin* struck down at the Spartan's left shoulder. The Spartan blocked the blow, then swapped the *xiphos* mid-air from his right hand to his left hand and stabbed the *jonin* below the left shoulder blade. The *jonin* screamed, but his discipline held. He managed to bring the Honjo Masamune diagonally across the Spartan's chest, slicing open his white shirt and exposing his body armor.

The *jonin* pressed his advantage. He kicked at the Spartan's legs, once, twice, sweeping his left leg out from under him. As the Spartan fell to the ground, the *jonin* attempted to skewer him two-handed. The Spartan rolled out of the way just in time as the point struck where his neck had been. He dodged again as the ninja's blade followed him.

The Spartan got to his feet, spun and delivered a roundhouse kick across the *jonin's* jaw. The ninja staggered back. The Spartan attempted to hack at the *jonin's* collarbone. The *jonin* sidestepped and struck the Spartan hard on the head with the pommel of the Honjo Masamune.

They were now both extremely close to each other – something the Spartan sought to capitalize upon. He stepped up to the *jonin's* face, preventing him from having the space to swing his blade, then head-butted his hated foe. And again. His *xiphos* ran against the *jonin's* ribs before the ninja could dodge more effectively.

A rumble from the ceiling drew their attention. Parts of the roof came down towards them, dislodged by the drone strikes. Both fighters dived out of the way as masonry fell between them. Distraction over, the pair closed the distance and resumed combat.

The Spartan aimed the point of his *xiphos* at the *jonin's* throat and thrust out. Yet the *jonin* spun, allowing the Spartan to pass him, got down on one knee and slashed the Spartan.

It was a deep blow, striking the Spartan's lower torso as the blade travelled downwards. Instantly the Spartan began bleeding, his white shirt soaked with red.

"Hurts, doesn't it?" taunted the *jonin*. "To be caught up in the gears of history."

The *jonin* stepped back, put his right foot forward and held the Honjo Masamune two-handed in front of him.

He said nothing, waiting for the Spartan to attack.

The Spartan rushed towards the *jonin*, hacking low.

The *jonin* passed him, delivering his own strike.

The Spartan's attack missed by a mere inch.

The *jonin's* attack had expertly cut the holster of the Spartan's Glock, sending the pistol tumbling to the floor.

The Spartan scowled. He took the *jonin's* implied lack of trust – that he'd pull a gun during a swordfight – as an unwelcome insult.

There were more insults to come. The *jonin* sheathed his sword behind his back, smiled and waved for the Spartan to attack him.

Which the Spartan did, aiming at the *jonin's* darting body with quick, angry strikes. Yet he might as well have been striking smoke. The *jonin* backflipped away from each attack, tumbling towards the front of the room. The Spartan gave chase, swinging all the while, blood flying off his *xiphos*. None of the blows landed home.

Then, with blinding speed, the *jonin* landed on his feet, dodged a strike aimed at his chest, quick-drew the Honjo Masamune, and struck the Spartan on his face and right arm.

Again, the wounds were deep. The Spartan was bleeding all over now ... and a man could easily bleed his last in mere minutes. The Tier 1 soldier realized he couldn't be hit many more times like that and still be standing. It was only a matter of time before the *jonin* hit a critical artery.

His strength was ebbing away. He felt the touch of the void, the beguiling voice that seemed to whisper *lay down your weapon and let go.*

The Spartan raised his *xiphos* once more.

Yet the *jonin* was everywhere again. The Spartan did his best to parry the blows, but the *jonin*, sensing the advantage was his, increased his tempo.

Swords locked, the *jonin* kicked the Spartan in the chest, sending him tumbling against chairs and tables. The ninja then kicked the Spartan in the face and attempted to deliver a fatal blow to the Spartan's neck.

The Spartan dodged, but the blade came down on his left hand.

The Honjo Masamune severed the Spartan's left pinkie finger and the digit next to it.

The Spartan was shocked, face turning white. The *jonin* was contemptuous.

"To think you're the man that killed my master," he spat. "Unbelievable."

The Spartan barely managed to fend off the ensuing attack, giving more ground as he stepped backwards.

With arrogant ease, the *jonin* made a fool of gravity and struck the Spartan in the chest with a flying kick, sending him tumbling across more chairs and past the desk signs of various countries.

If the politicians, diplomats and world leaders who had thrashed out the world's great affairs could see what was happening right now, what would they think? Would they be appalled that this sanctuary devoted to the harmonious running of international affairs – to the prevention of violent conflict – was being desecrated with real-life violence? Or would they appreciate the honesty of the battle: two world powers going at each other through their chosen paladins instead of fighting each other with carefully chosen words laden with double meanings?

For now, the chosen paladin of the US was on the back foot. The *jonin's* blade found the Spartan's flesh again, hacking his right leg just above the knee.

"White meat for dinner," hissed the *jonin*.

The *jonin* held the Honjo Masamune one-handed and punched the Spartan in the face, once, twice, and then a third, final time, sending the sagging Spartan sprawling over a table on the very front row. As the Spartan made to raise his weapon, the *jonin* sent a shikan-ken – a finger knuckle strike – into the Spartan's ribs, the pain forcing the Spartan to lower his *xiphos*.

The *jonin* used one hand to push the battered Spartan to the right, as if arranging him. Satisfied with his handiwork, he then raised the Honjo Masamune for the killing blow.

He swung down.

To strike thin air.

Then he looked down at his stomach.

No.

The Spartan had buried his *xiphos* there.

The *jonin* dropped the Honjo Masamune to the floor. The Spartan, now standing, pushed his blade from right to left, cutting through flesh and sinew and everything else. The last time the Spartan had stabbed a mortal enemy in the stomach the cur had survived, so he made sure to make a proper job of it this time, putting his arms and back into it. The *jonin's* face was a portrait of incredible pain; the Spartan's, a portrait of triumph.

Then, just as quickly as he had struck, he withdrew his *xiphos*.

The *jonin* collapsed to his knees. "You … you …"

The Spartan moved back from the *jonin*. As badly wounded as he was, the Spartan felt something else, too.

He felt good.

He tore a sign from the table and dropped it onto the *jonin*. The white writing on the sign said "People's Republic Of China".

"When you need to kill a man, don't get cute," said the Spartan. "Don't try and 'send a message'. Just point your weapon at his neck and finish the job." The Spartan kicked the Honjo Masamune out of reach behind the ninja.

"You didn't think I knew what you were doing?" said the Spartan, wrapping part of his shirt around his bleeding arm. "That you were going to execute me on the table next to the sign of your country?

"I'd done a recce of the room earlier. I remembered where most of the signs were. And I realized what a planner you were. What a *schemer*. So I knew where you were going to strike."

The *jonin* merely gaped.

"Yes, you cost me some fingers," said the Spartan, holding up the hand with the missing digits. "But that's a price I was willing to pay to finish you."

The Spartan wasn't usually one to gloat and crow, but he considered his current opponent worthy of both.

He continued: "That's the difference between us – you're a swordsman; hell, you're the best swordsman I've ever faced; but I'm a soldier. Soldiers are willing to make sacrifices to get the job done. Soldiers spend their time fighting other soldiers, not sneaking up on civilians and cutting their heads off. You've spent too much time trying to be clever and not enough time fighting armed men."

The *jonin* stared at the Spartan for a long time. Then he said: "I underestimated you."

"You're not the first," said the Spartan, applying more first aid to his wounds. "Won't be the last."

They paused as the building rumbled from another aerial attack.

"Then again, I did have some help," added the Spartan. "Your old friend the Monk told me all about you. His intel proved … useful."

If anything, the *jonin* looked even more pained at the mention of the Monk. "And you accuse me of scheming. I granted you a boon by facing you as a warrior. Now I want something from you, Spartan. You owe me that. Warrior to warrior."

The Spartan considered this as he applied first aid to his injuries. "Talk."

"Finish it. Finish me with the Honjo Masamune." The *jonin* stared at the Spartan with respect in his eyes at last. The hard arrogance had disappeared, to be replaced with something like resignation.

The Spartan stepped behind the *jonin* for a few moments.

The Spartan picked up the Honjo Masamune, staring at its exquisite edge. "Magnificent," he breathed.

The Spartan knew exactly what he was going to do with the legendary sword.

He spent another moment admiring this most coveted of weapons, feeling its weight in his hand, before stepping up to his fallen foe.

The *jonin* bowed his head. He felt the Honjo Masamune against his neck.

"To die by this blade could be considered an honor," said the Spartan. Then he withdrew the blade. "But it's an honor I choose to deny you."

No, thought the *jonin*.

Instead the Spartan raised his Glock and shot him the back of the head.

Chapter 85

If Vasquez had taken away anything useful from her battle with the *kunoichi*, it was the value of some kind of stealth climbing apparatus.

The cat's claws the *kunoichi* had used to scale the roof of Vasquez's room had intrigued her. It would have been impossible to incorporate those devices into her Ghost Armor without losing the invisibility function, so she had had to settle for some high-tech suction cups for her hands and knees. The benefit of those was that if she moved slowly enough, Vasquez could remain invisible. However, the suction cups would still be visible to the naked eye. A baffling sight for anyone who bothered to look up.

The suction cups had the added benefit of holding her in place by the knees while she did something else with her hands – like now.

Dangling from a ceiling, hoping to ambush a Chinese Premier surrounded by hostile bodyguards willing to die for and kill for him … it was a pretty crazy plan.

But it was the best one she had.

After a minute sneaking into position and then climbing the walls to the roof, she was now almost good to go. All she had to do was drop down on the Second Most Powerful Leader in the World, hold a phone to his head and tell him that the Most Powerful Leader in the World was on the line.

All without breaking her ankles from the fall and without being instantly murdered by his bodyguards.

Easy.

She put the hand cups in her pouch and removed both a loaded Glock and the cell phone.

"Are you there, sir?" she said into the cell phone, staring down at the melee below.

"Yes, Vasquez."

She tapped her throat mic. "Mancuso, I'm making my descent now. Stop firing and start popping smoke."

"Roger," replied Mancuso.

Vasquez watched as the Secret Service men stopped firing and instead lobbed in two smoke grenades, their tops fizzing out greyish smoke.

Chingalo. Fuck it.

She dropped from the ceiling.

Vasquez's plunge was near-perfect. She landed on her feet right next to the panicked Premier. Instantly she felt a crippling pain in her ankles.

Something felt fractured or broken.

But if she couldn't get on her feet, she was dead.

Yet by sheer willpower Vasquez made it up, wrapped one arm around the Premier's neck and held a phone next to his ear at the same time she held a Glock to his head.

Instantly there were screams and shouts, "don't move" and "let him go" yelled in both English and Mandarin.

"Mr Premier, the President is on the line," Vasquez shouted over the din, putting the phone into his nervous hands.

"Mr Premier, are you there?" said the President over the phone. "Can you hear me?"

It was the last thing Vasquez heard before strong hands grabbed her and hurled her to the floor. Guns were pointed in her face. It was over.

"Do not harm her yet," commanded the startled Premier, raising a hand.

"She's with me, Mr Premier!" shouted POTUS on the phone.

"Hold her for now," said the Premier. Hands pinned her down, her face against the floor.

"Don't hurt her!" yelled someone from the Secret Service side.

Both sides stopped firing.

"I can hear you, Mr President," said the Premier, moving to cover, followed by his guards. "Speak." Vasquez was dragged along the ground with them. She didn't resist.

"Mr Premier, the drone attack is being directed from China," said the President hurriedly. "We're running out of time. We need you to neutralize the controllers. Can you help us?"

The Premier paused, but only for a second. "Are you sure?"

"Yes, we're sure. We must act now. Please ... we need your help. *I* need your help."

There was another pause. The UN building groaned, metal creaking, as if the cumulative strikes on the structure had rendered it in danger of collapse. "I am forced to trust you, Mr President. Give me the co-ordinates." The Premier snapped his fingers for paper and pen, which were quickly supplied.

"Received." Fortunately, the location was deep in the Chinese countryside, away from the cities. Casualties would be minimal. The issue could be contained. He would have deniability in the press. "If this is a trick, Mr President, the consequences will be grave. You are asking me to bomb my own country."

"This is no trick, sir. You have to trust me."

Trust as a concept among humans had died the day they'd had to put tamper-proof packages on bottles of aspirin in case lunatics wanted to poison their fellow man. And yet, the Premier replied: "I will make the call."

"I am in your debt, Mr Premier."

"Yes, Mr President ... you are," came the cold reply. The Premier hung up the phone.

Then, using his own mobile, he called the commander of the Chinese air force.

* * *

The call was received.

The commander, once the situation had been explained, passed on the details to his subordinates. The pride of Chinese's air force, poised to strike American targets in the South China Sea, had new targets.

The planes were in the air in minutes.

The bombs were dropped.

The targets were neutralized. The attack was devastating, thorough. The Americans were told there would be no survivors.

The remaining drones ceased attacking the UN HQ, flying as straight arrows out towards the sea, rudderless and directionless.

Whereupon they were quickly shot down and destroyed by cannon and missile.

Chapter 86

The blond Secret Service agent steered his boss towards the armored limo in the underground car park of the UN HQ.

"The drones are taken care of, sir," he said, his hand on the shoulder of his charge. "The firing outside has stopped. We can leave now. We *should* leave now."

"Thank mercy for that," said the President.

The Secret Service agents opened the door of the Presidential limo and moved him inside.

The President scooted over in the back seat ... only to meet resistance.

A figure suddenly became visible. A ninja in silver.

A ninja holding a tanto.

The President didn't even have time to scream as the ninja plunged the razor-sharp tanto into the President's body. He struck again and again, starting with the neck.

Now the President screamed.

Bullets from Secret Service agents slammed into the ninja's body. The shinobi kept stabbing until he could stab no more.

He slumped over, face-first, against the front seats.

So did POTUS.

The Secret Service agents immediately attempted first aid on the President.

"Stay with me, sir," they said, before attempting resuscitation. Other agents powered up the vehicle's portable life-support machine. But it was too late. The ninja's stabs were too knowing, too deep, too numerous.

The incredible had happened.

The President of the United States had been assassinated.

Chapter 87

Eventually, once the all-clear was given, the Chinese Premier walked over to where Vasquez was being held by his security team. Her mask had been removed so that he could see her anxious face.

"I think you can release her now," he said. To Vasquez, he said: "Allow me to help you up, young lady." The Premier extended a hand, which Vasquez gratefully accepted. Vasquez could detect the strength of an experienced martial artist in his grip.

"Thank you, Mr Premier," she said as she got to her feet, wincing at the pain in her ankles.

"That was a brave thing you did," said the Premier, looking at Vasquez and then back at the ceiling. "I'm surprised you're still alive. But you have helped us avoid a major diplomatic incident. I thank you for my country."

"It was an honor and a privilege, Mr Premier." *Vasquez saves the day again*, she suddenly thought.

"May I ask your name?"

"Teresa, sir."

"Thank you again ... Teresa." The Premier stared at Vasquez again. "And I do believe you're wearing one of those troublesome invisibility suits." The Premier laughed at Vasquez's startled expression. "Yes, we've heard about them. Don't worry, Teresa ... I'm not going to order my men to rip it off you. Although they could."

"They'd have to tear it off my dead body, sir," said Vasquez suddenly.

The Premier smiled. "Yes, I can see that they would have to."

"We should leave now, sir," said one of the Premier's guards. In the background, men had already begun to carry their wounded colleagues to ambulances outside. EMTs attempted to work amid the blood, bodies, drone wreckage and rubble around the building.

"Soon," replied the Premier. He turned back to Vasquez. "Those suits have changed the game, don't you think? I wish they had never been invented. They have led to much misfortune. Pandora's Box is now open and spreading its evils among the world."

Vasquez stared around the room, with its terrible carnage. "That is sadly correct, sir."

"May I speak candidly?"

"I would welcome it, Mr Premier."

"But now that the suits have come into the world, you know that you won't be able to keep their secret forever. Now that America has them, we must have them. And others must have them, too. Others will make ... plans. Others will need to look into Pandora's Box. That is the problem with military escalation. We are all trapped in its gravity, whether we like it or not."

"You are undoubtedly right, sir."

"So hold your suit tight, Teresa. Sleep with it. Never abandon it for a moment. Because you will *need* to."

Vasquez stared at the Premier. There was no malice in his statement, rather a wistful sadness.

Just then, over the Premier's shoulder, Vasquez spotted a welcome sight. The Spartan. Tottering towards them with what seemed like sheer force of will.

His body bore numerous wounds and cuts, some bandaged, some not.

Yet on his back, sheathed in its scabbard, was the precious Honjo Masamune.

Which told Vasquez everything she needed to know about why he had disappeared, who he had fought and who he had subsequently killed.

The Premier's men sensed that, despite looking like the walking dead, the Spartan was dangerous. They made to surround the Premier.

Yet the Premier intuited that the Spartan meant him no harm and waved them away.

"He's with me," said Vasquez, turning to the Spartan. "So the *jonin's* dead?"

"You won't be seeing him again except in flashbacks."

Like a protective hoplite phalanx, the Secret Service men came closer, eager to take the Spartan and Vasquez away to safety. The Chinese security team let them approach.

"You need urgent medical attention," said the Premier, studying the Spartan's bloody appearance. "Both of you. My men will escort you outside."

The Spartan watched as Secret Service agents came forward until they were right next to him. "Thank you, sir, but I think our ride is already here."

"As you wish." The Premier nodded at Vasquez. "Fortune smile upon you, Vasquez. Perhaps we will meet again."

"I'd like that, Mr Premier," she replied. She turned to the Spartan. "Lean on me, soldier."

"Just this once," he replied. He put his injured arm around her shoulder. Vasquez noticed the bloody space where digits used to be.

"What happened to your hand?"

"The Honjo Masamune exacted a blood tithe."

Vasquez kept her eyes off the wound and on the eyes of the Spartan. "See what happens when you go off gallivanting without your partner?"

"Point. Meanwhile, you're limping."

"I think I've broken one of my ankles."

"We're a pair, aren't we?"

"The best of pairs, Spartan, The very best of pairs."

Together, they wandered out into the kind sun and into the future.

Chapter 88

New York, the city that never sleeps. And if it ever did sleep again after what had happened, it would be sleeping with one eye open and with a hatchet under its pillow.

The top of the UN HQ looked like Godzilla had taken a bite out of it, then, pleasantly surprised by its gritty taste, had gone back for more. Dozens had been killed inside, both from drone attacks and gunfights. The British Prime Minister and German Foreign Minister – those tireless champions of once-great empires – were among the VIP casualties.

Not to mention the many bodyguards, aides, police, emergency service workers and even members of the press both inside and outside.

All sacrificed on the altar of a madman's ambition.

Then there was the devastation of New York by the drone attacks. The casualties were expected to top four digits. The damage bill would be in the billions.

It was expected that the US would foot the bill for the restoration of the UN HQ.

The decent, hard-working people of America groaned under the weight of another unimaginable event.

This attack was a particularly savage and cruel psychological blow for a country just beginning to get over the trauma of a mass plague event.

The public howls of outrage were louder than any drone engine. Drones were supposed to be killing terrorists in Third World countries, not citizens of the Most Powerful Nation on Earth. It was more proof that the weapons of the surveillance state had outreached the controls of their masters. It hinted at the shape of things to come, a population kept compliant by the threat of armed drones constantly circling overhead, ready to kill by bullet or missile anyone who stepped out of line.

In short, it shouldn't have happened in the Land of the Free.

Lands in which drones struck with impunity held celebrations in the streets, complete with the burning of American flags. US military planners observed these outbreaks of schadenfreude and marked the countries down for future, possibly drone-related punishment.

The official narrative for the disaster was being carefully crafted. Early reports claimed the drones had been electronically hijacked by terrorists, but such detail-poor explanations failed to placate a grieving, terrified populace.

Civilian bodies had fallen. Thus government heads had to roll.

How did this happen, the public screamed to anyone and in any medium that would listen. *How could this happen? Who is responsible?*

And a final, plaintive complaint: why won't the President get on TV and address the nation?

Chapter 89

Colonel Garin puffed on his cheroot as he watched the large plasma TV screen.

"For a dead man you look pretty good on TV, Mr President," he said drolly.

POTUS, smoking a cigar, sat in a matching leather chair beside Garin in the President's lounge room. He paused his puffing to nod.

"I do, don't I? Still, I owe you my life, colonel. If I hadn't taken your call ..."

"It was my duty and my pleasure, sir," replied Garin. "Fortunately, ninjas aren't the only ones who know something about subterfuge and deception."

"That was a close-run thing. The plot only failed at the one-yard line. If either I or the Premier had been killed ..."

Garin put on his best concerned face. "It doesn't bear thinking about, sir."

"I owe the Premier a panda," said the President out of the corner of his mouth. "Maybe two."

"Pandas, sir?"

POTUS turned to face Garin. "Panda diplomacy. The worse the crisis, the more pandas you have to exchange with the aggrieved party."

"Oh."

"I wonder if two pandas will do. The Premier almost walked into a deathtrap."

"Almost being the operative word, sir."

"So where do we stand, colonel? What's the rest of the butcher's bill?"

"Well, sir, I think we have all the invisibility suits in our possession."

"*Think?*"

"Our best guesses suggest so, sir." Garin briefly thought of the missing soldier known as Monkey and his suspicion that he may have absconded to parts unknown with a set of Ghost Armor. Seeing POTUS watching him closely, Garin chose not to voice his suspicions, but instead said: "You know how things work in the real world, Mr President. Nothing is ever wrapped up neatly in a tight little bow. It's more tied together by the fingers of your drunken uncle as he tries to slip your present under the tree on Christmas Eve."

"Humfh. Charming uncle you have there."

"He's everyone's uncle, sir. Hopefully we've seen the last of those rogue invisibility suits."

"'Seen the last'? Is that a pun, colonel?"

"No, sir."

"Because you know how I feel about puns."

"You and *The New York Times*, sir. One thing we know is that no one will be making any more, seeing how we have rescued Professor Eisenstein."

Indeed, Eisenstein had been rescued from a group of half-dead ninjas by a special forces team. He was alive and relatively well. His first request had been to see his family.

"Eisenstein … let's hope we have him somewhere secure this time. Like in the very bowels of the earth."

"He is indeed being held underground, sir."

The President looked pensive. "Perhaps it would have been better … no, best not to even think it."

"Think what, sir?"

"Better that Eisenstein hadn't lived. He's the dictionary definition of an inconvenient man. The world might be better off with the Ghost Armor never having been invented in the first place. Eisenstein is the only person alive who understands how they can be built. No Eisenstein, no suits."

POTUS stared at Garin. *Holy shit*, thought Garin. *Is the President telling me to kill Eisenstein?*

"Never mind," said POTUS, as if putting such evil thoughts aside.

Just then the First Lady, clad in gym gear, came into the room with some cocktail sausages.

Garin had always found FLOTUS to be beautiful, gracious and charming in person. For her part, she seemed to more than tolerate the colonel. A formidable presence, there was talk that FLOTUS might even run for President once her husband's term was up.

The First Lady held her tray before Garin. "Weiner?"

"I'd love one, thanks," said the colonel. "Maybe two."

"Just one for me … I'm supposed to be on a low-sodium diet," said POTUS, winking at Garin.

Just then the First Dog, a small, brown excitable Belgian barge dog much pilloried in the press, rushed in and made a beeline for the President's wiener.

"Mr Willoughby, no!" said the First Lady as the First Dog snatched the wiener, then, cheekily, ran out of the room.

"Ahh, let him have it," said POTUS. "He's hungry." Garin wordlessly handed over one of his wieners to the President.

For a moment all three watched the President shaking hands with the Chinese Premier on TV. Words like "working to secure world peace" and "my good friend the Premier" echoed throughout the room.

"You do look fine," said FLOTUS, casting an admiring glance at her husband on the screen and then in the flesh. "But I should be mad at his security team, colonel. Those assassins thought they'd killed my husband."

"They were never supposed to get that close, ma'am," admitted Garin. "But just in case, I advised your husband to use his 'double'."

"And a good thing you did," said FLOTUS, putting a strong hand on Garin's shoulder. On the surface, the grasp seemed like a vote of confidence and appreciation. And yet, the subtext was, "Don't let my husband come so close to death again, asshole."

POTUS noticed the grasp and glanced up at his wife, who removed her hand with a final glance at POTUS. "Shame about Jerry," he said.

"Jerry" being the President's double, a salesman from Ohio, blessed – or cursed, considering events – with an uncanny resemblance to POTUS, a likeness made even more uncanny by surgery and prosthetics.

"Yes," replied Garin somberly, rubbing his shoulder. "He died a true patriot."

Words, no doubt, that would be cold comfort to Jerry's family.

There was a moment as Jerry's sacrifice was noted and remembered. His name would be inscribed on a wall somewhere as a new member of the secret fallen, one of the heroes and heroines who had died to make America safe.

The President closed his eyes. When he re-opened them, he said: "Quite a few other important people have died under strange circumstances, too. And not just at the UN. Scientists and engineers."

"Is that so?" replied Garin, raising an eyebrow. "Could be worth looking into."

"I'll leave you to running the free world, dear," said FLOTUS as she left the room. "Nice to see you, colonel. Don't be a stranger."

"I don't intend to be, ma'am."

The two worthies continued to watch the footage of the summit between POTUS and the Premier. The planet was happy that the leaders of the two most powerful nations on Earth had brought the world back from the brink of war.

"Moving on ... I gather we're confident the ninja cell has been eliminated."

"Yes, Mr President, barring those remaining in custody. The Spartan personally killed the ringleader in the UN building. The camera footage survived. I can show it to you later if you like. It was a hell of a fight."

"I'd like to see that. A useful soldier, your Spartan."

"I've always found him so, sir."

"And we have Vasquez to thank for getting me in phone contact with the Premier. So please pass on my thanks to her as well."

"Will do, sir."

The President took a contemplative puff of his cigar. "And of course, we've benched our entire drone fleet worldwide. Mostly as a sop to public opinion, but we really do need to look at them again to make sure they can never be hijacked and turned against us again."

"Once is more than enough, sir."

"Still, we're not about to get rid of the drones, are we? They're just too useful. Too … convenient."

"The armed forces would agree with you, sir."

"Drones are the future, not just for us but all the First World armies. Along with autonomous weapons systems. According to all my advisers, in the not-too-distance future warfare will be largely fought by non-human actors."

"Non-human actors … that sounds like you're describing half of Hollywood, sir." POTUS rewarded him with a slight chortle. "I hear you, sir. Anything that prevents our troops coming back in body bags is a good thing. No one is going to miss a machine if it gets destroyed."

"Still, we will always need men and women like the Spartan and Vasquez."

Garin smiled conspiratorially. "I concur, sir."

"What will the Spartan do for an encore, do you think?"

"'There is no hunting like the hunting of a man, and those who have hunted armed men long enough and liked it, never care for anything else thereafter.'"

"Hemingway?"

"Hemingway, wishing he was the Spartan."

"Heh." POTUS leaned in closer, giving Garin a whiff of expensive cologne. "And on a personal matter, colonel … I hope you're not too mad that I benched you," he said, his voice dropping, as if to denote a matter of great personal import. "The whole 'Colonel X' scandal made things difficult. And the Joint Chiefs were turning against you. I must listen to my advisers. I can't govern in a vacuum. It was …"

"A dick move, sir?" Garin immediately shot back.

POTUS guffawed in surprise. "In retrospect, it was indeed a 'dick move', wasn't it?"

Garin's face gave nothing away, not even a lingering sense of betrayal.

Seeing this, POTUS gently grasped Garin's elbow, as if to suggest a level of personal intimacy. "But you know I think you're a hell of a guy, on both a personal and professional level. I must know – do you hold a grudge against me?"

Garin was surprised by the question. He paused as he carefully assembled his thoughts. "A grudge? No, sir. A mutual friend told me that you hadn't abandoned me. That you hadn't lost faith."

POTUS smiled, knowing who the "mutual friend" was. "Yes. I'm glad you kept the faith, too, colonel. Otherwise I never would have taken your call. It could have been me stabbed to death. *Would* have been me stabbed to death."

There was a stage-like cough at the doorway. "Hug it out, bitches," smirked the First Lady.

Garin wondered how long she had been lurking there. Meanwhile, POTUS stood and extended his arms wide. "You heard the lady. So, no hard feelings? Hug on it?"

Garin stood and accepted the embrace eagerly. "Consider it hugged out, sir."

The First Lady clapped. "Peace in our time. My work here is done," she said, before leaving the room.

Both men sat down again with wide grins on their faces, like two schoolboys who had just successfully pulled off a prank.

Peace in our time had indeed been achieved.

Garin smiled, but his mind was working on a second track apart from the track conversing with the President. And that second track reminded him that the President, as personally amenable as he was, was a politician, not a soldier. He could only rely on a politician's grace and favor so far. A soldier could be relied on to follow orders and fight with you to the death, but a politician would only stick his or her neck out so far. That made them essentially untrustworthy.

So he would trust this President as far as he would trust any politician, but in the meantime, he would work behind the scenes to improve his influence and power so he would be immune from the changeability of politicians.

He would also consider how the Joint Chiefs had crossed him … and what he could do about that, too.

Outwardly, however, he continued to smile.

Chapter 90

The *kunoichi* stared up in surprise as Vasquez entered the rather Spartan interrogation room.

"You!" she shouted hoarsely.

"Yes, me. Hail Hydra."

The ninja's hands were chained to the table, which was the only thing preventing her from hurling herself at Vasquez. Nevertheless, she still tried to grasp at Vasquez as the latter took a seat in front of her, the thin yet sturdy chains making a loud rattle as she lunged out.

"Having fun there?" asked Vasquez. Undeterred, she kept the two warm coffees she held in her hands away from the moving metal and grasping hands.

The thrashing and grasping continued for a few seconds, the ninja's haggard face a picture of rage. Eventually the *kunoichi*, realizing the futility of her gesture, stopped struggling and placed her arms back on the table.

"I bet you feel better with that out of your system," said Vasquez.

The *kunoichi* eyed her warily. "What are you doing here, if not to put your neck in my hands? Have you come to laugh at my predicament?"

"No one's laughing after the shit you pulled."

"Have you come to offer me a deal?"

"No," came the firm answer.

"You've come to gloat, then."

"I've come to bring you coffee. Here. I know they haven't given you any." Vasquez pushed a coffee towards the *kunoichi*. The room was lit by a single bright bulb overhead, illuminating the *kunoichi's* features. Dressed in an orange prison jumpsuit, she looked tired, as if she had aged five years in the past week. Her hair was disheveled and lank.

The *kunoichi* rested her fingers on the disposable cup's warm surface. "How do I know you haven't drugged it?"

"I'm not here to interrogate you," said Vasquez. "I thought you might just want to talk."

"I won't tell you anything," said the ninja, who accepted the coffee and brought it to her lips. She downed half of the liquid quickly. She nodded to the door. "I won't tell them anything, either."

"I don't doubt you."

"They do things to me, you know," said the *kunoichi* conspiratorially. "Things while I sleep. They leave no marks, and yet ... I know. I know!" she shouted towards the door.

Vasquez said nothing, drinking her own coffee. She knew, too.

The ninja stared at Vasquez's legs, as if hoping to see something underneath the blue jeans. "You're injured."

"Fractured ankle."

"Good. You deserve to suffer. I should have killed you."

"You tried three times. You failed."

"I still don't know how you beat me."

"I've been eating my spinach."

The *kunoichi* sipped her coffee. "Why didn't you kill me?"

"Because I used to be a policewoman. We bring in suspects alive when we can."

"Unlike your partner." The *kunoichi* paused. "He killed him, didn't he?"

Vasquez didn't need to ask who he was. "Yes."

The ninja's eyes briefly flickered with constellations of pain. Then she sighed. "I knew it. I felt his death." The *kunoichi* said nothing for a good 30 seconds, staring down at the table. Not without empathy, Vasquez averted her eyes. Eventually, the *kunoichi* looked up and said: "The Spartan is the only one who could've beaten him."

"Special forces require special forces."

The *kunoichi* looked at Vasquez with something approaching respect. "Tell me how it happened."

"Swordfight at the UN. If it's any consolation, it was an epic battle. The immovable object meets the unstoppable force. The Spartan was badly wounded."

"I knew he would sell his life dearly."

"A lot of people died because of your man," said Vasquez, a touch of judgment in her voice.

"Don't expect me to apologize for his actions. And what of the rest of it? My pig captors have told me nothing."

"They wouldn't want me telling you this, but … both the President and the Premier are still alive. And the rest of your clan are dead or in custody. Your mission failed."

"Did it?" The ninja quickly finished her coffee. Vasquez may have imagined it, but she thought the *kunoichi's* quick movements with the cup hid a brief smile. "Again, I ask: why are you telling me this? Why are you here?"

Vasquez grew contemplative. "I must confess to some selfish reasons. There's something I want to talk to you about. I believe we have something in common. We both love men in love with violence. It's a reality that comes with its own complications."

The *kunoichi's* body language suggested curiosity. "Explain."

"No matter how much we care for them – how much we might want something different – there will always be a part of them that will refuse to settle down and give up war. That can make things difficult between a man and a woman. Particularly in the long term."

A look of understanding came over the *kunoichi's* face.

"Ah … the whole Happily Ever After thing. You want to know whether it's possible with a soldier. You desire another woman's perspective." She laughed bitterly. "Appealing to my 'womanly instincts' is a low trick, even in the eyes of a ninja."

"I'm not trying to trick you. As I said, I just want to chat."

"He must mean a lot to you, for you to come to me like this."

"He does. Enough for me to fail the Bechdel Test." The *kunoichi* stared at her, baffled. "Sorry. Bad joke."

"So why have you chosen me for this task?"

"Because I don't have anyone else I can talk to."

The ninja's eyes glittered with sudden interest. "You have no family?"

"They're … gone."

"I disappointed my own family. They expected me to get married, not to become" … the *kunoichi* raised her manacled hands … "this."

"It's a lonely life, that of the warrior woman. We must show no weakness, to be as tough as the men. Even tougher."

The *kunoichi* brushed her hair away from her eyes two-handed. "It is no different in China. My lover was my only comfort … and even with him I had to be careful." The ninja's façade seemed to crumble a little. "I think I understand where you are 'coming from'. So you will be expecting more of these 'chats'?"

"If you find them agreeable, then yes."

"Even though I despise America and its ways?"

"I'm actually Mexican."

"I will never tell you anything of operational use against my country." The *kunoichi* gestured towards the cell door with her head. "And you know that *they* won't be able to hold me here forever. When I escape and find you in the outside world, I will kill you. You and your 'Spartan'."

Vasquez nodded. "If I see you in the outside world, I'll shoot first and ask questions later. But I will bring coffee every time I visit you here."

"A feeble bribe. However, I do like coffee." The *kunoichi* half-smiled. "So be it. Let us talk of warrior women and the ways of the world … and how so few of us ever get what we really want."

Chapter 91

The Jaguar hurried along the secret underground passage in El Paso, joined by four of his most deadly and most trusted bodyguards. When his hired assassins had failed to kill Vasquez and the Spartan, he knew it was time to leave the US. Especially after the drone attack on the UN.

The hornet's nest had been disturbed – and the Jaguar didn't want to stick around to be stung.

He hadn't lived this long in the criminal underworld without knowing when to retreat.

This particular tunnel between El Paso and Mexico was reserved only for the most clandestine of drug deliveries and/ or the most important of people in the cartels. Constructed in great secrecy and care, it was reserved for special occasions.

Such as now.

The Jaguar was glad to leave North America. The insolent Vasquez would have to wait. But she would fall. Once a contract was issued, the target always did eventually. So it would be with this *puta* cop. But he was patient, unlike his former prodigy Fighting Dog.

Suddenly the lights in the tunnel flicked off.

That shouldn't have happened. Not with such a VIP as himself making the transit.

His men began yelling, confused. Yet the Jaguar refused to panic. He would embarrass himself in front of the men if he did so.

Just then there was an explosion in the tunnel. It was a precise explosion, designed for a specific purpose, more surgical than frightful. A careful demolition by experts. Rocks, dirt, wood and masonry fell to the ground.

Once the dust subsided and it was clear that there would be no more explosions, his men checked on the situation. The explosion had done its job. One end of the passage was now impassable.

Now the Jaguar began to panic.

Because the explosion came from the *Yankee* side of the border.

Which meant someone from the Mexican side was waiting for him. And they played by an entirely different, infinitely more brutal set of rules.

The Jaguar and his team watched in horror as men with flashlights came down the Mexican side of the tunnel towards them.

Chapter 92

The General drove his Bentley up the road towards his estate in Connecticut. It had belonged to his family for generations, a prized asset that had eventually been bequeathed to the General. He had other houses and apartments dotted around the US and the globe, but this was the one he returned to when he felt the need for safety.

And after the events in New York, he felt such a desire.

It was his sanctuary. His true home.

The Spartan would no doubt have sneered at the decadence of his estate, with its carefully clipped lawns and hedges, gardeners, maids and fine antique furniture. The General had learned that his enemy was recuperating in hospital. Too bad he hadn't been killed. However, he had been nicely sliced up by that ninja assassin, so it wasn't a complete loss.

The General touched his own facial scar. Now that bastard knows what it feels like to be violated by cold metal. The thought pleased him.

The General stopped at the guard gate. There was only one guard on tonight instead of the usual two.

"Good evening, sir," said the guard respectfully.

"Good evening, Mike. Where's Rocco?"

"Rocco's got a cold."

I don't give a shit if he's got a cold, thought the General. He paid good money for the benefit of security in the gated community. After what happened in New York, he wanted all the VIP protection he could get. He would be having words with someone later. But instead he said with faux sincerity: "I hope Rocco gets well soon."

"Have a good one, sir," said Mike as he activated the security barrier, letting the General drive through.

The streets looked strangely empty as he approached his estate. Normally they'd be a few security cars around. Or any cars, really.

Perhaps he felt their absence because he knew he was going to be alone tonight. His maid had gone home and he had no current plans for any other female companionship. Perhaps that would change later.

He keyed the security code into his gate and waited for the doors to swing open. He had a state-of-the-art system automatically linked to both the guard booth and the local police force. He could expect a very fast reaction time if his perimeter was breached. That had never happened, but he liked having peace of mind in any case. VIP membership had its privileges.

As he was halfway down his driveway, the phone rang. "Unknown ID" said the screen. He decided to answer it anyway.

"Yes?"

"Stop the car right there," ordered a harsh male voice.

For some reason the General complied. "Who is this?"

"I'm glad you answered your phone at last. You've been ducking me for days."

"*Garin.*"

"That's Colonel Garin to you."

"What the hell do you want?"

"We need to talk."

"We never need to talk, Garin."

"I think we do. I know you were behind the whole 'Colonel X' smear campaign."

"You're 'Colonel X'? Ouch."

"Like you didn't know. Like you didn't set it up."

The General smiled. "I have no idea what you're talking about. But the idea of you being troubled doesn't exactly displease me."

"And if I could prove you had anything to do with that surfer trying to kill the Spartan in my apartment, we'd be having a completely different conversation." Garin paused. "But still, I figure you deserve this. Look ahead."

The General complied.

Suddenly his beloved estate exploded. The concussion rocked his Bentley. By instinct the General ducked down as bits of flaming debris fell on the car's roof. After a few seconds, he lifted his head up to survey the damage. The main building of the estate resembled a flaming skull missing its forehead. His precious roses, the subject of hours of painstaking work, burnt before his eyes. An alarm rang out, only to become muted as its components melted. Four out of the five chimneys were destroyed, the lone survivor resembling a middle finger in the night sky. The flames illuminated the windshield of the Bentley and the General's terrified expression.

"Fuuucckkkk!" he screamed, ducking down in his seat.

"Must be a nice view from your Bentley."

"You ... you just blew up my home, Garin! You maniac!"

"Like I said, Charlton Heston, mess with the bull, get the horns. I'm just sorry I can't be there in person to cook a marshmallow on the fire. Now neither of us can go home."

"Fuuuccck!"

"That evens us up, I reckon … but you know we're going to continue this conversation another time."

The General continued to gape at his now-ruined home.

"Have a good night, General."

Click.

Chapter 93

Garin couldn't watch the General's bonfire of the vanities in person because he was miles away in an underground location, silenced pistol in his hand, watching Professor Eisenstein.

Garin stared through the one-way glass in the door as Eisenstein embraced his wife and two children. He could see the genuine love and joy on their faces. A happy occasion. A Kodak moment. The beleaguered genius reunited with kith and kin after his torment at the hands of the ninjas.

And yet – he still couldn't ignore what the President had said. That the world would be safer if the inventor of the Ghost Armor was no longer around to make any more.

Had the President truly wanted him to kill Eisenstein?

Was POTUS really that cold-blooded?

After New York, perhaps he was.

Garin held the pistol up.

Decision time.

It wouldn't be hard. How many men had Garin killed already? Eisenstein would just be another in a long list waiting to greet him in Hell. A familiar tug on the trigger and that would be it. All he would have to do would be to wait for the family to leave, thank Eisenstein for his service to his country ... and then.

And then.

Yet Garin found his arm lowering. The last time he had killed innocents, it had cost him his faith. If he killed another innocent, what would it cost him? His idea of himself? His pride? His soul?

No ... Eisenstein would live, no matter how inconvenient his existence was. If we became murderers, he thought, what was the point of fighting in the first place? We were no better than the other savages out there wanting to plunge the world into darkness. The professor's death was a bridge too far for him. A bridge too far for POTUS and, by extension, the country.

The General had it coming for his crimes, but Eisenstein's only crime was to serve the United States too well. And surely that was no crime at all.

So he would give the President not what he wanted but what he needed. He would not put a round into Eisenstein's wonderful, brilliant, outsized brain.

Garin holstered his weapon and made his way towards the elevator.

Maybe I'm getting too old for this shit, he thought.

Chapter 94

Professor Eisenstein hugged his wife tightly, feeling the heat from her body through his lab coat. Beside them, his two young children – a son and a daughter – hugged their legs, forming an intimate family circle.

Eisenstein relished the human contact after his captivity. And yet, as his family tearfully told him how grateful they were that he was alive, he stared over his wife's shoulder towards the door.

It was not the first time he had felt a malign presence there. And it probably wouldn't be the last.

Eisenstein was a brilliant man, but it didn't take a Mensa member to figure out that he proved a problem for his would-be saviors. The Ghost Armor suits, the fruits of his genius, had caused much unwelcome chaos on the world stage. It was one thing to build an exoskeleton or combat armor for grunts in Iraq or Afghanistan. It was quite another to construct a device that allowed the assassination of an American Vice President, the near-death of the actual President, the co-opting of American drones to attack New York, the sinking of a US aircraft carrier, and much more besides.

That was just ... too much chaos. More chaos than the people who ran the world liked to tolerate. And he was the only one who knew how to build the suits.

You do the math.

Eisenstein filled in the other part of the equation. How long would it take for his allies to figure out it might be better for everyone if he was no longer around? How long before the bureaucracy of death gave the order? How long before the man behind the door came in to finish the job?

Would it be weeks? Months?

Days?

The titan Prometheus had had his liver pecked out by eagles for eternity for sharing the secret of fire with man. As the man who "shared" the secret of the Ghost Armor with America's enemies, he suspected his punishment would be more prosaic: more likely a pillow over the face or a bullet in the dead of night.

Eisenstein hugged his family more closely. He'd had his fill as an operative for the Americans and a captive of the Chinese. Yet perhaps there was a third way. Perhaps he didn't have to serve either the Lord or the Devil.

Perhaps it was time for a new backer.

Perhaps it was time to reach out to Mother Russia.

Eisenstein decided to phone his old comrade and former KGB officer Marchenko the first chance he got.

Chapter 95

It pained the Spartan to read the assorted "get well" cards by his hospital bed. Not because of the sentiments inside, but rather because he was reading them with a hand that had just had two fingers surgically reattached.

Colonel Garin had tersely informed the doctors to "put those fingers back or I'll make sure you lose yours".

The Spartan was not entirely sure that Garin had been joking.

In any case, the fingers severed by the Honjo Masamune were back in place. The nerves were alive yet screaming in complaint as he held the cards. He did them a favor and swapped over to the other hand.

Jackson's postcard – featuring the cityscape of an unnamed Middle Eastern city, presumably where Jackson was now plying his new and lucrative trade as a mercenary – was pithy.

"I told you no one gets to kill you except for me," it said. The letter "J" was next to the handwriting.

There was also a thumbprint which may or may not have been made in blood.

Agent Mancuso had sent his own missive on Secret Service letterhead.

"Get well soon and stay the hell away from me." Like the Spartan, the Secret Service man was also recovering in a private hospital in one of New York City's five boroughs, guards posted outside his door.

The third missive – a postcard bearing a stamp from China – was the one that meant the most. It boasted a scene from the Chinese countryside, at once beautiful and moving. It merely had the Chinese character for strength in careful black ink on the bare reverse. The Spartan's fingers ran close to the bottom edge of the card, where his fingers detected a tiny raised bump.

A layman would think it was nothing. But the Spartan knew another message lay hidden there.

One he would pore over with much interest later.

He put the card aside. The Tier 1 soldier felt restless. He had a private room, so his only entertainment was various novels and his own thoughts. He had also had a television for a while, which he had used to watch Mexican soap operas. He told himself that he was watching them to improve his Spanish language skills, but he had found an odd pleasure watching those lurid tales of passion.

He'd skimmed through the news as well. No one was ready to admit the truth of what had happened, neither on the American or the Chinese side. Still, the Americans had pulled out all their ships and aircraft from the South China Sea, the Pacific Fleet sailing away to a respectful distance. Relieved, the Chinese had ordered their own forces to retreat and stand down.

The world would never know how much it owed to the actions of the Spartan, Vasquez, Garin and Mancuso. Such was the lot of special forces everywhere.

Eventually, the Spartan had grown tired of watching uniformed news anchors flounder in search of the truth and had requested that the television be taken away.

So he was bored again.

He knew he had to allow his body time to heal … and yet he craved activity. The soldier in him bade him to sit still, to ignore his overactive adrenal glands and allow his many wounds to knit and heal, but the Spartan in him demanded he get out of bed, collect his *xiphos* from under the mattress, and leave.

As Colonel Garin had told him: "In times of peace, the warlike man goes to war with himself."

Which is kind of how he felt right now.

At least the headaches had now stopped.

The nurses came in occasionally to check his wounds. Every now and then they'd ask him where and how he had received a particular scar. Sometimes he could tell them … or at least a classified version of the tale, recounting a date in time as if remarking upon the rings of an ancient tree. And sometimes he found he was unable to remember, he'd been wounded so often. Sometimes the tales all blurred into one.

His face suddenly complained of pain. He touched his face with his repaired fingers. The Spartan had needed plastic surgery after being slashed by the Honjo Masamune. The surgeons had done an excellent job, but he would always have a scar there. Not unlike the scar he had left on the General's face with his own *xiphos*.

Perhaps this was a form of karma. Or perhaps it was a question of mathematics, that the more combat situations he entered, the more likely it was he would be left with a facial scar or relieved of several fingers.

His thoughts returned to the *jonin*, of the supremely arrogant expression of his face, so sure he had been of victory.

The *jonin* had been a superb fighter. And like his battle with the Monk, the Spartan's victory had been as narrow as the Hot Gates at Thermopylae.

Was it his fate to one day meet a warrior he couldn't put down?

An image flickered in his mind, that of a strange man in a cave, predicting his future.

The image slipped away. He let it go like a leaf travelling down a stream.

Then there was his relationship with Vasquez. And it was indeed a relationship, not a "relationship" or a booty call situation or other modern euphemism.

It was a relationship that had been nourished by mutual experience and respect: something he would need to think about going forward. She had visited him regularly in the hospital. Maybe they would go on that holiday he had promised her.

And if she needed help chasing down the Jaguar, well, he'd help her with that, too.

But he didn't have any more time to think about such matters, because Vasquez herself came through the door, wearing blue jeans, a light shirt and a wide smile.

"Morning, sunshine," she said. "How's the patient today?"

"Bored."

"Fifty CCs of boredom won't kill you after what you've been through. Could even be relaxing." Vasquez pulled up a nearby chair, then retrieved a newspaper from out of her bag. "Here … I've brought you yesterday's news." The front page was dominated by an image of the ravaged UN HQ. The headline, in giant type, was simply: "Why?"

The answer, of course, being because someone could.

"I'll read it later. Thanks."

Vasquez studied the Spartan's medical chart before examining the man himself. As if observing the laws of cause and effect, she said: "That was some mission, wasn't it?"

"It's not every day ninjas try to kill you."

"Or drones."

The Spartan looked down. "How's the ankle?"

"Sore. Technically, I shouldn't be walking at all. But I can't sit still."

"I know the feeling."

"Are you in much pain?"

The Spartan merely shrugged.

"Your ability to endure suffering and keep going is almost Mexican," observed Vasquez.

"I'll take that as a compliment."

"It was meant to be." Vasquez put her hand in his. He knew she loved his rough hands. She then took the Spartan's face in her other hand. "What have they done to your handsome face?"

"Tried to keep me handsome."

"Your whole body is becoming one giant mass of scar tissue."

"There goes my career as a Calvin Klein underwear model."

Vasquez chuckled. "I should be mad at you. You left me behind to fight the *jonin*."

"Sorry, Vasquez. The heart wants what the heart wants."

"You're like a dog with a bone." Vasquez surveyed his wounded body, then snaked her hands underneath the white sheets. "Speaking of which … did any of the pretty gringa nurses try to touch your 'little *xiphos*'?"

"It has remained untouched and fully sheathed."

Vasquez's hand gently squeezed the "little *xiphos*". "Good. Because it belongs to me."

The Spartan seemed pleased by her sudden possessiveness. "Affirmative, ma'am."

Vasquez removed her hand, then lifted the Spartan's blue gown to look at his wounded torso. "Perhaps your injuries will teach you that it's better to fight as a team. Like a proper Spartan should."

The Spartan half-smiled. "I'll cover you with my shield any time, Vasquez. My heart also wants you, too."

Vasquez gave the Spartan's face a half-slap. "And don't you forget it."

"Hey," cried a voice from the doorway, "no hitting an injured man."

"Colonel!" replied Vasquez happily as Garin, dressed in civilian clothes, entered the room.

"How is our brave warrior feeling today?" asked Garin.

"Still bored."

Garin sat on the edge of the white sheets. "Of course you are. A Spartan has no business lollygagging around in bed." The colonel seemed chipper ... and well he should be. The word was he was back in favor with the President. That tended to happen when you saved a man's life and all.

Garin faced the Spartan. "What about your injuries? Give me your no-shit-assessment, son."

"My injuries won't kill me but the hospital food might."

"Good." Garin nodded towards the door. "I've got a surprise for you." Garin disappeared and returned with a man in a wheelchair: a pale-looking Shintaro, who looked like he was only being held together by stitches and willpower.

"We meet again, Spartan-san," said the patient solemnly.

"You survived," said the Spartan appreciatively.

"Just. It only hurts when I breathe."

"Join the club."

"I think you have powerful gods watching over you," observed Shintaro as he took in the Spartan's damaged but intact form. "The God Of War, perhaps."

"I think he watches over you, too, Shintaro."

At that, Shintaro smiled.

The Japanese government had flown in their best surgeons to work on Shintaro. They were proud of him and desperately wanted him to live. Which was good because Shintaro had desperately wanted to live, too. That last fact had made all the difference in his recovery.

"Death refused to release me until the Honjo Masamune was recovered," said Shintaro in a thin voice. "It is now in Japanese hands again. Mere words cannot express my gratitude, Spartan-san. You have made my country – and me, personally – very happy."

The appreciation of a peer filled the Sparta's soul with a rare form of glee. "Any man in my position would have done the same."

"I doubt that, Spartan-san." Shintaro leant closer, gripping the handles of the wheelchair. "The Honjo Masamune meant *everything*. Thanks to you, I can finally return home with honor."

The Spartan nodded. He got it. Return home with your shield or on it, went the Spartan credo. Only Shintaro was returning home alive and with the Honjo Masamune.

He regarded Shintaro. He thought that a certain satisfaction also hummed in the other man's soul. He wouldn't say that the Japanese agent was someone who came to happiness easily, but he did seem remarkably upbeat for someone who had been gutted by a samurai sword.

"I have seen the footage of your fight with the *jonin*," said Shintaro. "An impressive battle."

"Impressive but risky," chided Garin. "He was sliced up like deli meat."

"Nevertheless, my countrymen are pleased at how the fight ... concluded," added Shintaro.

"With a bullet rather than beheading with the Honjo Masamune?" offered the Spartan. "Didn't think he deserved the honor."

"Of that we are of one mind, Spartan-san. He violated all eight bushido virtues." The Japanese man became suddenly serious. "I feel a debt of *giri* – of obligation – towards you. You have suffered for another man's cause – and that man wishes to repay you."

"That's not necessary, Shintaro," said the Spartan.

Meanwhile, Garin and Vasquez looked on, intrigued by what Shintaro was going to say next.

"When I have healed I would like to train with you," said the Japanese agent. "Your bladework is excellent, but there is still more you could learn, if you would allow me to share my experience with you. I have spent my life following the Way of the Sword and would be grateful to share that wisdom with someone worthy. Someone like you."

He looked at the Spartan, trying to gauge his reaction to the offer. He continued: "In Japan there is a long tradition of an older man teaching a younger pupil his wisdom."

"Kind of did a bit of that with the Spartan myself," said Garin, in the tone of a proud father. "Made him the soldier he is today."

"So you did, sir." The Spartan turned to Shintaro. "I'd like that, Shintaro." Shintaro nodded. He seemed relieved that the Spartan had taken the offer as a welcome gift.

"See, Spartan ... you can make new friends after all," said Garin teasingly.

"He must be badly wounded if he's being all sociable," joked Vasquez.

The Spartan stared at Shintaro's waist, as if expecting to see a sword there. "Where is the Honjo Masamune?"

"At this moment it is being polished, sharpened and tended to by the finest swordsmiths in Japan," said Shintaro, with obvious satisfaction. "Its previous owner – God rot his soul – had no idea how to treat such a treasure."

The Spartan touched his wounded side. "He knew how to swing it, though."

"Obviously not well enough, as it is you sitting before us now and not him," replied Shintaro.

Garin reached forward and put a fatherly hand on the Spartan's shoulder. "The Honjo Masamune has been waiting for you, son. Waiting for you to be ready for a road trip, which the docs now tell me you'll be able to take. And we're all coming with you."

"Outstanding, sir. So tell me ... where are we going?"

Garin grinned. "Japan."

Chapter 96

Few foreigners had been inside this inner sanctum of the Imperial Palace in Tokyo.

And yet, today it held host to three *gaijin*.

Colonel Garin, dressed in full US military uniform.

Vasquez, the lone woman in the room, in a white kimono.

And finally, in a spectacular robe of black and gold, the Spartan.

In his hands he held the Honjo Masamune.

And in front of him, sitting on a magnificent chair, was the Emperor of Japan.

A land both ancient and modern was honoring a soldier both ancient and modern.

The room was silent. No words were said. In such a place, words had no meaning.

Now was the time for respect and ritual.

These were the moments the Spartan lived for.

With all due reverence, the Spartan made his way along the wooden floor towards the Emperor, passing spectacular imagery of ancient samurai battles along walls never seen by the general public.

As the soldier solemnly approached, watched silently and carefully by many luminaries including Shintaro and the Prime Minister of Japan, the Emperor stepped off his chair to greet the Spartan.

The Spartan, holding the Honjo Masamune towards him, bowed.

The Emperor accepted the precious weapon, long missing from its sacred homeland. Then he bowed to the Spartan: equally as deep, if not deeper.

The crowd burst in spontaneous and riotous applause.

Behind him, Vasquez gave him the thumbs-up.

Their adventure had ended in a way that would have been impossible to predict at the beginning ... which was the way all the best adventures ended.

A grand feeling of accomplishment swelled in the Spartan's chest. He felt caught up in a warrior tradition dating back centuries. He knew he had achieved something significant this day.

Today, he knew what it meant to be a man of honor.

Today, he knew what it meant to be a Spartan.

He smiled.